**W9-APH-168**

# SHATTERED
# ILLUSIONS

The wizard threw a gray-green leaf on a brazier and set a small, sparkling stone in a copper bowl and smashed it to fragments. "Thus we destroy the spell." His finger stabbed out toward the peaceful landscape ahead.

For a long moment, nothing happened. Then the air rippled, as if it were the surface of a rough-running stream. Krispos rubbed at his eyes. The wizard raised a fist, shouting in triumph. And while the landscape did not change, when the ripples cleared they revealed the enemy army drawn up in battle array . . .

By Harry Turtledove
*Published by Ballantine Books:*

# KRISPOS
# OF
# VIDESSOS

Book Two of
*The Tale of Videssos*

## Harry Turtledove

A Del Rey Book
BALLANTINE BOOKS • NEW YORK

A Del Rey Book
Published by Ballantine Books

Copyright © 1991 by Harry Turtledove

Library of Congress Catalog Card Number: 91-91890

ISBN 0-345-36119-9

Manufactured in the United States of America

First Edition: August 1991

Cover Art by Romas

To Constantine VII
(who liked rice pudding)
and Leo the Deacon

# I

THE GOLD FLAN WAS FLAT AND ROUND, ABOUT AS WIDE AS Krispos' thumb—a blank surface, about to become a coin. Krispos passed it to the mintmaster, who in turn carefully set it on the lower die of the press. "All ready, your Majesty," he said. "Pull this lever here, hard as you can."

*Your Majesty.* Krispos hid a smile. He'd been Avtokrator of the Videssians for only eight days, and still was far from used to hearing his new title in everyone's mouth.

He pulled the lever. The upper die came down hard on the flan, whose soft gold was squeezed and reshaped between it and the one beneath.

The mintmaster said, "Now if you please, your Majesty, just ease back there so the die lifts again." He waited until Krispos obeyed, then took out the newly struck goldpiece and examined it. "Excellent! Had you no other duties, your Majesty, you would be welcome to work for me." After laughing at his own joke, he handed Krispos the coin. "Here, your Majesty, the very first goldpiece of your reign."

Krispos held the coin in the palm of his hand. The obverse was uppermost: an image of Phos, stern in judgment. The good god had graced Videssos' coinage for centuries. Krispos turned the goldpiece over. His own face looked back at him, neatly bearded, a bit longer than most, nose high and proud. Yes, his image, wearing the domed imperial crown. A legend ran around his portrait, in letters tiny but perfect: KRISPOS AVTOKRATOR.

He shook his head. Seeing the goldpiece brought home once more that he *was* Emperor. He said, "Thank your die-maker

1

for me, excellent sir. To cut the die so fast, and to have the image look like me—he did splendidly.''

"I'll tell him what you've said, your Majesty. I'm sure he'll be pleased. We've had to work in a hurry here before, when one Avtokrator replaced another rather suddenly, so we, ah—''

The mintmaster found an abrupt, urgent reason to stare at the coin press. He knew he'd said too much, Krispos thought. Krispos' own ancestry was not remotely imperial; he'd grown to manhood on a peasant holding near Videssos' northern frontier—and spent several years north of that frontier, as a serf toiling for the nomads of Kubrat.

But after a cholera outbreak killed most of his family, he'd abandoned his village for Videssos the city, the great imperial capital. Here he'd risen by strength and guile to the post of vestiarios—chamberlain—to the Emperor Anthimos III. Anthimos had cared for pleasure more than for ruling; when Krispos sought to remind him of his duties, Anthimos tried to slay him by sorcery. He'd slain himself instead, with a bungled spell . . . *And so,* Krispos thought, *my face goes on goldpieces now.*

"We're cutting more dies every day, both for this mint and those out in the provinces,'' the mintmaster said, changing the subject. "Soon everyone will have the chance to know you through your coins, your Majesty.''

Krispos nodded. "Good. That's as it should be.'' He'd been a youth, he remembered, when he first saw Anthimos' face on a goldpiece.

"I'm glad you're pleased, your Majesty.'' The mintmaster bowed. "May your reign be long and happy, sir, and may our artisans design many more coins for you.''

"My thanks.'' Krispos had to stop himself from bowing in return, as he would have before the crown came to him. A bow from the Avtokrator would not have delighted the mintmaster; it would have frightened him out of his wits. As Krispos left the mint, he had to hold up a hand to keep all the workers from stopping their jobs to prostrate themselves before him. He was just learning how stifling imperial ceremony could be for the Emperor.

A squad of Halogai stood outside the mint. The imperial guardsmen swung up their axes in salute as Krispos emerged. Their captain held his horse's head to help him mount. The big blond northerner was red-faced and sweating on what seemed to Krispos no more than a moderately warm day; few of the fierce mercenaries took Videssos' summer heat well.

"Where to now, Majesty?" the officer asked.

Krispos glanced down at a sheet of parchment on which he'd scrawled a list of the things he had to do this morning. He'd had to do so much so fast since becoming Avtokrator that he'd given up trying to keep it all in his head. "To the patriarchal mansion, Thvari," he said. "I have to consult with Gnatios—again."

The guardsmen formed up around Krispos' big bay gelding. He touched the horse's flanks with his heels, twitched the reins. "Come on, Progress," he said. The imperial stables held many finer animals; Anthimos had fancied good horseflesh. But Progress had belonged to Krispos before he became Emperor, and that made the beast special.

When the Halogai reached the edge of the palace quarter and came to the plaza of Palamas, they menacingly raised their axes and shouted, "Way! Way for the Avtokrator of the Videssians!" As if by magic, a lane through the crowded square opened for them. That was an imperial perquisite Krispos enjoyed. Without it, he might have spent most of an hour getting to the other side of the plaza—he had, often enough. Half the people in the world, he sometimes thought, used the plaza of Palamas to try to sell things to the other half.

Though the presence of the Emperor—and the cold-eyed Halogai—inhibited hucksters and hagglers, the din was still dreadful. He rubbed an ear in relief as it faded behind him.

The Halogai tramped east down Middle Street, Videssos the city's chief thoroughfare. The Videssians loved spectacle. They stopped and stared and pointed and made rude remarks, as if Krispos could not see or hear them. Of course, he realized wryly, he was so new an Avtokrator as to be interesting for novelty's sake, if nothing else.

He and his guards turned north toward the High Temple, the grandest shrine to Phos in all the Empire. The patriarch's home stood close by. When it came into view, Krispos braced himself for another encounter with Gnatios.

The meeting began smoothly. The ecumenical patriarch's aide, a lesser priest named Badourios, met Krispos at the mansion door and escorted him to Gnatios' study. The patriarch sprang from his chair, then went to his knees and then to his belly in full proskynesis—so full, indeed, that Krispos wondered, as he often did with Gnatios, if he was being subtly mocked.

Though his shaven pate and bushy beard marked him as a cleric, they did not rob the patriarch of his individuality, as often happened with priests. Krispos always thought of him as foxlike, for he was clever, elegant, and devious, all at the same time. Had he been an ally, he would have been a mighty one. He was not an ally; Anthimos had been a cousin of his.

Krispos waited for Gnatios to rise from his prostration, then settled into a chair across the desk from the patriarch. He motioned Gnatios to sit and plunged in without preamble. "I hope, most holy sir, you've seen fit to reverse yourself on the matter we discussed yesterday."

"Your Majesty, I am still engaged in a search of Phos' holy scriptures and of canon law." Gnatios waved to the scrolls and codices piled high in front of him. "But I regret to say that as yet I have failed to find justification for performing the ceremony of marriage to join together you and the Empress Dara. Not only is her widowhood from his late Majesty the Avtokrator Anthimos extremely recent, but there is also the matter of your involvement in Anthimos' death."

Krispos drew in a long, angry breath. "Now see here, most holy sir, I did not slay Anthimos. I have sworn that again and again by the lord of the great and good mind, and sworn it truthfully." To emphasize his words, his hand moved in a quick circle over his heart, the symbol of Phos' sun. "May Skotos drag me down to the eternal ice if I lie."

"I do not doubt you, your Majesty," Gnatios said smoothly, also making the sun-sign. "Yet the fact remains, had you not been present when Anthimos died, he would still be among men today."

"Aye, so he would—and I would be dead. If he'd finished his spell at leisure, it would have closed on me instead of him. Where in Phos' holy scriptures does it say a man may not save his own life?"

"Nowhere," the patriarch answered at once. "I never claimed that. Yet a man may not hope to escape the ice if he takes to wife the widow of one he has slain, and by your own statements you were in some measure a cause of Anthimos' death. Thus my continued evaluation of your degree of responsibility for it, as measured against the strictures of canon law. When I have made my determination, I assure you I shall inform you immediately."

"Most holy sir, by *your* own statements there can be honest doubt about this—men can decide either way. If you find against me, I am sure I can discover another cleric to wear the patriarch's blue boots and decide for me. Do you understand?"

"Oh, indeed, painfully well," Gnatios said, putting a wry arch to one eyebrow.

"I'm sorry to be so blunt," Krispos said, "But it strikes me your delays have more to do with hindering me than with Phos' sacred words. I will not sit still for that. I told you the night you crowned me that I was going to be Emperor of all Videssos, including the temples. If you stand in my way, I will replace you."

"Your Majesty, I assure you this delay is unintentional," Gnatios said. He gestured once more to the stacks of volumes on his desk. "For all you say, your case is difficult and abstruse. By the good god, I promise to have a decision within two weeks' time. After you hear it, you may do with me as you will. Such is the privilege of Avtokrators." The patriarch bowed his head in resignation.

"Two weeks?" Krispos stroked his beard as he considered. "Very well, most holy sir. I trust you to use them wisely."

"Two weeks?" Dara gave her head a decisive shake. "No, that won't do. It gives Gnatios altogether too much time. Let him have three days to play with his scrolls if he must, but no more than that. Tomorrow would be better."

As he often had, Krispos wondered how Dara fit so much stubbornness into such a small frame. The crown of her head barely reached his shoulder, but once she made up her mind she was more immovable than the hugest Haloga. Now he placatingly spread his hands. "I was just pleased I got him to agree to decide within any set limit. And in the end I think he'll decide for us—he likes being patriarch and he knows I'll cast him from his throne if he tells us we may not wed. That amount of time we can afford."

"No," Dara said, even more firmly than before. "I grudge him every grain of sand in the glass. If he's going to find for us, he doesn't need weeks to do it."

"But why?" Krispos asked. "Since I've already agreed to this, I can't change my mind without good reason, not unless I want him preaching against me in the High Temple as soon as I leave him."

"I'll give you a good reason," Dara said: "I'm with child."

"You're—" Krispos stared at her, his mouth falling open. Then he asked the same foolish question almost every man asks his woman when she gives him that news: "Are you sure?"

Dara's lips quirked. "I'm sure enough. Not only have my

courses failed to come, but when I went to the privy this morning, the stench made me lose my breakfast.''

"You're with child, all right," Krispos agreed. "Wonderful!" He took her in his arms, running a hand through her thick black hair. Then he had another thought. It was not suited for the moment, but passed his lips before he could hold it back: "Is it mine?''

He felt her stiffen. The question, unfortunately, was neither idle nor, save in its timing, cruel. Dara had been his lover, aye, but she'd also been Anthimos' Empress. And Anthimos had not been immune to the pleasures of the flesh—far from it.

When at last she looked up at him, her dark eyes were troubled. "I think it's yours," she said slowly. "I wish I could say I was certain, but I can't, not really. You'd know I was lying.''

Krispos thought back to the time before he'd seized the throne; as vestiarios, he'd had the bedchamber next to the one Dara and Anthimos had shared. The Emperor had gone carousing and reveling many nights, but not all. Krispos sighed, stepping back and wishing life did not give him ambiguity where he most wanted to be sure.

He watched Dara's eyes narrow and her mouth thin in calculation. "Can you afford to disown a child of mine, no matter who it looks like in the end?'' she asked.

"I just asked myself the same question," he said, respect in his voice. Nothing was wrong with Dara's wits, and just as Gnatios liked being patriarch, she liked being Empress. She needed Krispos for that, but he knew he also needed her— because she was Anthimos' widow, she helped confer legitimacy on him by connecting him to the old imperial house. He sighed again. "No, I don't suppose I can.''

"By the good god, Krispos, I hope it's yours, and I think it is,'' Dara said earnestly. "After all, I was Anthimos' Empress for years without quickening. I never knew him to get bastards on any of his tarts, either, and he had enough of them. I have to wonder at the strength of his seed.''

"That's so,'' Krispos said. He felt relieved, but not completely. Phos he took on faith. His years in Videssos the city had taught him the danger of similar faith in anything merely human. Yet even if the child was not his by blood, he could set his mark on it. "If it's a boy, we'll name him Phostis, for my father.''

Dara considered, nodded. "It's a good name.'' She touched Krispos' arm. "But you do see the need for haste, not so? The sooner we're wed, the better; others can count months as well as we can. A babe a few weeks early will set no tongues wagging. Much more, though, especially if the child is big and robust—"

"Aye, you're right," Krispos said. "I'll speak to Gnatios. If he doesn't like being hurried, too bad. It's just deserts for surprising me and making me speak unprepared when he was crowning me. By the good god, I know he was hoping I'd flub."

"Just deserts for that piece of effrontery would be some time in the prisons under the government office buildings on Middle Street," Dara said. "I've thought so ever since you first told me of it."

"It may come to that, if he says me nay here," Krispos answered. "I know he'd sooner see Petronas come out of the monastery and take the throne than have me on it. Being Anthimos' cousin means he's Anthimos' uncle's cousin, too."

"He's not your cousin, that's for certain," Dara said grimly. "You ought to have your own man as patriarch, Krispos. One who's against you can cause you endless grief."

"I know. If Gnatios does tell me no, it'll give me the excuse I need to get rid of him. Trouble is, if I do, I'd likely have to replace him with Pyrrhos the abbot."

"He'd be loyal," Dara said.

"So he would." Krispos spoke without enthusiasm. Pyrrhos was earnest and able. He was also pious, fanatically so. He was a far better friend to Krispos than Gnatios ever would be, and far less comfortable to live with.

Dara said, "Now I hope Gnatios does stand up on his hind legs against you, if you truly mean to slap him down for it."

All at once, Krispos was tired of worrying about Gnatios and what he might do. Instead he thought of the child Dara would have—*his* child, he told himself firmly. He stepped forward to take her in his arms again. She squeaked in surprise as he bent his head to kiss her, but her lips were eager against his. The kiss went on and on.

When at last they separated, Krispos said, "Shall we go to the bedchamber?"

"What, in the afternoon? We'd scandalize the servants."

"Oh, nonsense," Krispos said. After Anthimos' antic reign, nothing save perhaps celibacy could scandalize the palace servants, though he did not say so aloud. "Besides, I have my reasons."

"Name two," Dara said, mischief in her voice.

"All right. For one, if you are pregnant, you're apt to lose interest for a while, so I'd best get while the getting's good, as they say. And for another, I've always wanted to make love with you with the sun shining in on us. That's one thing we never dared do before.''

She smiled. ''A nice mix of the practical and the romantic. Well, why not?''

They walked down the hall hand in hand. If maidservants or eunuch chamberlains gave them odd looks, neither one noticed.

Barsymes bowed to Krispos. ''The patriarch is here, your Majesty,'' the eunuch vestiarios announced in his not-quite-tenor, not-quite-alto voice. He did not sound impressed. Few things impressed Barsymes.

''Thank you, esteemed sir,'' Krispos answered; palace eunuchs had their own honorifics, different from those of the nobility. ''Show him in.''

Gnatios prostrated himself as he entered the chamber where Krispos had been wrestling with tax documents. ''Your Majesty,'' he murmured.

''Rise, most holy sir, rise by all means,'' Krispos said expansively. ''Please be seated; make yourself comfortable. Shall I send for wine and cakes?'' He waited for Gnatios' nod, then waved to Barsymes to fetch the refreshments.

When the patriarch had eaten and drunk, Krispos proceeded to business. ''Most holy sir, I regret summoning you so soon after I promised you would have your two weeks, but I must seek your ruling on whether Dara and I may lawfully wed.''

He had expected Gnatios to splutter and protest, but the patriarch beamed at him. ''What a pleasant coincidence, your Majesty. I was going to send you a message later in the day, for I have indeed reached my decision.''

''And?'' Krispos said. If Gnatios thought this affable front would make a rejection more palatable, Krispos thought, he was going to get a rude awakening.

But the ecumenical patriarch's smile only grew broader. ''I am delighted to be able to inform you, your Majesty, that I find no canonical impediments to your proposed union with the Empress. You may perhaps hear gossip at the haste of the match, but that has nothing to do with its permissibility under ecclesiastical law.''

''Really?'' Krispos said in glad surprise. ''Well, I'm delighted to hear you say so, most holy sir.'' He got up and poured more wine for the two of them with his own hands.

"I am pleased to be able to serve you with honor in this matter, your Majesty," Gnatios answered. He lifted his cup. "Your very good health."

"And yours." Avtokrator and patriarch drank together. Then Krispos said, "From what you've just told me, I don't suppose you'd mind celebrating the wedding yourself." If Gnatios was just going along for the sake of going along, Krispos thought, he ought to balk or at least hesitate.

But he replied at once, "It would be my privilege, your Majesty. Merely name the day. From your urgency, I suppose you will want it to come as soon as possible."

"Yes," Krispos said, still a bit taken aback at this whole-hearted cooperation. "Will you be able to make everything ready in—hmm—ten days' time?"

The patriarch's lips moved. "A couple of days after the full moon? I am your servant." He inclined his head to the Emperor.

"Splendid," Krispos said. When he rose this time, it was a sign Gnatios' audience was done. The patriarch did not miss the signal. He bowed himself out. Barsymes took charge of him and escorted him from the imperial residence.

Krispos gave his attention back to the cadasters. He smiled a little as he took up his stylus to scrawl a note on a waxed tablet. That had been easier than he'd figured it would be, he thought with a twinge of contempt for Gnatios. The patriarch seemed willing to pay whatever price he had to in order to keep his position. A firm line with him would get Krispos anything he required.

Nice to have one worry settled, he thought, and went on to the next tax register.

"Don't worry, your Majesty. We have plenty of time yet," Mavros said.

Krispos looked at his foster brother with mixed gratitude and exasperation. "Nice to hear someone say so, by the good god. All of Dara's seamstresses are having kittens, wailing that they'll never be able to have her dress ready on the day. And if they're having kittens, the mintmaster is having bears—big bears, with teeth. He says I can send him to Prista if I like, but that still won't get me enough goldpieces with my face on them to use for largess."

"Prista, he?" Amusement danced in Mavros' eyes. "Then he probably means it." The lonely outpost on the northern shore of the Videssian Sea housed the Empire's most incorrigible exiles. Few people went there willingly.

"I don't care if he means it," Krispos snapped. "I need to have that gold to pass out to the people. We grabbed power too quickly the night I was crowned. This is my next good chance. If I don't do it now, the city folk will think I'm mean, and I'll have no end of trouble from them."

"I daresay you're right," Mavros said, "but does it all have to be *your* gold? Aye, that would be nice, but you hold the treasury as well as the mint. So long as the coin is good, no one who gets it will care whose face it bears."

"Something to that," Krispos said after a moment's thought. "The mintmaster will be pleased. Tanilis would be, too, to hear you; you're your mother's son after all."

"I'll take that for a compliment," Mavros said.

"You'd better. I meant it for one." Krispos had nothing but admiration for Mavros' mother. Tanilis was one of the wealthiest nobles of the eastern town of Opsikion, and seer and mage, as well. She'd foretold Krispos' rise, helped him with money and good advice, and fostered Mavros to him. Though she was a decade older than Krispos, they'd also been lovers for half a year, until he had to return to Videssos the city—Mavros did not know about that. She was still the standard by which Krispos measured women, including Dara— Dara did not know about *that*.

Barsymes politely tapped at the open door of the chamber where Krispos and Mavros were talking. "Your Majesty, eminent sir, your presence is required for another rehearsal of assembling for the wedding procession." In matters of ceremony, the vestiarios ordered the Avtokrator about.

"We'll be with you shortly, Barsymes," Krispos promised. Barsymes withdrew, a couple of paces' length. He did not go away. Krispos turned back to Mavros. "I think I'll use the wedding to declare you Sevastos."

"You will? Me?" Mavros was in his mid-twenties, a few years younger than Krispos, and had a more openly excitable temperament. Now he could not keep his surprised delight from showing. "When did you decide to do that?"

"I've been thinking about it ever since this crown landed on my head. You act as my chief minister, so you should have the title that says what you do. And the wedding will be a good public occasion to give it to you."

Mavros bowed. "One of these days," he said slyly, "you ought to tell your face what you're thinking, so it'll know, too."

"Oh, go howl," Krispos said. "Naming you Sevastos will also make you rich, even apart from what you stand to inherit. It'll also set you up as my heir if I die without one." As he said that, he wondered again whether Dara's child was his. He suspected—he feared—he would keep on wondering until the baby came, and perhaps for years afterward as well.

"I see that, since you're Emperor, you don't have to listen to people anymore," Mavros said. Realizing he hadn't been listening and had missed something, Krispos felt himself flush. With the air of someone doing an unworthy subject a great favor, Mavros repeated himself. "I said that if you die without an heir, it will likely mean you've lost a civil war, in which case I'll be a head shorter myself and in no great position to assume the throne."

In his breezy way, Mavros had probably hit truth there, Krispos thought. He said, "If you don't want the honor, I could bestow it on Iakovitzes."

They both laughed. Mavros said, "I'll take it, then, just to save you from that. With his gift for getting people furious at him, you'd lose any civil war where he was on your side, because no one else would be." Then, as if afraid Krispos might take him seriously, he added, "He is in the wedding party, isn't he?"

"Of course he is," Krispos answered. "Do you think I want the rough side of his tongue for leaving him out? He gave it to me often enough in the days when I was one of his grooms— and to you, too, I'd bet."

"Who, me?" Mavros assumed a not altogether convincing expression of innocence.

Before Krispos could reply, Barsymes stepped back into view. Implacably courteous, he said, "Your Majesty, the rehearsal will commence at any moment. Your presence—and yours, eminent sir—" He turned to Mavros. "—would be appreciated."

"Coming," Krispos said obediently. He and Mavros followed the vestiarios down the hall.

Barsymes bustled up and down the line, clucking like a hen not sure all her chicks were where they belonged. His long face was set in doleful lines made more than commonly visible by his beardless cheeks. "Please, excellent sirs, eminent sirs, your Majesty, try to remember all we've practiced," he pleaded.

"If the army had its drill down as well as we do, Videssos

would rule the bloody world," Iakovitzes said, rolling his eyes. The noble stroked his graying beard. "Come on, let's get this nonsense done with, shall we?"

Barsymes took a deep breath and continued as if no one had spoken. "Smooth and steady and stately will most properly awe the people of Videssos the city."

"Phos coming down from behind the sun with Skotos all tied up in colored string wouldn't properly awe the people of Videssos the city," Mavros said, "so what hope have we?"

"Take no notice of any of my comrades," Krispos told Barsymes, who looked about ready to burst from nerves. "We are in your capable hands."

The vestiarios sniffed, but eased a little. Then he went from mother hen to drillmaster in one fell swoop. "We begin—now," he declared. "Forward to the plaza of Palamas." He marched east from the imperial residence, past lawns and gardens and groves, past the Grand Courtroom, past the Hall of the Nineteen Couches, past the other grand buildings of the palace quarter.

Dara and her companions, Krispos knew, were traversing the quarter by another route. If everything went as planned, his party and hers would meet at the edge of the plaza. It had happened in rehearsals. Barsymes acted convinced it would happen again. To Krispos, his confidence seemed based on sorcery, but so far as he knew, no one had used any.

Magic or not, when his party turned a last corner before the plaza of Palamas, he saw Dara and the noblewomen with her round an outbuilding and come straight toward him. Once they got a few steps closer, he also saw the relief on her face; evidently she'd worried, too, about whether their rendezvous would go as planned.

"You look lovely," he said as he took her right hand with his left. She smiled up at him. A light breeze played with her hair; like him, she wore no golden crown today. Her gown, though, was of dark gold silk that complemented her olive complexion. Fine lace decorated cuffs and bodice; the gown, cinched tight at the waist, displayed her fine figure.

"Forward!" Barsymes called again, and the newly united wedding party advanced into the plaza. The palace quarter had been empty. The plaza was packed with people. They cheered when they saw Krispos and his companions, and surged toward them. Only twin rows of streamers—and Halogai posted every ten feet or so along them—kept the way open.

Instead of his sword, Krispos wore a large leather sack on the right side of his belt. He reached into it, dug out a handful of goldpieces, and threw them into the crowd. The cheers got louder and more frantic. All his groomsmen were similarly equipped; they also flung largess far and wide. So did a dozen servants, who carried even larger bags of coins.

"Thou conquerest, Krispos!" people shouted. "Many years!" "The Avtokrator!" "Many sons!" "Hurrah for the Empress Dara!" "Happiness!" They also shouted other things: "More money!" "Throw it this way!" "Over here!" And someone yelled, "A joyous year to the Emperor and Empress for each goldpiece I get!"

"What an ingenious combination of flattery and greed," Iakovitzes said. "I wish I'd thought of it."

The fellow was close; Krispos saw him waving like a madman. He pulled on a servant's sleeve. "Give him a hundred goldpieces."

The man screamed with delight when the servant poured gold first into his hands, then into a pocket that looked hastily sewn onto his robe—he'd come ready for any good that might happen to him. "That was kindly done, Krispos," Dara said, "but however much we wish it, we won't have a hundred years."

"I'll bet that chap won't have a hundred goldpieces by the time he gets out of the plaza, either," Krispos answered. "But may he do well with those he manages to keep, and may we do well with so many years."

The wedding party pushed out of the plaza of Palamas onto Middle Street. Long colonnades shielded the throngs there from the sun. More servants—these accompanied by an escort of armored Halogai—brought up fresh bags of goldpieces. Krispos dug deep and threw coins as far as he could.

As he had when visiting Gnatios, he turned north off Middle Street with his companions. This time they bypassed the patriarchal mansion with its small dome of red brick for the High Temple close by. Mavros tapped Krispos on the shoulder. "Remember the last time we saw the forecourt here so packed with people?"

"I should hope so," Krispos said. That had been the day he'd taken the throne, the day Gnatios had set the crown on his head in the doorway to the High Temple.

Dara sighed. "I wish I could have been here to see you crowned."

"So do I," Krispos said. They both knew that would not have looked good, though, not when he was replacing the man to whom she'd been wed. Even this ceremony would stir gossip in every tavern and sewing circle in the city. But Dara was right—with a child in her belly, they could not afford to wait.

More Halogai stood on the steps of the High Temple, facing outward to protect Krispos and his comrades as they had when he'd been crowned. At the top of the steps, Gnatios stood waiting. The patriarch looked almost imperially splendid in his blue boots and pearl-encrusted robe of cloth-of-gold and blue. Mere priests in less magnificent raiment swung thuribles on either side of him; Krispos' nose twitched as he caught a whiff of the sweet smoke that wafted from them.

When he and Dara started to climb the low, broad stairs, he held her hand tightly. He wanted not the slightest risk of her falling, not when she was pregnant. The wedding party followed. Behind them, servants flung the last handsful of gold coins into the crowd.

Gnatios bowed when Krispos reached the top step but did not prostrate himself. The temple was, after all, his primary domain. Krispos returned the bow, but less deeply, to show he in fact held superior rank even here. Gnatios said, "Allow me to lead you within, your Majesty." He and his acolytes turned to enter the narthex. The last time Krispos had gone in there, it was for Barsymes to robe him in the coronation regalia.

"A moment," he said now, holding up a hand.

Gnatios stopped and turned back, a small frown on his face. "Is something wrong?"

"No, not at all. I just want to speak to the people before we go on."

The ecumenical patriarch's frown grew deeper. "Your doing so is not a planned part of the ceremony, your Majesty."

"No, eh? That didn't bother you when you asked me to speak before you would crown me." Krispos kept his tone light, but he was sure he was glaring at Gnatios. The patriarch had tried to ruin him then, to make him sound like a bumbler in front of the people of the city, the most critical and fickle audience in the world.

Now Gnatios could only bow in acquiescence. "What pleases the Avtokrator has the force of law," he murmured.

Krispos looked out to the packed forecourt and held up his hands. "People of Videssos," he called, then again, "People of Videssos!" Little by little they gave him quiet. He waited until it had grown still enough for everyone to hear. "People of

Videssos, this is a happy day for two reasons. Not only am I to be wed today—''

Cheers and applause drowned him out. He smiled and let them run their course. When they were through, he resumed, ''Not only that, but today before you all I can also name my new Sevastos.''

The crowd remained quiet, but suddenly the quiet became alert, electric. A new high minister was serious business, the more with a new, as yet little-known, and childless Emperor on the throne. Into that expectant hush, Krispos said, ''I give you as Sevastos my foster brother, the noble Mavros.''

''May his Highness be merciful!'' the people called, as if with one voice. Krispos blinked; he hadn't thought there would be a special cry for the proclamation of a Sevastos. He was beginning to suspect Videssian ceremonial had a special cry or ritual for everything.

Grinning enormously, Mavros waved to show himself to the crowd. Krispos nudged him. ''Say something,'' he whispered.

''Who, me?'' Mavros whispered back. At Krispos' nod, the new Sevastos waved again, this time for quiet. When he got it, or at least enough of it to speak through, he said, ''The good god willing, I will do as well in my office as our new Avtokrator does in his. Thank you all.'' As the crowd cheered, Mavros lowered his voice and told Krispos, ''Now it's on your shoulders, your Majesty. If you start going astray, I have every excuse to do the same thing.''

''Oh, to the ice with you,'' Krispos said. He dipped his head to Gnatios. ''Shall we get on with it?''

''Certainly, your Majesty. By all means.'' Gnatios' expression reminded Krispos the delay had not been his idea in the first place. Without another word, he strode into the High Temple.

As Krispos followed him into the narthex, his eyes needed a moment to adjust to the dimmer light. The antechamber was the least splendid portion of the High Temple; it was merely magnificent. On the far wall, a mosaic depicted Phos as a beardless youth, a shepherd guarding his flock against wolves that fled, tails between their legs, back to their dark-robed master Skotos. The evil god's face was full of chilling hate.

Other mosaics set into the ceiling showed those whom Skotos' blandishments had seduced. The souls of the lost stood frozen into eternal ice. Demons with outstretched black wings and mouths full of horrid fangs tormented the damned in ingenious ways.

Not an inch of the High Temple was without its ornament. Even the marble lintel of the doorway into the narthex was covered with reliefs. Phos' sun stood in the center, its rays nourishing a whole forest of broad-toothed pointed leaves that had been carved in intricate repeating interlaced patterns.

Krispos paused to glance over to a spot not far from the doors. There by torchlight Barsymes had invested him with the leggings and kilt, the tunic and cape, and the red boots that were all part of the imperial coronation regalia. The boots had been tight; Anthimos' feet turned out to be smaller than Krispos'. Krispos was still wearing tight boots, though the cordwainers promised him pairs cut to his measure any day now.

Gnatios took a couple of steps before he noticed Krispos had stopped. The patriarch turned back and asked, "Shall we get on with it?" He did such an exquisite job of keeping irony from his voice that it was all the more ironic for being less so.

Unable to take offense no matter how much he wanted to, Krispos followed Gnatios out of the narthex and into the main chamber of the High Temple. Seated within were the high secular lords and soldiers of Videssos and their ladies, as well as the leading prelates and abbots of the city. They all rose to salute the Avtokrator and patriarch.

The nobles' rich robes, brightly dyed, shot through with gold and silver thread, and encrusted with gems hardly less glittering than those that adorned the soft flesh and sparkled in the hair of their wives and consorts, would irresistibly have drawn the eye to them in any other setting in the world. Within the High Temple, they did not dominate. They had to struggle to be noticed.

Even the benches from which the lords and ladies rose were works of art in themselves. They were blond oak, waxed to shine almost as brightly as the sun, and inset with ebony and red, red sandalwood; with semiprecious stones; and with mother of pearl that caught and brightened every ray of light.

Indeed, the huge interior of the High Temple seemed awash with light, as was only fitting for a building dedicated to Phos. "Here," Krispos had read in a chronicle that dealt in part with the raising of the Temple, "the immaterial became material." Had he seen the phrase in some provincial town far from the capital, he never would have understood it. In Videssos the city, the example lay before him.

Silver foil and gold leaf worked together with the mother of pearl to reflect light softly into every corner of the High Temple, illuminating with an almost shadowless light the moss-agate-faced columns that supported the building's four wings. Looking down, Krispos could see himself reflected in the polished golden marble of the floor.

More marble, this white as snow, gleamed on the interior walls of the Temple. Together with sheets of turquoise and, low in the east and west, rose quartz and ruddy sardonyx, it reproduced indoors the brilliance and beauty of Phos' sky.

Viewing the sky led the eye imperceptibly upward, to the twin semidomes where mosaics commemorated holy men who had been great in the service of Phos. And from those semidomes, it was impossible not to look farther yet, up and up and up into the great central dome overhead, from which Phos himself surveyed his worshipers.

The base of the dome was pierced by dozens of windows. Sunlight streamed through them and coruscated off the walls below; the beams seemed to separate the dome from the rest of the Temple below. The first time Krispos saw it, he'd wondered if it really was linked to the building it surmounted or if, as felt more likely, it floated up there by itself, suspended, perhaps, from a chain that led straight up into the heavens.

Down from the heavens, then, through the shifting sunbeams, Phos gazed upon the mere mortals who had gathered in his temple. The Phos portrayed in the dome was no smiling youth. He was mature, bearded, his long face stern and somber, his eyes . . . The first time Krispos had gone into the High Temple to worship, not long after he came to Videssos the city, he had almost cringed from those eyes. Large and omniscient, they seemed to see straight through him.

That was proper, for the Phos in the dome was judge rather than shepherd. In the long, spidery fingers of his left hand, he held to his chest a bound volume wherein all of good and evil was inscribed. A man could but hope that good outweighed the other. If not, eternity in the ice awaited, for while this Phos was just, Krispos could not imagine him merciful.

The tesserae that surrounded the god's head and shoulders in the dome were glass filmed with gold, and set at slightly varying angles. Whenever the light shifted, or whenever an observer below moved, different tiny tiles gleamed forth, adding to the spiritual solemnity of the depiction.

As it always did, tearing his eyes away from Phos' face cost Krispos a distinct effort of will. Temples throughout the Empire of Videssos held in their central domes images modeled on the one in the High Temple. Krispos had seen several. None held a fraction of the brooding majesty, the severe nobility, of this archetype. Here the god had truly inspired those who portrayed him.

Even after Krispos looked to the great silver slab of the altar that stood below the center of the dome, he felt Phos' gaze pressing down on him with almost physical force. Not even sight of the patriarchal throne of carven ivory behind the altar, a breathtaking work of art in its own right, could bring Krispos fully back to himself, not while everyone stood in silent awe, waiting for the ceremony to proceed.

Then Gnatios raised his hands to the god in the dome and to the god beyond the dome and beyond the sky. "We bless thee, Phos, lord with the great and good mind," he intoned, "by thy grace our protector, watchful beforehand that the great test of life may be decided in our favor."

Krispos repeated Phos' creed along with the ecumenical patriarch. So did everyone else in the High Temple; beside him he heard Dara's clear soprano. His hand tightened on hers. She squeezed back. Out of the corner of his eye he saw her smile.

Gnatios lowered his hands. The assembled grandees seated themselves. Krispos felt their gaze on him, too, but in a way different from Phos'. They were still wondering what sort of Avtokrator he would make. The good god already knew, but left to Krispos the working out of his fate.

Gnatios waited for quiet, then said what had been in Krispos' thoughts: "The eyes of all the city are on us today. Today we see joined in marriage the Avtokrator Krispos and the Empress Dara. May Phos bless their union and make it long, happy, and fruitful."

The patriarch began to pray again, now and then pausing for responses from Krispos and Dara. Krispos had memorized some of his replies, for the long-set language of the liturgy was growing apart from the tongue spoken in the streets of the city.

Gnatios delivered a traditional wedding sermon, touching on the virtues that helped make a good marriage. Then the patriarch said, "Are the two of you prepared to cleave to these virtues, and to each other, so long as you both may live?"

"Yes," Krispos said, and then again, louder, so that people besides himself and Dara could hear, "Yes."

"Yes," Dara agreed, not loudly but firmly.

As they spoke the words that bound them together, Mavros

set a wreath of roses and myrtle on Krispos' head. One of Dara's
attendants did the same for her.

"Behold them decked in the crowns of marriage!" Gnatios
shouted. "Before the eyes of the entire city, they are shown to
be man and wife!"

The grandees and their ladies rose from their benches to applaud. Krispos hardly heard them. He cared only about Dara,
who was looking back at him with that same intent expression.
Although it was no part of the ceremony, he took her in his
arms. He smelled the sweet fragrance of her marriage crown as
she held him tightly.

The cheers got louder and more sincere. Someone shouted
bawdy advice. "Thou conquerest, Krispos!" someone else
yelled, in a tone of voice altogether different from the usual
solemn acclamation.

"Many heirs, Krispos!" another wit bawled.

Iakovitzes came up to Krispos. The noble was short and had
to stand on tiptoe to put his mouth near Krispos' ear. "The
ring, you idiot," he hissed. Perhaps because he had no interest
whatever in women, he was immune to the joy of the marriage
ceremony and cared only that it be correctly accomplished.

Krispos had forgotten the ring and was so relieved to be reminded of this that he took no notice of how Iakovitzes spoke
to him; for that matter, Iakovitzes relished playing the gadfly no
matter whom he was talking to. Krispos had the ring in a tiny
pouch he wore on the inside of his belt so it would not show.
He freed the heavy gold band and slipped it onto Dara's left
index finger. She hugged him with renewed strength.

"Before the eyes of the whole city, they are wed!" Gnatios
proclaimed. "Now let the people of the city see the happy pair!"

With the patriarch at their side, Krispos and Dara walked
down the aisle by which they had approached the altar, through
the narthex, and out onto the top of the stairway. The crowd in
the forecourt cheered as they came down the steps. It was a
smaller crowd now, even though the wedding attendants had
fresh, full bags in their hands. They would not fling gold, but
figs and nuts, fertility symbols from time out of mind.

Even the often dour Halogai were grinning as they formed up
around the wedding party. Geirrod, the first of the northerners
to acknowledge Krispos as Emperor, told him, "Do not fail
me, Majesty. I have big bet on how many times tonight."

Dara squawked in indignation. Krispos' own humor was
earthier, but he said, "How do you hope to settle that? By the

good god, it's something only the Empress and I will ever know.''

"Majesty, you served in the palaces before you ruled them," Geirrod said, his gray eyes knowing. "Was there anything servants could not learn when they needed to?''

"Not that," Krispos said, then stopped, suddenly unsure he was right. "At least, I hope not that.''

"Huh," was all Geirrod said.

Giving his guardsman the last word, Krispos paraded with his new bride and their companions back the way they had come. Even without expectations of more money, a fair crowd still lined the streets and filled the plaza of Palamas; the folk of the city loved spectacle almost as well as largess.

After the plaza, the calm of the palace quarter came as a relief. Most of the Halogai departed for their barracks; only the troops assigned to guard the imperial residence accompanied the wedding party there. Save for Krispos and Dara, everyone stopped at the bottom of the steps. They pelted the newlywed couple with leftover figs and gave Krispos more lewd advice.

He endured that with the good humor a new groom is supposed to show. When he didn't feel like waiting any longer, he slid his arm round Dara's waist. Led by Mavros, the groomsmen and bridesmaids whooped. Krispos stuck his nose in the air and turned away from them, drawing Dara with him. They whooped louder than ever.

The happy shouts of the wedding party followed Dara and him down the hall to the bedchamber. The doors were closed. He opened them and found that the servants had turned down the bedcovers and left a jar of wine and two cups on the night table by the bed. Smiling, he closed the doors and barred them.

Dara turned her back on him. "Would you unfasten me, please? The maidservant took half an hour getting me into his gown; it has enough hooks and eyelets and what-have-you for a jail, not something you'd wear.''

"I hope I can get you out of it faster than half an hour,'' Krispos said. He did, but not as fast as he might have; the more hooks he undid, the more attention his hands paid to the soft skin he was revealing and the less to the fasteners that remained.

Finally the job was done. Dara turned to him. They kissed for a long time. When at last they broke apart, she ruefully looked down at herself. "Every pearl, every gem, every metal thread on that robe of yours has stamped itself into me,'' she complained.

"And what will you do about that?" he asked.

A corner of her mouth quirked upward. "Let's see if I can keep it from happening again." Her disrobing of him also proceeded more slowly than it might have, but he did not mind.

The two of them hung their crowns of marriage on the bedposts for luck, then lay down together. Krispos caressed Dara's breasts, lowered his mouth to one of them. She stirred, but not altogether in pleasure. "Be gentle, if you can," she said. "They're sore."

"Are they?" Under the fine skin, he could see a new tracery of blue veins. He touched her again, as carefully as he could. "Another sign you're carrying a child."

"I don't have much doubt, not anymore," she said.

"All those nuts and figs did a better job than they know," he said, straight-faced.

Dara started to nod, then snorted and poked him in the ribs. He grabbed her and held her close to keep her from doing it again. They did not separate, not until they were both spent. Then, his breath still coming quick, Krispos reached for the wine jar and said, "Shall we see what they gave us to keep us going?"

"Why not?" Dara answered. "Pour a cup for me, too, please."

Thick and golden, the wine gurgled out of the jar. Krispos recognized the sweet, heady bouquet. "This is that Vaspurakaner vintage from Petronas' cellars," he said. When Anthimos broke his ambitious uncle's power, he'd confiscated all of Petronas' lands, his money, his horses, and his wines. Krispos had drunk this one before. He raised the cup to his lips. "As good as I remember it."

Dara sipped, raised an eyebrow. "Yes, that's quite fine—sweet and tart at the same time." She drank again.

Krispos held his cup high. "To you, your Majesty."

"And to you, your Majesty," Dara answered, returning his salute with vigor—so much that a few drops flew over the rim and splashed on the bedclothes. As she looked at the spreading stain, she started to laugh.

"What's funny?" Krispos said.

"I was just thinking that this time no one will expect to find a spot of blood on the sheet. After my first night with Anthimos, Skombros marched in, peeled that sheet off the bed—he almost dumped me out to get it—then took it outside and waved it about. Everyone cheered, but it was a ritual I could have done without. As if I were a piece of raw meat, checked to make sure I hadn't spoiled.''

"Ah, Skombros," Krispos said. The fat eunuch had been Anthimos' vestiarios before Petronas got Krispos the post. An Emperor's chamberlain was in a uniquely good position to influence him, and Petronas had wanted no one but himself influencing Anthimos. And so Skombros had gone from the imperial residence to a bare monastery cell; Krispos wondered if Petronas had ever thought the same fate could befall him.

"I liked you better than Skombros as vestiarios," Dara said with a sidelong look.

"I'm glad you did," Krispos answered mildly. All the same, he understood why imperial chamberlains were most of them eunuchs, and was not sorry his own vestiarios followed that rule. Since Dara had cheated for him, how could he be sure she would never cheat against him?

He glanced toward his Empress, wondering again whether the child she carried was his or Anthimos'. If even she could not say, how would he ever know?

He shook his head. Doubts at the very beginning of a marriage did not bode well for contentment to come. He tried to put them aside. If ever a husband had given his wife reason to be unfaithful, he told himself, Anthimos had provoked Dara with his orgies and his endless parade of paramours. As long as he treated her well himself, she should have no reason to stray.

He took her in his arms again. "So soon?" she said, startled but not displeased. "Here, let me set my wine down first." She giggled as his weight pressed her to the bed. "I hope your Haloga bet high."

"So do I," Krispos said. Then her lips silenced him.

Krispos woke, yawned, stretched, and rolled over onto his back. Dara was sitting up in bed beside him. By the look of her, she'd been awake for some time. Krispos sat up, too. He glanced at where sunbeams hit the far wall. "Phos!" he exclaimed. "What hour is it, anyway?"

"Somewhere in the fourth, I'd say—more than halfway to noon," Dara told him. The Videssians gave twelve hours to the day and another twelve to the night, reckoning them from sunrise and sunset respectively. Dara gave him a quizzical look. "What do you suppose you were doing last night that left you so tired?"

"I can't imagine," Krispos said, only partly in irony. He'd

grown up a peasant, after all, and what labor was more exhausting than farming? Yet he'd risen with the sun every day. On the other hand, he'd gone to bed with the sun, too, and he'd been up considerably later than that the night before.

Yawning again, he got up, ambled over to the bureau to put on some drawers, then opened a tall wardrobe, picked out a robe, and pulled it on over his head. Dara watched him bemusedly. He was reaching for a pair of red boots when she asked, "Have you forgotten you have a vestiarios to help you with such things?"

He paused. "As a matter of fact, I did," he said sheepishly. "That was foolish of me, wasn't it? But it's also foolish for Barsymes to help me just because I'm Avtokrator. I didn't need his help before." As if to defy custom, he tugged on his own boots.

"It's also foolish not to let Barsymes do his job, which is to serve you," Dara said. "If you don't allow him to perform his proper function, then he has none. Is that what you want?"

"No," Krispos admitted. But having done entirely without service most of his life, and having given it first as groom in Iakovitzes' and Petronas' stables, then as Anthimos' vestiarios, he still felt odd about receiving it.

Dara, a western noble's daughter, had no such qualms. She reached for a green cord that hung by her side of the bed and pulled down on it. A couple of rooms away, a bell tinkled. Moments later, a maidservant tried to open the doors to the imperial bedchambers. "They're still locked, your Majesties," she said.

Krispos walked over and lifted the bar. "Come in, Verina," he said.

"Thank you, your Majesty." The serving maid stared at him in surprise and no little indignation. "You're dressed!" she blurted. "What are you doing being dressed?"

He did not turn around to see the I-told-you-so look in Dara's eyes, but he was sure it was there. "I'm sorry, Verina," he said mildly. "I won't let it happen again." A scarlet bellpull dangled next to his side of the bed. He pulled it. This bell was easier to hear—the vestiarios' chamber, the chamber that had until recently been his, was next door to the bedchamber.

Barsymes' long pale face grew longer when he saw Krispos. "Your Majesty," he said, making the title into one of reproach.

"I'm sorry," Krispos said again; though he ruled the Empire of Videssos, he wondered if he was truly master of the palaces.

"Even if I did dress myself, I'm sure I'm no cook. Will you be less angry at me after you escort me to breakfast?"

The vestiarios' mouth twitched. It could have been a smile. "Possible a trifle, your Majesty. If you'll come with me?"

Krispos followed Barsymes out of the bedchamber. "I'll join you soon," Dara said. She was standing nude in front of her wardrobe, chattering with Verina about which gown she should wear today. Barsymes' eyes never went her way. Not all eunuchs were immune from desire, even if they lacked the capacity to satisfy it. Krispos wondered whether the vestiarios felt no stirring or was just a discreetly excellent servant. He knew he could never ask.

Barsymes fussed over seating him in a small dining room. "And how would you care to break your fast this day, your Majesty?"

"A big hot bowl of porridge, a chunk of bread and some honey, and a couple of rashers of bacon would do me very well," Krispos said. That was the sort of hearty breakfast he'd had back in his home village when times were good. Times hadn't been good often enough. Sometimes breakfast had been a small bowl of porridge, sometimes nothing at all.

"As you wish, your Majesty," Barsymes said tonelessly, "though Phestos may be disappointed at having nothing more elaborate to prepare."

"Ah," Krispos said. Anthimos had gloried in the exotic; he'd thought his own more mundane tastes would be a relief to everyone. But if Phestos wanted a challenge . . . "Tell him to make the goat seethed in fermented fish sauce and leeks tonight, then."

Barsymes nodded. "A good choice."

Dara came in, asked for a stewed muskmelon. The vestiarios went to take her request and Krispos' to the cook. With a wry smile, she patted her belly. "I just hope it stays down. The past couple of days, I've hardly wanted to look at food."

"You have to eat," Krispos said.

"I know it full well. My stomach's the one that's not convinced."

Before long, Barsymes brought in the food. Krispos happily dug in and finished his own breakfast while Dara picked at her melon. When Barsymes saw Krispos was done, he whisked away his dishes and set in front of him a silver tray full of scrolls. "The morning's correspondence, your Majesty."

"All right," Krispos said without enthusiasm. Anthimos, he

knew, would have pitched a fit at the idea of handling business before noon—or after noon, for that matter. But Krispos had impressed on his servants that he intended to be a working Avtokrator. This was his reward for their taking him at his word.

He pawed through the proposals, petitions, and reports, hoping to begin with something moderately interesting. When he found a letter still sealed, his eyebrows rose. How had the secretaries who scribbled away in the wings that flanked the Grand Courtroom let it slip past them unopened? Then he exclaimed in pleasure.

Dara gave him a curious look. "You don't usually sound so gleeful when you go over those parchments."

"It's a letter from Tanilis," he said. Then he remembered that, for a variety of reasons, he'd told Dara little about Tanilis, so he added, "She's Mavros' mother, you know. She and Mavros were both kind to me when I went there with Iakovitzes a few years ago; I'm glad to hear from her."

"Oh. All right." Dara took another bite of muskmelon. Krispos supposed that hearing Tanilis described—truthfully—as Mavros' mother made her picture the noblewoman—most untruthfully—as plump, comfortable, and middle-aged. Though she had to be nearly forty now, Krispos was sure Tanilis retained all the elegant sculpted beauty she'd had when he knew her.

He began to read aloud. " 'The lady Tanilis to his Imperial Majesty Krispos, Avtokrator of the Videssians: My deepest congratulations on your accession to the throne and on your marriage to the Empress Dara. May your reign be long and prosperous.' " Then his glance happened to stray to the date above the salutation. "By the good god," he said softly, and sketched Phos' sun-circle above his heart.

"What is it?" Dara asked.

He passed her the letter. "See for yourself." He pointed to the date.

For a moment, it meant nothing to her. He watched her eyes widen. She made the sun-sign, too. "That's the day *before* you took the throne," she whispered.

"So it is," he said, nodding. "Tanilis—sees things. When I was in Opsikion, she foresaw that I might become Emperor. By then I was Iakovitzes' spatharios—his aide. A couple of years before, I'd been a farmer laboring in the field. I thought I'd already risen as high as I could." Some days he could still be surprised he was Avtokrator. This was one of them. He reached across the table and took Dara's hand. A brief squeeze reminded him this was no dream.

She gave the letter back to him. "Read it out loud, if you don't mind."

"Of course." He found his place and resumed. " 'May your reign be long and prosperous. My gratitude for your naming Mavros Sevastos—' " He broke off again.

"If she knew the rest, no reason she wouldn't know that," Dara pointed out.

"I suppose not. Here, I'll go on: '. . . for your naming Mavros Sevastos. I am sure he will serve you to the best of his ability. One favor I would beg of you in regard to my son. Should he ever desire to lead troops against the northern barbarians, I pray that you tell him no. While he may win glory and acclaim in that pursuit, I fear he will not have the enjoyment of them. Farewell, and may Phos bless you always.' "

Krispos set down the parchment. "I don't know that Mavros ever would want to go out on campaign, but if he does, telling him no won't be easy." He made a troubled sound with tongue and teeth.

"Not even after this?" Dara's finger found the relevant passage in the letter. "Surely he knows his mother's powers. Would he risk defying them?"

"I've known Mavros a good many years now," Krispos said. "All I can say is that he'll do as he pleases, no matter who or what gets defied in the doing. The lord with the great and good mind willing, the matter won't ever come up. Tanilis didn't say it was certain."

"That's true," Dara agreed.

But Krispos knew—and knew also Dara knew—the matter might very well arise. Having overthrown the khagan of Kubrat on Videssos' northern frontier, an adventurer called Harvas Black-Robe and his band of Haloga mercenaries had begun raiding the Empire, as well. The generals on the border had been having little luck with them; before too long, someone would have to drive them back where they belonged.

One of the palace eunuchs stuck his head into the dining chamber. "What is it, Tyrovitzes?" Krispos asked.

"The abbot Pyrrhos is outside the residence, your Majesty," Tyrovitzes said, puffing a little—he was as fat as Barsymes was lean. "He wants to speak with you, at once, and will not speak with anyone else. For your ears alone, he insists."

"Does he?" Krispos frowned. He found Pyrrhos' narrow

piety harsh and oppressive, but the abbot was no one's fool. "Very well, fetch him in. I'll hear him."

Tyrovitzes bowed as deeply as his rotund frame would permit, then hurried away. He soon returned with Pyrrhos. The abbot bowed low to Dara, then prostrated himself before Krispos. He did not seek to rise, but stayed on his belly. "I abase myself before you, your Majesty. The fault is mine, and let my head answer for it if that be your will."

"What fault?" Krispos said testily. "Holy sir, will you please get up and talk sense?"

Pyrrhos rose. Though a graybeard, he was limber as a youth, a kinder reward of the asceticism that also thinned his face to almost skeletal leanness and left his eyes dark burning coals. "As I told your Majesty, the fault is mine," he said. "Through some error, whether accidental or otherwise I am investigating, the count of the monks in the monastery dedicated to the memory of the holy Skirios may have been inaccurate last night. It was surely one too low this morning. We do indeed have a runaway monk."

"And who might this runaway be?" Krispos inquired, though he was sickly certain he knew the answer without having to ask. No trivial disappearance would make the abbot hotfoot it to the imperial residence with the news.

Pyrrhos saw his certainty and gave a grim nod. "Aye, your Majesty, it is as you fear—Petronas has escaped."

# II

Trying to meet bad news with equanimity, Krispos said, "I don't think he's going to be very pleased with me."

Only after the words were out of his mouth did he realize what an understatement that was. Petronas had virtually ruled the Empire for a decade and more while his nephew Anthimos reveled; he had raised Krispos to the post of vestiarios. Finally Anthimos, worried lest his uncle supplant him on the throne, a worry abetted by Krispos and Dara, clapped him into the monastery . . . for good, Krispos had thought.

Dara said bitterly, "While all the eyes of the city were on us yesterday, Petronas took the chance to get out."

Krispos knew she was just echoing Gnatios' words, but what she said raised echoes in his own mind, echoes of suspicion. He'd wondered why Gnatios had suddenly become so obliging about the wedding. Now maybe he knew. "The patriarch did keep harping on that, didn't he? He and Petronas are cousins, too, and if anyone could arrange to have a monk taken from his monastery without the abbot's knowledge, who better than Gnatios?"

"No one better, your Majesty," Pyrrhos said, following Krispos' line of thought. His sharp-curved nose, fierce eyes, and shaven head made him resemble a bird of prey.

"Tyrovitzes!" Krispos shouted. When the fat eunuch reappeared, Krispos told him, "Take a squad of Halogai and fetch Gnatios here at once, no matter what he's doing."

"Your Majesty?" Tyrovitzes said. At Krispos' answering glare, he gulped and said, "Yes, your Majesty."

Tyrovitzes had hardly left before Krispos shouted, "Longinos!'' As soon as that eunuch responded, Krispos said, ''Go to Captain Thvari. Take all the Halogai save enough to guard me here, take whatever other troops are in the city, and start a search. Maybe Petronas has gone to ground inside the walls.''

''Petronas?'' Longinos said, staring.

''Yes; he's escaped, curse him,'' Krispos answered impatiently. The chamberlain started to go. Then Krispos had an afterthought. ''If Thvari does use our own troops along with the northerners, have him make sure he puts more Halogai than Videssians in each party. I know his men are loyal.''

''As you say, your Majesty.'' Longionos bowed deeply and departed.

*He* was scarcely gone when Krispos yelled, ''Barsymes!'' The vestiarios might have been waiting right outside; he came in almost at once. ''Go to the house of Trokoundos the wizard and bring him here, if you please.''

''Certainly, your Majesty. I suppose you'll want him to interrogate Gnatios,'' Barsymes said calmly. At Krispos' expression of surprise, he went on, ''You have not kept your voice down, you know, your Majesty.''

Krispos thought about that. ''No, I suppose I haven't. Go get me Trokoundos now, if you please. If Gnatios did have a hand in Petronas' escape—'' He pounded a clenched fist down on the tabletop. ''If that's so, we'll have a new ecumenical patriarch before the day is out.''

''Your pardon, Majesty, but perhaps not so quickly as that,'' Pyrrhos said. ''You may of course remove a prelate as you wish, but the naming of his successor lies in the hands of a synod of clerics, to whom you submit a list of three candidates for their formal selection.''

''You understand that all that rigmarole would just delay your own choice,'' Krispos said.

Pyrrhos bowed. ''Your Majesty is gracious. All the same, however, observances must be fulfilled to ensure the validity of any patriarchal enthronement.''

''If Gnatios helped Petronas get away, he deserves worse than being deposed,'' Dara said. ''Some time with the torturers might be a fit answer for his treason.''

''We'll worry about that later,'' Krispos said. With peasant patience, he settled down to see whether Gnatios or Trokoundos would be brought to the imperial residence first. When Pyrrhos began to look restive, he sent him back to his monastery. Sitting quietly, he kept on waiting.

"How can you be so easy about this?" demanded Dara, who was pacing back and forth.

"Nothing would change if I fussed," he said. Dara snorted and kept pacing.

Rather to Krispos' surprise, Tyrovitzes' party fetched back Gnatios before Barsymes arrived with Trokoundos. "Your Majesty, what is the meaning of this?" the patriarch said indignantly after the eunuch chamberlain escorted him into Krispos' presence. "I find it humiliating to be seized in the street like some low footpad and fetched here with no more consideration for my feelings than such a criminal would receive."

"Where's Petronas, Gnatios?" Krispos asked in a voice like iron.

"Why, in the monastery sacred to the holy Skirios." Gnatios' eyebrows rose. "Or are you telling me he is not? If you are, I have no idea where he is."

The patriarch sounded surprised and curious, just as he would if he were innocent. But Krispos knew he had no small rhetorical talents; sounding innocent was child's play for him. "While all the eyes of the city were on us yesterday, Gnatios, Petronas was spirited out of the monastery. To be blunt, I know you have scant love for me. Do you wonder that I have doubts about you?"

"Your Majesty, I can see that you might." Gnatios smiled his most engaging smile. "But after all, your Majesty, you know where I was yesterday. I could hardly have helped Petronas escape at the same time as I was performing the wedding ceremony for you and your new Empress." He smiled again, this time at Dara. She stared stonily back. His smile faded.

"No, but you could have planned and arranged a rescue," Krispos said. "Will you take oath on your fear of Skotos' ice that you had no part of any sort in Petronas' getting out of the monastery?"

"Your Majesty, I will swear any oath you wish," Gnatios answered at once.

Just then, Krispos saw Barsymes standing in the hall with a short spare man who shaved his head like a priest but wore a red tunic and green trousers. He carried a bulging carpetbag.

"Your Majesty," Trokoundos said. The mage started a proskynesis, but Krispos waved for him not to bother. "How may I serve you, your Majesty?" he asked, straightening. His voice was deep and rich, the voice to be expected of a man a head taller and twice as wide through the shoulders.

"Most holy sir, I will require no oath of you at all," Krispos said to Gnatios. "You might throw away your soul for the sake of advantage in this world, and that would be very sad. Instead, I will ask you the same questions you have already heard, but with this wizard standing by to make sure you speak the truth."

"I will need a little while to ready myself, your Majesty," Trokoundos said. "I have here some of the things I may use, if your vestiarios spoke accurately about your requirements." He began taking mirrors, candles, and stoppered glass vials of various sizes and colors out of the carpetbag.

Gnatios watched him prepare with indignation but no visible fear. "Your Majesty, I will even submit to this outrage, but I must inform you that I protest it," he said. "Surely you cannot imagine that I would violate my oath."

"*I* can," Dara said.

Krispos took a different line. "I can imagine many things, most holy sir," he told the patriarch. "I can even imagine giving you over to the torturers to find out what I must know. A mage, I think, will hurt your body and your pride less, but I can go the other way if you'd rather."

"As you will, your Majesty," Gnatios said, so boldly that Krispos wondered if he was indeed innocent. The patriarch added, "My thanks for showing consideration for me, at least to the extent you have."

"Just stay right there, if you would, most holy sir," Trokoundos said. Gnatios nodded regally as the mage set up a mirror on a jointed stand a few feet in front of him. Between mirror and patriarch, Trokoundos lit a candle. He opened a couple of his vials and shook powder from them onto the flame, which changed color and sent up a large cloud of surprisingly sweet-smelling smoke.

Muttering to himself, Trokoundos set up another mirror a few feet behind Gnatios and slightly to one side: this one faced the one he'd set up before. He fussily adjusted the two squares of polished silver until Gnatios' face, reflected from the first, was visible in the second. Then he lit another candle between the second mirror and Gnatios' back. He sprinkled different powders over this flame, whose smoke proved as noxious as the other's had been pleasant.

Coughing a little, the mage said, "Go ahead, your Majesty; ask what you will."

"Thank you." Krispos turned to the patriarch. "Most holy

sir, did you help Petronas escape from the monastery dedicated to the holy Skirios?"

He watched Gnatios' lips shape the word "No" but did not hear him speak it. At the same time, the patriarch's second reflection, the one in the mirror behind him, loudly and clearly said, "Yes."

Gnatios jerked as if stung. Krispos asked, "How did you do it?"

He thought the patriarch tried to say "I had nothing to do with it." The reflection answered for him: "I sent in a monk who rather resembled him to take his place while he was at solitary prayer and to stay into the evening. Then, last night, I sent a priest who asked for the substituted monk by his proper name and brought him out of the monastery once more."

"What is the name of this monk?" Krispos demanded.

This time Gnatios stood mute. His reflection answered for him nonetheless. "Harmosounos."

Krispos nodded to Trokoundos. "This is an excellent magic." The wizard's heavy-lidded eyes lit up.

Gnatios shifted from foot to foot, awaiting the next question. "Where did Petronas plan to go?" Krispos asked him.

"I do not know," he answered, out of his own mouth.

"A moment, your Majesty," Trokoundos said sharply. He fiddled with the mirrors again. "He sought to move enough to shift his image from the second mirror."

"Don't play such games again, most holy sir. I promise you would regret it," Krispos told Gnatios. "Now I will ask once more, where did Petronas plan to go?"

"I do not know," Gnatios repeated. This time, strangely, Krispos heard the words both straight from him and from the mirror at his back. He glanced toward Trokoundos.

"He speaks the truth, your Majesty," the wizard said.

"I was afraid that was what that meant," Krispos said. "Let's try something else, then. Answer me this, most holy sir: you being kinsman to Petronas, where would you go in his boots?"

Gnatios plainly tried to lie again; his lips moved, but no sound came out of his mouth. Instead, his doubly reflected image replied, "Petronas' greatest estates are in the westlands, between the towns of Garsavra and Resaina. There he would find the most support for any bid to take the crown."

"You expect him to do that, eh?" Krispos said.

The answer to that question was so obvious, Krispos did not expect Gnatios to bother giving it aloud. And, indeed, the patriarch stayed silent. But under Trokoundos' spell, his second image spoke for him. "Don't you expect it, your Majesty?"

Krispos' chuckle was dry. "Well, yes, as a matter of fact." He turned to Trokoundos. "I'm in your debt once more, it seems."

Trokoundos waved that away. "I'm happy to do what I can for you, your Majesty. Your warning saved me from Anthimos' wrath a couple of years ago."

"And your wizardry let me live through the enchantment with which Petronas would have killed me otherwise," Krispos said. "Don't be shy when you name your fee for today."

"Your Majesty, people have accused me of many things, but never of being shy about my fees," Trokoundos said.

Whether anxious over his fate or simply resentful at being forgotten for the moment, Gnatios burst out, "What will you do with me, your Majesty?"

"A good question," Krispos said musingly. "If helping to set up a rival Emperor isn't treason, what is? Shall I put your head on the Milestone as a warning to others, Gnatios?"

"I'd rather you didn't," the patriarch answered, coolly enough to win Krispos' reluctant admiration.

"I think you should, Krispos," Dara said. Gnatios winced as she went on, "What does a traitor deserve but the axe? What would Petronas do to you, and to me, and to our child, if—Phos prevent it—he beat you?"

Gnatios missed very little. Though he could not have known of Dara's pregnancy before she mentioned it, he used it at once, saying, "Your Majesty, would you slay the man who performed your marriage ceremony and so made your heir legitimate?"

"Why not," Dara shot back, "when part of the reason you married us was to draw attention away from the holy Skirios' monastery so you could loose Petronas against us?" The patriarch winced again.

"I don't think I'll kill you now," Krispos said. Gnatios looked delighted, Dara disappointed. Krispos went on, "I do cast you down from the patriarchal throne. In your place I intend to propose the name of the abbot Pyrrhos."

Gnatios winced a third time. "I'd almost rather you killed me, if afterwards you named in my place someone not a fanatic."

"I can trust the clerics of his faction. If I thought I could trust one from yours, I'd take you up on that."

"I did say 'almost,' your Majesty," the patriarch reminded him quickly.

"So you did. Here's what I will do. Till the synod names Pyrrhos, I will send you to the monastery of the holy Skirios. There you will be under his hand as abbot. That should be enough to keep you out of mischief for the time being." Krispos watched Gnatios open his mouth to speak. "Think twice if you are about to say again that you'd rather be dead, most holy sir— no, holy sir, for you are but a monk now. I just may oblige you."

Gnatios glared at him but said nothing.

Krispos turned to Tyrovitzes. "You heard what I ordered?" The eunuch nodded. "Good. Take this monk to the monastery, then, and tell the abbot he is not to leave no matter what happens. Take the Halogai with you as you go, too, to make sure the man doesn't get stolen on the way."

"As you say, your Majesty." Tyrovitzes nodded to Gnatios. "If you will come with me, holy sir?" Unlike Krispos, Tyrovitzes adjusted to changing honorifics without having to think twice. Still in his patriarch robe, Gnatios followed the chamberlain away.

"I wish you'd slain him," Dara said.

"He may still have some use alive," Krispos said. "Besides, I don't think he'll be going anywhere, not now. He and Pyrrhos have despised each other for years. Now that he's in Pyrrhos' clutches, he'll be locked up tighter and watched better than if he was in prison—and fed worse, too, I'd wager."

He sighed. "All this would be much easier if I really believed the soldiers would turn up Petronas still inside the city. If they don't—" Krispos stood thinking for a while, trying to work out what he would have to do to hunt down Petronas loose in the countryside.

"I fear they won't," Dara said.

"So do I," Krispos told her. Petronas was both clever and nervy. The only flaw Krispos had ever noted in him was a streak of vanity; because he could do so much, he thought he could do anything. Some time in the monastery might even have cured him of that, Krispos reflected gloomily.

"You should proclaim him outlaw," Dara said. "A price on his head will make folk more likely to betray him to you."

"Aye, I'll do that," Krispos said. "I'll also send a troop of cavalry out to the estates that used to be his. Though Anthimos took them over, I expect most of the men on them will still be people Petronas chose, and they may still be loyal to him."

"Be careful of the officer you choose to command that troop," Dara warned. "You won't want anyone who served under him."

"You're right," Krispos said. But Petronas had headed the imperial army while his nephew frittered away the days. That meant every Videssian officer had served under him, at least indirectly. The commanders in the city had sworn oaths of loyalty to Krispos. Those in the field were sending in written pledges; a couple arrived every day. How much would such pledges mean, when measured against years of allegiance to a longtime leader? Krispos was convinced oaths and pledges were only as reliable as the men who gave them. He wished he'd had time to learn more about his officers before facing a challenge like this.

As is the way of such things, wishing failed to furnish him the time he needed. He sighed again. "I'll pick as carefully as I can."

Days passed. The search of the city failed to yield any trace of Petronas. At Krispos' order, scribes calloused their fingers writing scores of copies of a proclamation that branded Petronas outlaw, rebel, and renegade monk. They posted them in the plaza of Palamas, in the lesser square called the forum of the Ox, in the forecourts to the High Temple, and at each of the gates in Videssos the city's walls. Before long, dozens of people claimed to have seen Petronas. So far as Krispos could tell, no one really had.

Imperial couriers galloped east and west from the city with more copies of the proclamation. A cavalry troop also galloped west. Other couriers took ship to carry word of Petronas' escape to coastal towns more quickly than horses could reach them.

Despite the worry that gnawed at him, Krispos carried on with the routine business of the Empire. Indeed, he threw himself into it; the busier he was, the less chance he had to notice Petronas was still free.

He also wasted no time in organizing the synod that would ratify his choice of Pyrrhos to succeed Gnatios as ecumenical patriarch. That was connected to Petronas' disappearance, but gave Krispos satisfaction nonetheless; on Gnatios, at least, he could take proper vengeance.

Yet even the synod proved more complicated than he'd expected. As custom required, he summoned to it abbots and high-ranking priests from the capital, as well as the prelates of the larger suburbs on both sides of the Cattle-Crossing, the strait that separated Videssos the city from its western provinces. Having summoned them, he assumed the rest of the process would be a formality. After all, as Avtokrator he headed the ecclesiastical hierarchy no less than he did the state.

But many of the prelates who gathered at his command in the chapel in the palace quarter owed their own appointments to Gnatios, were of his moderate theological bent, and did not take kindly to choosing the head of the more zealous faction to replace him.

"May it please your Majesty," said Savianos, prelate of the western suburb known simply as Across because it lay directly opposite Videssos the city, "but the abbot Pyrrhos, holy though he is, is also a man of harsh and severe temper, perhaps not ideally suited to administering all aspects of ecclesiastical affairs." By the way Savianos' bushy eyebrows twitched, he would have said a good deal more than that had he dared. Talking to his fellow clerics, he probably had said a good deal more than that.

Krispos said politely, "I have, after all, submitted three names to this holy synod." He and all the clerics knew he'd done so only because the law required it of him. Moreover, he'd taken no chances with his other two candidates.

Savianos understood that, too. "Oh, aye, your Majesty, Traianos and Rhepordenes are very pious," he said. Now his eyebrows leapt instead of twitching. The two clerics, one the prelate of the provincial town of Develtos, the other an abbot in the semidesert far southwest, were fanatical enough to make even Pyrrhos seem mild by comparison.

"Never having known discipline, the holy Savianos may fear it more than is warranted," observed a priest named Lournes, one of Pyrrhos' backers. "The experience, though novel, should prove salutary."

"To the ice with you," Savianos snapped.

"You are the one who will know the ice," Lournes retorted. The clerics on either side yelled and shook their fists at those on the other. Krispos had seen little of prelates till now, save in purely ceremonial roles. Away from such ceremony, he discovered, they seemed men like any others, if louder than most.

He listened for a little while, then slammed the flat of his hand down on the table in front of him. Into sudden quiet he said, "Holy sirs, I didn't think I'd need the Halogai to keep you from one another's throats." The hierarchs looked briefly shamefaced. He went on. "If you reckon the holy Pyrrhos a heretic or an enemy of the faith, do your duty, vote him down, and give the blue boots to one of the other men I've offered you. If not, make that plain with your vote, as well.''

"May it please your Majesty," Savianos said, "my questions about the holy Pyrrhos do not pertain to his orthodoxy; though I love him not, I will confess he is most perfectly orthodox. I only fear that he will not recognize as orthodox anyone who fails to share his beliefs to the last jot and tittle.''

"That is as it should be," said Visandos, an abbot who supported Pyrrhos. "The truth being by definition unique, any deviation from it is unacceptable.''

Savianos shot back, "The principle of theological economy grants latitude of opinion on issues not relating directly to the destination of one's soul, as you know perfectly well.''

"*No* issue is unrelated to the destination of one's soul," Visandos said. The ecclesiastics started yelling louder than ever.

Krispos whacked the table again. Silence came more slowly this time, but he eventually won it. He said, "Holy sirs, you have more wisdom than I in these matters, but I did not summon you here to discuss them. Gnatios has shown himself a traitor to me. I need a patriarch I can rely on. Will you give him to me?''

Since even Savianos had admitted Pyrrhos was orthodox, the result of the synod was a foregone conclusion. And since no cleric cared to risk the Avtokrator's wrath, the vote for Pyrrhos was unanimous. The priests and abbots began arguing all over again, though, as they filed out of the chapel.

As Savianos rose to depart, he told Krispos, "Majesty, I pray that you always recall we did this only at your bidding.''

"Why? Do you think I will regret it?" Krispos said.

Savianos did not reply, but his eyebrows were eloquent.

In spite of the prelate's forebodings, Krispos remained convinced he had done a good day's work. But his satisfaction lasted only until he finished the walk from the chapel to the imperial residence. There he found an imperial courier waiting for him. The man's face was drawn with fatigue and pain; a bloodstained bandage wrapped his left shoulder.

Looking at him, Krispos wondered where disaster had struck now. The last time a courier had waited for him like this, it was with word that Harvas Black-Robe's savage followers had destroyed the village where he'd grown up and that his sister, brother-in-law, and two nieces were gone forever. Did this man bring more bad news from the north, or had things gone wrong in the west?

"You'd best tell me," Krispos said quietly.

The courier saluted like a soldier, setting his clenched right fist over his heart. "Aye, your Majesty. The troops you sent to Petronas' estates—well, sir, they found him there. And their captain and most of the men . . ." He paused, shook his head, and went on as he had to: "They went over to him, sir. A few fled that night. I heard what happened from one of those. We were being pursued; we separated to try to make sure one of us got to you with the news. I see I'm the first, sir. I'm sorry."

Krispos did his best to straighten his face; he hadn't realized he'd let his dismay show. "Thank you for staying loyal and bringing it to me . . ." He paused to let the courier give his name.

"I'm called Themistios, your Majesty," the fellow said, saluting again.

"I'm in your debt, Themistios. First find yourself a healer-priest and have that shoulder seen to." Krispos pulled a three-leafed tablet from the pouch on his belt. He used a stylus to write an order. Then he drew out the imperial sunburst seal and pushed it into the wax below what he had written. He closed the tablet, handing it to Themistios. "Take this to the treasury. They'll give you a pound of gold. And if anyone tries to keep you from getting it, find out his name and give it to me. He won't try twice, I promise."

Themistios bowed. "I was afraid my head might answer for bringing you bad news, your Majesty. I didn't expect to be rewarded for it."

"Why not?" Krispos said. "How soon good news comes makes no difference; good news takes care of itself. But the sooner I hear of anything bad, the longer I have to do something about it. Now go find a healer-priest, as I told you. You look as if you're about to fall over where you stand."

Themistios saluted once more and hurried away. One of the Halogai with Krispos asked, "Now that you know where Petronas is, Majesty, and now you have longer to do something about it, what will you do?"

Krispos had always admired the big, fair-haired barbarians' most un-Videssian way of coming straight to the point. He did his best to match it. "I aim to go out and fight him, Vagn."

Vagn and the rest of the guardsmen shouted approval, raising their axes high. Vagn said, "While you were still vestiarios,

Majesty, I told you you thought like a Haloga. I am glad to see you do not change now that you are Avtokrator.''

The other northerners loudly agreed. Forgetting Krispos' imperial dignity, they pounded him on the back and boasted of how they would hack their way through whatever puny forces Petronas managed to gather, and how they would chop the rebel himself into pieces small enough for dogs to eat. "Small enough for baby dogs," Vagn declared grandly. "For puppies straight from bitches' teats."

For as long as he listened to them, Krispos grinned and, buoyed by their ferocity, almost believed disposing of Petronas would be as easy as they thought. But his smile was gone by the time he got to the top of the stairs that led into the imperial residence.

Barsymes stood behind Krispos' back, fumbling with unfamiliar catches. "There," he said at last. "You look most martial, your Majesty."

"I do, don't I?" Krispos sounded surprised, even to himself. His shoulders tightened to bear the weight of the mail shirt the vestiarios had just finished fastening. He suspected he'd ache by the time he took it off. He had fought before, against Kubrati raiders, but he'd never worn armor.

And such armor! His was no ordinary mail shirt. Even in the pale light that sifted through the alabaster ceiling panels of the imperial residence, its gilding made it gleam and sparkle. When the Avtokrator of the Videssians went on campaign with his troops, no one could doubt for an instant who was in command.

He set his conical helmet on his head, fiddled with it until it fit comfortably over his ears. The helmet was gilded, too, with a real gold circlet soldered around it at about the level of the top of his forehead. His scabbard and sword belt were also gilded, as was the hilt of the sword. About the only things he had that were not gilded were the sword's blade, his red boots, and the stout spear in his right hand. He'd carried that spear with him when he walked from his native village to Videssos the city. Along with a lucky goldpiece he wore on a chain round his neck, it was all he had left of the place where he'd grown up.

Dara threw her arms around him. Through the mail and the padding beneath it, he could not feel her body. He hugged her, too, gently, so as not to hurt her. "Come back soon and safe," she said—the same wish women always send with their men who ride to war.

"I'll come back soon enough," he answered. "I'll have to. With summer almost gone, the fighting season won't last much longer. I only hope I'll be able to beat Petronas before the rains come and turn the roads to glue."

"I wish you weren't going at all," Dara said.

"So do I." Krispos still had a peasant farmer's distaste for soldiering and the destruction it brought. "But the soldiers will perform better under my eye than they would otherwise." Better than they would under some general who might decide to turn his coat, Krispos meant. The officers of the regiment he would lead out were all of them young and ambitious, men who would rise faster under a young Emperor weeding rebels from the army than they could hope to if an old soldier with old cronies wore the crown. Krispos hoped that would keep them loyal. He avoided thinking about his likely fate if it didn't.

Dara understood that, too. "The good god keep you."

"May that prayer fly from your mouth to Phos' ear." Krispos walked down the hall toward the doorway. As he passed one of the many imperial portraits that hung on the walls, he paused for a moment. The long-dead Emperor Stavrakios was shown wearing much the same gear Krispos had on. Blade naked in his hand, Stavrakios looked like a soldier; in fact, he looked like one of the veterans who had taught Krispos what he knew of war. Measuring himself against that tough, ready countenance, he felt like a fraud.

Fraud or not, though, he had to do his best. He walked on, pausing in the doorway to let his eyes get used to the bright sunshine outside—and to take a handkerchief from his belt pouch to wipe sweat from his face. In Videssos the city's humid summer heat, chain mail was a good substitute for a bathhouse steam room.

A company of Halogai, two hundred men strong, saluted with their axes as Krispos appeared. They were fully armored, too, and sweating worse than he was. He wished he could have brought the whole regiment of northerners to the westlands with him; he knew they were loyal. But he had to leave a garrison he could trust in the city, or it might not be his when he returned.

A groom led Progress to the foot of the steps. The big bay gelding stood quietly as Krispos lifted his left foot into the stirrups and swung aboard. He waved to the Halogai. "To the harbor of Kontoskalion," he called, touching his heels to Progress' flanks. The horse moved forward at a walk. The imperial guards formed up around Krispos.

People cheered as the Emperor and his Halogai paraded through the plaza of Palamas and onto Middle Street. This time they turned south off the thoroughfare. The sound of the sea, never absent in Videssos the city, grew steadily louder in Krispos' ears. When he first came to the capital, he'd needed some little while to get used to the endless murmur of waves and their slap against stone. Now he wondered how he would adjust to true quiet once more.

Another crowd waited by the docks, gawking at the Videssian troops drawn up on foot there. Sailors were loading their horses onto big, beamy transports for the trip to the west side of the Cattle-Crossing; every so often, a sharp curse cut through the low-voiced muttering of the crowd. Off to one side, doing their best to look inconspicuous, were Trokoundos and a couple of other wizards.

Along with the waiting soldiers stood the new patriarch Pyrrhos. He raised his hands in benediction as he saw Krispos approach. The soldiers stiffened to attention and saluted. The noise from the crowd got louder. Because the horses did not care that the Emperor had come, the sailors coaxing them onto and along the gangplanks did not care, either.

The Halogai in front of Krispos moved aside to let him ride up to the ecumenical patriarch. Leaning down from the saddle, he told Pyrrhos, "I'm sorry we had to rush the ceremony of your investiture the other day, most holy sir. What with trying to deal with Petronas and everything else, I know I didn't have time to do it properly."

Pyrrhos waved aside the apology. "The synod that chose me was well and truly made, your Majesty," he said, "so in the eyes of Phos I have been properly chosen. Next to that, the pomp of a ceremony matters not at all; indeed, I am just as well pleased not to have endured it."

Only so thoroughgoing an ascetic as Pyrrhos could have expressed such an un-Videssian sentiment, Krispos thought; to most imperials, ceremony was as vital as breath. Krispos said, "Will you bless me and my warriors now, most holy sir?"

"I shall bless you, and pray for your victory against the rebel," Pyrrhos proclaimed, loud enough for the soldiers and city folk to hear. More softly, for Krispos' ears alone, he went on, "I first blessed you twenty years ago, on the platform in Kubrat. I shall not change my mind now."

"You and Iakovitzes," Krispos said, remembering. The noble had gone north to ransom the farmers the Kubratoi had stolen; Pyrrhos and a Kubrati shaman were there to make sure Phos and the nomads' false gods heard the bargain.

"Aye." The patriarch touched the head of his staff, a gilded sphere as big as a fist, to Krispos' shoulder. Raising his voice, he declared, "The Avtokrator of the Videssians is the good god's vice-regent on earth. Whoso opposes him opposes the will of Phos. Thou conquerest, Krispos!"

"Thou conquerest!" people and soldiers shouted together. Krispos waved in acknowledgment, glad Pyrrhos was unreservedly on his side. Of course, if Petronas ended up beating him, that would only prove Phos' will had been that he lose, and then Pyrrhos would serve a new master. Or if he refused, it would be from distaste at Petronas' way of life, not because Petronas had vanquished Krispos. Determining Phos' will could be a subtle art.

Krispos did not intend that Pyrrhos would have to weigh such subtleties. He aimed to beat Petronas, not to be beaten. He rode down the dock to the *Suncircle*, the ship that would carry him across to the westlands. The captain, a short, thickset man named Nikoulitzas, and his sailors came to attention and saluted as Krispos drew near. When he dismounted, a groom hurried forward to take charge of Progress and lead the horse aboard.

Once on the *Suncircle*, Progress snorted and rolled his eyes, not much caring for the gently shifting planks under his feet. Krispos did not much care for them, either. He'd never been on a ship before. He told his stomach to behave itself; the imperial dignity would not survive hanging over the rail and giving the fish his breakfast. After a few more internal mutterings, his stomach decided to obey.

Nikoulitzas was very tan, but years of sun and sea spray had bleached his hair almost as light as a Haloga's. Saluting again, he said, "We are ready to sail when you give the word, your Majesty."

"Then sail," Krispos said. "Soonest begun, soonest done."

"Aye, your Majesty." Nikoulitzas shouted orders. The *Suncircle*'s crew cast off lines. Along with its sail, the ship had half a dozen oars on each side for getting into and out of harbors. The sailors dug in at them. That changed the motion of the *Suncircle* and Progress snorted again and laid his ears back. Krispos spoke soothingly to the horse—and to his stomach. He fed Progress a couple of dried apricots. The horse ate them, then peered at his hands for more. Nothing was wrong with *his* digestion, at any rate.

The voyage over the Cattle-Crossing took less than half an hour. The *Suncircle* beached itself a little north of the western suburb called Across; none of Videssos the city's suburbs had docks of their own, lest they compete with the capital for trade. The sailors took out a section of rail and ran out the gangplank from the *Suncircle*'s gunwale to the sand. Leading Progress by the rein, Krispos walked down to the beach. His feet and the horse's hooves echoed on the planks.

The rest of the transports went aground to either side of the *Suncircle*. Some Halogai had sailed on Krispos' ship; those who had not hurried up to join their countrymen and form a protective ring around him. The Videssian troops, by contrast, paid more attention to recovering their horses. The afternoon was well along before the regimental commander rode up to Krispos and announced, "We are ready to advance, your Majesty."

"Onward, then, Sarkis," Krispos said.

Sarkis saluted. "Aye, your Majesty." He shouted orders to his men. His Videssian had a slight throaty accent; that, along with his wide face, thick beard, and imperious promontory of a nose, said he was from Vaspurakan. So were a good many of his troopers—the mountain land bred fine fighting men.

A small strain of Vaspurakaner blood also flowed in Krispos' veins, or so his father had always said. That was one of the reasons Krispos had chosen Sarkis' regiment. Another was that the "princes"—for so every Vaspurakaner reckoned himself—were heretics in Videssian eyes and found fault, themselves, with the imperial version of Phos' faith. As outsiders in Videssos, they, like the Halogai, had little reason to favor an old-line noble like Petronas—or so Krispos hoped.

Scouts trotted ahead of the main line of soldiers. Still surrounded by the Halogai, Krispos rode along near the middle of that line. Mule-drawn baggage wagons rattled along behind him, followed by the rearguard.

The Cattle-Crossing and its beach vanished as they moved west down a dirt road toward Petronas' lands. From the road, Krispos could see farms and farming villages as far as his eyes reached; the western coastal lowlands held perhaps the most fertile soil in all the Empire. After a while Krispos dismounted, stepped into a field, and dug his hand deeps in to the rich black earth. He felt of it, smelled it, tasted it, and shook his head.

"By the good god," he said, as much to himself as to any of his companions, "if I'd worked soil like this, nothing could have made me leave it." Had the soil of his native village been half this good, he and his fellows there could easily have grown enough to meet the tax bill that forced him to seek his fortune in the city. On the other hand, had the soil there been better, the tax bill undoubtedly would have been worse. Videssos' tax collectors let nothing slip through their fingers.

A few farmers and a fair number of small boys stayed in the fields to gape at the soldiers and Avtokrator as they went by. More did what Krispos would have done had he worn their sandals: they turned and fled. Soldiers did not always plunder, rape, and kill, but the danger of it was too great to be taken lightly.

As the crimson ball of the sun neared the western horizon, the army camped in a field of clover not far from a grove of fragrant orange trees. Cookfires drew moths, and the bats and nightjars that preyed on them.

Krispos had ordered that he be fed the same as any soldier. He stood in line for hard cheese, harder bread, a cup of rough red wine, and bowl of stew made from smoked pork, garlic, and onions. The cook who ladled out the stew looked nervous. "Begging your pardon, your Majesty, but I'm afraid this isn't so fine as what you're used to."

Krispos laughed at him. "The gravy's thicker than what I grew up with, by the good god, and there's more in the kettle here, too." He spooned out a piece of pork and chewed thoughtfully. "My mother would have thrown in some thyme, I think, if she had it. Otherwise I can't complain."

"He's an army cook, your Majesty," one of the Videssian cavalrymen said. "You expect him to know what he's doing?" Everyone who heard jeered at the cook. Krispos finished quickly and held out his bowl for a second helping. That seemed to make the luckless fellow sweating over his pots a little happier.

Three mornings later, as the army drew near a small town or large village called Patrodoton, one of the scouts came riding back at a gallop. He spoke briefly to Sarkis, who led him to Krispos. "You'd best hear this yourself, your Majesty," the general said.

At Krispos' nod, the scout said, "A couple of the farmers up ahead warned me there's already soldiers in that town."

"Did they?" Krispos clicked his tongue between his teeth.

"Can't expect Petronas just to sit back and let us do as we like," Sarkis remarked.

"No, I suppose not. I wish we could." Krispos thought for

a few seconds. He asked the scout, "Did these farmers say how many men were there?"

The scout shook his head. "Can't be too many, though, I figure, or we'd have some idea they were around before this."

"I think you're right." Krispos turned to Sarkis. "Excellent sir, what if we take a couple of companies of our horsemen here and . . ." He spent a couple of minutes explaining what he had in mind.

But for one broken tooth in front, Sarkis' smile was even and very white. His closed fist thumped against his mail shirt over his heart as he saluted Krispos. "Your Majesty, I think I just may enjoy serving under you."

At the general's command, the panpipers blew "Halt." Sarkis chose his two best company commanders and gave them their orders. They grinned, too; like Sarkis and Krispos, they were young enough to enjoy cleverness for its own sake. Before long, their two contingents trotted down the road toward Patrodoton. The men rode along in loose order, as if they had not a care in the world.

The rest of the army settled down to wait. After a bit, Sarkis ordered them into a defensive position, with the Halogai in the center blocking the road and the remaining Videssian cavalry on either wing. Glancing apologetically over at Krispos, the general said, "We ought to be ready in case it goes wrong."

Krispos nodded. "By all means." Both Tanilis and Petronas had taught him not to take success for granted. But he'd never led large numbers of troops before; he didn't automatically know the right way to insure against mischance. That was why he had Sarkis along. He was glad the general had prudence to go with his dash.

Waiting stretched. The soldiers drank wine, gnawed bread, sang songs, and told each other lies. Krispos stroked his beard and worried. Then one of the Halogai pointed southwest, in the direction of Patrodoton. Krispos saw the dust rising over the roadway. A good many men were heading this way. The Halogai raised their axes to the ready. The Videssians were first and foremost archers. They quickly strung their bows, set arrows to them, and made sure sabers were loose in their scabbards.

But one of Sarkis' two picked company commanders, a small, lean fellow named Zeugmas, rode in front of the oncoming horsemen. His wave was full of exuberance. "We've got 'em!" he shouted. "Come see!"

Krispos touched his heels to Progress' flanks. The horse started forward. Thvari and several other Halogai stepped close together to keep Krispos from advancing. "Let me through!" he said angrily.

The northerner's captain shook his head. "No, Majesty, not by yourself, not when it could be a trap."

"I thought you were my guards, not my jailers," Krispos said. Thvari and the others stood implacable. Krispos sighed. In his younger days, he hadn't wanted to be a soldier, but if he had taken up sword and spear, no one would have kept him from risking his life. Now that he wanted to go into action, the Halogai would not let him. He sighed again, struck by the absurdity of it, but could only yield. "As you wish, gentlemen. Will you come with me?"

Thvari saluted. "Aye, Majesty. We come."

Accompanied by a squad of Halogai—*not that they'll do me much good if the bowmen shoot a volley at me*, he thought— Krispos went out to see what the companies he'd sent out had accomplished. The troopers didn't seem to find that cowardly. They yelled and grinned and waved—and laughed at the glum, disarmed riders in their midst.

"There, you see?" Krispos told Thvari. "It's safe enough."

Thvari's broad shoulders went up and down in a slow, deliberate shrug. "We did not know. Your duty is to rule, Majesty. Ours is to guard." Shamed by the reproach in the captain's voice, Krispos had to nod.

Then Zeugmas came up. "Couldn't have worked better, your Majesty," he said happily. "We bagged the lot of 'em and didn't lose a man doing it. Just like you said, we rode on in cursing you for a bloody usurper and everything else we could think of, and their leader—that sour-faced bastard with the thick mustaches over there; his name's Physakis—figured we'd come to join the rebels, too. Seeing as we had twice his numbers, he was glad to see us. He posted us with his men and didn't take any precautions. We just passed the word along, made sure we got the drop on 'em all at the same time, and—well, here we are."

"Wonderful." Krispos found himself grinning, too. He was no professional soldier, but his stratagem had taken in a man who was. He pointed to Physakis. "Bring him here. Let's see what he knows."

At Zeugmas' orders, a couple of troopers made the rebel officer dismount and marched him over to Krispos. He peered up at Krispos from under lowered brows. "Your Majesty," he mumbled. As Zeugmas had said, his mustaches were luxuriant; Krispos could hardly see his lips move when he spoke.

"You didn't call me 'Majesty' before you got caught," Krispos said. "What shall I do with you now?"

"Whatever you want, of course," Physakis answered. He did indeed look sour, not, Krispos judged, from fear, but more as if his stomach pained him.

"If I decide your parole is good, I'll send you north to serve against Harvas Black-Robe and his cutthroats," Krispos said.

Physakis brightened; he must have expected to meet the axe traitors deserved. With the threat Harvas posed, though, Krispos could not afford to rid himself of every officer who chose Petronas. "You have mages with you, then?" Physakis asked.

"Aye." Krispos contented himself with the bare word. He'd almost gone west without sorcerous aid. Because of the passions that filled men in combat, battle magic was notoriously unreliable. But Petronas had tried before to slay him with sorcery; he wanted protection close at hand if Anthimos' uncle tried again. Wizards were also useful for such noncombat tasks as testing the sincerity of paroles and oaths.

The troopers took Physakis back to Trokoundos and his comrades. One by one, the rest of the captured officers and underofficers of the troop followed him. The common soldiers were another matter. Krispos did not merely want their pledge to fight him no more; he wanted them to take service with him.

When he put that to them, most agreed at once. So long as they had leadership and food, they cared little as to which side they were on. A few, stubbornly loyal to Petronas, refused. As Physakis had before them, they waited nervously for Krispos to decree their fate.

"Take their horses, their mail shirts, and all their weapons but one dagger each," he told his own men. "Then let them go. I don't think they'll be able to do us much harm after that."

"Leave us our money, too, Majesty?" one of them called.

Krispos shook his head. "You earned it by opposing me. But you've shown yourselves to be honest men. You'll find the chance to make more."

While his soldiers disarmed those of Krispos' men who refused to go over to him, the wizards listened to the rest of the troopers from Patrodoton give their oaths of allegiance. When that ceremony was done, Trokoundos approached Krispos. A squad of Halogai followed, along with three increasingly unhappy-looking Videssians.

Trokoundos pointed to them, each in turn. "These three, Majesty, swore falsely, I am sorry to say. While they granted you their pledges, in their hearts they still intended to betray you."

"I might have guessed that would happen," Krispos said. He turned to the Halogai. "Strip them, give them a dozen lashes well laid on, and send them on their way naked. Such traitors are worse than honest foes."

"Aye, Majesty," said Narvikka, the leader of the squad. One of the Videssians tried to bolt. The Halogai grabbed him before he could even break out of their circle. They drove tent pegs into the ground, tied the three captives to them facedown, and swung the whip. The troopers' shrieks punctuated its harsh, flat cracks. When the strokes were done, the Halogai cut the men loose and let them stagger away.

That night the wind began to blow from the northwest. It swept away the hot, humid air that had hung over the coastal lowlands and had made travel in armor an even worse torment than usual. When Krispos came out of his tent the next morning, he saw dirty gray clouds stacked along the northern horizon.

He frowned. Back in his village, fall was on the way when those clouds started piling up over the Paristrian Mountains. And with fall came the fall rains that turned dirt roads to quagmires. "They'd be early if they started so soon."

He didn't realize he'd spoken aloud until Sarkis, who was emerging from the tent next to his, nodded and answered, "Aye, so they would, Majesty. And wouldn't we have a jolly time trying to run Petronas down when we're all squelching through mush?"

Krispos spat, rejecting Sarkis' words as if the officer had invoked Skotos. Sarkis laughed, but they both knew it was no joke. Krispos said, "We'll have to push harder, that's all. The lord with the great and good mind willing, I want to bring Petronas to bay now, while he's still on the run. I don't want him to have the winter to get in touch with all his old cronies and build up his strength."

"Sensible." Sarkis nodded. "Aye, sensible, Majesty. Come next year, you'll have Harvas Black-Robe to worry about; you won't want to split time between Petronas and him."

"Exactly." Krispos' estimation of Sarkis went up a notch. Not many soldiers worried about Harvas, or about the northern frontier in general, as much as he did. Then he wondered if Sarkis was agreeing with his concern just to curry favor. Being Avtokrator meant making an unending string of such judgments. He hadn't expected that. He didn't care for it, either.

He lined up for breakfast, taking a thick slice of bread and a handful of salted olives. He spat out the last olive pit from atop Progress. His soldiers drove toward Petronas' estates as fast as they could. The suddenly milder weather helped keep men and horses fresh, but every time Krispos looked northward over his shoulder he saw more clouds building up. He could not even urge the troops to better speed, not unless he wanted to leave the Halogai in the cavalry's dust. He could grumble, and he did.

Nor were his spirits lifted when an imperial courier caught up with the army from behind; that only reminded him he could have been going faster. The rolled-up parchment the rider delivered was sealed with sky-blue wax. "From the patriarch, eh?" Krispos said to the courier. "Did he give you the gist of it?" People who sent messages sometimes did, to make sure that what they had to say got through even if their written words were lost.

But the courier shook his head. "No, your Majesty."

"All right, I'll see for myself." Krispos broke the seal. Florid salutations and greetings from Pyrrhos took up half the sheet. Krispos skipped over them, looking for meat. At last he found it, two chunks: Gnatios was still immured in the monastery, where he had begun to compile a chronicle to help pass the time, and Pyrrhos had seen fit to depose an abbot and two prelates for false doctrines and another abbot for refusing to acknowledge his authority.

Krispos rubbed the side of his head with his hand. He'd expected Pyrrhos to be contentious; why should he be surprised now to have the man prove him right?

"Is there a reply, Majesty?" the courier asked. He took out a waxed tablet and stylus.

"Yes." Krispos paused to order his thoughts, then said, " 'Avtokrator Krispos to the patriarch Pyrrhos: Greetings. I hope you will keep peace among the priests and monks, prelates and abbots of the temples. With a rebel in the field and an enemy on our border, we have no need for more strife.' That's all. Let me hear it, if you would."

The courier read the message back. At Krispos' nod, he closed the tablet. He carried a stick of sealing wax. Someone not far away had a torch going; easier to bring fire along than to start it fresh every night. The soldier fetched the torch; in a moment, melted wax dripped down onto the closed tablet. While the wax was still soft, Krispos sealed it with the imperial sunburst. The courier saluted and rode away.

Because of his complete success at Patrodoton, Krispos gained another day and a half to advance unopposed. He knew he was nearing Petronas' estates. He also knew that was fortunate. Rain began to fall toward evening of the first day out of Patrodoton and showed no sign of letting up during the night.

At first the rain was welcome, for it kept down the choking clouds of dust the horses would otherwise have raised. But as the next day wore on and the rain kept coming, Krispos felt Progress begin to work to pick up his feet and heard the horse's hooves pull loose from the thickening mud with wet, sucking sounds.

In the fields, farmers worked like men possessed as they battled to get in their crops before the rains ruined them. They were even too frantic to be afraid of Krispos' army. Remembering the desperation the folk of his village had felt once or twice because of early fall rains, he knew what they were going through and wished them well.

Just after noon on the second day of the rains, Krispos and his soldiers came to the Eriza River, a fair-size stream that ran south into the Arandos. A wooden bridge should have spanned the Eriza. In spite of the rain, the bridge was burned. Peering across to the western bank, Krispos made out patrolling riders.

In spite of the rain, they saw him and his men, too. They shook their fists and shouted insults Krispos could barely hear through the rain and across a hundred years of water. One cry, though, he made out clearly: "Petronas Avtokrator!"

Rage ripped through him. "Give them a volley," he barked to Sarkis.

The general's bushy eyebrows came together above his nose as he frowned. "With the bows we have, the range isn't short, and we'll get our bowstrings wet when we shoot," he said. "If they have men on this side of the river, too, that could leave us in a nasty spot."

Reluctantly, Krispos nodded. "A company, then," he said. "Just something to shut their mouths."

"Aye, why not?" Sarkis rode down the line to the troopers Zeugmas led. Krispos watched Zeugmas object as the regimental commander had, watched Sarkis talk him round. The horsemen in Zeugmas' company quickly strung their bows, plucked arrows from quivers, and let fly. Some tried second shots, a few third. Then, fast as they'd taken them out, they put away their bowstrings to protect them from the rain.

On the far side of the Eriza, the jeers abruptly turned to cries of alarm and pain. Krispos saw one man slide from the saddle. The rest set spur to their horses and drew away from the riverbank. A couple of Petronas' troopers shot back. An arrow buried itself in the mud not far from Krispos. Another clattered off a Haloga's axe. No one on this side of the river seemed hurt.

"We can't cross here," Krispos said.

"Not unless we want to swim," Sarkis agreed, watching the brown waters of the Eriza foam creamily against the pilings of the burned bridge. The regimental commander was not downhearted. "The farmers hereabouts will know where the fords are, I expect."

"So they will," Krispos said; he'd known all the best places to cross the streams near his old village. "But we'd best not waste time finding one. This river's going to start rising, and it's big enough that if it does, we won't be able to cross anywhere."

The peasants hereabouts were stolid, serious people, altogether unlike the clever magpie men who called Videssos the city home. The sight of gold in Krispos' palm quickly turned them voluble, though. "Aye, lord, there's a good place to ford half a league north of here, there is, by the dead elm tree," a farmer said. "And there's another, not so good, rather more than that southward, where the Eriza takes a little jog, if you know what I mean."

"My thanks." Krispos gave the peasant two goldpieces. To his embarrassment, the fellow clumsily prostrated himself in the mud. "Get up, you fool! Ten years ago I was just a farmer myself, working a field not near so fine as this one."

The peasant scrambled to his feet, filthy and dripping, his eyes puzzled. "You—were a farmer, lord? How could you be a farmer? You are Avtokrator!"

Krispos gave it up. He would only be sure of staying Avtokrator if he got across the Eriza. He turned Progress away from the farmer. His captains, who had gathered round to hear his exchange with the man, were already shouting orders. "North half a league to a dead elm tree!"

They squelched along by the river, moving more slowly than they would have when the weather was good. Normally, a local landmark like a dead elm would have been easy to find. In the rain, they almost rode past it. Krispos urged Progress into the river. The water rose to the horse's belly before he was a quarter of the way across. "This isn't as easy as that peasant made it out to be," he said.

"So it isn't." Sarkis pointed across to the western bank of the river. Horsemen with bows and lances waited there. More came trotting up while he and Krispos watched.

"We outnumber them," Krispos said without conviction.

"So we do." Sarkis sounded unhappy, too. He pointed out what Krispos had also seen. "We can't bring our numbers to bear, though, not by way of a narrow ford. Where numbers count, they have more than we do."

"They knew where this ford was," Krispos said, thinking aloud. "As soon as we came to the bridge, they started gathering here."

Sarkis nodded mournfully. "They're probably at the other one, as well, the one where the Eriza jogs."

"Curse these early rains!" Krispos snarled.

"Just have to hunt up some more farmers," Sarkis said. "Sooner or later we'll find a ford that's unguarded. Once we're across, we may be able to roll up the rebels all along the river." The regimental commander was not one to stay downcast long.

Krispos' spirits lifted more slowly. The rain that splashed against his face and trickled through his beard did nothing to improve his mood. "If the river keeps rising, there won't be any fords, no matter what we learn from the farmers."

"True enough," Sarkis said, "but if we can't get at them for a while, they can't get at us, either."

Though Krispos nodded, that thought consoled him less than it did Sarkis. As was fitting and proper, the regimental commander thought like a soldier. As Avtokrator, Krispos had to achieve a wider vision. All the Empire of Videssos was his by right; any part that did not obey his will diminished his rule, in an odd way diminished him personally.

"We'll find a ford," Sarkis said.

Finding one that Petronas' men were not covering took two days and wore Krispos' patience to rags. At last, though, squad by squad, his troopers began making their way across the Eriza. Though the peasant who'd told of the ford swore it was an easy one, the horses had to fight to move forward against the rain-swollen stream.

The Halogai waited with Krispos. When they crossed, they would hang onto the tails of the last cavalry company's horses; the Eriza might well have swept away a man who tried that ford afoot. They found the fall rains funny. "In our country, Majesty, rain is for the end of spring and for summer," Vagn said. The rest of the northerners around Krispos chorused agreement.

"No wonder so many of you come south," he said.

"Aye, that's the way of it, Majesty," Vagn said. "To a Haloga, even the weather in Kubrat would seem good."

Having spent several years in Kubrat, Krispos found that prospect appalling. It gave him a measure of how harsh life in Halogaland had to be—and a new worry. He asked, "With Harvas Black-Robe and his mercenaries holding Kubrat, does that mean more Halogai might come south to settle there?"

"It could, Majesty," Vagn said after a thoughtful pause. "That would bear hard on Videssos, were it so."

"Yes," was all Krispos answered. He already knew he could not rely on all his Videssian soldiers against Petronas. When he took the field against Harvas, would he be able to trust his own Haloga guards?

One thing at a time, he told himself. After he dealt with Petronas, almost all the rank-and-file troopers in Videssian service would rally to him, especially if he campaigned against a foreign foe.

"Your Majesty?" someone called. "Your Majesty?"

"Here," Krispos answered. The Halogai who had been about to cross the Eriza turned back and formed up around him, weapons ready. That unthinking protective move told him more plainly than any oaths that these were loyal troops.

The man who asked for Krispos proved to be an imperial courier who sat soaked and bedraggled atop a blowing horse. "I have a dispatch from the Sevastos Mavros, your Majesty," he said, holding out a tube of waxed and oiled leather. "If you like, I can give you the news it bears. I must tell you, it is not good."

"Let me hear it, and I will judge," Krispos said, wondering how bad it would be. It was bad enough, he saw, to make the courier nervous. "Speak! By the good god, I know you only bring news; you don't cause it."

"Thank you, your Majesty." Even in the rain, the courier licked his lips before he went on. And when he did, the word he gave was worse than any Krispos had imagined. "Majesty, Harvas and his raiders have sacked the town of Develtos."

# III

KRISPOS NOTICED HE WAS GRINDING HIS TEETH. HE MADE HIM-
self stop. All the same, he felt pulled apart. How was he supposed to deal with Petronas if Harvas Black-Robe invaded the
Empire? And how could he deal with Harvas if Petronas clung
to his revolt?

"Majesty?" the courier said when he was some time silent.
"What is your will, Majesty?"

*A good question*, Krispos thought. He laughed harshly. "My
will is that Harvas go to Skotos' ice, and Petronas with him.
Neither of them seems as interested in my will as you do, though,
worse luck for me."

Taking the liberty the courier dared not, Sarkis asked, "What
will you do, Majesty?"

Krispos pondered that while the rain muttered down all
around. Not the least part of his pondering was Sarkis himself.
If he left the regimental commander here by the Eriza alone,
would he stay loyal or desert to Petronas? If he did go over, all
the westlands save perhaps the suburbs across from Videssos the
city would be lost. But if Krispos gave his attention solely to
overthrowing Petronas, how much of the Empire would Harvas
ravage while he was doing it?

He realized that was but a different phrasing for the unpalatable questions he'd asked himself before. As if he had no doubt
Sarkis would remain true—as if the notion that Sarkis could do
otherwise had never crossed his mind—he said, "I'll go back
to the city. I can best deal with Harvas from there. Now that
we've pushed over the Eriza, I want you to go after Petronas

with everything you have. If you can seize him this winter, few rewards would be big enough.''

The regimental commander's eyes were dark and fathomless as twin pools reflecting the midnight sky. Nevertheless, Krispos thought he saw a faint light in them, as if a star were shining on those midnight pools. Saluting, Sarkis said, ''You may rely on me, your Majesty.''

''I do,'' Krispos said simply. He wished he did not have to. He hoped Sarkis did not know that, but suspected—half feared— the Vaspurakaner soldier was clever enough to grasp it.

Thvari said, ''My men will escort you back to the city, Majesty.''

''A squad will do,'' Krispos said. ''I want the rest of you to stay with Sarkis and help him run Petronas to earth.''

But Thvari shook his head. ''We are your guardsmen, Majesty. We took oath by our gods to ward your body. Ward it we shall; our duty is to you, not to Videssos.''

''The eunuchs in the palace think they have the right to tell the Avtokrator what to do,'' Krispos said, his voice somewhere between amusement and chagrin. ''Do you claim it, too, Thvari?''

The Haloga captain folded his arms across his broad chest. ''In this, Majesty, aye. Think you—you travel a land in revolt. A squad, even a troop, is not enough to assure your safety.''

Krispos saw Thvari would not yield. ''As you wish,'' he said, reflecting that the longer he held the throne, the less absolute his power looked.

As it happened, he and the Halogai met not a single foeman on their long, muddy slog back to Videssos the city. They did see one fellow, though, who plainly took them for enemies: a monk going west on muleback, the hood of his blue robe drawn up over his shaven pate to protect him from the rain. He kicked his mount into a stiff-legged trot and rode far around the oncoming soldiers before he dared return to the highway.

The Halogai snickered at the monk's fear. With delicate irony, Krispos asked, ''Bold captain Thvari, do you think a squad of your heroes would have been enough to save me from that desperado?''

Thvari refused to be baited. ''By the look of him, Majesty, belike he would have set on a mere squad.'' Krispos had to laugh. The northerner went on more seriously. ''Besides, who's to say that if you had only the squad, you mightn't have come across a whole horde of Petronas' rogues? The gods delight in sending woe to folk who scant their safety. No man outwits his fate, but it may entrap him before his time.''

"I know why that monk turned aside from us," Krispos said: "for fear of having to argue theology with you."

"Few Halogai turn to Phos, but not for the priests' lack of trying," Thvari said. "Your god suits you of the Empire, and our gods suit us." Krispos remained convinced the northerners' gods were false, but could not deny the quality of the men who followed them.

He and his guards reached the suburbs across from the imperial city two days later. The courier had preceded them; boats were waiting to take them over the Cattle-Crossing. The short trip left Krispos green-faced and gulping, for the northerly winds that brought the fall rains had also turned the strait choppy. He sketched the sun-circle over his heart when he was back on dry land. Through the thick, gray rain clouds, though, Phos' sun could not be seen.

Long faces greeted him when he entered the imperial residence. "Cheer up," he said. "The world hasn't ended." He tapped the message tube the courier had brought him. "I know losing Develtos is a hard blow, but I think I have a way around it, or at least a way to keep Harvas quiet until I've settled Petronas."

"Very good, your Majesty. I am pleased to hear it." But Barsymes did not seem pleased, nor did his features lighten. *Well*, Krispos told himself, *that's just his way—he never looks happy*. Then the vestiarios said, "Majesty, I fear the evil news does not stop at Develtos."

Krispos stiffened. Just when he could hope he'd solved one problem, another came along to throw him back again. "You'd better tell me," he said heavily.

"I hear and obey, Majesty. No doubt you can comprehend that the most holy Pyrrhos' elevation to the patriarchate entailed some confusion for the monastery dedicated to the memory of the holy Skirios. So forceful an abbot as Pyrrhos, I daresay, would not have suffered others there to gain or exercise much authority. Thus no one, it appears, paid close enough attention to the comings and goings of the monks. In fine, your Majesty, the former patriarch Gnatios is nowhere to be found."

Krispos grunted as if he'd taken a blow in the belly. All at once he remembered the westbound monk who'd been so skittish on seeing him and the Halogai. He had no way of knowing whether that was Gnatios, but the fellow had been going where

Gnatios, if free, was likeliest to go—toward land Petronas controlled. He said that aloud, adding, "So now Petronas will have a patriarch of his own, to crown him properly and to call Pyrrhos' appointment illegal."

"That does seem probable," Barsymes agreed. He dipped his head to Krispos. "For one new to the throne—indeed, to the city and its intrigues—you show a distinct gift for such maneuvers."

"It's what I'd do, were I in Petronas' boots," Krispos said, shrugging.

"Indeed. Well, Petronas is no mean schemer, so you have not contradicted me."

"I know that only too well. From whom do you think I learned?" Krispos thought for a while, then went on. "When you go, Barsymes, send in a secretary. I'll draft a proclamation of outlawry against Gnatios and offer a reward for his capture or death. I suppose I should also have Pyrrhos condemn him on behalf of the temples."

"The ecumenical patriarch has already seen to that, your Majesty," Barsymes said. "Yesterday he issued an anathema against Gnatios and read it publicly at the High Temple. It was quite a vituperative document, I must say, even for one of that sort. Some of the phrases that stick in the mind are 'perverter of the patriarchate,' 'spiritual leper,' and 'viper vilely hissing at the altar.' "

"They never were fond of each other," Krispos observed. Barsymes let one eyebrow rise in understated appreciation for the understatement. Sighing, Krispos continued, "Trouble is, Gnatios will just fling his own anathemas right back at Pyrrhos, so neither set will end up accomplishing anything."

"Pyrrhos' will appear first, and he does control the ecclesiastical hierarchy and preach from the High Temple. His words should carry the greater weight," Barsymes said.

"That's true," Krispos said. The thought consoled him a little. As it was the only consolation he'd had for the last several days, he cherished it as long as he could.

The general Agapetos rubbed a raw new pink scar that puckered his right cheek. In size and placement, it almost matched an old pale one on the other side of his face. He looked relieved to be reporting his failure in a chamber off the Grand Courtroom rather than from a prison cell to an unsympathetic jailer. "By the good god, Majesty, I still don't know how the bugger got past me to Develtos with so many men," he said, his deep voice querulous. "I don't know how he took the place so quick, either."

"That puzzles me, too," Krispos said. He'd been through Develtos, a cheerless gray fortress town that helped ward the road between the capital and the eastern port of Opsikion. Its walls had seemed forbiddingly tall and solid.

"I hear magic toppled one of the towers and let the savages in," Iakovitzes said.

Agapetos snorted. "That's always the excuse of those who run first and fastest. They lie as fast as they run, too. If battle magic worked even a quarter of the time, wizards would fight wars and soldiers could go home and tend their gardens."

"As far as I know, the only ones who got out of Develtos alive were the ones who ran first and fastest," Mavros put in. "All the rest are dead."

"Aye, that's so," Agapetos said. "The Halogai are bloodthirsty devils, and this Harvas strikes me as downright vicious. Still and all, my lads were keeping the raiders to their side of the frontier. Then somehow he slid a whole army past us. Maybe it *was* magic, your Majesty. I don't see how else he could have done it. May the ice take me if I lie."

"I've heard that claimed of Harvas before," Krispos said. "I never really believed it; whenever a man has great good fortune, people naturally think he's a mage. But now I do begin to wonder."

"The Halogai slew all the priests in the city, it's said," Mavros observed. "If Harvas is a wizard, he is not one who works by the power of Phos."

"Of course a heathen Haloga doesn't work magic by the power of Phos," Iakovitzes said. "And if the savages were killing everyone in the city, I doubt they'd have bothered to spare anyone just because he was wearing a blue robe. Would you?" He lifted an elegantly arched eyebrow.

Mavros knew better than to take him seriously. "I'm sorry, excellent sir, but I must confess that, never having sacked a town, I really couldn't say."

A little of Iakovitzes' sarcasm was bracing. More than a little had a way of disrupting things. Not wanting that to happen now, Krispos said, "The real question is, what to do next? If I fight Petronas and Harvas at the same time, I split my forces and can't concentrate on either one. But if I neglect one and just fight the other, the one I ignore has free rein."

"Are you wondering why you ever wanted to be Avtokrator in the first place?" Iakovitzes asked with malicious relish.

"I didn't particularly want to be Avtokrator," Krispos retorted, "but letting Anthimos go ahead and kill me didn't look all that good, either."

"You're going to have to buy time with one of your foes so you can crush the other one, Krispos," Mavros said. "If you hadn't already been at war with Petronas, I could have led a fresh force out from the city and joined Agapetos against Harvas. As it was, I didn't dare, in case you were defeated in the westlands and needed aid."

"I'm glad you stayed here," Krispos said quickly, remembering Tanilis' letter. He went on, "It galls me, but I fear you're right. And it galls me worse that the one I'll have to buy off is Harvas. Petronas paid him to invade Kubrat, so I know he takes gold. And once I've beaten Petronas—why, then, the good god willing, master Harvas may just have to give that gold back, among other things. If he thinks I'll ever forget Develtos, or forgive, he's mistaken."

"Still, you're making the right choice," Iakovitzes said, nodding vigorously. "You can't afford to treat with Petronas; that would be as much as recognizing him as your equal. A reigning Avtokrator has no equals inside Videssos. But paying off a foreign prince who's made a nuisance of himself—why, it happens all the time."

Krispos glanced to Mavros, who also nodded. Agapetos said, "Aye, Majesty, settle the civil war first. Once the whole Empire is behind you, then you can have another go at Harvas when the time is ripe."

"How much did Petronas pay Harvas to bring his murderers south into Kubrat?" Krispos asked.

"Fifty pounds of gold—thirty-six hundred goldpieces," Iakovitzes answered at once.

"Then you can offer him up to twice that much if you have to, and buy me a year's peace with him," Krispos said. "I trust you'll be able to get him to settle for less, though, being the able dickerer you are."

Iakovitzes glared at him. "I was afraid you were leading up to that."

"You're the best envoy I have," Krispos said. "How many embassies to the folk of the north have you headed? We first met in Kubrat, remember? I still wear that goldpiece you gave the old khagan Omurtag when you were ransoming the lot of kidnapped peasants I was part of. So you know what you need to do, and I know I can rely on you.''

''If it were a mission to the Kubrat that was, or to Khatrish, or even Thatagush, I'd say aye without thinking twice, though all those lands are bloody barbarous,'' Iakovtizes said slowly. ''Harvas, now . . . Harvas is something else. I tell you frankly, Krispos—your Majesty—he alarms me. He wants more than just plunder. He wants slaughter, and maybe more than that.''

''Harvas alarms me, too,'' Krispos admitted. ''If you think you're going into danger, Iakovtizes, I won't send you.''

''No, I'll go.'' Iakovtizes ran a hand through his graying hair. ''After all, what could he do? For one thing, he may have to send an embassy here one fine day, and I know—and he'd know—you'd avenge any harm that came to me. And for another, I'm coming to pay him tribute, lots of tribute. How could I making him angry doing that?''

Mavros leered at the short, feisty noble. ''If anyone could manage, Iakovtizes, you're the man.''

''Ah, your Highness,'' Iakovtizes said in a tone of sweet regret, ''were you not suddenly become second lord in all the land, be assured I would tell you precisely what sort of cocky, impertinent, jumped-up little snipsnap bastard son of a snake and a cuckoo you really are.'' By the time he finished, he was shouting, red-faced, his eyes bulging.

''Kind and gracious as always,'' Krispos told him, doing his best not to laugh.

''You, too, eh?'' Iakovtizes growled. ''Well, you'd just better watch out, your Majesty. As best I can tell, I can call *you* anything I bloody well please for a while and not worry a bit about lèse majesté, because if you send me to the chap with the axe, you can't send me to Harvas.''

''That depends on where I tell him to cut,'' Krispos said.

Iakovtizes grabbed his crotch in mock horror. Just then Barsymes brought in a fresh jar of wine and a plate of smoked octopus tentacles. The eunuch looked down his long nose at Iakovtizes. ''There are not many men to whom I would say this, excellent sir, but I suspect you would be as much a scandal without your stones as with them.''

''Why, thank you,'' Iakovitzes said, which made even the imperturbable vestiarios blink. Krispos raised his cup in salute. So long as Iakovitzes had his tongue, he was armed and dangerous.

* * *

Iakovitzes set out on his mission to Harvas a few days later. Krispos promptly put him in a back corner of his mind; what with the state of the roads during the fall rains and the blizzards that would follow them, he did not expect the noble to be back before spring.

Of more immediate concern was Sarkis' continuing campaign against Petronas. By his dispatches, the regimental commander was making progress, but at a snail's pace thanks to the weather. The rains were still falling when he reached the first of Petronas' estates. "Drove off to westward the cavalry who sought to oppose us," he wrote, "then attempted to fire the villa and outbuildings we had taken. Too wet for a truly satisfactory job, but no one will be able to use them for a good long while yet."

When Krispos was a youth, the world in winter had seemed to contract to no more than his village and the fields around it. Even as Avtokrator, something similar happened. Though news came in from all over the Empire, everything beyond Videssos the city seemed dim and distant, as if seen through thick fog. Not least because of that, he paid more attention to the people closest to him.

By Midwinter's Day, Dara was visibly pregnant, though not in the thick robes she wore to the Amphitheater to watch the skits that celebrated the sun's swing back toward the north. Midwinter's Day was a time of license; a couple of the pantomime shows lewdly speculated on what Dara's relationship with Krispos had been before Anthimos died. Krispos laughed even when the jokes on him weren't funny. After looking angry at first, Dara went along, though she said, "Some of those so-called clowns should be horsewhipped through the plaza of Palamas."

"It's Midwinter's Day," Krispos said, as if that explained everything. To him, it did.

Some of the servants had started a bonfire in front of the steps that led into the imperial residence. It still blazed brightly when the imperial party returned from the Amphitheater. Krispos dismounted from Progress. He tossed the reins to a groom. Then, holding the crown on his head with one hand, he dashed toward the fire, sprang into the air. "Burn, ill luck!" he shouted as he flew over the flames.

A moment later he heard more running feet. "Burn, ill luck!" Dara called. Her jump barely carried her across the fire. She staggered when she landed. She might have fallen, had Krispos not reached out a quick hand to steady her.

"That was foolish," he said, angry now himself. "Why have

you been traveling in a litter the past month, but to keep you from wearing yourself out or hurting yourself? Then you go and risk it all—and for what? Holiday hijinks!''

She pulled away from him. ''I'm not made of pottery, you know. I won't shatter if you look at me sideways. And besides—'' She lowered her voice. ''—what with Petronas, Gnatios, and Harvas Black-Robe, don't you think more ill luck is out there than one alone can easily burn away?''

His anger melted, as the snow had around the campfire. ''Aye, that's so.'' He put an arm round her shoulder. ''But I wish you'd be more careful.''

She shook him off. He saw he'd somehow annoyed her again. Then she said, ''Is that for my sake, or just on account of the child in my belly?''

''For both,'' he answered honestly. Her eyes stayed narrowed as she studied him. He said, ''Come on, now. Have you seen me building any minnow ponds?''

She blinked, then found herself laughing. ''No, I suppose not.'' Minnows had been a euphemism Anthimos used for one of the last of his debauched schemes—one of the few times Anthimos bothered with euphemism, Krispos thought. Dara went on, ''After living with such worries so long, do you wonder that I have trouble trusting?''

By way of answer, he put his arm around her again. This time she let it stay. They walked up the steps and down the hallway together. When they got to their bedchamber, she closed and barred the doors behind them. At his quizzical look, she said, ''You were the one who was talking about it being Midwinter's Day.''

They wasted no time undressing and sliding under the blankets. Though brick-lined ducts under the floor brought warm air from a central furnace, the bedchamber was still chilly. Krispos' hand traced the small bulge rising around Dara's navel. Her mouth twisted into a peculiar expression, half pride, half pout. ''I liked myself better flat-bellied,'' she said.

''I like you fine the way you are.'' To prove what he said, Krispos let his hand linger.

She scowled ferociously. ''Did you like me throwing up every morning and every other afternoon? I'm not doing that as often now, the good god be praised.''

''I'm glad you're not,'' Krispos said. ''I—'' He stopped. Under his palm, something—fluttered? rolled? twisted? He could not find the right word. Wonder in his voice, he asked, "Was that the baby?"

Dara nodded. "I've felt him—" She always called the child to come *him*. "—moving for a week or ten days now. That's the hardest wiggle yet, though. I'm not surprised you noticed it."

"What does it feel like to you?" he asked, all at once more curious than aroused. He pressed lightly on her belly, hoping the baby inside would stir again.

"It's rather like—" Dara frowned, shook her head. "I started to say it felt like gas, like what would happen if I ate too much cucumber and octopus salad. It did, when he first started moving. But these bigger squirmings don't feel *like* anything, if you know what I mean. You'd understand, if you were a woman."

"Yes, I suppose I would. But since I'm not, I have to ask foolish questions." As if on cue, the baby moved again. Krispos hugged Dara close. "*We* did that!" he exclaimed, before he recalled he might not have had anything to do with it at all.

If Dara remembered that, too, she gave no sign. "*We* may have started it," she said tartly, "but *I'm* the one who has to do the rest of the work."

"Oh, hush." The feel of Dara's warm, smooth body pressed against his own reminded Krispos why they were in bed together. He rolled her onto her back. As they joined, he looked down at her and said, "Since you're complaining, I'll do the work tonight."

"Fair enough," she said, her eyes glowing in the lamplight. "We won't be able to do it this way too much longer anyhow—someone coming between us, you might say. So let's—" She paused, her breath going short for a moment. "—enjoy it while we can."

"Oh, yes," he said, "Oh, yes."

The message Iakovitzes had sent out well before Midwinter's Day arrived several weeks after the festival was over. All the same, Krispos was glad to have it. "Harvas wants to take the tribute. We've been haggling over how much. His is not simple Haloga greed; he fights for every copper like a prawn-seller in the city (not a prawn to be had here, worse luck—nothing but bloody mutton and bloody beef). By the lord with the great and good mind, Majesty, he nearly frightens me: he is very fierce and very clever. But I give as good as I get, I think. Yours in frigid resignation from the blizzards of Pliskavos—"

Krispos smiled as he rolled up the parchment. He could easily summon a picture of Iakovitzes' sharp tongue carving strips off a barbarous warlord too slow-witted to realize he'd been insulted. Then Krispos read the letter again. If Harvas Black-Robe was clever—and everything Krispos knew of him pointed that way—Iakovitzes' acid barbs might sink deep.

He closed the letter once more and tied a ribbon around it. Iakovitzes had been treating with barbarians for close to thirty years—for as long as Krispos had been alive. He'd know not to go too far.

What had been a quiet winter in matters ecclesiastical heated up when Pyrrhos abruptly expelled four priests from their temples. Seeing the blunt announcement in with the rest of the paperwork, Krispos summoned the patriarch. "What's all this in aid of?" he asked, tapping the parchment. "I thought I told you I wanted quiet in the temples."

"So you did, Majesty, but without true doctrine and fidelity, what value has mere quiet?" Pyrrhos, as Krispos had long known, was not one to compromise. The patriarch went on, "As you will note in my memorandum there, I had reason in each case. Bryones of the temple of the holy Nestorios was heard to preach that you were a false Avtokrator and I a false patriarch."

"Can't have that," Krispos agreed. He wished Gnatios had never gotten out of his monastic cell. Not only did he confer legitimacy on Petronas' revolt, but as patriarch-in-exile he also provided a focus for clerics who found Pyrrhos' strict interpretation of ecclesiastical law and custom unbearable.

"To continue," the patriarch said, ticking off the errant priests' transgressions on his fingers, "Norikos of the temple of the holy Thelalaios flagrantly cohabited with a woman, an abuse apparently long tolerated thanks to the laxness that prevailed under Gnatios. The priest Loutzoulos had the habit of wearing robes with silk in the weave, vestments entirely too luxurious for one of his station. And Savianos . . ." Pyrrhos' voice sank in horror to a hoarse whisper. "Savianos has espoused the Balancer heresy."

"Has he?" Krispos remembered Savianos speaking out against Pyrrhos' nomination as patriarch. He was sure Pyrrhos had not forgotten, either. "How do you know?" he asked, wondering how vindictive Pyrrhos was: more than a little, he suspected.

"By his own words I shall convict him, Majesty," Pyrrhos said. "In his sermons he has declared that Skotos darkens Phos' radiant glory. How could this be so unless the good god and the master of evil—" He spat in renunciation of Skotos. "—stand equally matched in the Eternal Balance?"

Imperial orthodoxy preached that in the end Phos was sure to vanquish Skotos. The eastern lands of Khatrish and Thatagush also worshiped Phos, but their priests maintained no man could know whether good or evil would triumph in the end—thus their concept of the Balance.

Krispos knew the Balance had its attractions even for some Videssian theologians. But he asked, "Are you sure that's the only meaning you can put on what Savianos said?"

Pyrrhos' eyes glittered dangerously. "Name another."

Not for the first time, Krispos wished his formal education went farther than reading and writing, adding and subtracting. "Maybe it was just a fancy way of saying there is still evil in the world. Phos hasn't won yet, you know."

"Given the sad state of sinfulness I see all around me, I am but too aware of that." Pyrrhos shook his head. "No, Majesty, I fear Savianos' speech cannot be interpreted so innocently. When a man of that stripe admires Skotos' strength, his remarks must have a sinister import."

"Suppose a priest who had always supported you spoke in the same way," Krispos said. "What would you do then?"

"Upbraid him, chastise him, and expel him," Pyrrhos said at once. "Evil is evil, no matter from whose lips it comes. May the lord with the great and good mind guard against it." He drew the sun-circle over his heart.

Krispos also signed himself. He studied the ecumenical patriarch he had created. At last, reluctantly, he decided he had to believe Pyrrhos. The patriarch was narrow, aye, but within his limits just. Sighing, Krispos said, "Very well, then, most holy sir, act as you think best."

"I shall, your Majesty, I assure you. These four are but the snow-covered tip of a mountain of corruption. They are the ones who shine most brightly when Phos' sun lights their misdeeds, but their glitter shall not blind me to the rest of the mountain, either."

"Now wait one moment, if you please," Krispos said hastily, holding up his hand. "I did not name you to your office to have you spread chaos through the temples."

"What is the function of the patriarch but to root out sin where he finds it?" Pyrrhos said. "If you think some other duty comes before it, then cast me down now." He bowed his head to show his acceptance of that imperial prerogative.

Krispos realized that in Pyrrhos he had at last found someone more stubborn than he was. Seeing that, he also realized he had been naive to hope the greater responsibilities of the patriarchate would temper Pyrrhos' pious obstinacy. And finally, he understood that since he could not afford to oust Pyrrhos from the blue boots—no other man, hastily set in place, could serve as much of a counterweight to Gnatios—he was stuck with him for the time being.

"As I told you, most holy sir, you must act as you think best," he said. "But, I pray you, remember also the—" What had Savianos called it? "—the principle of theological economy."

"Where the principle applies, Majesty, rest assured that I shall," Pyrrhos said. "I must warn you, though, its application is less sweeping than some would claim."

No, Krispos thought, Pyrrhos was not a man to yield much ground. He gave a sharp, short nod to show the audience was over. Pyrrhos prostrated himself—whatever his flaws, disrespect for the imperial office was not one of them—and departed. As soon as he was gone, Krispos shouted for a jar of wine.

Looking at a map of the Empire, Krispos observed, "I'm just glad Harvas' murderers decided to withdraw after they took Develtos. If they'd pressed on, they could have reached the Sailors' Sea and cut the eastern provinces in half."

"Yes, that would have spilled the chamber pot into the soup, wouldn't it?" Mavros said. "As is, though, you're still going to have to restore the town, you know."

"I've already begun to take care of it," Krispos said. "I've sent word out through the city guilds that the fisc will pay double the usual daily rate for potters and plasterers and tilemakers and carpenters and stonecutters and what have you willing to go to Develtos for the summer. From what the guildmasters say, we'll have enough volunteers to make the place a going concern again by fall."

"The guilds are the best way to get the people you'll need," Mavros agreed. Labor in Videssos the city was as minutely regulated as everything else; the guildmasters reported to the eparch of the city, as if they were government functionaries themselves. Mavros pursed his lips, then went on. "Stonecutters, aye; they'll need more than a few of those, considering what happened to Develtos' wall."

"Yes," Krispos said somberly. The reports from survivors of the attack and later witnesses told how one whole side of the fortifications had been blasted down, most likely by magic. Afterwards Harvas' northern mercenaries swarmed into the stunned town and began their massacre. "Till now, I thought battle magic was supposed to be a waste of time, that it didn't work well with folk all keyed up to fight."

"I thought the same thing," Mavros said. "I talked with your friend Trokoundos and a couple of other mages. From what they say, the spell that knocked over the wall wasn't battle magic, strictly speaking. Harvas or whoever did it must have spirited his soldiers past the frontier and got them to Develtos with no one the wiser. That made the sorcery a lot easier, because the garrison wasn't expecting attack and didn't get into that excited state until the stones came crashing down onto them."

"Which was too late," Krispos said. Mavros nodded. Krispos added, "The next question is, how did Harvas get his army over the border like that?"

Mavros had no answer. Neither did anyone else. Krispos knew Trokoundos had interrogated Agapetos with the same double mirror arrangement he'd used on Gnatios. Even sorcerously prodded, the general had no idea how Harvas' men eluded his. Maybe magic had played a part there, too, but nobody could be sure.

Krispos said, "By the good god, I hope Harvas and his murderers can't spring out of nowhere in front of Videssos the city and smash through the walls here." The imperial capital's walls were far stronger than those of a provincial town like Develtos, so much so that no foreign foe had ever taken the city. Nor had any Videssians, save by treachery. Harvas Black-Robe, though, was looking like a foe of an uncommon sort.

"Now we'll have wizards ever on the alert here," Mavros said. "Taking us by surprise won't be as easy as it was in Develtos. And surprise, the mages say, was the main reason he succeeded there."

"Yes, yes." Krispos still fretted. Maybe that was because he was so new on the throne, he thought; with more experience, he might have a better sense of just how dangerous Harvas truly was. All the same, like any sensible man, he preferred to be ready for a threat that wasn't there than to ignore one that was. He said, "I wish Petronas wouldn't have picked now to rebel. If he gave up, I'd be happy to let him keep his head. Harvas worries me more."

"Even after you're buying Harvas off?"

"Especially after I'm buying Harvas off." Krispos plucked at his thick, curly beard, then snapped his fingers in sudden decision. "I'll even tell Petronas as much, in writing. If he and Gnatios will come back to the monastery, I won't take any measures against them." He raised his voice to call for a secretary.

Before the scribe arrived, Mavros asked, "And if he says no?"

"Then he says no. How am I worse off?"

Mavros considered, then judiciously pursed his lips. "Put that way, I don't suppose you are."

When the secretary came in, he set down his tablet and stylus so he could prostrate himself before Krispos. Krispos waited impatiently till the man had got to his feet and taken up his writing tools once more. He had given up on telling underlings not to bother with the proskynesis. All it did was make them uneasy. He was the Avtokrator, and the proskynesis was the way they were accustomed to showing the Avtokrator their respect.

After he was done dictating, Krispos said, "Let me hear that once more, please." The secretary read him his words. He glanced over at Mavros. The Sevastor nodded. Krispos said, "Good enough. Give me a fair copy of that, on parchment. I'll want it today." The scribe bowed and hurried away.

Krispos rose, stretched. "All that talking has made me thirsty. What do you say to a cup of wine?"

"I generally say yes, and any excuse will do nicely," Mavros answered, grinning. "Are you telling me your poor voice is too worn and threadbare to call Barsymes? I'll do it for you, then."

"No, wait," Krispos said. "Let's scandalize him and get it ourselves." He knew it was a tiny rebellion against the stifling ceremony that hedged him round, but even a tiny rebellion was better than none.

Mavros rolled his eyes. "The foundations of the state may crumble." Not least because he had trouble taking things seriously himself, he sympathized with his foster brother's efforts to keep some of his humanity intact.

Chuckling like a couple of small boys sneaking out to play at night, Avtokrator and the Sevastos tiptoed down the hall toward the larder. They even stopped chuckling as they sneaked past the chamber where Barsymes was directing a cleaning crew. The vestiarios' back was to them; he did not notice them go by. The cleaners needed his direction, for thick dust lay over the furnishings inside the chamber and the red-glazed tile that covered its floor and walls. The Red Room was only used—indeed, was only opened—when the Empress was with child. The baby— Krispos' heir, if it was a boy—would be born there.

*I wonder if it's mine*, he thought for the thousandth time. For the thousandth time, he told himself it did not matter—and tried to make himself believe it.

The wine, successfully gained and successfully drunk, helped him shove the unanswerable question to the back of his mind once more. He picked up the jar. "Another cup?" he asked Mavros.

"Thank you. That would be lovely."

Barsymes stalked into the larder while Krispos was still pouring. The eunuch's long smooth disapproving face got longer and more disapproving. "Your Majesty, you have servants precisely for the purpose of serving you."

Had he sounded angry, Krispos would have gotten angry in return. But he only sounded sad. Absurdly, Krispos felt guilty. Then he *was* angry, angry at his own feeling of guilt. "You'd like to wipe my arse for me, too, wouldn't you?" he snarled.

The vestiarios said nothing, did not even change his expression. Krispos felt his own face go hot with shame. Barsymes and the other chamberlains *had* wiped his arse for him, and tended all his other needs, no matter how ignoble, a couple of summers before when he lay paralyzed from Petronas' wizardry. He hung his head. "I'm sorry," he mumbled.

"Many men would not have remembered," Barsymes said evenly. "I see you do. Can we bargain, your Majesty? If your need to be free of us grows so pressing from time to time, will you tolerate us more readily the rest of the time on account of these occasional escapes?"

"I think so," Krispos said.

"Then I will essay not to be aggrieved when I see you occasionally serving yourself, and I hope you will remain sanguine when I and the rest of your servants perform our office." Bowing, Barsymes withdrew.

Once the vestiarios was gone, Mavros said, "Who rules here, you or him?"

"I notice you lowered your voice before you asked me that," Krispos said, laughing. "Is it for fear he'll hear?"

Mavros laughed, too, but soon sobered. "There have been vestiarioi who controlled affairs far beyond the palaces—Skombros, for one."

"Me for another," Krispos reminded him. "I haven't seen any of that from Barsymes, the lord with the great and good mind be praised. As long as he runs the palace, he's content to let me have the rest of the Empire."

"Generous of him." Mavros emptied his cup and picked up the jar of wine. "I'm going to pour myself another. Can I do the same for you? That way he'll have nothing with which to be offended."

Krispos held out his own cup. "Go right ahead."

The imperial courier sat gratefully in front of a roaring fire. Outside, mixed sleet and rain poured down. Krispos knew that meant spring was getting closer. Given a choice between snow and this horrible stuff, he would have preferred snow. Instead, he would get weeks of slush and glare ice and mud.

The courier undid his waterproof message pouch and handed Krispos a rolled parchment. "Here you are, your Majesty."

Even had the fellow's face not warned Krispos that Petronas was not about to come back to his monastery, the parchment would have done the job by itself. It was bound with a scarlet ribbon and sealed with scarlet wax, into which had been pressed a sunburst signet. It was not *the* imperial seal—Krispos wore that on the middle finger of his right hand—but it was an imperial seal.

"He says no, does he?" Krispos asked.

The courier set down the goblet of hot wine laced with cinnamon from which he'd been drinking. "Aye, Majesty, that much I can tell you. I haven't seen the actual message, though."

"Let's see how he says no, then." Krispos cracked the sealing wax, slid the ribbon off the parchment, and unrolled it. He recognized Petronas' firm, bold script at once—his rival had responded to him in person.

The response sounded like Petronas, too, Petronas in an overbearing mood: " 'Avtokrator of the Videssians Petronas, son of Agarenos Avtokrator, brother of Rhaptes Avtokrator, uncle to Anthimos Avtokrator, crowned without duress by the true most holy ecumenical patriarch of the Videssians Gnatios, to the baseborn rebel, tyrant, and usurper Krispos: Greetings.' ''

Krispos found reading easier if he did it aloud in a low voice. He didn't realize the courier was listening until the man remarked, "I guess he wouldn't say you aye after a start like that, would he?"

"Doesn't seem likely." Krispos read on: " 'I know that advice is a good and goodly thing: I have, after all, read the books of the learned ancients and Phos' holy scriptures. But at the same time, I reckon that this condition obtains when matters may be remedied. But when the times themselves are dangerous and drive one into the worst and most terrible circumstances, then, I think, advice is no longer so useful. This is most true of advice from you, impious and murderous wretch, for not only did you conspire to confine me unjustly in a monastery, but you also pitilessly slew my nephew the Avtokrator.'

"That, by the way, is not so," Krispos put in for the courier's benefit. He resumed. " 'So, accursed enemy, do not urge me to deliver my life into your hands once more. You will not persuade me. I, too, am a man with a sword at my belt, and I will struggle against one who has sought to lay my family low. For either I shall regain the imperial glory and furnish you, murderer, a full requital, or I shall perish and gain freedom from a disgusting and unholy tyranny.' ''

The courier's eyes were wide by the time Krispos rolled up the parchment once more. "That's the fanciest, nastiest 'no' I ever heard, your Majesty."

"Me, too." Krispos shook his head. "I didn't really think he'd say yes. A pity you and your comrades got drenched carrying the letters there and back again, but it was worth a try."

"Oh, aye, Majesty," the courier said, "I've done my soldiering time, fighting against Makuran on the Vaspurakaner frontier. Anything you can try to keep from having a war is worth doing."

"Yes." But Krispos had begun to wonder just how true that was. He'd certainly believed it back in his days at the farming village. Now, though, he was sure he would have to fight Petronas. Just as Petronas could not trust him, he knew a victory by his former patron would only bring him to a quick end, or more likely a slow one.

And he would have to fight a war against Harvas Black-Robe. Though he paid Harvas tribute for the moment, that was only buying time, not solving the problem. If he let a wild wolf like Harvas run loose on his border, more peasants who wanted nothing but peace would be slaughtered or ruined than if he fought to keep them safe. He also knew the ones who were ruined and the loved ones of those slaughtered in his war would never understand that. He wouldn't have himself, back in the days before he wore a crown.

"That's why the Empire needs an Emperor," he said to himself: "to see farther and wider than the peasants can."

"Aye, Majesty. Phos grant that you do," the courier said. Krispos sketched the sun-circle over his heart, hoping the good god would hear the fellow's words.

The rains dragged on. In spite of them, Krispos sent out couriers ordering his forces to assemble at Videssos the city and in the westlands. Spies reported that Petronas were also mustering troops. Krispos was glumly certain Petronas had spies of his own. He did his best to confuse them, shuttling companies back and forth and using regimental standards for companies and the other way round.

Thanks to the civil war, his strength in the north and east were less than it should have been. Thus he breathed a long sigh of relief when Iakovitzes wrote: "Harvas has agreed to a year's truce, at the highest price you would suffer me to pay him. By the lord with the great and good mind, Majesty, I would sooner gallop a ten-mile steeplechase with a galloping case of the piles than chaffer again with that black-robed bandit. I told him as much, in so many words. He laughed. His laugh, Majesty, is not a pleasant thing. Skotos might laugh so, to greet a damned soul new-come to the ice. Never shall I be so glad as the day I leave his court to return to the city. Phos be praised, that day will come soon."

When Krispos showed Mavros the letter, the Sevastos whistled softly. "We've both seen Iakovitzes furious often enough, but I don't think I ever heard him sound frightened before."

"Harvas has done it to him," Krispos said. "It's been building all winter. Just one more sign we should be fighting Harvas now. May the ice take Petronas for keeping me from what truly needs doing."

"We settle him this year," Mavros said. "After that, Harvas will have his turn."

"So he will." Krispos glanced outside. The sky was still cloudy, but held patches of blue. "Before long we can move on Petronas. One thing at a time, I learned on the farm. If you try to do a lot of things at once, you end up botching all of them."

Mavros glanced at him, mobile features sly. "Perhaps Videssos should draw its Emperors from the peasantry more often. Where would a man like Anthimos have learned such a simple lesson?"

"A man like Anthimos wouldn't have learned it on the farm, either. He'd have been one of the kind—and there are plenty of them, the good god knows—who go hungry at the end of winter because they haven't raised enough to carry them through till spring, or because they were careless with their storage pits and let half their grain spoil."

"You're probably right," Mavros said. "I've always thought—"

Krispos never found out what his foster brother had always thought. Barsymes came into the chamber and said, "Forgive me, your Majesty, but her Majesty the Empress must see you at once."

"I'll come as soon as I'm done with Mavros here," Krispos said.

"This is not a matter that will wait on your convenience, your Majesty," Barsymes said. "I've sent for the midwife."

"The—" Krispos found his mouth hanging open. He made himself shut it, then tried again to speak. "The midwife? The baby's not due for another month."

"So her Majesty said." Barsymes' smile was always wintry, but now, like the weather, it held a promise of spring. "The baby, I fear, is not listening."

Mavros clapped Krispos on the shoulder. "May Phos grant you a son."

"Yes," Krispos said absently. How was he supposed to stick to his one-thing-at-a-time dictum if events kept getting ahead of him? With some effort, he figured out the one thing he was supposed to do next. He turned to Barsymes. "Take me to Dara."

"Come with me," the vestiarios said.

They walked down the hall together. As they neared the imperial bedchamber, Krispos saw a serving maid mopping up a puddle. "The roof stayed sound all winter," he said, puzzled, "and it's not even raining now."

"Nor is that rain," Barsymes answered. "Her Majesty's bag of waters broke there."

Krispos remembered births back in his old village. "No wonder you called the midwife."

"Exactly so, your Majesty. Fear not—Thekla has been at her trade more than twenty years. She is the finest midwife in the city; were it otherwise, I should have sent for someone else, I assure you." Barsymes stopped outside the bedchamber door. "I will leave you here until I come to take her Majesty to the Red Room."

Krispos went in. He expected to find Dara lying in bed, but instead she was pacing up and down. "I thought I would wait longer," she said. "I'd felt my womb tightening more often than usual the last couple of days, but I didn't think anything of it. Then—" She laughed. "It was very strange—it was as if I was making water and couldn't stop myself. And after I was done dripping . . . now I know why they call them labor pains."

No sooner had she finished speaking than another one took her. Her face grew closed, secret, and intent. Her hands found Krispos' arms and squeezed hard. When the pain passed, she said, "I can tolerate that, but my labor's just begun. I'm afraid, Krispos. How much worse will they get?"

Krispos helplessly spread his hands, feeling foolish and useless and male. He had no idea how bad labor pains got—how could he? He remembered village women shrieking as they gave birth, but that did not seem likely to reassure Dara. He said, "Women are meant to bear children. It won't be worse than you can take."

"What do you know?" she snapped. "You're a man." Since he had just told himself the same thing, he shut up. Nothing he said was apt to be right, so he leaned over her swollen belly to hug her. That was a better idea.

They waited together. After a while, a pain gripped Dara. She clenched her teeth and rode it out. Once it had passed, though, she lay down. She twisted back and forth, trying to find a comfortable position. With her abdomen enormous and labor upon her, there were no comfortable positions to find. Another pain washed over her, and another, and another. Krispos wished he could do something more useful than hold her hand and make reassuring noises, but he had no idea what that something might be.

Some time later—he had no idea how long—someone tapped on the bedchamber door. Krispos got up from the bed to open it. Barsymes stood there with a handsome middle-aged woman whose short hair was so black, Krispos was sure it was dyed. She wore a plain, cheap linen dress. The vestiarios said, "Your Majesty, the midwife Thekla."

Thekla had a no-nonsense air about her that Krispos liked. She did not waste time with a proskynesis, but pushed past Krispos to Dara. "And how are we today, dearie?" she asked.

"I don't know about you, but I'm bloody awful," Dara said.

Unoffended, Thekla laughed. "Your waters broke, right? Are the pangs coming closer together?"

"Yes, and they're getting harder, too."

"They're supposed to, dearie. That's how the baby comes out, after all," Thekla said. Just then Dara's face twisted as another pain began. Thekla reached under Dara's robes to feel how tight her belly grew. Nodding in satisfaction, she told Dara, "You're doing fine." Then she turned to Barsymes. "I don't want her walking to the Red Room. She's too far along for that. Go fetch the litter."

"Aye, mistress." Barsymes hurried away. Krispos judged Thekla's skill by the unquestioning obedience she won from the vestiarios.

Barsymes and a couple of the other chamberlains soon returned. "Put the edge of the litter right next to the side of the bed," Thekla directed. "Now, dearie, you just slide over. Go easy, go easy—there! That's fine. All right, lads, off we go with her." The eunuchs, faces red but step steady, carried the Empress out the door, down the hall, and to the Red Room.

Krispos followed. When he got to the entrance of the Red Room, Thekla said firmly, "You wait outside, if you please, your Majesty."

"I want to be with her," Krispos said.

"You wait outside, your Majesty," Thelka repeated.

This time the midwife's words carried the snap of command. Krispos said, "I am the Avtokrator. I give orders here. Why should I stay out?"

Thekla set hands on hips. "Because, your most imperial Majesty, sir, you are a pest-taken man, that's why." Krispos stared at her; no one had spoken to him like that since he wore the crown, and not for a while before then, either. In slightly more reasonable tones, Thekla went on, "And because it's woman's work, your Majesty. Look, before this is done, your wife is liable to shit and piss and puke, maybe all three at once. She's sure to scream, likely a lot. And I'll have my hands deeper inside her than you ever dreamed of being. Do you really want to watch?"

"It is not customary, your Majesty," Barsymes said. For him, that settled the matter.

Krispos yielded. "Phos be with you," he called to Dara, who was carefully wiggling from the litter to the bed in the Red Room. She started to smile at him, but a pain caught her and turned the expression to a grimace.

"Here, your Majesty, come with me," Barsymes said soothingly. "Come sit down and wait. I'll bring you some wine; it will help ease your worry."

Krispos let himself be led away. As he'd told Mavros, he ruled the Empire but his servants ruled the palaces. He drank the wine Barsymes set before him without noticing if it was white or red, tart or sweet. Then he simply sat.

Barsymes brought in a game board and pieces. "Would your Majesty care to play?" he asked. "It might help pass the time."

"No, not now, thank you." Krispos' laugh was ragged. "Besides, Barsymes, you'd have a hard time losing gracefully today, for my mind wouldn't be on the board."

"If you notice how I lose, Majesty, then I don't do so gracefully enough," the vestiarios said. He seemed chagrined, Krispos noted, as if he thought he had failed in the quest for perfect service.

"Esteemed sir, just let me be, if you would," Krispos said. Barsymes bowed and withdrew.

Time crawled by. Krispos watched a sunbeam slide across the floor and start to climb the far wall. A servant came in to light lamps. Krispos only noticed him after he was gone.

He was not close to the Red Room. Barsymes, clever as usual, had made sure of that. Moreover, the door to the birthing chamber was closed. Whatever cries and groans Dara made, for a long time he did not hear them. But as the lamps' flickering light grew brighter than the failing day, she shrieked with such anguish that he sprang from his chair and dashed down the hall.

Thekla was indeed a veteran of her trade. She knew who pounded on that door, and why. "Nothing to worry about, your

Majesty," she called. "I was just turning the baby's head a little so it'll pass through more easily. The babe has dark hair, a lot of it. Won't be too much longer now."

He stood outside the door, clenching and unclenching his fists. Against Petronas or Harvas, he could have charged home at the head of his troops. Here he could do nothing—as Thekla had said, this was woman's work. Waiting seemed harder to bear than battle.

Dara made a noise he had never heard before, part grunt, part squeal, a sound of ultimate effort. "Again!" he heard Thekla say. "Hold your breath as long as you can, dearie—it helps the push." That sound burst from Dara once more. "Again!" Thekla urged. "Yes, that's the way."

Krispos heard Dara gasp, strain—and then exclaim in excitement. "Your Majesty, you have a son," Thekla said loudly. A moment later, the high, thin, furious cry of a newborn baby filled Krispos' ears.

He tried the door. It was locked. "We're not ready for you yet, your Majesty," Thekla said, annoyance and amusement mixed in her voice. "She still has the afterbirth to pass. You'll see the lad soon enough, I promise. What will you call him?"

"Phostis," Krispos answered. He heard Dara say the name inside the Red Room, too. Sudden tears stung his eyes. He wished his father had lived to see a grandson named for him.

A few minutes later Thekla opened the door. The lamplight showed her dress splashed with blood—no wonder she hadn't worn anything fancy, Krispos realized. Then Thekla held out to him his newborn son, and all such thoughts vanished from his mind.

The baby was swaddled in a blanket of soft lamb's wool. "Five fingers on each hand, five toes on each foot," Thekla said. "A little on the scrawny side, maybe, but that's to be expected when a child comes early." The midwife fell silent when she saw Krispos wasn't listening.

He peered down at Phostis' red, wrinkled little face. Part of that was the awe any new father feels on holding his firstborn for the first time. Part, though, was something else, something colder. He searched those tiny, new-formed features, trying to see in them either Anthimos' smooth, smiling good looks or his own rather craggier appearance. So far as he could tell, the baby looked like neither of its possible fathers. Phostis' eyes seemed shaped like Dara's, with the inner corner of each lid folding down very slightly.

When he said that out loud, Thekla laughed. "No law says a boy child can't favor his mother, your Majesty," she said. "Speaking of which, she'll want another look at the baby, too, I expect, and maybe a first try at nursing him." She stepped aside to let Krispos go into the Red Room.

The chamber stank; Thekla had meant her warning. Krispos did not care. "How are you?" he asked Dara, who was still lying on the bed on which she had given birth. She looked pale and utterly exhausted; her hair, soaked with sweat, hung limply. But she managed a worn smile and held out her hands for Phostis. Krispos gave her the baby.

"He doesn't weigh anything," Dara exclaimed.

Krispos nodded; his arms hardly noticed Phostis was gone. He saw Dara giving Phostis the same careful scrutiny he had, no doubt for the same reason. He said, "I think he looks like you."

Dara's eyes went wary as she glanced at him. He smiled back, though he wondered if he would ever be sure who Phostis' father really was. As he had so often before, he told himself it did not matter. As he had so often before, he almost made himself believe it.

"Hold him again, will you?" Dara said. Phostis squalled at being passed back and forth. Krispos clumsily rocked him in his arms. Dara unfastened her dress and tugged it off one shoulder to bare a breast. "I'll take him now. Let's see if this will make him happy."

Phostis rooted, found the nipple, and began to suck. "He likes them," Krispos said. "I don't blame him—I like them, too."

Dara snorted. Then she said, "Ask the kitchen to send me supper, would you, Krispos? I'm hungry now, though I wouldn't have believed it if you'd told me I would be."

"You haven't eaten for quite a while," Krispos said. As he hurried off to do what Dara had asked, he paused and thanked Thekla.

"My pleasure, your Majesty," the midwife said. "Phos grant that the Empress and your son do well. No reason she shouldn't, and he's not too small to thrive, I'd say."

Chamberlains and maidservants congratulated Krispos on having a son as he walked to the kitchens. He wondered how they knew; a baby girl's cry would have sounded the same as Phostis'. But palace servants had their own kind of magic. The moment Krispos walked through the door, a grinning cook pressed into his hands a tray with a jar of wine, some bread, and a covered silver dish on it. "For your lady," the fellow said.

Krispos carried the tray to Dara himself. Barsymes saw him and said not a word. When he got back to the Red Room, he helped her sit up and poured wine for her. He poured for himself, as well; the cook had thoughtfully set two goblets on the tray. He raised his. "To Phostis," he said.

"To our son," Dara agreed. That was not quite what Krispos had said, but he drank her toast.

Dara attacked her meal—it proved to be roast kid in fermented fish sauce and garlic—as if she'd had nothing for days. Krispos watched her eat and watched Phostis, who was dozing on the bed next to her, turn his head from side to side. Thekla had been right; for a baby, Phostis did have a lot of hair. Krispos stood up and reached out a gentle hand to touch it. It was soft and fine as goose down. Phostis squirmed. Krispos took his hand away.

Dara sopped up the last of the sauce with the heel of her bread. She finished her wine and set the goblet down with a sigh. "That helped," she said. "A bath and about a month of sleep and I'll be—not good as new, but close enough." She sighed again. "Thekla says it's better for a baby to nurse with his own mother the first few days, so I won't get that sleep right away. Afterward, though, a wet nurse can get up with him when he howls."

"I've been thinking," Krispos said in an abstracted tone that showed he'd hardly heard what she said.

"What about?" she asked cautiously. Without seeming to notice what she did, she moved closer to Phostis, as if to protect him.

"I think we ought to declare the baby co-Avtokrator even before I go out on campaign against Petronas," he answered. "It will let the whole Empire know I intend my family to hold this throne for a long time."

Dara's face lit up. "Yes, let's do that," she said at once. Even more gently than Krispos had, she touched Phostis' head, murmuring, "Sleep well, my tiny Emperor." Then, after a little while, she added, "I was afraid you were thinking something else."

Krispos shook his head. Even since he'd known Dara was pregnant, he'd also known he'd have to act as if her child was surely his. Now that the boy was born, he would not stint. If anything, he would make a show of favoring him, to make sure no one else had any doubts—or at least any public doubts—about Phostis' paternity.

What he did was everyone's affair. What he thought was his own.

ment and was gained for never suspicious. The magic broke...
"Quite right, your Majesty. If that pow"dark stroke," he said, I
shall thing it in a—

# IV

Barsymes carried a medium-size silver box and a folded sheet of parchment in to Krispos. The vestiarios looked puzzled and a bit worried. "The Halogai just found this on the steps, your Majesty. As they do not read, they asked me what the parchment said. I saw it had your name on the outside, so I brought it here."

"Thank you," Krispos said. Then he frowned. "What do you mean, the Halogai found it on the steps? Who brought it there?"

"I don't know, your Majesty. Neither do the guardsmen. From what they say, it wasn't there one moment and was the next."

"Magic," Krispos said. He stared suspiciously at the box. After almost killing him once by sorcery, did Petronas think he would fall into the trap again? If so, he would be disappointed. "Send someone for Trokoundos, Barsymes. Until he tells me it's all right, that box will stay closed."

"No doubt you are wise, your Majesty. I shall send someone directly."

Krispos even wondered if unfolding the parchment was safe. He grew impatient waiting for Trokoundos to come, though, and opened it up. Nothing lethal or sorcerous—nothing at all—happened when he did. The note inscribed within was written in a crabbed, antique hand. Though it was not signed, it could only have come from Harvas Black-Robe; it read: "I accept your purchase of a year's peace with gold. Your envoy has left my court and wends his way homeward. I believe you will find him much improved on account of that which is enclosed herewith."

When Trokoundos arrived, Krispos showed him the parchment and explained his own suspicions. The mage nodded. "Quite right, your Majesty. If that box hides sorcery, be sure I shall bring it to light."

He set to work with powders and jars of bright-colored liquids. After a few minutes one of the liquids suddenly went from blue to red. Trokoundos grunted. "Ha! There *is* magic here, your Majesty." He made quick passes, all the while chanting under his breath.

Krispos watched the red liquid turn blue again. He asked, "Does that mean the spell is gone?"

"It should, your Majesty." But Trokoundos did not sound sure. He explained. "The only spell I detected was one of preservation, such as some fancy fruiterers use to let rich clients have their wares fresh but out of season. Forgive me, but I cannot imagine how such a spell could be harmful in any way. Whether it was or not, though, I have dispersed it."

"Then nothing should happen if I open the box?" Krispos persisted.

"Nothing *should*." Trokoundos took out more sorcerous apparatus. "If anything does, I am prepared to meet it."

"Good." Krispos flipped the catch that held the box shut. As he did so, Trokoundos stepped up to protect him from whatever was inside. He opened the lid. Inside the box was a curiously curved piece of meat, bloody at the thick end.

Trokoundos' brows came together at the anticlimax. "What is that?" he demanded.

Krispos needed a minute to recognize it, too. But he had butchered a good many cows and sheep and goats in his farming days. This was too small to have come from a cow, but a sheep had one much like it . . . "It's a tongue," he said. Then horror ran through him as he remembered the note that had accompanied this gift. "It's—Iakovitzes' tongue," he choked out. He slammed the lid shut, turned his head, and vomited on the fine mosaic floor.

Near the south end of Videssos the city's wall was a broad field where soldiers often exercised. Several regiments of horsemen, lancers and archers both, were drawn up in formation there. Their banners rippled in the spring breeze. They saluted as Krispos and Agapetos rode past in review.

Krispos was saying "Draw out whatever garrison troops you think the towns can spare, if they're men who'd be any good in the field. The Kubrati nomads always liked to play the raid-and-run game. Now it'll be our turn. If Harvas thinks he can sell us peace at the price of maiming an ambassador, we'll teach him different. The way I see it, he's stolen a hundred pounds of gold. We'll take it back from his land.''

"Aye, Majesty," Agapetos said. "But what happens if one of my raiding bands comes up against too many men for them to handle?''

"Then pull back," Krispos told him. "Your job is to keep Harvas and his cutthroats too busy in their own country to come down into the Empire. I won't be able to send you much support, not until Petronas is beaten. After that, the whole army will move to the northern frontier, but until then, you're on your own.''

"Aye, Majesty. I shall do as you require." Agapetos saluted, then raised his right arm high. Trumpets brayed brassily, pipes skirled, and drums thuttered. The cavalry regiments rolled forward. Krispos knew they were good troops. Agapetos was a good soldier, too; Videssian generals made a study of the art of war and learned scores of tricks for gaining the most with the smallest expenditure of manpower.

*Then why am I worried?* Krispos asked himself. Maybe it was because the competent, serious Videssian soldiers had not faced warriors like Harvas' Halogai before. Maybe it was because competent, serious Agapetos had already let Harvas trick him once. *And maybe,* Krispos thought, *it's for no reason at all. No matter how well he acts the part, Harvas isn't Skotos come again. He can be beaten. In the end, even Skotos will be beaten.*

*Then why am I worried?* he asked again. Angry at himself, he yanked Progress' head around sharply enough to draw a reproachful snort from the horse. He rode back to the city at a fast trot. He knew he should already have been in the westlands, moving against Petronas. But for Harvas' latest outrage, that campaign would have begun a fortnight before.

Krispos rode not to the palaces, but to the Sorcerers' Collegium north of the palace quarter. Iakovitzes had reached the capital the night before, more dead than alive. The Empire's most skillful healer-priests taught at the Collegium, passing on their art to each new generation in turn. The desperately ill came there, too, in hope of cures no one less skilled could give. Iakovitzes fell into the latter group.

"How is he?" Krispos demanded of Damasos, the head of the healing faculty.

The skin under Damasos' eyes was smudged with fatigue, part of the price a healer-priest paid for his gift. "Majesty," he began, and then paused to yawn. "Your pardon, Majesty. I think he may yet recover, Majesty. We are at last to the point where we may attempt the healing of the wound itself."

"He's been here most of a day now," Krispos said. "Why haven't you done anything before this?"

"We have done a great deal, Majesty," Damasos said stiffly. He was of middle height and middle years, his pate tan, his untrimmed beard going gray. He continued, "We've had to do a great deal, much of it in conjunction with sorcerers who are not healers, for added to this mutilation was something I have never before encountered and pray to the good god I never see again: a spell specifically intended to thwart healing. First discovering and then defeating that spell has occupied us up to this time."

"A spell *against* healing?" Krispos felt queasy; the very idea was an abomination worse than the torture Harvas had inflicted on Iakovitzes. "Who could conceive such a wicked thing?"

"For too long, we did not, Majesty," Damasos said. "Even after we realized what we faced, we needed no small space of time to overcome the wizardry. Whoever set it on the wound bound it with the power of the victim's blood, making it doubly hard to banish. It was, in effect, a deliberate perversion of my own ritual." Tired though he was, Damasos set his jaw in outrage.

Krispos asked, "You are ready to heal now, you say?" At the healer-priest's nod, he went on. "Take me to Iakovitzes. I would see him healed, as best he may be." He also wanted Iakovitzes to see him, to know how guilty he felt for sending him on an embassy about which he'd had misgivings.

He gasped when Damasos ushered him into Iakovitzes' chamber. The little noble, usually so plump and dapper, was thin, ragged, and filthy. Krispos coughed at the foul odor that rose from him: not just that of a body long unwashed, but worse, a ripe stench like rotting meat. Yellow pus dribbled from the corner of his mouth. His eyes were wide and blank with fever.

Those blank eyes slid past Krispos without recognizing him. A healer-priest sat beside the bed where Iakovitzes thrashed. Four beefy attendants stood close by. Damasos spoke to the priest. "Are you ready, Nazares?"

"Aye, holy sir." Nazares' glance rested on Krispos for a moment. When Krispos showed no sign of leaving, the healer-priest shrugged and nodded to the attendants. "Commence, lads."

Two of the men seized Iakovitzes' arms. A third grabbed his head to pull down his lower jaw, then wedged a stout stick padded with cloth between his teeth. Iakovitzes had not seemed aware of his surroundings till then. But the instant the stick touched his lips, he began to struggle like a man possessed, letting out blood-curdling shrieks and a string of gurgles that tried to be words.

"Poor fellow," Damasos whispered to Krispos. "In his delirium, he must think we're about to cut him again." Krispos' nails bit into his palms.

In spite of the battle Iakovitzes put up, the fourth attendant forced a metal gag into his mouth, of the sort horse doctors used to hold an animal's jaws apart so they could trim its teeth. When the gag was in place, Nazares reached into Iakovitzes' forcibly opened mouth. Seeing Krispos still watching, the healer-priest explained, "For proper healing, I must touch the wound itself."

Krispos started to answer, then saw Nazares was dropping into a healer's trance. "We bless thee, Phos, lord with the great and good mind, watchful beforehand that the great test of life may be decided in our favor." The priest repeated the creed again and again, using it to distract his conscious mind and to concentrate his will solely on the task of healing before him.

As always, Krispos felt awed to watch a healer-priest at work. He could tell just when Nazares began to heal by the way the man suddenly went rigid. Iakovitzes continued to moan and kick, but he could have burst into flames without turning Nazares from his purpose. Almost as if lightning were in the air, Krispos felt the current of healing as it passed from Nazares to Iakovitzes.

Then, all at once, Iakovitzes quit struggling. Krispos took a step forward in alarm, afraid his one-time patron's heart had given out. But Iakovitzes continued to breathe and Nazares continued to heal; had something been wrong, the healer-priest surely would have sensed it.

At last Nazares withdrew his hand. He wiped pus-smeared fingers on his robe. The attendant removed the gag from Iakovitzes' mouth. Krispos saw the noble was in full possession of his senses again. Now when he moved in the grip of the two men who held him, they let him go.

He bowed low to the healer-priest, then made a series of yammering noises. After a moment, he realized no one could understand him. He signed for something to write with. One of the attendants brought him a waxed wooden tablet and stylus. He scribbled and handed the tablet to Nazares.

" 'What are you all standing around for?' " Nazares read, his voice slow and dragging from the crushing fatigue that followed healing. " 'Take me to the baths—I stink like a latrine. I could use some food, too, about a year's worth.' "

Krispos could not help smiling—Iakovitzes might never speak an intelligible word again, but he still sounded like himself. Then Iakovitzes wrote some more and handed the tablet to him. "Next time, send someone else."

Sobered, he nodded, saying "I know gold and honor will never give you back what you have lost, Iakovitzes, but what they can give, you will have."

"I'd better. I earned them," Iakovitzes wrote.

He felt inside his mouth with his fingers, poking and prodding, then let out a soft grunt of wonder and bowed again to Nazares. He scrawled again, then handed the healer-priest the tablet. " 'Holy sir, the wound feels as if it happened years ago. Only the memory is yet green,' " Nazares read. Behind the brassy front Iakovitzes habitually assumed, Krispos saw the terror that still lived in his eyes

An attendant touched Iakovitzes on the arm. He flinched, then scowled at himself and dipped his head in apology to the man. "Excellent sir, I just wanted to tell you I would take you to a bathhouse now, if you like," the attendant said. "There's one close by the Sorcerers' Collegium here."

Iakovitzes tried to speak, scowled again, and nodded. Before he left with the attendant, though, Krispos said, "A moment, Iakovitzes, please. I want to ask you something." Iakovitzes paused. Krispos went on. "By the messages you sent me, you and Harvas traded barbs all winter long. What did you finally say that made him do—that—to you?"

The noble flinched again, this time from his own thoughts. But he bent over the tablet and wrote out his reply. He gave it to Krispos when he was done. "I didn't even intend to insult him, worse luck. We'd settled on a price for the year's truce and were swearing oaths to secure it. Harvas would not swear by the spirits, Kubrati-style, nor would he take oath by the Haloga gods of his followers. 'Swear by Phos, then,' I told him—a truce is no truce without oaths, as any child knows. Better I had told him to go swive his mother, I think. In a voice like thunder, he cried out, 'That name shall never be in my mouth again, nor in yours either.' And then—'' The writing stopped there, but Kris-pos knew what had happened then.

He sketched the sun-sign over his heart. Iakovitzes did the same. Krispos promised, "We'll avenge you, avenge this. I've just sent out a force under Agapetos to harry Harvas' land. When I'm done with Petronas, Harvas will face the whole army."

Again Iakovitzes tried to reply with spoken words, again he had to stop in frustration. He nodded instead, held up one finger while he pointed to the west, then two while he pointed north-eastward. He nodded again, to show he approved of Krispos' course. Krispos was glad of that; while Iakovitzes had helped him form his priorities the winter before, he could hardly have blamed the noble for changing his mind after what had befallen him. That he hadn't helped convince Krispos he was on the right course.

Iakovitzes turned to the attendant and mimed scrubbing himself. The man led him out of the chamber.

"I am in your debt," Krispos said to Nazares.

"Nonsense." The healer-priest waved his words away. "I praise the good god that I was able to end Iakovitzes' agony. I only regret his injury is such that it will continue to trouble him greatly despite being healed. And the charm set on the wound to keep from healing it . . . that was most wicked, your Majesty."

"I know." Krispos opened the waxed tablet and read again the words that had cost Iakovitzes his tongue. No man unwilling to say Phos' name, or even to hear it, was likely to be good. *If only Harvas were as inept as he was evil*, Krispos thought, *and if only Petronas would disappear, and if only Pyrrhos would grow mild, and if only I could be certain I'm Phostis' father, and if only I could rule by thinking "if only"* . . .

Even in early spring, the coastal lowlands were hot and sticky. The roads were still moist enough, though, that armies on the march kicked up only a little dust—as good a reason as any for campaigning in the spring, Krispos thought as he trotted along on Progress toward the Eriza River.

The army in whose midst he traveled was the biggest he had ever seen, more than ten thousand men. Had Sarkis captured or killed Petronas over the winter, this new round of civil war would not have been needed. By keeping Anthimos' uncle from gaining ground, though, the Vaspurakaner soldier had managed the next best thing: he'd convinced the generals of the local provinces that Krispos was the better bet. Those generals and their troopers rode with the force from Videssos the city now.

Krispos saw the inevitable host of farmers busy in their fields on either side of the road. Though the force with which he traveled was far larger than the one that had fought Petronas the previous fall, fewer farmers fled. He took that for a good sign. "They know we'll keep good order," he remarked to Trokoundos, who rode nearby. "Peasants shouldn't fear soldiers."

"This far before harvest, they have little to steal anyhow," Trokoundos said. "They know that, too, and take courage from it."

"You've been drinking sour wine this morning," Krispos said, a trifle startled; such cynicism was worthy of Iakovitzes.

"Maybe so," Trokoundos said. "We also have supplies for the army well arranged, this being territory that stayed loyal to you. We'll see how the men behave when we enter country that had been under Petronas' hand."

"Oh, aye, we'll do a bit of plundering if our supply train has trouble," said Mammianos, one of the provincial generals who had at last cast his lot with Krispos. He was in his mid-fifties and quite round, but a fine horseman for all that. "But we'll do a bit of fighting, too, which makes up for a lot."

Krispos started to say nothing could make plundering his own people right. He kept the words to himself. If folk farther westward worked for his rival and against him, they and their fields became fair targets for his soldiers—Petronas' men, he was sure, would not hold back if they reached territory he controlled. Either way, the Empire and the fisc would suffer.

When he did speak aloud, he said, "Civil war," as if it were a curse.

"Aye, the times are hard," Mammianos agreed. "There's but one thing worse than fighting a civil war, and that's losing it." Krispos nodded.

Two days later he and his army forded the Eriza—the ruined bridges were yet to be rebuilt. This time the crossing was unopposed, though Krispos found himself looking back over his shoulder lest some imperial courier come riding up with word of a new disaster. But no couriers appeared. That in itself buoyed Krispos' spirits.

. He began seeing traces of the fighting Sarkis had done the previous winter: wrecked villages, fields standing idle and unplanted, the shells of burned-out buildings. Peasants on this side of the Eriza, those who were left, fled his soldiers as if they were so many demons.

The land began to rise toward the westlands' rugged central plateau. The rich, deep black earth of the lowlands grew thinner, dustier, grayer. Because of the early season, the countryside was still bright green, but Krispos knew the sun would bake it dry long before summer was done. In the lowlands, they sometimes raised two crops a year. On the central plateau, they were lucky to get one; broad stretches of land were better suited to grazing cattle than growing crops.

Krispos' advance stopped being a walkover about halfway between the Eriza and the town of Resaina. He had started to wonder if Petronas would ever stand and fight. Then, all at once, the scouts who rode ahead of his army came pelting back toward the main body of men. He watched them turn to shoot arrows back over their shoulders, then saw other horsemen pursuing them.

"Those must be Petronas' men!" he exclaimed, pointing. Only by the way they attacked his own cavalry could he be sure: Their gear was identical to what his own forces used. One more hazard of civil war that hadn't occurred to him, he thought uneasily.

"Aye, by the good god, those are the rebels," Mammianos said. "A whole bloody great lot of them, too." He turned his head to shout orders to the musicians whose calls set the army in motion. As martial music blared out and units hurried from column to line of battle, Mammianos sped them into place with bellowed commands. "Faster there, the ice take you! Here's the fight we've been waiting for, the chance to smash the stinking traitor once for all. Come on, deploy, deploy, deploy!"

The fat general showed more energy in a couple of minutes than he had used all through the campaign thus far, so much more that Krispos stared at him in surprise. The curses he kept calling down on Petronas' head, and the spleen with which he hurled them forth, were also something new. When Mammianos paused to draw breath, Krispos said, "General, forgive me for ever having doubted your loyalty."

Mammianos' eyes were shrewd. "In your boots, Majesty, I'd doubt my own shadow if it wasn't in front of me. May I speak frankly?"

"I hope you will."

"Aye, you seem to," Mammianos said judiciously. "I know I didn't lend you much aid last fall."

"No, but you didn't aid Petronas, either, for which I'm grateful."

"As well you might be. Truth to tell, I was sitting tight. I won't apologize for it, either. If you'd stolen the throne without deserving it, Petronas would've made quick hash of you. Likely I would have joined him afterward, too; the Empire doesn't need a weakling Avtokrator now. But since you did well enough against him, and since most of the decrees you've issued have made sense—" Mammianos clapped his hands together in savage glee. "—I'll help you nail the whoreson's hide to the wall instead. Put me on the shelf, will he?"

"On the shelf?" Krispos echoed, perplexed. "But you're the general of—"

"—a province that usually needs a general about as much as a lizard needs a bathtub," Mammianos interrupted. "I was with Petronas when he invaded Vaspurakan a couple of years ago. I told him to his face he didn't have the wherewithal to push the Makuraners out."

"I told him the same, back at the palaces," Krispos said.

"What'd he do to you?" Mammianos asked.

"He tried to kill me." Krispos shivered, remembering Petronas' sorcerous assault. "He almost did, too."

Mammianos grunted. "He told me that if I didn't want to fight, he'd send me someplace where I wouldn't have to, which is how I got stuck in the lowlands where nothing ever happens. Except now it has, and I get a chance to pay the bastard back." He shook his fist at Petronas' horsemen. "You'll get yours, you lice!"

Krispos watched the oncoming soldiers, too. His military eye was still unpracticed, but he thought his rival's army was about the size of his own. His lips skinned back from his teeth. That was only likely to make the battle more expensive but less decisive.

A blue banner with gold sunburst flew above the center of Petronas' force, a twin to the one a standardbearer carried not far from Krispos. He shook his head. This sort of fight was worse than confusing. It was as if he battled himself in a mirror.

A great shout rose from his men: "Krispos! Krispos Avtokrator!" Petronas' men shouted back, crying out the name of their commander.

Krispos drew his sword. He was no skilled soldier, but had learned that did not always matter in the confusion of the battlefield. A company of Halogai, the sharpened edges of their axe blades glittering in the spring sunshine, formed up in front of him to try to make sure he did no fighting in any case. He'd given up arguing with them. He knew he might see action in spite of them; not even a captain of guardsmen could always outguess combat.

Arrows flew in beautiful, deadly arcs. Men fell from their saddles. Some thrashed and tried to rise; others lay still. Horses fell, too, crushing riders beneath them. Animals and men screamed together. More horses, wounded but not felled, ran wild, carrying the soldiers on them out of the fight and injecting chaos into their comrades' neat ranks.

The two lines closed with each other. Now, here and there, men thrust with light lances and slashed with sabers rather than shooting arrows at one another. The din of shouts and shrieks, drumming hooves, and clashing metal was deafening. Peering this way and that, Krispos could see no great advantage for either side.

He looked across the line, toward that other imperial banner. With a small shock, he recognized Petronas, partly by the gilded armor and red boots his rival also wore, more by the arrogant ease with which Anthimos' uncle sat his horse. Petronas saw him, too; though they were a couple of hundred yards apart, Krispos felt their eyes lock. Petronas swung his sword down, straight at Krispos. He and the men around him spurred their mounts forward.

Krispos dug his roweled heels into Progress' flanks. The big bay gelding squealed in pain and fury and bounded ahead. The Halogai, though, were waiting for Krispos. One big man after another grabbed at Progress' reins, at his bridle, at the rest of his trappings. "Let me through, curse you!" Krispos raged.

"No, Majesty, no," the northerners yelled back. "We will settle the rebel for you."

Petronas and his companions were very close now. He had no Haloga guards, but the men who rode with him had to be his closest retainers, the bravest and most loyal of his host. Sabers upraised and gleaming, lances poised and ready, they crashed into the ranks of the imperial bodyguards.

For all the tales he had heard, Krispos had never actually seen the Halogai fight before. Their first couple of ranks simply went down, bowled over by their foes' horses or speared before they were close enough to swing their axes. But Petronas' men fell, too; their chain mail might have been linen for all it did to keep those great axes from their flesh. Their horses, which wore no

armor, suffered worse. The axes abbatoir workers used to
slaughter beeves were shorter, lighter, and less keen than the
ones in the northerners' strong hands. One well-placed blow
dropped any horse in its tracks; another usually sufficed for its
rider.

A barricade of flesh, some dead, some writhing, quickly
formed between Krispos' men and Petronas'. The Halogai
hacked over it. Petronas' mounted men kept trying to bull their
way through. The ranks of the guardsmen thinned. Krispos
found himself ever closer to the fighting front. Now the Halogai,
battling for survival themselves, could not keep him away.

And there was Petronas! Red smeared his saber; no one had
told him he was too precious to risk. Krispos spurred Progress
toward him. With warrior's instinct, Petronas' head whipped
round. He snarled at Krispos, blocked his cut, and returned one
that clattered off Krispos' helmet.

They cursed each other, the same words in both their mouths.
"Thief! Bandit! Bastard! Robber! Whoreson!"

More Halogai still stood than Petronas' companions. Shouting Krispos' name, they surged toward the rebel. Petronas was
too old a soldier to stay and be slaughtered. Along with those
of his guards who yet lived, he pulled back, pausing only to
shake his fist one last time at Krispos. Krispos answered with a
two-fingered gesture he'd learned on the streets of Videssos the
city.

The center had held. Krispos looked round to see how the
rest of the battle was doing. It still hung in the balance. His own
line sagged a little on the left, Petronas' on the right. Neither
commander had enough troops to pull some out of line and
exploit his small advantage without the risk of giving his foe a
bigger one. And so men hacked and thrust and hit and swore
and bled, all to keep matters exactly as they had been before the
battle started.

That tore at Krispos. To his way of thinking, if war had any
purpose whatsoever, it was to make change quick and decisive.
Such suffering with nothing to show for it seemed a cruel waste.

But when he said as much to Mammianos, the general shook
his head. "Petronas has to go through you before he can move
on the capital. A drawn fight gains him nothing. This is the first
real test of fighting skill and loyalty for your men. A draw for
you is near as good as a win, because you show the Empire you
match him in those things. Given that, and given that you hold
Videssos the city, I like your chances pretty well."

Reluctantly Krispos nodded. Mammianos' cool good sense was something he tried to cultivate in himself. Applying it to this wholesale production of human agony before him, though, took more self-possession than he could easily find.

He started to tell that to Mammianos, but Mammianos was not listening. Like a farmer who scents a change in the wind at harvesttime and fears for his crop, the general peered to the left. "Something's happened there," he said, certainty in his voice.

Krispos also stared leftward. He needed longer than Mammianos to recognize a new clumping of men at the wing, to hear the new shouts of alarm and fury and, a moment later, triumph. The sweat that dripped from the end of his nose suddenly went cold. "Someone's turned traitor."

"Aye." Mammianos packed a world of meaning into a single word. He bellowed for a courier and started a series of frantic orders to plug the gap. Then he broke off and looked again. As if against his will, a grin of disbelief stretched itself over his fat face. "By the good god," he said softly. "It's one of theirs, going over to us."

Since he felt it himself, Krispos understood Mammianos' surprise. He'd feared the reliability of his own troops, not Petronas'. But sure enough, a sizable section—more than a company, perhaps as much as a regiment—of Petronas' army was now shouting "Krispos!"

And the defectors did more than shout. They turned on the men to their immediate right, the men who held the rightmost position in Petronas' line. Beset by them as well as by Krispos' own supporters, the flank guards broke and fled in wild confusion.

Mammianos' amazement did not paralyze him for long. Though he'd done nothing to force the break in Petronas' line, he knew how to exploit it once it was there. He sent the left wing of Krispos' army around Petronas' shattered right, seeking to roll up the whole rebel army.

But Petronas also knew his business. He did not try to salvage a battle already lost. Instead, he dropped a thin line back from the stump of his army's broken right wing, preventing Krispos' men from surrounding too many more of his own. His forces gave ground all along their line now, but nowhere except on the far right did they yield to panic. They were beaten, but remained an army. Breaking off combat a little at a time, they retreated west toward Resaina.

Krispos wanted to press the pursuit hard, but still did not feel sure enough of himself as battlefield commander to override Mammianos, who kept the army under tight control. The bulk of Petronas' troops escaped to the camp they had occupied before they came out to fight, leaving Krispos' men in possession of the field.

Healer-priests went from man to wounded man, first at a run, then at a walk, and finally at a drunken shamble as the exhaustion of their trade took its toll on them. More mundane leeches, men who worked without the aid of magic, saw to soldiers with minor wounds, here sewing up a cut, there splashing an astringent lotion onto flesh lacerated when chain mail was driven through padding and leather undertunic alike.

And Krispos, surrounded not only by the surviving Halogai of the imperial guard but also by most of Sarkis' cavalry regiment, approached the troopers whose defection had cost Petronas the fight. He and all his men stayed ready for anything; Petronas was devious enough to throw away a battle to set up an assassination.

The leader of the units that had changed sides saw Krispos coming. He rode toward him. Krispos had the odd feeling he'd seen the fellow before, though he was sure he had not. The middle-age officer, plainly a noble, was short and slim, with a narrow face, a thin arched nose, and a neat beard the color of his iron helmet. He set his right fist over his heart in salute to Krispos. "Your Majesty," he said. His voice was a resonant tenor.

"My thanks for your aid there, excellent sir," Krispos said. He wondered how big a reward the officer would want for it. "I fear I don't know your name."

"I am Rhisoulphos," the fellow said, as if Krispos ought to know who Rhisoulphos was.

After a moment, he did. "You're Dara's father," he blurted. No wonder the man looked familiar! "Your daughter takes after you, excellent sir."

"So I've been told." Rhisoulphos let out a short bark of laughter. "I daresay she wears the face better than I do, though."

Mammianos studied Dara's father, then said, "What was the Avtokrator's kinsman by marriage doing in the ranks of the Avtokrator's foes?" Suspicion made his tone harsh. Krispos leaned forward in his saddle to hear how Rhisoulphos would reply.

The noble dipped his head first to Mammianos, then to Krispos. "Please recall that, until Anthimos walked the bridge between light and ice, I was also Petronas' kinsman by marriage. And after Anthimos did die—" Rhisoulphos looked Krispos full in the face. "—I was not sure what sort of arrangement you had with my daughter, your Majesty."

Sometimes Krispos also wondered what sort of arrangement he had with Dara. He said, "You have a grandson who will be Emperor, excellent sir." That remained true no matter who Phostis' father was, he thought. He felt like giving his head a wry shake, but was too well schooled to reveal himself so in front of Rhisoulphos.

He saw he had said the right thing. Rhisoulphos' eyes, so like Dara's with their slightly folded inner lids, softened. His father-in-law said, "So I heard, and it set me thinking: what would that boy be if Petronas won the throne? The only answer I saw was an obstacle and a danger to him. I showed Petronas none of my thoughts, of course. I pledged him my loyalty again and again, loudly and rather stupidly."

"A nice touch," Mammianos said. His eyes slid toward Krispos. Krispos read them without difficulty: if Rhisoulphos could befool Petronas, he was a man who needed watching.

Krispos had already worked that out for himself. Now, though, he could only acknowledge Rhisoulphos' aid. "Our first meeting was well timed, excellent sir," he said. "After Petronas is beaten, I will show you all the honor the Avtokrator's father-in-law deserves."

Rhisoulphos bowed in the saddle. "I will do my best to earn that honor on the field, your Majesty. I know my soldiers will support me—and you."

"I'm sure they will," Krispos said, resolving to use Rhisoulphos' men but not to trust them with any truly vital task until Petronas was no longer a threat. "Now perhaps you will join my other advisors as we plan how to take advantage of what we've won with your help."

"I am at your service, your Majesty." Rhisoulphos slid down from his horse and walked over to the imperial tent. Seeing that Krispos did not object, the Halogai in front of the entrance bowed and let him pass. Krispos also dismounted. Grunting and wheezing with effort, so did Mammianos.

Along with Rhisoulphos, Sarkis and Trokoundos the mage waited inside the tent for Krispos. They rose and bowed when he came in. "A fine fight, your Majesty," Sarkis said enthusiastically. "One more like it and we'll smash this rebellion to bloody bits." The rest of the soldiers loudly agreed. Even Trokoundos nodded.

"I don't want another battle, not if I can help it," Krispos said. The other men in the tent stared at him. He continued. "If I can, I want to make Petronas give up without more fighting. Everyone who falls in the civil war, on my side or his, could have fought for me against Harvas. The fewer who fall, then, the better."

"Admirable, your Majesty," Mammianos rumbled. "How do you propose to bring it off?" His expression said he did not think Krispos could.

Krispos spoke for several minutes. By the time he was done, he saw Rhisoulphos and Sarkis running absentminded fingers through their beards as they thought. Finally Rhisoulphos said, "It might work, at that."

"So it might," Sarkis said. He grinned at Krispos. "I wasn't wrong, your Majesty—you are a lively man to serve under. We have a saying in Vaspurakan about your kind—'sneaky as a prince out to sleep with another man's princess.' "

Everyone in the tent laughed. "I have a princess of my own, thank you," Krispos said, which won him an approving glance from Rhisoulphos. His own mirth soon faded, though; he remembered the days when Dara had not been his, and how the two of them had both done some sneaking to be able to sleep with each other. Sarkis' Vaspurakaner saying held teeth the officer did not know about.

Mammianos' yawn almost split his head in two. "Let's get on with it," he said. "The Emperor's scheme has to move tonight if it moves at all, and afterward I aim to sleep. If the scheme doesn't come off—maybe even if it does—we'll have more fighting in the morning, and I for one am not so young as I used to be. I need rests between rounds, in battle as in other things."

"Sad but true," said Rhisoulphos, who was within a few years of the fat general's age. He yawned, too, less cavernously.

"Go get some of your scouts, Sarkis," Krispos said. "They're the proper men for the plan." Sarkis saluted and hurried away. Along with the rest of his companions, Krispos stepped outside the tent to await his return. A couple of Halogai stayed almost within arm's length of him, their axes at the ready, their eyes never leaving Rhisoulphos. He must have known they were watching him, and why, but gave no sign. Krispos admired his sangfroid.

A few minutes later Sarkis returned with fifteen or twenty soldiers. "All young and unmarried, as you asked," he told Krispos. "They don't care if they live or die."

The scouts thought that was very funny. Their teeth gleamed whitely in their dirty faces as they chuckled. Krispos realized that what Sarkis had said was literally true for most of them; they did not believe in the possibility of their own deaths, not down deep. Had he been so foolish himself, ten or twelve years before? He probably had.

"Here's what I want you to do," he said, and the scouts drew closer to listen. "I want you to get into Petronas' camp tonight, when everything there is still in disorder. I don't care whether you pretend to be his soldiers or you take off your armor and make as if you're farmers from around here. Whatever you do, you need to get among his men. I don't order this of you. Anyone who doesn't care to risk it may leave now."

No one left. "What do we do once we're in there, Majesty?" one of the scouts asked. The light from the campfires played up the glitter of excitement in his eyes. To him it was all a game, Krispos thought. He breathed a prayer to Phos that the youngster would come through safe.

"Here's what," he answered. "Remind Petronas' soldiers that I offered him amnesty, and tell them they can have it, too, for the asking . . . if they don't wait too long. Tell them I'll give them three days. After that, we'll attack again, and we'll treat any we capture as enemies."

The young men looked at one another. "Sneaky as a prince out to sleep with another man's princess," one of them said with a strong Vaspurakaner accent. As Sarkis had, he sounded admiring.

When they saw Krispos was done, the scouts scattered. Krispos watched them slip out of camp, heading west. Some rode out, armed and armored; others left on foot, wearing knee-length linen tunics and sandals.

Mammianos watched them go, too. After the last one was gone, he turned to Krispos and asked, "Now what?"

"Now," Krispos said, picking a phrase more likely in Barsymes' mouth than his own, "we await developments."

The flood of deserters he'd hoped for did not materialize. A few riders came over from the rebel camp, but Petronas' cavalry pickets stayed alert and aggressive. If they'd given up on the chief they followed, they showed no sign of it.

To Krispos' relief, all his own scouts managed to return safely. He would have felt dreadful, sacrificing them without gaining the advantage he'd expected. On the third day after he'd sent them out, he began readying his forces for an attack on the morrow. "Since I warned Petronas' men, I can't make myself out a liar now," he told Mammianos.

"No, your Majesty," Mammianos agreed mournfully. "I might wish, though, that you hadn't been so exact. Since Petronas must know we're coming, who can guess what sort of mischief he'll have waiting for us?" Without words, his round face said, *You wouldn't be in this mess if you'd listened to me.*

Krispos did not need to be reminded of that. Thinking to save lives, he'd probably cost Videssos—and his own side in particular—a good many men instead. As he sought his tent that evening, he told himself that he had generals along for a reason, and kicked himself for ignoring Mammianos' sage advice to pursue his own scheme.

Thanks to his worry, he took awhile to fall asleep. Once slumber took him, he slept soundly; he had long since learned to ignore the usual run of camp noises. The commotion that woke him was nothing usual. He grabbed sword and shield and clapped a helmet on his head before he peered out through the tentflap to see what was going on.

His first thought was that Petronas had decided to beat him to the punch with a night attack. But while the noise outside was tremendous, it was not the din of battle. "It sounds like a festival," he said, more than a little indignant.

Geirrod and Vagn stood guard in front of his tent. They turned to look at him. "Good you're up, Majesty," Geirrod said. "We'd have roused you any time now, had the clamor not done it for us. Two of Petronas' best generals just came into camp."

"*Did* they?" Krispos said softly. "Well, by the good god." Just then Mammianos came out of his tent, which was next to Krispos'. Krispos felt like putting his thumbs in his ears, twiddling his fingers, and sticking out his tongue at the fat general. Instead, he simply waited for Mammianos to notice him.

The general's own guards must have given him the news. He glanced over toward the imperial tent and saw Krispos there. Slowly and deliberately, he came to attention and saluted. A moment later, as if deciding that was not enough, he doffed his helm as well.

Krispos waved back, then asked the guards, "Who are these generals, anyway?"

"Vlases and Dardaparos, their names are, Majesty," Geirrod said.

To Krispos they were only names. He said, "Have them

fetched here. What they can tell me of Petronas and his army will be beyond price.'' As the Haloga walked off to do his bidding, Krispos waved Mammianos over. He was sure his general would know everything worth knowing about them.

Guards brought up the pair of deserters within a couple of minutes. One officer was tall and thickset, though muscular rather than fat like Mammianos. He proved to be Vlases. Dardaparos, on the other hand, was small, skinny, and bowlegged from a lifetime spent in the saddle; by looks, he might have been father to some of Sarkis' scouts. He and his comrade both went down in proskynesis before Krispos, touching their foreheads to the ground. ''Majesty,'' they said together.

Krispos let them stay prostrate a beat longer than he would have with men he fully trusted. After he told them to rise, he asked, ''How long ago did you last give Petronas imperial honors?''

Dardaparos spoke for both of them. ''Earlier this evening. But we came here trusting your amnesty, your Majesty. We'll serve you as loyally as ever we served him.''

''There's a fine promise,'' Mammianos growled. ''Does it mean you'll desert the Avtokrator just when he needs you most?''

''Surely not, Mammianos,'' Krispos said smoothly, seeing Dardaparos and Vlases stiffen. To them he added, ''And my promise is good—you'll not be harmed. Tell me, though, what made you decide to come over to me now?''

''Majesty, we decided you'd likely win with us or without us,'' Vlases answered. His voice made Krispos blink. It was a high, sweet tenor, as surprising from such a big man as Trokoundos' bass from a small one. He went on. ''Petronas said you were nothing but a jumped-up stable boy, begging your pardon, your Majesty. The campaign you've run against him showed us different, though.''

Dardaparos nodded. ''Aye, that's how it was, your Majesty. Any time an able man holds Videssos the city, a rebel's in deep from the get-go. You're abler than we thought when we first picked Petronas. We were wrong, and own it now.''

Krispos drew Mammianos to one side. ''What do you think?'' he asked quietly.

''I'm inclined to believe them.'' Mammianos sounded as if he regretted his inclination. ''If they'd told you they couldn't stand the idea of being traitors any more, or some such high-sounding tripe, I'd keep 'em under guard—in irons, too, most likely. But I've known both of 'em for years, and they have a keen-honed sense of where their interest lies.''

"That's about as I saw it." Krispos walked back over to the generals. "Very well, excellent sirs, I welcome you to my cause. Now tell me how you think Petronas will dispose his forces to meet the attack I intend to make tomorrow."

"He won't dispose them so well, with us gone," Dardaperos said at once. Krispos had no idea how good a general he was, but he certainly had a high officer's sense of self-worth.

"Likely he won't," Krispos said. He found himself yawning enormously. "Excellent sirs, on second thought I'm going to leave the rest of your questioning to Mammianos here. And I hope you will forgive me, but I intend to keep you under guard until after the fighting is done tomorrow. I don't know what harm you could do me there, but I'd sooner not find out."

"Spoken like a sensible man, your Majesty," Vlases said. "You may welcome us, but you have no reason to trust us. By the lord with the great and good mind, we'll give you reason soon enough."

He stooped, found a twig, and started drawing in the dirt. Grunting with the effort it cost him, Mammianos also stooped. Krispos watched for a few minutes as Vlases laid out Petronas' plans, then yawned again, even more widely than before. By the time he sought his cot, though, he'd learned enough to decide that the movements he and Mammianos had already devised would still serve his aims.

They would, that is, if Vlases and Dardaperos spoke the truth. He suddenly realized he could find out if they did. He sprang from bed once more, shouting for Trokoundos. The mage appeared shortly, dapper as ever. Krispos explained what he wanted.

"Aye, the two-mirror trick will tell whether they lie," Trokoundos said, "but it may not tell you everything you need to know. It won't tell you what changes Petronas has made in his plans because they deserted. And it won't tell whether he encouraged them to go over to you, maybe so subtly they don't even grasp it themselves, just for the sake of putting you in confusion and doubt like this."

"I can't believe that. They're two of his best men." But Krispos sounded unsure, even to himself. Petronas was a master of the game of glove within glove within glove. He'd twisted Anthimos round his finger for years. If he wanted to manipulate a couple of his generals, Krispos was convinced he could.

Angrily Krispos shook his head. A fine state of affairs, when even learning the truth could not tell him whether to change his plans or keep them. "Find out what you can," he told Trokoundos.

Once Trokoundos had gone, Krispos lay down again. Now, though, sleep was slower coming. And after Krispos' eyes closed and his breathing grew deep and regular, he dreamed he followed Petronas down a path that twisted back on itself until Petronas was following him . . .

After a night of such dreams, waking to the certainty of morning was a relief. Krispos found himself looking forward to battle in a way he never had before. For good or ill, battle would yield but one outcome, not the endlessly entrapping webs of possibility through which he had struggled in the darkness.

As Krispos gnawed a hard roll and drank sour wine from a leather jack, Trokoundos came up to report: "So far as Dardaparos and Vlases know, they're honest traitors, at any rate."

"Good," Krispos said. Trokoundos, duty done, departed, leaving Krispos to chew on his phrasing. Honest traitors? The words could have come straight from his near nightmare.

Scrambling up into Progress' saddle gave him the same feeling of release he'd known on waking, the feeling that something definite was about to happen. The Haloga guardsmen had to stay tight around him to keep him from spurring ahead of the army to the scouts who led its advance.

Before the day was very old, those scouts began trading arrows with the ones Petronas had sent out. Petronas' men drew back; they were far in advance of their own army, while Krispos' main body of troops trotted on, close behind his scouting parties. Had he not already known where Petronas' force lay, the retreating scouts would have led him to it.

Petronas' camp was in the middle of a broad, scrubby pasture, placed so no one could take it unawares. The rebel's forces stood in line of battle half a mile in front of their tents and pavilions. Petronas' imperial banner flapped defiantly at the center of their line.

Mammianos glanced at Krispos. "As we set it up?"

"Aye," Krispos said. "I think we'll keep him too busy to cut us in half." He showed his teeth in what was almost a smile. "We'd better."

"That's true enough." Mammianos half grunted, half chuckled. He yelled to the army musicians. Horns, drums, and pipes sent companies of horsemen galloping from the second rank to either wing as they bore down on Petronas' force.

The rebels were also moving forward; the momentum of horse and rider played a vital part in mounted warfare. Petronas had musicians of his own. Their martial blare shifted his deployments to match Krispos'.

"Good," Krispos said. "He's dancing to our tune for a change." He'd most feared Petronas trying to smash through his army's deliberately weakened center. Now—he hoped—the fight would be on his terms.

Arrows flew. So did war cries. The rebels still acclaimed Petronas. Along with Krispos' name, his men had others to hurl at their foes—those of Rhisoulphos, Vlases, and Dardaperos. They also shouted one thing more. "Amnesty! We spare those who yield!"

The armies collided first at the wings. Saber and lance took over for the bow. Despite defections, Petronas' men fought fiercely. Krispos bit his lip as he watched his own troops held in place. The treachery he'd looked for simply was not there.

When he complained of that, Mammianos said, "Can't be helped, your Majesty. But aren't you glad to be worrying over the loyalty of the other fellow's army and not your own?"

"Yes, as a matter of fact," Krispos said. Only last fall he'd wondered if any Videssian soldiers at all would cleave to him. Only days before he'd wondered if his army would hold together through combat. Now Petronas' bowels were the ones that griped at each collision of men. Amazing what a victory could do, Krispos thought.

The fight ground on. Thanks to Rhisoulphos' defection, Krispos had more men in it than Petronas. Rhisoulphos' men were not in a hotly engaged part of the line—they held the middle of the right wing. But their presence freed up other warriors for the attack. The men on the extreme right of Petronas' line found themselves first outnumbered, then outflanked.

They bent back. That was not enough to save them; Krispos' horsemen, scenting victory, folded round them like a wolf's jaws closing on a tasty gobbet of meat. Petronas' men were brave and loyal. For half an hour and more, they fought desperately, selling themselves dear for their comrades' sake. But flesh and blood will only bear so much. Soldiers began casting swords and lances to the ground and raising their hands in token of surrender.

Once the yielding started—and once Petronas' men saw that, as promised, those who yielded were not butchered—it ran from the end of Petronas' line toward the middle. The line shook, like a man with an ague. Shouting, Krispos' warriors pressed hard.

All at once Petronas' army broke into fragments. Some men fled the field, singly and in small groups. More, sometimes whole companies at a time, threw down their weapons and surrendered. A hard core of perhaps three thousand men, Petronas' firmest followers, withdrew in a body toward hill country that corrugated the horizon toward the northwest.

"After them!" Krispos cried in high excitement, pounding his fist against Mammianos' armored shoulder. "Don't let a one of them get away!"

"Aye, Majesty." Mammianos shouted for couriers and stabbed his finger out toward Petronas' retreating soldiers. He roared orders that, properly carried out, would have bagged every fugitive.

Somehow, though, the pursuit did not quite come off. Some of Krispos' men rode after Petronas' hard core of strength. But others were still busy accepting surrenders, or relieving of their portable property soldiers who had surrendered. Still others made for Petronas' camp, which lay before them, tempting as a naked woman with an inviting smile. And so Petronas' followers, though in a running fight all the way, reached the hills and set up a rear guard to hold the gap through which they fled.

By the time the column that had given chase to Petronas returned empty-handed, night was falling. Krispos swore when he found out they had failed. "By the lord with the great and good mind, I'd like to send the fools who stopped to plunder straight to the ice," he raged.

"And if you did, you'd have hardly more men left than those who escaped with Petronas," Sarkis said.

"They should have chased Petronas first and plundered later," Krispos said.

Sarkis answered with a shrug. "Common soldiers don't grow rich on army pay, your Majesty. They're lucky to hold their own. If they see the chance to steal something worth stealing, they're going to do it."

"And think, your Majesty," Mammianos added soothingly, "had everyone gone after Petronas, who would have protected you if his men decided all at once to remember their allegiance?"

"I should have gone after Petronas myself," Krispos said, but then he let the matter drop. What was done was done; no matter how he complained, he could not bring back an opportunity lost. That did not mean he forgot. He filed the failure away in his mind, resolving not to let it happen again with any army of his.

"Any way you look at it, Majesty, we won quite a victory," Mammianos said. "Here's a great haul of prisoners, Petronas' camp taken—"

"I'll not deny it," Krispos said. He'd hoped to win the whole war today, not just a battle, but, as he'd just reminded himself, one took what one got. He was not so mean-spirited as to forget that. He undid his tin canteen from his belt, raised it, then swigged a big gulp of the rough wine the army drank. "To victory!" he shouted.

Everyone who heard him—which meant a good part of the army—turned at the sound of his voice. In a moment, bedlam filled the camp. "To victory!' soldiers roared. Some, like Krispos, toasted it. Others capered round campfires, filled with triumph or simple relief at being alive.

And others, the crueler few, taunted the prisoners they had taken. The former followers of Petronas, disarmed now, dared not reply. From taunts, some of the ruffians moved on to roughing up their captives. Krispos did not care to think about how far their ingenuity might take them if he gave them free rein.

Hand on sword hilt, he stalked toward the nastiest of the little games nearby. Without his asking, Halogai formed up around him. Narvikka said, "Aye, Majesty, there's a deal of us in you, I t'ink. You look like a man about to go killing mad."

"That's how I feel." Krispos grabbed the shoulder of a trooper who had been amusing himself by stomping on a prisoner's toes. The man whirled round angrily when his sport was interrupted. The curse in his mouth died unspoken. Quickly, shaking with fear, he prostrated himself.

Krispos waited till he was flat on his belly, then kicked him in the ribs. Pain shot up his leg—the fellow wore chain mail. By the way he twisted and grabbed at himself, he felt the kick, too, through links, leather, and padding. Krispos said, "Is that how you give amnesty: tormenting a man who can't fight back?"

"N-no, Majesty," the fellow got out. "Just—having a little fun, is all."

"Maybe you were. I don't think he was." Krispos kicked the trooper again, not quite so hard this time. The man grunted, but otherwise bore it without flinching. Krispos drew back his foot and asked, "Or do you enjoy it when I do this? Answer me!"

"No, Majesty." Overbearing while on top, the soldier shrank in on himself when confronted with power greater than his petty share.

"All right, then. If you ever want to get mercy, or deserve it, you'd best give it when you can. Now get out of here." The soldier scrambled to his feet and fled. Krispos glared around. "Hurting a man who's yielded, especially one who's promised amnesty, is Skotos' work. The next trooper who's caught at it gets stripes and dismissal without pay. Does everyone understand?"

If anybody had doubts, he kept them to himself. In the face of Krispos' anger, the camp went from boisterous to solemn and quiet in moments. Into that sudden silence, the fellow he'd rescued said, "Phos bless you, your Majesty. That was done like an Avtokrator."

"Aye." Several Halogai rumbled agreement.

"If I have the job, I should live up to it." Krispos glanced over at the prisoner. "Why did you fight against me in the first place?"

"I come from Petronas' estates. He is my master. He was always good to me; I figured he'd be good for the Empire." He studied Krispos, his head cocked to one side. "I still reckon that might be so, but looks to me now like he's not the only one."

"I hope not." Krispos wondered how many men throughout the Empire of Videssos could run it capably if they somehow found themselves on the throne. He'd never had that thought before. More than a few, he decided, a little bemused. But he was the one with the job, and he aimed to keep it.

"What is it, Majesty?" Narvikka asked. "By the furrow of your brow, I'd guess a weighty thought."

"Not really." Laughing, Krispos explained.

Narvikka said, "Bethink yourself on your good fortune, Majesty: of all those might-be Avtokrators, only Petronas wears the red boots in your despite."

"Even Petronas is one man too many in them." Krispos turned to go back to his tent, then stopped. A grin of pure mischief slowly spread over his face. "I know just how to get him out of them, too." His voice rose. "Trokoundos!"

The mage hurried over to him. "How may I serve your Majesty?" he asked, bowing.

Krispos told Trokoundos what he needed, then said anxiously, "This isn't battle magic, is it?"

Trokoundos' heavy-lidded eyes half closed as he considered. At last he said, "It shouldn't be. And even if Petronas' person is warded, as it's sure to be, who would think of protecting his boots?" His smile was a slyer version of Krispos'. "The more so as we won't do them a bit of harm."

"So we won't," Krispos said. "But, the lord with the great and good mind willing, we'll do some to Petronas."

# V

Petronas, as was his habit, woke soon after dawn. His back and shoulders ached; too many years of sleeping soft in Videssos the city—aye, and even when he took the field—left him unused to making do with a single blanket for a bedroll. At that, he was luckier than most of the men who still clove to him, for he had a tent to shelter him from the nighttime chill. Theirs were lost, booty now for the army that followed Krispos.

"Krispos!" Petronas mouthed the name, making it into a curse. He cursed himself, too, for he had first taken Krispos into his own household, then introduced him into Anthimos'.

He'd never imagined Krispos' influence with his nephew could rival his own—till the day he found himself, his head shorn, cast into the monastery of the holy Skirios. He ran a hand through his hair. Only now, most of a year after he'd slipped out of the monastery, did he have a proper man's growth once more.

He'd never imagined Krispos would dare seize the throne, or that Krispos could govern once he had it—everyone, he'd been sure, would flock to his own banner. But it had not happened so. Petronas cursed himself again, for putting that fat fool of a Mammianos in a place that had proven so important.

And with that fat fool, Krispos had beaten him twice now—and by the good god, Petronas had never imagined *that*! Just how badly he'd underestimated Krispos, and Krispos' knack for getting other people to do what he needed, was only now sinking in, when it was on the very edge of being too late.

Petronas clenched a fist. "No, by Phos, not too late!" he said out loud. He pissed in a chamber pot—likely the last of those left to his army—then decked himself in the full imperial regalia.

Seeing him in the raiment rightfully his could only hearten his men, he told himself.

He stooped to go out through the tent flap and walked over to his horse, which was tied nearby. He sprang onto the beast's back with a surge of pride—he might be nearing sixty, but he could still ride. He smiled maliciously to think of Gnatios, who quivered atop anything bigger than a mule.

But as Petronas rode through the camp, his smile faded. Years of gauging armies' tempers made him worry about this one. The men were restive and discouraged; he did not like the way they refused to meet his eye. When a soldier did look his way, he liked the fellow's stare even less. "By the ice, what are you gaping at?" he snarled.

The trooper looked apprehensive at being singled out. "B-begging your pardon, your Majesty, but why did you don black boots to wear with your fine robe and crown?"

"Are you mad?" Petronas took his left foot from the stirrup and kicked his leg up and down. "This boot's as red as a man's arse after a week in the saddle."

"Begging your pardon again, Majesty, but it looks black to me. So does the right one, sir—uh, sire. May the ice take me if I lie."

"Are you telling me I don't know red when I see it?" Petronas asked dangerously. He looked down at his boots. They were both a most satisfactory crimson, the exact imperial shade. Petronas had seen it worn by his father, by his brother, and by his nephew; it was as familiar to him as the back of his hand— more familiar than his own face, for sometimes he did not see a mirror for weeks at a stretch.

Instead of answering him directly, the trooper turned to his mates. "Tell his Majesty, lads. Are those boots red or are they black?"

"They're black," the soldiers said in one voice. Now it was Petronas' turn to stare at them; he could not doubt they meant what they said. One man added, "Seems an unchancy thing to me, wearing a private citizen's boots with all that fancy imperial gear."

Another said, "Aye, there's no good omen in that." Several troopers drew Phos' sun-circle over their hearts.

Petronas glanced at his boots again. They still looked red to him. If his men did not see them so—he shivered. That omen seemed bad to him, too, as if he had no right to the imperial throne. He clenched his teeth against the idea that

Phos had turned away from him and toward that accursed upstart Krispos . . .

The moment his rival's name entered his mind, he knew Phos was not the one who had arranged the omen. He shouted for his wizard. "Skeparnas!" When the mage did not appear at once, he shouted again, louder this time. *"Skeparnas!"*

Skeparnas picked his way through the soldiers. He was a tall, thin man with a long, lean face, a beard waxed to a point, and the longest fingers Petronas had ever seen. "How may I serve you, your Majesty?"

"What color are my boots?" Petronas demanded.

He'd seldom seen Skeparnas taken aback, but now the wizard blinked and drew back half a step. "To me, your Majesty, they look red," he said cautiously.

"To me, too," Petronas said. But before the words were out of his mouth, the soldiers all around set up a clamor, insisting they were black. "Shut up!" he roared at them. To Skeparnas he went on, more quietly, "I think Krispos magicked them, the stinking son of a spotted snake."

"Ahh." Skeparnas leaned forward, like a tower tilting after an earthquake. "Yes, that would be a clever ploy, wouldn't it?" His hands writhed in quick passes; those spidery fingers seemed almost to knot themselves together.

Suddenly Petronas' soldiers called out: "They're red now, your Majesty!"

"There, you see?" Petronas said triumphantly.

"A lovely spell, most marvelously subtle," Skeparnas said with a connoisseur's appreciation. "Not only did it have no hold on you, it was also made to be invisible to anyone who perceived it with a mage's eye, thus perhaps delaying its discovery and allowing it to work the maximum amount of confusion."

"Very fornicating lovely," Petronas snapped. He raised his voice to address his men. "You see, my heroes, there's no omen here. This was just more of Krispos' vile work, aiming to make you think something's wrong when it's not. Just a cheap, miserable trick, not worth fretting over."

He waited, hoping for an answering cheer. It did not come. Determinedly, though, he rode through the army as if it had. He waved to the men, making his horse rear and caracole.

"How do we know those boots weren't really black till the mage spelled 'em red again?" one soldier asked another as he came by. He rode on, but keeping his face still after that was as hard as if he'd taken a lance in the guts.

* * *

Trokoundos staggered, then steadied himself. "They've broken the spell," he gasped. "By the good god, I could do with a cup of wine." Greasy sweat covered his fine-drawn features.

Krispos poured with his own hand. "How much good do you think it's done?"

"No way to guess," Trokoundos said, gasping again after he'd drained the cup at a single long draft. "You know how it is, Majesty: If the soldiers are truly strong for Petronas, they'll stay with him come what may. If they're wavering, the least little thing could seem a bad omen to 'em."

"Aye." More and more, Krispos was coming to believe the art of leading men was a kind of magic, though not one sorcerers studied. What folk thought of a ruler, oftentimes, seemed more important than what he really was.

"Shall I try the spell again this afternoon, Majesty, or maybe tomorrow morning?" Trokoundos asked.

After some thought, Krispos shook his head. "That would make them sure it was our sorcery, I think. If it only happens the once, they can't be certain quite what it is."

"As you wish, of course," Trokoundos said. "What then?"

"I'm going to let Petronas stew in his own juice for a couple of days," Krispos answered. "When I do hit him again, I'll hit hard. People who know this country have already told me of other passes through the hills, and he doesn't have enough men to cover them all. If he stays where he is, I can leave enough men here to keep him from bursting out onto the plain again, while I take the rest around to hit him from behind."

"What if he flees?"

"If he flees now, after losing to me twice, he's mine," Krispos said. "Then it's just a matter of running him to earth."

While Petronas—he hoped—stewed, Krispos spent the next few days catching up on the dispatches that never stopped coming from the capital. He approved a commercial treaty with Khatrish, scribbled minor changes on an inheritance law before he affixed his seal to it, commuted one death sentence where the evidence looked flimsy, and let another stand.

He wrote to Mavros of his second victory, then read through his foster brother's gossipy reports of doings in Videssos the city. From them, and from Dara's occasional shorter notes, he gathered that Phostis, while still small, was doing well. That filled him with sober satisfaction; whether a baby lived to grow up was always a roll of the dice.

Mavros also forwarded dispatches from the war against Harvas Black-Robe. Krispos read and reread those. Agapetos' preemptive attack had bogged down, but he still stood on enemy soil. Maybe, Krispos thought, the peasants near the northern border would be able to get in a crop in peace.

Other documents also came from the city. Krispos began to dread opening the ones sealed with sky-blue wax. Every time he did, he read that Pyrrhos had deposed another priest or abbot for infractions that seemed ever more trivial. Casting a man from his temple for trimming his beard too close, for instance, left Krispos shaking his head. He wrote a series of increasingly blunt notes to the patriarch, urging Pyrrhos to show restraint.

But restraint did not seem to be part of Pyrrhos' vocabulary. Letters of protest also came to Krispos from ousted clerics, from clerics afraid they would be ousted, and from delegations of prominent citizens from several towns seeking protection for their local priests.

More and more, Krispos wished he could have retained Gnatios as ecumenical patriarch. He'd never imagined that one of his strongest allies could become one of his greatest embarrassments. And yet Pyrrhos remained zealous in his behalf. With Petronas and Gnatios still to worry about, Krispos put off a decision on his rigorist patriarch.

He sent a holding force under Sarkis against the pass through which Petronas had fled, then led the rest of the army north and west through another gap to get behind his rival. His part of the army was just entering that second pass when a courier from Sarkis galloped up on a blowing, foam-spattered horse. The man was panting as hard as if he'd done all that running himself. "Majesty!" he called. "Rejoice, Majesty! We're through!"

"You're through?" Krispos stared at him. "Sarkis forced the pass, you mean?" That was good luck past all expectation. Petronas knew how to find defensive positions. A handful of determined men could have held the pass for days, so long as they were not outflanked.

But the courier said, "Looks like Petronas' army's gone belly-up, the lord Sarkis told me to tell you. Some have fled, more are yielding themselves up. The fight isn't in 'em anymore, Majesty."

"By the good god," Krispos said softly. He wondered what part—if any—the magic he'd suggested had played. *Have to ask some prisoners*, he told himself before more urgent concerns drove the matter from his mind. "What's become of Petronas, then? Has he surrendered?"

"No, Majesty, no sign of him, nor of Gnatios, either. The lord Sarkis urges speed on you, to help round up as many flying soldiers as we may."

"Yes." Krispos turned to Thvari, the captain of his Haloga guards. "Will you and your men ride pack horses, brave sir, to help us move the faster?"

Thvari spoke to the guardsmen in their own slow, rolling speech. They shouted back, grinning and waving their axes. "Aye," Thvari said unnecessarily. He added, "We would not miss being in at the kill."

"Good." Krispos called orders to the army musicians. The long column briefly halted. The baggage-train handlers shifted burdens on their animals, freeing up enough to accommodate the Halogai. They waved away soldiers who wanted to help; men without their long-practiced skill at lashing and unlashing bundles would only have slowed them down.

The musicians blew *At the trot*. The army started forward again. The Halogai were no horsemen, but most managed to stay on their mounts and keep them headed in the right direction. That was plenty, Krispos thought. If they needed to fight, they would dismount.

"Where do you think Petronas will go if his army has broken up?" Krispos asked Mammianos.

The fat general tugged at his beard as he thought. "Some failed rebels might flee to Makuran, but I can't see Petronas as cat's-paw for the King of Kings. He'd sooner leap off a cliff, I think. He might do that anyway, your Majesty, to keep you from gloating over him."

"I wouldn't gloat," Krispos said.

Mammianos studied him. "Mmm, maybe not. But he would if *he* caught *you*, and we always reckon others from ourselves. Likeliest, though, Petronas'll try and hole himself up somewhere, do what he can against you. Let me think . . . There's an old fortress not too far from here, place called—what in the name of the ice *is* the place called? Antigonos, that's what it is. That's as good a guess as any, and better than most."

"We'll head there, then," Krispos said. "Do you know the way?"

"I expect I could find it, but you'll have men who could do it quicker, I'll tell you that."

A few questions called to the soldiers showed Krispos that

Mammianos was right. With a couple of locally raised men in the lead, the army pounded toward Antigonos. Krispos spent a while worrying what to do if Petronas was not in the fortress. Then he stopped worrying. His column was heading in the right direction to cut off fugitives anyhow.

The riders ran into several bands from Petronas' disintegrating army. None included the rival Emperor; none of his men admitted knowing where he had gone. From what they said, he and some of his closest followers had simply disappeared the morning before, leaving the rest of the men to fend for themselves. One trooper said bitterly, "If I'd known the bugger'd run like that, I never would have followed him."

"Petronas thinks of his own neck first," Mammianos said. Remembering his own dealings with Anthimos' uncle, Krispos nodded.

He and his men reached the fortress of Antigonos a little before sunset. The fortress perched atop a tall hill and surveyed the surrounding countryside like a vulture peering out from a branch on top of a high tree. The iron-faced wooden gate was slammed shut; a thin column of cooksmoke rose into the sky from the citadel.

"Somebody's home," Krispos said. "I wonder who." Beside him, Mammianos barked laughter. Krispos turned to the musicians. "Blow *Parley*."

The call rang out several times before anyone appeared on the wall to answer it. "Will you yield?" Krispos called, a minor magic of Trokoundos' projecting his voice beyond bowshot. "I still offer amnesty to soldiers and safe passage back to the monastery for Petronas and Gnatios."

"I'll never trust myself to you, wretch," shouted the man on the wall.

Krispos started slightly to recognize Petronas' voice. It, too, carried; *Well*, Krispos thought, *I've known he had a mage along since he broke the spell on his boots*. He touched the amulet he wore with his lucky goldpiece. Petronas used wizards for purposes darker than extending the range of his voice. Without Trokoundos by him, Krispos would have feared to confront his foe so closely.

"I could have ordered you killed the moment I took the throne." Krispos wondered if he should have done just that. Shrugging to himself, he went on, "I have no special yen for your blood. Only pledge you'll live quietly among the monks and let me get on with running the Empire."

"*My* Empire," Petronas roared.

"Your empire is that fortress you're huddling in," Krispos said. "The rest of Videssos acknowledges me—and my patriarch." If he was stuck with Pyrrhos, he thought, he ought to get some use out of him, even if only to make Petronas writhe in his cage.

"To the ice with your patriarch, the Phos-drunk fanatic!"

Krispos smiled. For once, he and Petronas agreed on something. He had no intention of letting his rival know it. He said, "You're walled up as tightly here as you would be in the monastery of the holy Skirios. How do you propose to get away? You might as well give up and go back to the monastery."

"Never!" Petronas stamped down off the wall. His curses remained audible. He must have noticed that and signaled to his magician, for they cut off in the middle of a foul word.

Krispos nodded to Trokoundos, who chanted a brief spell. When Krispos spoke again, a moment later, his voice had only its usual power once more. "He won't be easy to pry out of there."

"Not without a siege train, which we don't have with us," Mammianos agreed. "Not unless we can starve him out, anyway."

Rhisoulphos stood close by, looking up at the spot on the wall that Petronas had just vacated. He shook his head at Mammianos' words. "He has supplies for months in there. He spent the winter strengthening the place against the chance that the war would turn against him."

"Smart of him." Mammianos also glanced toward the fortress of Antigonos. "Aye, he's near as clever as he thinks he is."

"We'll send for a siege train, by the good god, and sit round the fortress till it gets here," Krispos said. "If Petronas wants to play at being Avtokrator inside till the rams start pounding on the walls, that's all right with me."

"Your sitting here may be just what he wants," Trokoundos said. "Remember that he tried once to slay you by sorcery. Such an effort would be all the easier to repeat with you close by. We've just seen his mage is still with him."

"I can't very well leave before he's taken, not if I intend to leave men of mine behind here," Krispos said.

Mammianos and Rhisoulphos both saluted him, then looked at each other as if taken by surprise. Mammianos said, "Majesty, you may not be trained to command, but you have a gift for it.''

"As may be." Krispos did not show how pleased he was. He turned to Trokoundos. "I trust you have me better warded than I was that night."

"Oh, indeed. The protections I gave you then were the hasty sort one uses in an emergency. I thank the lord with the great and good mind that they sufficed. But since you gained the throne, I and my colleagues have hedged you round with far more apotropaic incantations."

"With what?" Krispos wanted to see if the wizard could repeat himself without tripping over his tongue.

But Trokoundos chose to explain instead: "Protective spells. I believe they will serve. With magecraft, one is seldom as sure as one would like."

"Come to that, we aren't sure Petronas and his wizard will attack me," Krispos said.

"He will, your Majesty," Rhisoulphos said positively. "What other chance in all the world has he now to become Avtokrator?"

"Put that way—" Krispos clicked his tongue between his teeth. "Aye, likely he will. Here I stay, even so. Trokoundos will keep me safe." What he did not mention was his fear that, if he returned to Videssos the city, Petronas might suborn some soldiers and get free once more.

"Maybe," Mammianos said hopefully, "he hasn't had the chance to fill the cisterns in there too full. Summers hereabouts are hot and dry. With luck, his men will get thirsty soon and make him yield."

"Maybe." But Krispos doubted it. He'd seen that Petronas could be matched as a combat soldier. For keeping an army in supplies, though, he had few peers. If he'd taken refuge in the fortress of Antigonos, he was ready to stand siege there.

Krispos ringed his own army round the base of the fortress' hill. He staged mock attacks by night and day, seeking to wear down the defenders. Trokoundos wore himself into exhaustion casting one protective spell after another over Krispos and over the army as a whole. That Petronas' mage bided his time only made Trokoundos certain the stroke would be deadly when it came.

The siege dragged on. The healer-priests were much busier with cases of dysentery than with wounds. A letter let Krispos know that a train of rams and catapults had set out from Videssos the city for Antigonos. Behind a white-painted shield of truce, a captain approached the fortress and read the letter in a loud voice, finishing "Beware, rebels! Your hour of justice approaches!" Petronas' men jeered him from the walls.

Trokoundos redoubled his precautions, festooning Krispos with charms and amulets until their chains seemed heavier than chain mail. "How am I supposed to sleep, wearing all this?" Krispos complained. "The ones that don't gouge my back gouge my chest."

With a look of martyred patience, Trokoundos said, "Your Majesty, Petronas must know he cannot hope to last long once the siege engines arrive. Therefore he will surely try to strike you down before that time. We must be ready."

"Not only will I be ready, I'll be stoop-shouldered, as well," Krispos said. Trokoundos' martyred look did not change. Krispos threw his hands in the air and walked off, clanking as he went.

But that night, alone at last in his tent, he tossed and turned until a sharp-pointed amethyst crystal on one of his new amulets stabbed him just above his right shoulder blade. He swore and clapped his other hand to the injury. When he took it away, his palm was wet with blood.

"That fornicating does it!" he snarled. He threw aside the light silk coverlet and jumped to his feet. He took off the offending chain and flung it on the floor. It knocked over one of the other charms that ringed the bed like a fortress' wall. Finally, breathing hard, Krispos lay down again. "Maybe Petronas' wizard will pick tonight to try to kill me," he muttered, "but one piece more or less shouldn't matter much. And if he does get me, at least I'll die sound asleep."

What with his fury, naturally, he had trouble drifting off even after the chain was gone. He tossed and turned, dozed and half woke. His shoulder still hurt, too.

Some time toward morning, a tiny crunch made him open his eyes yet again. He was frowning even as he came fully awake—the crunch had sounded very close, as if it was inside the tent. A servant who disturbed him in the middle of the night—especially the middle of this miserable night—would regret the day he was born.

But the man crouching not three paces away was no servant of his. He was all in black—even his face was blacked, likely with charcoal. His right hand held a long knife. And under one of his black boots lay the crushed remains of one of Trokoundos' charms. Had he not trod on it, Krispos would never have known he was there until that knife slid between his ribs or across his throat.

The knifeman's dark face twisted in dismay as he saw Krispos wake. Krispos' face twisted, too. The assassin sprang toward him. Krispos flung his coverlet in the fellow's face and shouted as loud as he could. Outside the tent, his Haloga guard also cried out.

While the assassin was clawing free of the coverlet, Krispos seized his knife arm with both hands. His foe kicked him in the shin, hard enough to make his teeth click together in anguish. He tried to knee the knifeman in the crotch. The fellow twisted to one side and took the blow on the point of his hip.

With a sudden wrench, he tried to break Krispos' grip on his wrist. But Krispos had wrestled since before his beard came in. He hung on grimly. The assassin could do what he pleased, so long as he did not get that dagger free.

*Thunnk!* The abrupt sound of blade biting into flesh filled Krispos' ears and seemed to fill the whole tent. Hot blood sprayed his belly. The assassin convulsed in his arms. A latrine stench said the man's bowels had let go. The knife dropped from his hands. He crumpled to the ground.

"Majesty!" Vagn cried, horror on his face as he saw Krispos spattered with blood. "Are you hale, Majesty?"

"If my leg's not broken, yes," Krispos said, giving it a gingerly try. The pain did not get worse, so he supposed he'd taken no real damage. He looked down at the knifeman and at the spreading pool of blood. He whistled softly. "By the good god, Vagn, you almost cut him in two."

Instead of warming to the praise, the Haloga hung his head. He thrust his dripping axe into Krispos' hands. "Kill me now, Majesty, I beg you, for I failed to ward you from this, this—" His Videssian failed him; to show what he meant, he bent down and spat in the dead assassin's face. "Kill me, I beg you."

Krispos saw he meant it. "I'll do no such thing," he said.

"Then I have no honor." Vagn drew himself up, absolute determination on his face. "Since you do not grant me this boon, I shall slay myself."

"No, you—" Krispos stopped before he called Vagn an idiot. Filled with shame as he was, the northerner would only bear up under insults like a man bearing up under archery and would think he deserved each wound he took. Krispos tried to get the shock of battling the assassin out of his mind, tried to think clearly. The harsh Haloga notion of honor served him well most of the time; now he had to find a way around it. He said, "If you didn't ward me, who did? The knifeman lies dead at your feet. I didn't kill him."

Vagn shook his head. "It means nothing. Never should he have come into this tent."

"You were at the front. He must have got in at the back, under the canvas." Krispos looked at the assassin's contorted body. He thought about what it must have taken, even dressed in clothes that left him part of the night, to come down from the fortress and sneak through the enemy camp to its very heart. "In his own way, he was a brave man."

Vagn spat again. "He was a skulking murderer and should have had worse and slower than I gave him. Please, Majesty, I beg once more, slay me, that I may die clean."

"No, curse it!" Krispos said. Vagn turned and walked to the tent flap. If he left, Krispos was sure he would never return alive. He said quickly, "Here, wait. I know what I'll do—I'll give you a chance to redeem yourself in your own eyes."

"In no way can I do that," Vagn declared.

"Hear me out," Krispos said. When Vagn took another step toward the flap, he snapped, "I order you to listen." Reluctantly the Haloga stopped. Krispos went on, "Here's what I'd have you do: first, take this man's head. Then, unarmored if you like, carry it up to the gates of Antigonos and leave it there to show Petronas the fate his assassin earned. Will that give you back your honor?"

Vagn was some time silent, which only made the growing hubbub outside the imperial tent seem louder. Then, with a grunt, the Haloga chopped at the knifeman's neck. The roof of the tent was too low to let him take big, full swings with his ax, so the beheading required several strokes.

Krispos turned away from the gory job. He threw on a robe and went out to show the army he was still alive. The men whom his outcry had aroused shouted furiously when he told how the assassin had crept into his tent. He was just finishing the tale when Vagn emerged, holding the man's head by the hair. The soldiers let out such a lusty cheer that the guardsman blinked in surprise. Their approval seemed to reach him where Krispos' had not; as the cheering went on and on, he stood taller and straighter. Without a word, he began to tramp toward the fortress of Antigonos.

"Wait," Krispos called. "Do it by daylight, so Petronas can see just what gift you bring him."

"Aye," Vagn said after a moment's thought. "I will wait." He set down the assassin's head, lightly prodding it with his foot. "So will he." The joke struck Krispos as being in poor taste, but he was glad to hear the Haloga make it.

Trokoundos plucked at Krispos' sleeve. "We were right in guessing Petronas aimed to treacherously slay you," he said, "wrong only in his choice of stealth over sorcery. But had we relied on his using stealth, he surely would have tried with magic."

"I suppose so," Krispos said. "And as for that, you can cheer up. Without your magecraft, I'd be a dead man right now."

"What do you mean?" Trokoundos scratched his shaven head. "After all, Petronas did but send a simple knifeman against you."

"I know, but if the fellow hadn't stepped on one of those charms you insisted on scattering everywhere, I never would have woke up in time to yell."

"Happy to be of service, your Majesty," Trokoundos said in a strangled voice. Then he saw how hard Krispos' face was set against laughter. He allowed himself a dry chuckle or two, but still maintained his dignity.

*Too bad for him*, Krispos thought. He laughed out loud.

When the siege train reached the fortress of Antigonos, Krispos watched the soldiers on the walls watching his artisans assemble the frames for stone-throwing engines, the sheds that would protect the men who swung rams against stones or boiling oil from above.

The assassin's head still lay outside the gate. Petronas' men had let Vagn come and go. By now even the flies had tired of it.

As soon as the first catapult was done, the craftsmen who had built it recruited a squad of common soldiers to drag up a large stone and set it in the leathern sling at the end of the machine's throwing arm. Winches creaked as the crew tightened the ropes that gave the catapult its hurling power.

The throwing arm jerked forward. The catapult bucked. The stone flew through the air. It crashed against the wall of the fortress with a noise like thunder. The soldiers began to haul another rock into place.

Krispos sent a runner to the engines' crew with a single word: "Wait." Then one of his men advanced toward the fortress with a white-painted shield of truce. After some shouting back and forth, Petronas came up to the battlements.

"What do you want of me?" he called to Krispos, or rather toward Krispos' banner. As at the last parley, his wizard amplified his voice to carry so far.

Trokoundos stood by Krispos to perform the same service for him. "I want you to take a good look around, Petronas. Look carefully—I give you this last chance to yield and save your life. See the engines all around. The rams and stone-throwers will pound down your walls while the dart-shooters pick off your men from farther than they can shoot back."

Petronas shook his fist. "I told you I would never yield to you!"

"Look around," Krispos said again. "You're a soldier, Petronas. Look around and see what chance you have of holding out. I tell you this: once we breach your walls—and we will—we'll show no mercy to you or anyone else." Maybe, he thought, Petronas' men would force him to give up even if he did not want to.

But Petronas led his tiny empire still. He made a slow circuit of the wall, then returned at last to the spot from which he had set out. "I see the engines," he said. By his tone, he might have been discussing the heat of the day.

"What will you do, Petronas?" Krispos asked.

Petronas did not answer, not with words. He scrambled up from the walkway to the wall itself and stood there for most of a minute looking out at the broad expanse of land that, so unaccountably, he did not rule. Then, slowly and deliberately, with the same care he gave to everything he did, he dove off.

Inside and outside the fortress of Antigonos, men cried out in dismay. But when some of Krispos' soldiers rushed toward the crumpled shape at the base of the wall, Petronas' men shot at them. "The truce is still good," Krispos shouted. "We won't hurt him further, by the good god—we'll save him if we can."

"There's a foolish promise," Mammianos observed. "Better to put him out of his misery and have done. I daresay that's what he'd want."

Krispos realized he was right. The pledge, though, was enough to give the rebels an excuse to hold their fire. When his own men did nothing but crowd round Petronas, Krispos thought they were only showing their share of Mammianos' rough wisdom. Then a sweating, panting trooper ran up to him and gasped out, "Majesty, he landed on his head, poor sod."

Of itself, Krispos' hand shaped the sun-circle over his heart. "The war is over," he said. He did not know what to feel. Relief, yes, that so dangerous a foe was gone. But Petronas had also raised him high, in his own household and then in Anthimos'. That had been in Petronas' interest, too, but Krispos could not help remembering it, could not help remembering the years in which he and Petronas had worked together to manage Anthimos. He sketched the sun-sign again. "I would have let him live," he murmured, as much to himself as to the men around him.

"He gave you his answer to that," Mammianos said. Krispos had to nod.

Without their leader, Petronas' men felt the urge to save their lives. The strong gate to the fortress of Antigonos opened. A soldier came out with a shield of truce. The rest of the garrison filed slowly after him. Krispos sent in troopers to make Antigonos his own once more.

The gleam of a shaven pate caught his eye. He smiled, not altogether kindly. To his bodyguards, he said, "Fetch me Gnatios."

Now in sandals and a simple blue monk's robe rather than the patriarchal regalia Krispos would have bet he'd had inside the fortress, Gnatios looked small, frail, and frightened between the two burly Halogai who marched him away from his fellows. He cast himself down on the ground in front of Krispos. "May your Majesty's will be done with me," he said, not lifting his face from the dust.

"Get up, holy sir," Krispos said. As Gnatios rose, he went on, "You would have done better to keep faith with me. You would still wear the blue boots now, not Pyrrhos."

A spark of malicious amusement flared in Gnatios' eyes. "From all I've heard, Majesty, your patriarch has not succeeded in delighting you."

"He's not betrayed me, either," Krispos said coldly.

Gnatios wilted again. "What will you do with me, your Majesty?" His voice was tiny.

"Taking your head here and now would likely cause me more scandal than you're worth. I think I'll bring you back to the city. Recant—say, in the Amphitheater, with enough people watching so you can't go back on your word again—and publicly recognize Pyrrhos as patriarch, and for all of me you can live out the rest of your days in the monastery of the holy Skirios."

Gnatios bowed in submission. Krispos had been sure he

would. Pyrrhos now, Pyrrhos would have gone to the headsman singing hymns before he changed his views by the breadth of a fingernail paring. That made him stronger than Gnatios; Krispos was less ready to say it made him better. It certainly made him harder to work with.

"If ever you're outside the monastery without written leave from me and Pyrrhos both, Gnatios, you'll meet the man with the axe then and there," Krispos warned.

"That walls me up for life," Gnatios said, a last, faint protest.

"Likely it does." Krispos folded his arms. He was ready to summon an executioner at another word from Gnatios. Gnatios saw that. He bit his lip till a bead of blood showed at the corner of his mouth, but he nodded.

"Take him away," Krispos told the Halogai. "While you're about it, put him in irons." Gnatios made an indignant noise. Krispos ignored it, continuing, "He's already escaped once, so I'd sooner not give him another chance." Then he turned to Gnatios. "Holy sir, I pledged I would not harm you. I said nothing of your dignity."

"I can see why," Gnatios said resentfully.

"A chopped dignity grows back better than a chopped neck," Krispos said. "Remember that. Soon enough you'll be back at your chronicle."

"There is that." Krispos was amused to see Gnatios brighten at the thought. Political priest and born intriguer though he was, he was also a true scholar. He went off with the Halogai without another word of complaint.

Krispos scanned the men still emerging from the fortress of Antigonos. When at last they stopped coming, he frowned. He walked toward them. Halogai fell in around him. "Where's Petronas' wizard?" he demanded.

The men looked around among themselves, then back toward the fortress. "Skeparnas?" one said with a shrug. "I thought he was with us, but he doesn't seem to be." Others spoke up in agreement.

"I want him," Krispos said. He wondered if he looked as savagely eager as he felt. Petronas' wizard had cost him a season of lying in bed limp as a dead fish; only Trokoundos' countermagic kept the fellow from taking his life. Sorcery that aimed at causing death was a capital offense.

When Krispos summoned him, Trokoundos studied with narrowed eyes the group of ragged, none too clean men who had come out of the fortress. "He might be hiding in plain sight," he explained to Krispos, "using another man's semblance to keep from being seen."

The mage took out two coins. "The one in my left hand is gilded lead. When I touch it against the true goldpiece in my right hand while reciting the proper spell, by the law of similarity other counterfeits will also be exposed."

He began to chant, then touched the two coins, false and true, together. A couple of men's hair suddenly went from black to gray, which made the Halogai round Krispos guffaw. But other than that, no one's features changed. "He is not here," Trokoundos said. He frowned, his eyes suddenly doubtful. "I do not think he is here—"

He touched the coins of gold and lead against each other once more and held them in his closed fist. Now he used a new chant, harsh and sonorous, insisting, demanding.

"By the good god," Krispos whispered. In the crowd of soldiers and others who had come out of the fortress, one man's features were running like wax over a fire. Before his eyes, the fellow grew taller, leaner. Trokoundos let out a hoarse shout of triumph.

The disguised wizard's face worked horribly as he realized he was discovered. His talonlike fingers stabbed at Trokoundos. The smaller mage groaned and staggered; goldpiece and lead counterfeit fell to the ground. But Trokoundos, too, was a master mage: had he been less, Anthimos would never have chosen him as instructor in the sorcerous arts. He braced himself against empty air and fought back. A moment later Skeparnas bent as if under a heavy weight.

The sorcerers' duel caught up both men—they were so perfectly matched that neither could work great harm unless the other blundered. Neither had any thought for his surroundings; each, of necessity, focused solely on his foe.

Krispos shoved his Halogai toward Skeparnas. "Capture or slay that man!" The imperial guardsmen obeyed without question or hesitation.

They were almost upon the wizard before he knew they were there. He started to send a spell their way, but in tearing his attention from Trokoundos, he left himself vulnerable to the other mage's sorcery. He was screaming as he turned and tried to run. The axes of the Halogai rose and fell. The scream abruptly died.

Trokoundos lurched like a drunken man. "Wine, someone, I beg," he croaked. Krispos undid his own canteen and passed it to the mage. Trokoundos drained it dry. He sank to his knees, then to his haunches. Worried, Krispos sat beside him. He had to lean close to hear Trokoundos whisper, "Now I understand what getting caught in an avalanche must be like."

"Are you all right?" Krispos asked. "What do you need?"

"A new carcass, for starters." With visible effort, Trokoundos drew up the corners of his mouth. "He was strong as a plow mule, was Skeparnas. Had the northerners not distracted him . . . well, your Majesty, let me just say I'm glad they did."

"So am I." Krispos glanced over to Skeparnas' body. The rest of the men from the fortress had pulled back as if the wizard were dead of plague. "I think we can guess his conscience was troubling him."

"He didn't seem anxious to meet you, did he?" Trokoundos' smile, though still strained, seemed more firmly attached to his face now. He got to his feet, waving off Krispos' effort to help. Trokoundos' gaze also went to Skeparnas' sprawled corpse. He wearily shook his head. "Aye, your Majesty, I'm very glad the Halogai distracted him."

Krispos looked over the Cattle-Crossing east to Videssos the city. Behind its seawalls, nearly as massive as the great double rampart that shielded its landward side, the city reared on seven hills. Gilded spheres atop the spires of innumerable temples to Phos shone under the warm summer sun, as if they were so many tiny suns themselves.

As he climbed down into the imperial barge that would carry him across the strait to the capital, Krispos thought, *I'm going home.* The notion still felt strange to him. He'd needed many years in Videssos the city before it, rather than the village from which he sprang, seemed his right and proper place in the world. But his dwelling was there, his wife, his child. Probably his child, at any rate—certainly his heir. Sure as sure, that all made home.

The rowers dug in. The barge glided through the light chop of the Cattle-Crossing toward the city. Krispos was so happy to see it draw near that he ignored his stomach's misgivings over being at sea.

The barge drew to a halt in front of the westernmost gate in the seawall, the gate closest to the palaces. The two valves swung open just as the barge arrived. By now Krispos had come to expect imperial ceremonial to operate so smoothly. The barge captain waved to his sailors. They tied up the barge, set a gangplank in place, then turned and nodded to Krispos. He strode up the plank and into the city.

Along with some of his palace servitors, a delegation of nobles awaited Krispos within the gate. They prostrated themselves before him, shouting, "Thou conquerest, Krispos Avtokrator!" For once, he thought, bemused, the ancient acclamation was literally true. "Thou conquerest!" his greeters cried again as they rose.

Among them he saw Iakovitzes. Clad in bright silks, impeccably groomed, the noble looked himself again, though he was no longer plump. But he perforce stood mute while his companions cried out praise for the Emperor. The unfairness of that tore at Krispos. He beckoned to Iakovitzes, giving him favor in the eyes of his fellows. Iakovitzes' chest puffed out with pride as he came up to Krispos and bowed before him.

"Now the small war, the needful war, is done," Krispos said. "Now we can start the greater fight and give you the vengeance you deserve. By the lord with the great and good mind, I pledge again that you will have it."

He'd thought that would give the nobles and servants another chance to cheer. Instead they stood silently, as if bereft of their tongues as Iakovitzes. Iakovitzes himself unhooked from his belt a tablet ornamented with enamelwork and precious stones; his stylus looked to be made of gold. When the noble opened the tablet, Krispos' nose told him the wax was perfumed. Maimed Iakovitzes might be, but he'd adapted to his injury with panache.

He wrote quickly. "Then you haven't heard, your Majesty? How could you not have?"

"Heard what?" Krispos said when he'd read the words.

Several people guessed what he meant and started to answer, but Iakovitzes waved them to silence. His stylus raced over the wax with tiny slithery sounds. When he was done, he handed the tablet to Krispos. "About ten days ago, Agapetos was heavily defeated north of Imbros. Mavros gathered what force he could and set out to avenge the loss."

Krispos stared at the tablet as if the words on it had betrayed him. "The good god knows, enough couriers brought me dispatches from the city while I was in the westlands. Set against this news, every word they carried was so much gossip and fiddle-faddle. *So why was I not told?*" His gaze fastened on Barsymes.

The vestiarios' face went pale as milk. "But Majesty," he

quavered, "the Sevastos assured me he was keeping you fully informed before he departed for the frontier and promised to continue doing so while on campaign."

"I don't believe you," Krispos said. "Why would he do anything so—" He groped for a word "—so foolhardy?" But that was hardly out of his mouth before he saw an answer. His foster brother had known Krispos did not want him to go out of the city to fight, but not why. If Mavros thought Krispos doubted his courage or ability, he might well have wanted to win a victory just to prove him wrong. And he would have to do it secretly, to keep Krispos from stopping him.

But Krispos knew Mavros was able and brave—would he have named him Sevastos otherwise? What he feared was for his foster brother's safety. Tanilis was not the sort to send idle warnings.

The taste of triumph turned bitter in his mouth. He turned and dashed back through the seawall gate, ignoring the startled cries that rose behind him. The captain and crew of the imperial barge gaped to see him reappear. He ignored their surprise, too. "Row back across the Cattle-Crossing fast as you can," he told the captain. "Order Mammianos to ready the whole army to cross to this side as fast as boats can bring it here. Tell him I intend to move north against Harvas the instant the whole force is here. Do you have all that?"

"I—think so, your Majesty." Stammering a little, the barge captain repeated his orders. Krispos nodded curtly. The captain bawled orders to his men. They cast off the ropes that held the barge next to the wall, then backed oars. As if it were a fighting galley, the imperial barge pivoted almost in its own length, then streaked toward the westlands.

Krispos stood back. Barsymes stood in the gateway. "What of the celebratory procession down Middle Street tomorrow, your Majesty?" he said. "What of the festival of thanksgiving at the High Temple? What of the distribution of largess to the people?"

"Cancel everything," Krispos snapped. After a moment he reconsidered. "No, go on and pay out the largess—that'll keep the city folk happy enough for a while. But with the northern frontier coming to pieces, I don't think we have much to celebrate."

"As you wish, your Majesty," Barsymes said with a sorrowful bow: he lived for ceremonial. "What will you do with your brief time in the city, then?"

"Talk with my generals," Krispos said—the first thing that entered his mind. He went on, "See Dara for a bit." Not only did he miss her, he knew he had to stay on good terms with her, the more so now that her father was with him. As something close to an afterthought, he added, "I'll see Phostis, too."

"Very well, your Majesty." Now Barsymes sounded as if all was very well; with no chance for a child of his own, the eunuch doted on Phostis. "As your generals are still on the far side of the Cattle-Crossing, shall I conduct you to the imperial residence in the meantime?"

"Good enough." Krispos smiled at the vestiarios' unflagging efficiency. Barsymes waved. A dozen parasol-bearers—the imperial number—lined up in front of Krispos. He followed the colorful silk canopies toward the grove of cherry trees that surrounded his private chambers—not, he thought, that anything having to do with the Emperor's person was what would be reckoned private for anyone else.

The Halogai outside the residence sprang to attention when they saw the parasol-bearers. "Majesty!" they shouted.

"Your brothers fought bravely, battling the rebel," Krispos said.

Grins split the northerners' faces. "Hear how he speaks in our style," one said. Krispos grinned, too, glad they'd noticed. He climbed the steps and strode into the imperial residence.

Barsymes bustled past him. "Let me fetch the nurse, your Majesty, with your son." He hurried down the hall, calling for the woman. She came out of a doorway. Phostis was in her arms. She squeaked when she saw Krispos. "Your Majesty! We hadn't looked for you so soon. But come see what a fine lad your son's gotten to be." She held out the baby invitingly. Krispos took him. The bit of practice he'd had holding Phostis before he went on campaign came back to him. He had a good deal more to hold now.

He lifted the baby up close to his face. As he always did, he tried to decide whom Phostis resembled. As if deliberately to keep him in the dark, Phostis still looked like his mother—and like himself. His features seemed far more distinctly his own than they had when he was newborn. He did have his mother's eyes, though—and his grandfather's.

Phostis was looking at Krispos, too, without recognition but with interest. When his eyes met Krispos', he smiled. Delighted, Krispos smiled back.

"See how he takes to you?" the nurse crooned. "Isn't that sweet?"

The baby's face scrunched up in fierce concentration. Krispos felt the arm he had under Phostis' bottom grow warm and damp. He handed him back to the nurse. "I think he's made a mess." A moment later any possible doubt left him.

"They have a habit of doing that," the nurse said. Krispos nodded; with a farm upbringing, he was intimately familiar with messes of every variety. The nurse went on, "I'll clean him up. I expect you want to see your lady, anyhow."

"Yes," Krispos said. "I don't think I'll be in the city very long." That did not surprise the nurse, but then, she'd known about the disaster near Imbros longer than he had.

Barsymes said, "Her Majesty will be at the needle this time of day." He led Krispos past the portrait of Stavrakios. Krispos wondered how the tough old Avtokrator would have judged his first war.

The sewing room had a fine north-facing window. Dara sat by it, bent close to her work. The tapestry on which she labored might not be finished in her lifetime; when one day it was, it would hang in the Grand Courtroom. She knew sober pride that the finest embroiderers in the city judged her skill great enough to merit inclusion in such a project.

She did not notice the door open behind her. Only when Krispos stepped between her and the window and made the light change did she look up; even after that, she needed a moment to return from the peacock whose shining feathers spread wider with each stitch she took.

"It's beautiful work," Krispos said.

She heard the praise in his voice, nodded without false modesty. "It was going well today, I thought." She jabbed needle into linen, set the tapestry aside, and got to her feet. "Which doesn't mean I can't put it down to hail a conqueror." Smiling now, she squeezed him hard enough to make the air whoosh from her lungs, then tilted her face up for a kiss.

"Aye, one victory won," he said after a bit. His hands lingered, not wanting to draw away from her. He saw that pleased her, but saw also by the way her eyebrows lowered slightly and pinched together that she was not altogether content. He thought he knew why. His tone roughened. "But, also, I learn just now, a loss in the north to balance it."

That further sobered her. "Yes," she said. Then, after a pause, she asked, "How do you mean, you just now learn?

Surely Mavros sent word on to you of what had happened to Agapetos.''

"Not a whisper of it," Krispos said angrily, "nor that he aimed to take the field himself. I think he hid it from me on purpose because he knew I'd forbid him on account of his mother's letter."

"I'd forgotten that." Dara's eyes went wide. "What will you do, then?"

"Go after him and—I hope—rescue him from his folly." Krispos scowled, irritated as much with himself as with Mavros. "I wish I'd flat-out told him what Tanilis wrote. But I was afraid he'd sally forth then just to prove he wouldn't let her run his life. And so I didn't spell things out—and he's sallied forth anyhow."

He misliked that; it had the air of the working out of some malign fate. He drew the sun-circle over his heart to turn aside the evil omen.

Dara also signed herself. She said, "Not all foretelling is truth, for which the lord with the great and good mind be praised. Who could bear to live, knowing that someone less than the good god knew what was to come? Maybe Tanilis felt a mother's fear and made too much of it. Now that I have Phostis, I know how that can be."

"Maybe." But Krispos did not believe it. Tanilis had called him "Majesty" when only a madman could have imagined he would ever dwell in the imperial residence, wearing imperial robes. Only a madman—or one who saw true.

"Have you further need for my services, Majesties?" Barsymes asked. Krispos and Dara, their eyes on each other, shook their heads at the same time. "Then if you will excuse me—" The vestiarios bowed his way out.

No sooner had he gone than Dara demanded, "And how many willing, pretty country girls kept your bed warm while you were away in the westlands?"

It might have been a joke; she kept her tone light. But Krispos did not think it was. After being married to Anthimos, Dara could hardly be blamed for doubting his fidelity when he was not under her eye—maybe even when he was. After a little thought he answered, "Do you think I'd be stupid enough to do anything like that when your father was in camp with me for most of the campaign?"

"No, I suppose not," she said judiciously. She set hands on hips and looked up as she had to do to meet his eyes. "You slept alone, then, all the time you were away from the city?"

"I said so."

"Prove it."

Krispos let a long, exasperated breath hiss out. "How am I supposed to—?" In the middle of his sentence, he saw a way. Four quick steps took him to the door. He slammed and barred it. As quickly, he returned to her side and took her in his arms. His lips came down on hers.

Some while later she said, "Get off me, will you? Not only is the floor hard, it's cold, and I expect I have the marks of mosaic tiles on my backside, too."

Krispos sat back on his haunches. Dara drew one leg up past him and rolled away. He said, "Yes, as a matter of fact, you do."

"I thought as much," she said darkly. But in spite of herself, she could not contrive to sound annoyed. "I hadn't looked for your proof to be so—vehement."

"That?" Krispos raised an eyebrow. "After going without for so long, that was just the beginning of my proof."

"Braggart," she said before her eyes left his face. Then her brows also lifted. "What have we here?" Smiling, she reached out a hand to discover what they had there. That, too, rose to the occasion. Before they began again, she said, "Can the second part of your proof wait till we go to the bedchamber? It would be more comfortable there."

"So it would," Krispos said. "Why not?" An advantage of the imperial robes was that they slid off—and now on—quickly and easily. Their principal disadvantage became obvious when the weather got cold. Peasants sensibly labored in tunics and trousers. Krispos shivered when he thought of rounding up sheep in winter with an icy wind whistling up a robe and howling around his private parts.

That was not a worry at the moment. Serving maids grinned as Krispos and Dara headed for the bedchamber hand in hand. Krispos carefully took no notice of the grins. He had begun to resign himself to the prospect of a life led with scant privacy. That had been easy for Anthimos, who'd owned no inhibitions of any sort. It could still sometimes unnerve Krispos. He wondered if the servants kept count.

When he was behind a closed door again, such trivial concerns vanished. He doffed his robe a second time, then helped Dara off with hers. They lay down together. This time they made slower, less driven love, kissing, caressing, joining together, and then separating once more to spin it out and make it last.

As the afterglow faded, Krispos said, "I think I'll bring your father along with me when I take the army north."

Beside him, Dara laughed. "You needn't do it for my sake. I couldn't hope for more or better proof than you've given me. Or could I?" Her hand lazily toyed with him. "Shall we see what comes up?"

"I think you'll have to get your comeuppance another time," he said.

She snorted, gave him an almost painful squeeze, then sat up. Abruptly she was serious. "As I think on it, having my father with you might be a good idea. If he stayed here in the city while you were away, he could forget on whose head the crown properly belongs."

"I can see that," Krispos said. "He's an able man, and able, too, to keep his own counsel. Maybe that comes of his living by the western frontier; from all I've seen, it's rare among folk here in the city. People here show off what they know, to make themselves seem important."

"You've always been able to keep secret what needs keeping," Dara said. Krispos nodded; the very bed in which they lay testified to that. Dara went on, "Why are you surprised others can do the same?"

"I didn't say that." Krispos paused to put what he felt into words. "It was easier for me because people looked down at me for so long. They didn't take me seriously for a long time— I don't think Petronas took me seriously until the siege train came up to Antigonos. But he'd known your father for years, and your father managed to keep his trust till the instant he came over to me."

"He's always held things to himself," Dara said. "He can be . . . surprising."

"I believe you." Krispos did not want Rhisoulphos to surprise him. The more he thought about it, the more keeping his father-in-law under his eye seemed a good idea. He let out a long sigh.

"What's the matter?" Dara asked in some concern. "You're not usually one to be sad afterward."

"I'm not—not about that. I just wish I could have more than moments stolen now and again when I didn't have to fret about every single thing that went on in the palaces and in the city and in the Empire and in all the lands that touch on the Empire— and in all the lands that touch on those lands, too, by the good god," Krispos added, remembering that the first he'd heard of

Harvas Black-Robe was when his raiders ravaged Thatagush, far to the northeast of Videssian territory.

Dara said, "You could do as Anthimos did, and simply not fret about things."

"Look where that got Anthimos—aye, and the Empire, too," Krispos said. "No, I'm made so I have to fret over anything I know of that needs fretting over."

"And over things you don't know but wish you could find out," Dara said.

Krispos' wry chuckle acknowledged the hit. "Think how much grief I could have saved everyone if I'd known Gnatios was going to help Petronas escape from his monastery. As it worked out in the end, I'd even have saved Petronas grief."

Dara shook her head. "No. He lived for power, not for the trappings but for the thing itself. You saw that. You would have let him live on as a monk, but he'd sooner have died—and he did."

Krispos thought about it and decided she was right. "If he'd given me the same choice, I'd have yielded up my hair and forgotten the world."

"Even though that means giving up women, as well?" Dara asked slyly. She slid her thigh over till it brushed against his.

He blinked at her. "Which of us missed the other more?"

"I don't know. That we missed each other at all strikes me as a good sign. We have to live with each other; more pleasant if we're able to enjoy it."

"Something to that," Krispos admitted. He took stock of himself. "If you wait just a bit longer, I might manage another round of proof."

"Might you indeed?" Dara got up on hands and knees, bent her head over him. "Maybe I can help speed that wait along."

"Maybe you can . . . Oh, yes." He reached out to stroke her. Her curls twisted round his fingers like black snakes.

Later, he lay back and watched the bedchamber grow shadowy as afternoon slid toward evening. Hunger eventually overcame his lassitude. He started to reach up to the scarlet bellpull, then stopped and got into his robe first. He was not Anthimos, after all.

Moving just as slowly, Dara also dressed. "What will you do after supper?" she asked once he'd told Barsymes what he wanted.

"Spend the night staring at maps with my generals," Krispos said. To please her, he tried to sound glum. But he looked forward, not to the campaign that lay ahead, but to the planning that went into it. He'd never seen a map before he came to Videssos the city. That there could be pictures of the world fascinated him; establishing on one of those pictures where he would be day by day gave him a truly imperial feeling of power.

"Think what you could be doing instead," Dara said.

"If you think so, you flatter me," he told her. "I'm surprised I can walk." She stuck out her tongue at him. He laughed. Despite the hard news that began it, this had not been a bad day.

# VI

Krispos shaded his eyes with a hand as he looked northward. The horizon ahead was still smooth. He sighed and shook his head. "When I start seeing the mountains, I'll know I'm close to the country where I grew up," he said.

"Close also to where the trouble is," Sarkis observed.

"Aye." Krispos' brief nostalgia deepened to true pain and anger. The summer before, Harvas' raiders had gone through the village where he'd grown up. His sister, her husband, and their two girls had still lived in the village. No one lived there now.

Ungreased wheels squeaked—sometimes screamed—as supply wagons rattled along. Horses, mules, and men afoot kicked up choking clouds of dust. Soldiers sang and joked. *Why not?* Krispos thought. *They're still in their own country.* If they sang as they came home again, he would have done something worth remembering.

Sarkis said, "The riders we sent ahead toward Mavros' army should get back to us in the next couple of days. Then we'll know how things stand."

"They'll get back to us in a couple of days if all's gone well and Mavros has pressed forward," Mammianos said. "If he's taken a reverse, they won't have had so far to travel to meet up with him, so they'll be back sooner."

But none of them—Mammianos, Sarkis, or Krispos—expected the riders to begin coming back that afternoon, the third of their march out from Videssos the city. Yet come back they did, with horses driven to bloody-mouthed exhaustion and with faces grim and drawn. And behind them, first by ones and twos, then in larger groups, came the shattered remains of Mavros' army.

Krispos ordered an early halt for his troops as evening neared. Advancing farther would have been like trying to make headway against a strong-flowing stream. A stream, though, did not infect with fear the men who moved against it. Seeing what had befallen their fellows, Krispos' soldiers warily eyed every lengthening shadow, as if screaming northern warriors might erupt from it at any moment.

While the army's healer-priests did what they could for the wounded, Krispos and his generals questioned haler survivors, trying to sift fragments of order from catastrophe. Not much was to be found. A young lieutenant named Zernes told the tale as well as anyone. "Majesty, they caught us by surprise. They waited in the brush along either side of the road south of Imbros and hit us as we passed them by."

"By the good god!" Mammianos exploded. "Didn't you have scouts out?" He muttered something into his beard about puppies who imagined they were generals.

"The scouts *were* out," Zernes insisted. "They *were*, by the lord with the great and good mind. The Sevastos knew he was not fully trained to command and left all such details to his officers. They might not have been so many Stavrakioi come again, but they knew their craft. The scouts found nothing."

Mammianos wheezed laughter at the lieutenant's youthful indiscretion. Krispos had ears only for the long string of past tenses the man used. "The Sevastos knew? He left these details? Where is Mavros now?"

"Majesty, on that I cannot take oath," Zernes said carefully. "But I do not think he was one of the people lucky enough to break free from the trap. And from what we saw, the Halogai wasted time with few prisoners."

"May he bask in Phos' light forevermore," Mammianos said. He sketched the sun-sign over his breast.

Mechanically Krispos did the same. The young officer's words seemed to reach him from far away. Even with the foreboding he'd had since he learned Mavros was on campaign, he could not believe his foster brother dead. Mavros had been always at his side for years, had fought Anthimos with him, had been first to acknowledge him as Avtokrator. How could he be gone?

Then he found another question, a worse one because it dealt with the living. How was he to tell Tanilis?

While he grappled with that, Mammianos asked Zernes,

"Were you pursued? Or don't you know, having fled so fast no foes afoot could keep up with you?"

The lieutenant bristled as he set a hand to the hilt of his saber. He forced himself to ease. "There was no pursuit, excellent sir," he said icily. "Aye, we were mauled, but we hurt the northerners, too. When they broke off with us, they headed back toward the mountains, not south on our tails."

"Something," Mammianos grunted. "What of Imbros, then?"

"Excellent sir, that I could not say, for we never reached Imbros," Zernes answered. "But since Agapetos was beaten north of the town and we to the south, I fear the worst."

"Thank you, Lieutenant. You may go," Krispos said, trying to make himself function in the face of disaster. First Mavros throwing his life away, now Imbros almost surely lost . . . Imbros, the only city he'd ever known till he left his village and came south to the capital. He'd sometimes sold pigs there, and thought it a very grand place, though the whole town was not much larger than the plaza of Palamas in Videssos the city.

"What do we do now, your Majesty?" Mammianos asked.

"We go on," Krispos said. "What other choice have we?"

As the army advanced, scouts not only examined stands of brush and other places that might hold an ambush—they also shot arrows into them. Some of the lesser mages who served under Trokoundos rode with the scouting parties to sniff out sorcerous concealments. They found none. As Zernes said, Harvas' army had headed back to its northern home after crushing Mavros.

Flocks of ravens and vultures and crows, disturbed from their feasting, rose into the air like black clouds when Krispos' men came to that dolorous field. The birds circled overhead, screeching and cawing resentfully. "Burial parties," Krispos ordered.

"It will cost us the rest of the day," Mammianos said.

"Let it. I don't think we'll catch them on this side of the frontier anyhow," Krispos said. Mammianos nodded and passed the command along. As the soldiers began their grim task, a twist of breeze brought Krispos the battlefield stench, worse than he had ever smelled it before. He coughed and shook his head.

He walked the field despite the stench, to see if he could find Mavros' body. He could not tell it by robes or fine armor; Harvas' men had stayed long enough to loot. After several days of hot sun and carrion birds, no corpse was easy to identify. He saw several that might have been his foster brother, but was sure of none.

The soldiers were quiet in camp that night, so quiet that Krispos wondered if pausing to bury Mavros' dead had been wise. A sudden attack might well have broken them. But the night passed peacefully. When morning came, priests led the men in prayers of greeting to Phos' new-risen sun. Perhaps heartened by that, they seemed in better spirits than they had before.

Before the morning was very old, a pair of scouts came galloping back to the main body of men. They rode straight to Krispos. Saluting, one said, "Majesty, ahead is something you must see."

"What is it?" Krispos asked.

The scout spat in the dust of the roadway, as if to show his rejection of Skotos. "I won't dirty my tongue with the words to tell you, your Majesty. My eyes have been soiled; let my mouth stay clean." His comrade nodded vigorously. Neither would say more.

Krispos traded glances with his officers. After a moment he nodded and urged Progress forward. The Halogai of the imperial guard came with him. So did Trokoundos. The wizard muttered to himself, choosing charms and readying them in advance against need.

"How far is it?" Krispos asked the scouts.

"Round this bend in the road here, your Majesty," answered the horseman who had spoken before. "Just past these oaks."

While the fellow was not watching, Krispos made sure his saber was loose in its scabbard. A troop of guardsmen pushed ahead of him as the party swung past the trees. Even so, from atop his horse he could see well enough.

First he noticed only the bodies, a hundred or so, and that their gear proclaimed them to be Videssian soldiers. Then he saw that each man's hands had been tied behind his back. The dead soldiers' feet were toward him, so he needed a few seconds more than he might have otherwise for his eyes to travel beyond the bodies to the neat pyramid of heads that lay beyond them.

"You see, your Majesty," said the scout who liked to talk.

"I see," Krispos answered. "I see helpless prisoners butchered for the sport of it." He clutched Progress' reins so hard, his knuckles whitened.

"Butchered, aye. That is well said, Majesty." Krispos had never heard a Haloga recoil from war and its consequences.

Now Geirrod did. Without prompting, the guardsman explained why: "Where is the honor, where even is the rightness, in using captives so? This is the work of one more used to slaying cattle than men."

"It's of a piece with what we've seen from Harvas and those who follow him." Krispos hesitated before he went on, but what he had to say needed saying sooner or later. "Most of those who follow Harvas come out of Halogaland. Will you have qualms about fighting them?"

The guardsmen shouted angrily. Geirrod said, "Majesty, we knew this. We talked among ourselves, aye we did, on how such a fight might be, swapping axe strokes with our own kind. But no man who could slaughter so, or stand by to see others slaying, is kin of mine." The other northerners shouted again, this time in loud agreement.

"Shall we start burying this lot, Majesty?" the scout asked.

Krispos slowly shook his head. "No. Let the whole army see them, and with them the sort of foe we fight." He knew he was running a risk. The massacred prisoners had been set in the road to terrify, and his men were none too steady after listening to the survivors from Mavros' force. But he thought—he hoped—this cold-blooded killing would raise in all his soldiers the same fury he and the Halogai felt.

A few minutes later the head of the long column rounded that bend in the road. Krispos gave the guards quick orders. They formed up in the roadway and directed the leading horsemen off the track and onto the grass and shrubs that grew alongside. Some of the troopers began to argue until they saw Krispos with the Halogai, also waving them off.

He watch closely as his men came upon the grisly warning Harvas had left behind. They all stared. Horror filled their faces, as was only natural, but on most outrage soon ousted it. Some soldiers swore, others sketched the sun-sign; not a few did both at once.

Their eyes swung from the bodies—and from that ghastly pyramid beyond them—to Krispos. He raised his voice. "This is the enemy we have loose in our land. Shall we run back to Videssos the city now, with our tails between our legs, and let him do as he likes in the northlands?"

"No." The word came, deep and determined, from many throats at once, like the growl of some enormous wolf. Krispos wished Harvas could have heard it. Soon enough, in effect, he would. Krispos set clenched right fist over his heart to salute his soldiers.

He stayed by the slain Videssians until the last wagon jounced past. The troops from the middle and back of the column had an idea of what lay ahead of them; if armies traveled at the speed of whispers, they could cross the Empire in a day and a night. But knowing and seeing were not the same. Company by company, men stared at the sorry spectacle—first, even knowing, in disbelief, then with ever-growing anger.

"Now we may bury them," Krispos said when everyone had seen. "They've given us their last service by showing what our enemy is like." He saluted the dead men before he rode on to retake his place in the advance.

The mood in camp that night was savage. No speech Krispos made could have inspired his troops like the fate of their fellows. Hoping against hope, he asked his generals, "Is there any chance we'll catch up with Harvas' men on our side of the mountains?"

Mammianos plucked at his beard as he examined the map. "Hard to say. They're footsoldiers, so we move faster than they do. But they have some days' start on us, too."

"Much depends on what's happened at Imbros," Sarkis added. "If the garrison there still holds firm, that might help delay the raiders' retreat."

"I think Imbros still stands," Krispos said. "If it had fallen, wouldn't we be seeing fugitives from the sack, the way we did from Mavros' army?" Even now, a day after he knew the worst, he found himself forgetting his foster brother was dead, only to be brought up short every so often when he was reminded of it: As if he had taken a wound, he thought, and the injured part pained him every time he tried to use it.

Rhisoulphos said, "My best guess is that you're right, your Majesty. There are always refugees from a city that falls: the lucky; the old; sometimes the young, if an enemy has more mercy than Harvas looks to own." His mouth tightened as he went on, "That we've seen no one from Imbros at all tells me its people are still safe behind their wall." He waved to a plan of the town. "It seems well enough fortified."

"It's like your holding, Rhisoulphos," Mammianos said. "On the border, we still need our walls. Some of the towns in the lowlands in the west, though, where they haven't seen war for a couple of hundred years, they've knocked most of 'em down and used the stone for houses."

"Fools," Rhisoulphos said succinctly.

Krispos turned the talk back to the issue at hand. "Suppose we find Harvas' men, or some of them, still besieging Imbros? What's the best way to hurt them then?"

"Pray to Phos the Lord who made the princes first that we catch them so, your Majesty," Sarkis said; the strange epithet he used for the good god made Krispos recall his Vaspurakaner blood. He went on, "If we do, they'll be smashed between our hammer and an anvil of the garrison."

"May it be so," Krispos said. All the generals murmured in agreement.

Pragmatic as usual, Rhisoulphos had the last word. "One way or the other, we'll know for certain in a couple of days."

Half a day south of Imbros, the land began to look familiar to Krispos. That was as far as he'd ever traveled, back in the days before he set out for Videssos the city. He took it as a signal to order the army to full battle alert. That brought less change than it might have under other circumstances, for the men had kept themselves ready to fight since they'd seen the slaughtered prisoners.

Scouts darted ahead to sniff out the enemy. When they returned, their news brought a sober smile to Krispos' face, for they'd spied hundreds, perhaps thousands of people outside Imbros. "What could that be, save Harvas' besieging force?" he exulted. "We have them!"

Trumpets shouted. Krispos' army knew what that meant, knew what it had to mean. The Videssian soldiers, thoroughgoing professionals the lot of them, waved their lances and yowled like so many horse nomads off the steppes of Pardraya. Against a foe like Harvas, even professionals grew eager to fight.

Smooth with long practice, the troops swung themselves from column to line of battle. *Forward!* cried horns and drums. The army surged ahead, wild and irresistible as the sea. Officers shouted, warning men to keep horses fresh for combat.

"We have them!" Krispos said again. He drew his saber and brandished it over his head.

Mammianos stared, a trifle goggle-eyed at the ferocity the soldiers displayed. "Aye, Majesty, if Harvas truly did sit down in front of Imbros, we just may. I'd not reckoned him so foolish."

The general's words set off a warning bell in Krispos' mind. Harvas had shown himself cruel and vicious. Never yet, so far as Krispos could see, had he been foolish. Counting on his stupidity now struck Krispos as dangerous.

He said as much to Mammianos. The fat general looked thoughtful. "I see what you mean, Majesty. Maybe he wants us to come haring along so he can serve us as he did Mavros. If we miss an ambush—"

"Just what I'm thinking," Krispos said. He called to the musicians. Soldiers cursed and shouted when *At a walk* rang out. Krispos yelled for Trokoundos. When the mage rode up, he told him, "I want you out in front of the army. If you can't sense sorcerous screening for an ambush, no one can."

"As may be so, your Majesty," Trokoundos answered soberly. "Harvas has uncommon—and unpleasant—magical skill. Nevertheless, I shall do what I can for you." He clucked to his horse, using reins and his boot heels to urge the animal into a trot. With the rest of the army walking, he was soon up among the scouts. The advance continued, though more slowly than before.

No cunningly hidden sorcerous pit yawned in the roadway. No hordes of Halogai charged roaring from the shelter of brush or trees. The only damage was to the fields the army trampled as it moved ahead in line of battle. Looking off to left and right, Krispos saw ruined villages and suspected few farmers were left to work those fields in any case.

A gray smudge on the northern horizon, light against the green woods and purple mountains behind it: Imbros' wall. Now it was Krispos' turn to yowl. He turned to Mammianos and showed his teeth like a wolf. "We're here, excellent sir, in spite of all our worries."

"By the good god, so we are." Mammianos glanced first to Krispos, then to the musicians. Krispos nodded. "*At the trot*, gentlemen," Mammianos said. The musicians passed along the command. The soldiers cheered.

Imbros drew nearer. Krispos saw in the distance the people outside the walls that his scouts had reported. His wolf's grin grew wider . . . but then slipped from his face. Why did Harvas' men simply hold their position? If he saw them, surely they had seen him. But no one around the walls moved, nor did anyone seem to be *on* those walls.

Up ahead with the scouts, Trokoundos suddenly wheeled his horse and galloped back toward Krispos. He was shouting something. Over the noise any moving army makes, Krispos needed a few seconds to hear what it was. "Dead! They're all dead!"

"Who? Who's dead?" troopers yelled at the wizard. Krispos echoed them. For a heady moment, he imagined disease had struck down Harvas' host where they stood. They deserved nothing better, he thought with somber glee.

But Trokoundos answered, "The folk of Imbros, all piteously slain." He reined in, leaned down onto his horse's neck, and wept without shame or restraint.

Krispos spurred his horse forward. After Trokoundos' warning, after the way the wizard, usually so self-controlled, had broken down, he thought he was braced for the worst. He needed only moments to discover how little he had imagined what the worst might be. The people of Imbros were not merely slain. They had been impaled, thousands of them—men, women, and children—each on his own separate stake. The stakes were uniformly black all the way to the ground with old dried blood.

The soldiers who advanced with Krispos stared in disbelieving horror at the spectacle Harvas had left behind for them. They were no strangers to dealing out death; some of them, perhaps, were no strangers to massacre, on the sordid but human scale of the butchered prisoners farther south. But at Imbros the size of the massacre was enough to daunt even a monster of a man.

Sarkis swatted at the flies that rose in buzzing clouds from the swollen, stinking corpses. "Well, your Majesty, now we know why no fugitives came south from Imbros to warn us of its fall," he said. "No one was able to flee."

"This can't be everyone who lived in Imbros," Krispos protested. He knew his heart was speaking, not his mind; he could see how many people squatted on their stakes in a ghastly parody of alertness.

In a way, though, he was proven right. As the army made its way through the neat concentric rows of bodies to Imbros' wall, the men soon discovered how Harvas' warriors had entered the city: the northern quadrant of those walls was cast down in ruins, down to the very ground.

"Like Develtos," Trokoundos said. His eyes were red; tears still tracked his cheeks. He held his voice steady by force of will, like a man controlling a restive horse. "Like Develtos, save that they must have been hurried there. Here they had the time to do their proper job."

When Krispos entered Imbros, he found what had befallen the rest of the folk who had dwelt there. They lay dead in the streets; the town had been burned over their heads after they fell.

"Mostly men in here, I'd say," Mammianos observed. "And look—here's a mail shirt that missed getting stolen. These must have been the ones who tried to fight back. Once they were gone, looks like Harvas had his filthy fun with everyone else."

"Aye," Krispos said. Calmly discussing the hows and whys of wholesale slaughter as he went through its aftermath struck him as grotesque. But if he was to understand—as well as an ordinary man could ever grasp such destruction—what else were he and his followers to do?

He walked the dead streets of the murdered city, Trokoundos at his side and a troop of Halogai all around him to protect against anything that might lurk there yet. The northerners peered every which way, their pale eyes wide. They muttered to themselves in their own tongue.

At last Narvikka asked, "Majesty, why all this—this making into nothing? To sack a town, to despoil a town, is all very well, but for what purpose did our cousins slay this town and then cast the corpse onto the fire?"

"I'd hoped you could tell me," Krispos said. The guardsman, as was the Haloga way, had stripped the problem to its core. War for loot, war for belief, war for territory made sense to Krispos. But what reason could lie behind war for the sake of utter devastation?

Narvikka made a sign with his fingers—had he been a Vides-sian, Krispos guessed he would have drawn the sun-circle over his heart. That guard said, "Majesty, I cannot fathom the minds of the men who fought here. That they are of my folk raises only shame in me. Renegades and outlawed men would not act so, much less warriors from honest holdings." Other northerners nodded.

"But they did act so," Krispos said. Every time he breathed, he took in the miasma of dead flesh and old smoke. He let his feet lead him through Imbros; even after so many years away, they seemed to remember how the bigger streets ran. Before long, he found himself in the central market square, looking across it toward the temple.

Once he'd thought that temple the grandest building he'd ever seen. Now he knew it was but a provincial imitation of Phos' High Temple in Videssos the city, and not a particularly im-pressive one, either. But even fire-ravaged as it was now, it still raised memories in him, memories of awe and faith and belief.

Those memories clashed terribly with the row of impaled bodies in front of the temple, the first he'd seen inside Imbros who had received that treatment rather than the quicker, cleaner death of axe or sword or fire. What with the stains of blood and smoke, he needed a moment to realize those victims all wore the blue robe. He sketched the sun-sign.

So did Trokoundos beside him. "Did I not hear they were savage to priests in Develtos, as well?" the wizard asked quietly.

"Aye, so they were." Krispos' boots clicked on flagstones as he walked across the square toward the temple. He stepped around a couple of corpses of the ordinary, crumpled sort. By now, numb with the scale of the butchery here, he found them hardly more than obstacles in his path.

But what the priests had suffered penetrated even that numbness. Though some days dead, their bodies still gave mute testimony to those special torments. As if impalement were insufficient anguish, some had had their manhood cut away, other their guts stretched along the ground for the carrion birds, still others their beards—and their faces—burned away.

Krispos turned his back on them, then made himself look their way once more. "May Phos take their souls into the light."

"So may it be," Trokoundos said. "But Skotos seems to have had his way with their bodies." Together, he and Krispos spat.

Krispos said, "All this ground will have to be blessed before we can rebuild. Who would want to live here otherwise, after this?" He nodded to himself. "I'll suspend taxes for the new folk I move in, and keep them off for a while, to try another way to make people want to stay once they've come."

"Spoken like an Emperor," Trokoundos said.

"Spoken like a man who wants Imbros to be a living city again soon," Krispos said impatiently. "It's a bulwark against whoever raids down from Kubrat, and in peacetime it's the main market town for the land near the mountains."

"And now, Majesty?" Trokoudnos said. "Will you pause to bury the dead here?"

"No," Krispos said, impatient still. "I want to come to grips with Harvas as soon as I can." He glanced toward the sun, which stood low in the west—days were shorter now than they had been while he laid siege to Petronas. Again he cursed the time he'd had to spend in civil war. "There's not a lot of summer left to waste."

"No denying that, your Majesty," Trokoundos said. "But—" He let the word hang.

Krispos had no trouble finishing for him. "But Harvas knows that, too. Aye, I'm all too sure he does. I'm all too sure he has some deviltry brewing, too, just waiting for us. I trust my soldiers to match his. As for magic—how strong can Harvas be?"

Trokoundos' lips twisted in a grin that seemed gayer than it was. "I expect, your Majesty, that before too long I shall find out."

More eager for fighting than any army Krispos had known, his force stormed north up the highway after Harvas' raiders. "Imbros!" was their cry; the name of the murdered city was never far from their lips.

The Paristrian Mountains towered against the northern horizon now, the highest peaks still snow-covered even in later summer. Some of the men from the western lowlands exclaimed at them. To Krispos they were—not old friends, for he remembered the kind of weather that blew over them through half the year, but a presence to which he was accustomed all the same.

Everything hereabouts seemed familiar, from the quality of the light, paler and grayer than it was in Videssos the city, to the fields of ripening wheat and barley and oats—worked now only by the few farmers lucky enough to have escaped Harvas' men—to the way little tracks ran off the highway, now to the east, now to the west.

Krispos pulled Progress out of the line of march when he came to one of those roads. He stared west along it for a long time, his mind ranging farther than his eyes could reach.

"What is it, Majesty?" Geirrod asked at last. He had to speak twice before Krispos heard him.

"My village lies down this road," Krispos answered. "Or rather it did; Harvas' bandits went through here last year." He shook his head. "When I left, I hoped I'd come back with money in my belt pouch. I never dreamed it would be as Avtokrator—or that the people I grew up with wouldn't be here to greet me."

"The world is as it is, Majesty, not always as we dream it will be."

"Too true. Well, enough time wasted here." Krispos tapped Progress' flanks with his heels. The big bay gelding walked, then went into a trot that soon brought Krispos back to his proper place in the column.

The road ran straight up toward the gap in the mountains, past empty fields, past stands of oak and maple and pine, past a small chuckling stream, and, as the ground grew higher, past more and more outcroppings of cold gray stone. Though Krispos had not seen it since he was perhaps nine years old, the gray land-scape seemed eerily familiar. He and his parents and sisters had come down this road after Iakovitzes ransomed them and hun-dreds of other Videssian peasants from captivity in Kubrat. He must have been keyed up almost to fever pitch then, for fear the Kubratoi would change their minds and swoop down again, for everything on that journey remained as vivid in his mind as if he'd lived it yesterday. The way water splashed from that clump of rocks in the stream had not changed at all in the two decades since, save that frogs had perched on them then.

The mountains themselves . . . *I've always been happier to see them getting smaller*, Krispos thought. They were not get-ting smaller now, worse luck. Krispos peered up and ahead. Now he could see the opening of the pass that led to Kubrat. *Agapetos got through with less force than I have*, he thought. *I will, too.*

When he said that aloud, Mammianos grunted. "Aye, Aga-patos got through, but he couldn't maintain himself north of the mountains. And Harvas beat him again on this side, then came down first on Imbros and then onto Mavros' army. Strikes me he's been able to defeat us in detail, if you know what I mean."

"Are you telling me I shouldn't attack?" Krispos asked, scowling. "After all he's done to us, how can I halt now?"

The image of thousands of bodies, each gruesomely buggered by its own stake, shoved itself forward in his mind. With it came a new vision, that of hundreds of men matter-of-factly cutting and sharpening those stakes. How could they have kept to their work, knowing what the stakes would be used for? Even Kubra-toi would have gagged on such cruelty, he thought. And Halo-gai, judging by long experience with the imperial guards, were harsh but rarely vicious. What made Harvas' men so different?

Mammianos' reply brought him back to the here-and-now. "All I'm saying, your Majesty, is that Harvas strikes me as dangerous enough to need hitting with everything the Empire has. The more I see, the more I think that. What we have with us is strong, aye, but is it strong enough?"

"By the good god, Mammianos, I aim to find out," Krispos said. Mammianos bowed his head in submission. He could sug-gest, but when the Avtokrator decided, his lot was to obey. *Or to mutiny*, Krispos thought. But Mammianos had seen plenty of better chances than this for mutiny. His disagreement with Kris-pos lay in how best to hurt Harvas, not whether to.

The army camped just out of bowshot of the foothills that night. Peering north in the darkness, Krispos saw the slopes of the mountains ahead dimly illuminated by orange, flickering light. He summoned Mammianos and pointed. "Does that mean what I think?"

"Bide a moment, Majesty, while the campfire glare leaves my eyes." Like Krispos, Mammianos stood with his back to the imperial camp. At last he said, "Aye, it does. They're encamped there, waiting for us."

"Forcing the pass won't be easy," Krispos said.

"No, it won't," the general agreed. "All kinds of things can go wrong when you try to barge through a defended pass. A holding force at the narrowest part will plug it up while they roll rocks down from either side, or maybe come charging down from ambush—that'd be easy for Harvas' buggers, because they're footsoldiers."

"Perhaps I should have listened to you before," Krispos said.

"Aye, Majesty, perhaps you should," Mammianos said—as close to criticism of the Emperor as he would let himself come.

Krispos plucked at his beard. He could not pull back, not having come so far, not having seen Imbros, not unless he wanted to forfeit the army's faith in him forevermore. Going blindly forward, though, was a recipe for disaster. If he had some idea of what lay ahead . . . He whistled to one of his guardsmen. "Fetch me Trokoundos," he said.

The wizard was yawning when he arrived, but cast off sleepiness like an old tunic when Krispos explained what he wanted. He nodded thoughtfully. "I know a scrying spell that should serve, your Majesty, one subtle enough that no barbarian mage, no mage not formally trained, should even be able to detect it, let alone counteract it. Against Petronas it would not have sufficed, for Skeparnas was my match, near enough. But against Harvas it should do very well; however strong in magic he may be, he is bound to be unschooled. If you will excuse me—"

When Trokoundos returned, he held in his hand a bronze bracelet. "Haloga workmanship," he explained as he showed it to Krispos. "I found it outside of Imbros; I think we may take it as proven that one of Harvas' raiders lost it. By the law of contagion, it is still bonded to its one-time owner, a bond we may now use to our advantage."

"Spare the lecture, sir mage," Mammianos said. "So long as you learn what we need to know, I care not how you do it."

"Very well," Trokoundos said stiffly. He held the bracelet

out at arm's length toward the north, then started a slow, soft chant. The chant went on and on. Krispos was beginning to get both worried and annoyed when Trokoundos finally lowered the bracelet. As he turned, the campfire shadowed the lines of puzzlement on his face. "Let me try again, with a variant of the spell. Perhaps the owner of the bracelet was slain; nonetheless, it remains affiliated, albeit more loosely, with the army as a whole."

He began to chant once more. Krispos could not tell any difference between this version of the spell and the other, but was willing to believe it was there. But he found no difference in the result: after some time, Trokoundos halted in baffled frustration.

"Majesty," he said, "so far as I can tell by my sorcery, there's no one at all up ahead."

"What? That's absurd," Krispos said. "We can see the fires—"

"They could be a bluff, your Majesty," Mammianos put in.

"You don't believe that," Krispos said.

"No, your Majesty, I don't, but it could be so. I tell you what, though: I'll send out a couple of scouts. They'll come back with what we need to know."

"Good. Do it," Krispos said.

"Aye, do it," Trokoundos agreed. "By the good god, excellent sir, I hope it is a bluff ahead, as you say. The alternative is believing that Harvas has a renegade Videssian mage in his service, and after Imbros I would sooner not believe that." The wizard made a sour face, decisively shook his head. "No, it can't be. I'd have sensed that my spell was being masked. I didn't have that feeling, only the emptiness I'd get if there truly were no men ahead."

The scouts slipped out of camp. They looked to be ideal soldiers for their task; had Krispos met them on the streets of Videssos the city, he would have unhesitatingly guessed they were thieves. Small, lithe, and wary, they carried only daggers and vanished into the night without a sound.

Yawning, Krispos said, "Wake me as soon as they get back." Worn though he was, he did not sleep well. Thoughts of Imbros would not leave his mind or, worse, his dreams. He was relieved when a guardsman came in to rouse him and tell him the scouts had returned.

A thin crescent moon had risen in the east; dawn was not far away. The scouts—there were three of them—prostrated themselves before him. "Get up, get up," he said impatiently. "What did you see?"

"A whole great lot of Halogai, your Majesty," one of them answered in a flat, up-country accent like the one Krispos had had before he came to Videssos the city. The other two scouts nodded to confirm his words. He went on, "And you know how the pass jogs westward so you can't see all the way up it from here? Just past the jog, they've gone and built themselves a breastwork. Be nasty getting past there, your Majesty."

"Their army's real, then," Krispos said, more than a little surprised. Trokoundos would not be pleased to learn his sorcery had gone astray.

"Majesty, we sneaked close enough to smell the shit in their slit trenches," the scout answered. "You don't get a whole lot realer than that."

Krispos laughed. "True enough. Two goldpieces to each of you for your courage. Now go get what rest you can."

The scouts saluted and hurried off toward their tents. Krispos thought about going back to bed, too, decided not to bother. Better to watch the sun come up than to toss and turn and think about stakes . . .

The eastern rim of the sky grew gray, then the pale bluish-white that seems to stretch the eye to some infinite distance, then pink. When the sun crawled above the horizon, Krispos bowed to it as if to Phos himself, recited the creed, and spat between his feet to show he rejected Skotos. Most of the time, he hardly thought about that part of the ritual. Not now. Imbros reminded him of what he was rejecting.

The camp stirred with the sun, at first slowly, blindly, like a plant's silent striving toward light, but then with greater purpose as horns rang out to rout sleepers from tents and prod them into the routine of another day. They lined up with bowls in front of cookpots where barley porridge bubbled; gnawed at hard bread, cheese, and onions; gulped wine under the watchful eyes of underofficers who made sure they did not gulp too much; and tended to their horses so the animals would also be ready for the day's work ahead.

Krispos went back to his tent and armed himself. He swung himself up onto Progress and rode over to the musicians. At his command, they played *Assemble*. The troopers gathered before them. Krispos raised a hand for silence and waited until he had it.

"Soldiers of Videssos," he said, hoping everyone could hear him, "the enemy waits for us ahead. You've seen the kind of foe he is, how he loves to slay those who can't fight back." A low growl ran through the army. Krispos went on, "Now we can pay Harvas back for everything, for the slaughters in Develtos last year and Imbros now, and for Agapetos' men, and Mavros', too. Will we turn aside?"

"No!" the men roared. "Never!"

"Then forward, and fight bravely!" Krispos drew his saber and held it high overhead. The soldiers whooped and cheered. They were eager to fight; Krispos needed no fancy turns of phrase to inspire them today. That was as well—he knew Anthimos, for instance, had been a far better speaker than he would ever be. He owned neither the gift nor the inclination for wrapping around his ideas of the flights of fancy that Videssian rhetoric demanded. His only gift, such as it was, was for plain thoughts plainly spoken.

As the army left camp, Krispos told Sarkis, "We'll want plenty of scouts out in front of us, and farther ahead than usual."

"It's taken care of, your Majesty," the Vaspurakaner officer said with a small, tight smile. "The country ahead reminds me all too much of the land where I grew up. You soon learn to check out a pass before you send everyone through, or you die young." He chuckled. "I suppose, over the generations, it improves the breed."

"Dismount some of those scouts, too," Krispos said as a new worry struck him. "We'll want to spy out the sides of the pass, not just the bottom, and they can't very well do that very well from horseback." He stopped, flustered. So much for plain thoughts plainly spoken. "You know what I mean."

"Aye, your Majesty. It's taken care of," Sarkis repeated. He sketched a salute. "For one who came so late to soldiering, you've learned a good deal. Have I told you of the saying of my people, 'Sneaky as a prince—?' "

Krispos cut him off. "Yes, you have." He knew he was rude, but he was also nervous. The scouts had just followed the western jog of the pass and disappeared from sight. He clucked to Progress, leaned forward in the saddle, and urged the gelding up to a fast trot with the pressure of knees and heels.

Then he rounded that jog himself. The breastwork, of turf and stones and brush and whatever else had been handy, stood a few hundred yards ahead, blocking the narrowest part of the pass.

Behind it, Krispos saw at last the warriors who had ravaged the Empire so savagely.

The big, fierce, fair-haired men saw him, too, or the imperial banner that floated near him. They jeered and brandished— weapons? No, Krispos saw; Harvas' men were holding up stout stakes carved to a point at both ends—impaling stakes.

Fury filled him, rage more perfect and absolute than any he had ever known. He wanted to slay with his own sword every marauder in front of him. Only a wild charge by all his men seemed a bearable second best. He filled his lungs to cry out the order.

But something cold and calculating dwelt within him, too, something that would not let him give way to impulse, no matter how tempting. He thought again and shouted, "Arrows!"

Bowstrings thrummed as the Videssian archers went to work from horseback. Instead of their stakes, the Halogai lifted yard-wide shields of wood to turn aside the shafts. They were not bowmen; they could not reply.

Here and there, all along the enemy line, men crumpled or lurched backward, clutching at their wounds and shrieking. But the raiders wore mail shirts and helms; even shafts that slipped between shields and over the rampart were no sure kills. And however steeped in wickedness they might have been, Harvas' followers were not cowards. The archery stung them. It could do no more.

By the time he saw that, Krispos had full control of himself once more. "Can we flank them out?" he demanded of Mammianos.

"It's steep, broken ground to either side of that breastwork," the general answered. "Better going for foot than for horse. Still, worth a try, I suppose, and the cheapest way to go about it. If we can get in their rear, they're done for."

Despite his doubts, the general yelled orders. Couriers dashed off to relay them to the soldiers on both wings. Several companies peeled off to try the rough terrain on the flanks. Harvas' Halogai rushed men up the slopes of the pass to head them off.

The northerners had known what they were about when they built their barricade; they had walled off all the ground worth fighting on. The horses of their Videssian foes had to pick their way forward step by step. Afoot, Harvas' men were rather more agile, but they, too, scrambled, stumbled, and often fell.

Some did not get up again; now that the foe was away from cover and concerned more with his footing than his shield, he grew more vulnerable to archery. But the Videssians could not simply shoot their way to victory. They had to force the north-erners from their ground. And at close quarters, the footsoldiers gave as good as they got, or better.

Saber and light lance against axe and slashing sword—Krispos watched his men battle the Halogai who followed Har-vas. Sudden pain made him wonder if he was wounded until he realized he had his lip tight between his teeth. With a distinct effort of will, he made himself relax. A moment later the pain returned. This time he ignored it.

For all the encouragement he shouted, for all the courage the Videssian cavalry displayed, the terrain proved too rugged for them to advance against determined foes. Krispos wished Har-vas' northerners were less brave than his own guardsmen. They did not seem so. He watched a Haloga with a lance driven deep into his side hack from the saddle the man who had skewered him before he, too, toppled.

"No help for it," Mammianos bawled in his ear. "If we want 'em, we'll have to go through 'em, not around."

"We want 'em," Krispos said. Mammianos nodded and turned to the musicians. They raised horns and pipes to their lips, poised sticks over drums. The wild notes of the charge echoed brassily from the boulders that studded both slopes of the pass. The Videssians in the front rank raised a cheer and spurred toward the breastwork that barred their way north.

The front was too narrow for more than a fraction of the imperial army to engage the enemy at once. Rhisoulphos, who led the regiments just behind the van, shouted for his troops to hold up. A gap opened between them and the men ahead.

When Krispos looked back and saw that gap, his own suspi-cions about his father-in-law and Dara's warning came together in a hard certainty of treason. He slapped a courier on the shoul-der. "Fetch me Rhisoulphos, at once. If he won't come, either drag him here or kill him." The rider stared, then set spurs to his horse. With an angry squeal, the beast bounded away.

Krispos' fist gripped the hilt of his saber as tightly as if that were Rhisoulphos' neck. Leave the head of the army to face Harvas' howling killers by itself, would he? Krispos was so sure Rhisoulphos would not willingly accompany his courier that, when his father-in-law did ride up to him, the best he could do was splutter, "By the good god, what are you playing at?"

"Giving our troops room to retreat in, of course, your Maj-esty," Rhisoulphos answered. If he was a traitor, he did it marvelously well. *So what? I already know he's good at that*, Krispos thought. But Rhisoulphos went on, "It's a standard ploy when fighting Halogai, your Majesty. Feigning a withdrawal will often lure them out of their position so we can wheel about and take them while they're in disorder."

Krispos glanced over at Mammianos. The fat general nodded. "Oh," Krispos said. "Good enough." His ears were hot, but his helmet covered them so no one could see the flame.

The Videssians at the barriers slashed and thrust at Harvas' men, who chopped at them and their horses both. The shrieks and oaths dinned through the pass. Then above them rose a long, mournful call. The horsemen wheeled their mounts and broke off combat.

The northerners screamed abuse in their own language, in the speech of the Kubratoi, and in broken Videssian. A couple of men started to scramble over the breastwork to pursue the retreating imperials. Their own comrades dragged them back by main force.

"Oh, a plague on them!" Mammianos said when he saw that. "Why can't they make it easy for us?"

"That's better discipline than they usually show," Rhisoulphos said. "The military manuals claim that tactic hardly ever fails against the northerners."

"I don't think Harvas shows up in the military manuals," Krispos said.

One corner of Rhisoulphos' mouth twitched upward. "I suspect you're right, your Majesty." He pointed. "But there he stands, whether he's in the manuals or not."

Krispos' eyes followed Rhisoulphos' finger. Of course that tall figure behind the enemy line had to be Harvas Black-Robe; none of his followers was garbed in similar style. Despite the chieftain's sobriquet, Krispos had looked for someone gaudily clad—a ruler needed to stand out from his subjects. So Harvas did, but by virtue of plainness rather than splendor. Had his hooded robe been blue rather than black, he could have passed for a Videssian priest.

Regardless of how he dressed, no doubt he led. Halogai heavily ran here and there at his bidding, doing their best to ignore the weight of mail on their shoulders. And when Harvas raised his arms—those wide black sleeves flapped like vultures' wings—the northerners held their places. For Halogai, that was the more remarkable.

Mammianos glowered at the northerners as if their good order personally affronted him. With a wheezy sigh, he said, "If they won't come out after us, we'll have to get in there nose to nose with them and drive them away." The words plainly tasted bad in his mouth; getting in there nose to nose was not a style of fighting upon which the subtle imperials looked kindly.

But when subtlety failed, brute force remained. As captains dressed their lines and troopers reached over their shoulders to see how many arrows their quivers held, the fierce notes of the charge rang out once more. The Videssians thundered toward the breastwork ahead. "Krispos!" they shouted, and "Imbros!"

Harvas raised his arms. This time he pointed not toward his soldiers or their rampart, but up the slope of the pass. Not far from Krispos, Trokoundos reeled in the saddle. "Call the men back, Majesty!" he cried, clinging to his seat more by determination than anything else. "Call them back!"

Krispos and his generals stared at the mage. "By the good god, why should I?" Krispos demanded angrily.

"Battle magic," Trokoundos croaked. The roar of boulders bounding downslope drowned him out.

Because he was looking at Trokoundos, Krispos did not see the first great stones leap free of the ground on which they had placidly rested for years, perhaps for centuries. That night one of the soldiers who had seen them said, "You ever watch a rabbit that's all of a sudden spooked by a hound? That's what those rocks were doing, except they didn't jump every which way. They came down on us."

The noise the boulders made as they crashed into the Videssian cavalrymen was the noise that might have come from a smithy in the instant a giant stepped on it. Horses went down as if scythed, pitching riders off their backs. The beasts behind them could not stop fast enough and crashed into them and into the stones. That only made the chaos worse.

The men and horses of the very foremost ranks were almost upon the breastwork when the avalanche began. Soldiers turned their heads to gape at what had happened to their comrades. Some drew rein in consternation; other pressed on toward the barricade. Now the Halogai, howling with ferocious glee, swarmed over it to meet them. The imperials at the head of the charge fought back desperately. No one could come to their aid through the writhing tangle behind them.

Krispos watched and cursed and slammed a fist against his thigh as Harvas' northerners overwhelmed his men one by one.

Harvas raised his arms and pointed again. More boulders sprang from their proper places and crashed down on the Videssian army's van.

"Make them stop!" Krispos screamed to Trokoundos.

"I wish I could." The wizard's face was haggard, his eyes wild. "He shouldn't be able to do this. The stress, the excitement of combat weaken magic's grip, even if the sorceries are readied in advance. I've tried counterspells—they go awry, as they should."

"What can we do, then?"

"Majesty, I have not the power to stand against Harvas, not even with my colleagues here." Trokoundos sounded as if admitting that cost him physical pain. "Perhaps with more mages, masters from the Sorcerers' Collegium, he may yet be defeated."

"But not now," Krispos said.

"No, Majesty, not now. He screened his encamped army so I could not detect it, he works battle magic so strong and unexpected that it almost broke me when he unleashed it . . . Majesty, a good many years have passed since I owned myself daunted by any sorcerer, but today Harvas daunts me."

Ahead at the barricade, almost all the Videssians were down. They and the crushed soldiers behind them blocked the army's way forward. Krispos' glance slid to the slopes of the pass. Who could guess how many more boulders needed only Harvas' sorcerous command to smash into the imperials, or what other magics Harvas had waiting?

"We retreat," Krispos said, tasting gall.

"Good for you, your Majesty," Mammianos said. Startled, Krispos turned in the saddle to stare at him. "Good for you," the fat general repeated. "Knowing when to cut your losses is a big part of this business. I feared you'd order us to press on regardless, and turn a defeat into a disaster."

"It's already a disaster," Krispos said.

Even as the call to retreat rang mournfully through the pass, Mammianos shook his head. "No, Majesty. We're still in decent order, there's no panic, and the men will be ready to fight another day—well, maybe another season. But if that he-witch ahead does much more to us, they'll turn tail every time they see his ruffians, whether he's with 'em or not."

Cold comfort, but better—a bit better—than none. Krispos' own Halogai closed around him as rearguard while the army withdrew from the pass. If the northerners wanted to slay him and go over to their countrymen, they would never have a better chance. The imperial guardsmen looked back only to shake fists at Videssos' foes.

And yet, in a way, the guards were the least of Krispos' worries. His eyes, like those of so many others with him, kept sliding up the sides of the pass while he wondered whether more great stones would smash men and horses to jelly. If Harvas had time to ready stones through the whole length of the pass, disaster great enough to satisfy even Mammianos' criteria might yet befall the army.

Somehow, retreat did not become rout. The boulders on the slopes held their places. At last those slopes grew lower and farther apart as the pass opened out into the country below the mountains. "Back to our old campsite?" Mammianos asked.

"Why not?" Krispos said bitterly. "That way we can pretend today never happened—those of us who are still alive, at any rate."

Mammianos tried to console him. "We can't do these little tricks without losses."

"Seems we can't even do them *with* losses," Krispos said, to which the general only grunted by way of reply.

Any camp is joyless after a defeat. Wounded men scream round winners' tents, too, but they and their comrades who come through whole know they have accomplished what they set out to do. Losers enjoy no such consolation. Not only have they suffered, they have suffered and failed.

Failure, Krispos remembered, made Petronas' army break up. He ordered stronger sentry detachments posted south of the camp than to the north. The officers to whom he gave the command did not remark on it, but nodded knowingly as they saw to carrying it out.

Krispos walked to the outskirts of the camp, where badly wounded men lay waiting for healer-priests to attend to them. The soldiers not too far gone in their own anguish saluted him and tried to smile, which made him feel worse than he had before. But he made sure he saw all of them and spoke to as many as he could before he went back to his own tent.

Darkness had fallen by then. Krispos wanted nothing more than to sleep, to forget about the day's misfortunes, if only for a few hours. But a duty harder even than visiting the wounded lay ahead of him. He'd kept putting off writing to Tanilis of Mavros' death; he'd hoped to be able to say he had avenged it. Now that hope had vanished—and how much, in any case, would it have mattered to her? Her only son was gone. Krispos inked his pen and sat staring at the blank parchment in front of him. How to begin?

"Krispos Avtokrator of the Videssians to the excellent and noble lady Tanilis: Greetings." Thus far formula took him, but no farther. He needed the smooth phrases that came naturally to anyone who had the rhetorical training that went with a proper education. He did not have them, and would not entrust this letter to a secretary.

"Majesty?" Geirrod's deep voice came from outside the tent.

"What is it?" Krispos put down the pen with a strange mixture of relief and guilt.

The guardsman's reply warned him he had known relief too soon. "A matter of honor, Majesty."

The last Haloga to speak of honor in that tone of voice had been Vagn, talking about killing himself. Krispos ducked out through the tent flap in a hurry. "What's touched your honor, Geirrod?" he asked.

"Not my honor alone, your Majesty, but the honor of all my folk who take your gold," Geirrod said. Krispos was tall for a Videssian. He still had to look up at Geirrod as the stern northerner went on, "I am chosen to stand for all of us, since I was first to bow before you as lord."

"So you were," Krispos agreed, "and I honor you for that. Do you doubt it?" Geirrod shook his massive head. Exasperated, Krispos snapped, "Then how have I failed you—aye, and all the other Halogai, too?"

"By not sending us forth in combat this day against those who follow Harvas, and holding us back despite what we told you on the road south of Imbros," Geirrod said. "It struck many among us as a slur, as a token you lack trust in us. Better we fare home to Halogaland than carry our axes where we may not blood them. Videssians delight in having troops for show. We took oath to fight for you, Majesty, not to look grand in your processions."

"If you truly think I held you back for fear you would betray me, blood your axe now, Geirrod." Not without second thoughts—the Halogai could be grimly literal—Krispos bent his head and waited. When no blow came, he straightened up and looked at Geirrod again. "Since you do not think so, how can you have lost any honor on account of me?"

The guardsman stiffened to attention. "Majesty, you speak sooth. I see this cannot be so. I shall say as much to my countrymen. Any who doubt me may measure their doubt against this.'' He hefted his axe.

"Good enough," Krispos said. "Tell them also that I didn't send them forward because I hoped I could clear the Halogai—Harvas' Halogai, I mean—away from the barricade with archery. If it had worked, we would have won the fight without costing ourselves too dear.''

Geirrod let out a loud snort. "You may think partway as we Halogai do, Majesty, but I see that at bottom you're a Videssian after all. As it should be, I guess; can't be helped, come what may. But a fight has worth for its own sweet sake. The time for reckoning up the cost is afterward, not before.''

"As you say, Geirrod.'' To Krispos, the northerner's words were insanely reckless. He knew the Halogai knew most Videssians thought as he did, and also knew the Halogai reckoned imperials overcautious at best in war, at worst simply dull. The Halogai fought for the red joy of it, not to gain advantage. That, he supposed, was why no Videssians served a northern chieftain as bodyguards, nor likely ever would.

As he went back into the tent, Geirrod resumed his post outside, evidently satisfied with their exchange. Krispos allowed himself the luxury of a long, quiet sigh. He hadn't lied to Geirrod, not quite, but he had entertained doubts about the Halogai. But by asking Geirrod if *he* believed his countrymen were held back from fear of treachery, Krispos had taken the onus off himself. The next time he faced Harvas' men, though, he did not think he would have to hold back his guardsmen.

He sat down at the little folding table that served him for a desk in the field. Parchment and pen were where he'd left them when Geirrod called. But for the salutation, the parchment remained blank. Krispos sighed again. He wished Trokoundos knew a spell to make unpleasant letters write themselves, but that probably went beyond sorcery into out-and-out miracle-working.

After one more sigh, Krispos inked the pen again. As was his habit, he plunged straight ahead with what he had to say. "My lady, while I was fighting Petronas in the westlands, Mavros heard Agapetos had been beaten and took an army north from Videssos the city to stop Harvas Black-Robe from moving farther forward. I grieve to have to tell you that, as you foresaw, your son was also beaten and was killed.''

Setting down the words brought back to him afresh the loss of his foster brother. He studied what he'd written. Was it too bald? He decided it was not. Tanilis approved of straightforward truth . . . and in any case, he thought, she might well already know Mavros was dead, being who and what she was.

He thought for a while before he wrote more. "I loved Mavros as if he were my brother by birth. I would have kept him from attacking Harvas if I'd known that was in his mind, but he hid it from me till too late. You will know better than I do that going ahead no matter what was always his way."

He spread fine sand over the letter to dry the ink. Then he turned over the parchment and wrote on the reverse, "The excellent and noble lady Tanilis, on her estate outside Opsikion." He sanded those words dry, too, then rolled the letter up into a small tube with them on the outside. After tying it shut, he let several large drops of sealing wax fall across the ribbon that closed it. While the wax was still soft, he pressed his signet into it. He stared at the imperial sunburst for a long time. It remained as perfect as if his armies had won three great victories instead of being thrashed three times running and seeing a city sacked and its populace destroyed.

He stuck his head out of the tent to call for a courier. As the fellow stuffed the letter into a waterproof tube, Krispos promised himself that before the war with Harvas was done, the Empire would again become as whole and complete as its seal. He was glad he'd made the vow, but would have felt easier about it had he been surer he could bring it to pass.

# VII

VIDESSOS THE CITY MOURNED. ALONG WITH THE MOURNING came no little fear. Not since the wild days three centuries before, when the Khamorth tribes swarmed off the steppes of Pardraya to carve Kubrat, Khatrish, and Thatagush from the Empire of Videssos, had the folk of the capital felt threatened from the north.

"People act as if we're going to be besieged tomorrow," Krispos complained to Iakovitzes a few days after he'd returned to the city. "Harvas' killers are on their own side of the Paristrian Mountains; they'll likely stay there till spring."

Iakovitzes scribbled in his tablet and passed it to Krispos. "Not even Harvas is wizard enough to stop the fall rains." He pointed upward, cocking a hand behind his ear.

Krispos nodded; raindrops were drumming on the roof. "Last year I cursed the rains when they came early, because they kept me from going after Petronas. Now I bless them, because they keep Harvas out of the Empire."

Iakovitzes took back the tablet and wrote some more. "Phos closes his ears to curses and blessing both, as far as weather goes. He hears too many of each."

"No doubt you're right," Krispos said. "It doesn't stop people from sending them up, though. And Harvas' being a couple of hundred miles from here doesn't stop people from looking north over their shoulders every time they hear a loud noise in the next street."

"It won't last," Iakovitzes wrote with confident cynicism. "Remember, city folk are fickle. Pyrrhos will give them something new to think about soon enough."

Krispos winced. "Don't remind me." More than ever, he wished Gnatios had stayed loyal to him. Gnatios was politician as well as priest, which made him pliable. Pyrrhos chose a course and pursued it with all the power he had—and as ecumenical patriarch he had more power, perhaps, than anyone save Krispos. He also cared not a copper whether the course he chose raised the hackles of every other ecclesiastic in the Empire. Sometimes Krispos thought he aimed at just that. Whether he did or not, he was accomplishing it.

"I've known him longer than you have, if you'll remember," Iakovitzes wrote. "After all, he's my cousin. He doesn't approve of me, either. Of course, he doesn't approve of anything much, as you'll have noticed." He made the throaty noise he used for laughter.

"No wonder he doesn't approve of you!" Krispos laughed, too. Iakovitzes' sybaritic habits and unending pursuit of handsome youths did not endear him to his stern, ascetic cousin. Krispos went on, "I notice you haven't slowed down, either. If anything, you're squiring more lads around than ever." Krispos wondered if, after his mutilation, Iakovitzes had plunged so deeply back into the world of the senses to remind himself he was still alive.

The noble made that throaty noise again. "Backward, your Majesty," he wrote. "These days they squire me."

Krispos started to laugh once more, too, but stopped when he saw Iakovitzes' face. "By the good god, you mean it," he said slowly. "But how—why? You know I mean you no disrespect, excellent sir, but you've baffled me."

Iakovitzes wrote one word, in big letters: "UNIQUE." Grinning, he pointed to himself, then wrote again. "Where else would they find the like? And like it they do." He leered at Krispos.

Krispos did not quite know whether to laugh some more or to be revolted. Barsymes came in and saved him from his dilemma. "I have here a petition for your Majesty," the vestiarios said, holding out a folded piece of parchment. "It is from the monk Gnatios." Nothing in his voice showed that Gnatios had ever held high rank.

"Speak of him and he pops up," Krispos observed. He took the parchment from Barsymes. The eunuch bowed his way out. Krispos glanced toward Iakovitzes as he opened the petition. "Do you want to hear this?"

At Iakovitzes' nod, Krispos read aloud: " 'The humble, sinful, and repentant monk Gnatios to his radiant and imperial Majesty Krispos, Avtokrator of the Videssians: Greetings.' '' He snorted. "Likes to lay it on thick, doesn't he?"

"He's a courtier," Iakovitzes wrote, which seemed to say everything he thought necessary.

Krispos resumed. " 'I beg leave to request the inestimable privilege of a brief interruption in my sojourn in the monastery dedicated to the memory of the holy Skirios so that I might enjoy the boon of your presence and acquaint you with the results of certain of my historical researches, these having been resumed at your behest, as the said results, reflections of antiquity though they be, also appear of significance in the Empire's current condition.' '' He put down the parchment. "Whew! If I have trouble understanding his request, why should I expect his historical researches, whatever those are, to make any better sense?"

"Gnatios is no one's fool," Iakovitzes wrote.

"I know that," Krispos said. "So why does he take me for one? This must be some sort of scheme to have him escape again. He'd pop up all over the countryside till we caught him again; he'd preach against Pyrrhos and do his best to raise a schism among the priests. With Harvas to worry about, trouble in the temples is the last thing I need. That can lead to civil war."

"You won't hear him?" Iakovitzes wrote.

"No, by the lord with the great and good mind." Krispos raised his voice: "Barsymes, fetch me pen and ink, please." When he had the writing tools, he scrawled "I FORBID IT—K." at the bottom of Gnatios' petition, using letters even bolder than the ones Iakovitzes had employed to call himself unique. Then he folded the parchment and handed it to Barsymes. "See that this is delivered back to the monk Gnatios." He made Gnatios' title deliberately dismissive.

"It shall be done, your Majesty," the vestiarios said.

"Thank you, Barsymes." As the eunuch chamberlain started to leave, Krispos added, "When you're done with that, could you bring me something from the kitchen? I don't much care what, but I feel like a snack. You, too, excellent sir?"

Iakovitzes nodded. "And some wine, if you would, esteemed sir," he wrote, holding up his tablet so Barsymes could read it.

Before long, the vestiarios carried in a silver tray with a jar of wine, two cups, and a covered serving dish. When he lifted the cover, savory steam rose. "Quails cooked in a sauce of cheese, garlic, and oregano, your Majesty. I hope they will do?"

"Fine," Krispos assured him. He attacked his little bird with gusto and finished it in a few bites.

Iakovitzes made slower going of his quail. He had to cut the meat into very small pieces, and he washed down each little mouthful by tilting back his head and taking a swallow of wine: without a tongue, he could not push food around inside his mouth or move it toward his throat. Here, though, as in other things, he evidently managed, for he'd regained most of the weight his ordeal had taken from him.

As the noble sucked the last scrap of meat from a leg bone, Krispos raised his cup in salute. "I'm glad to see you doing so well," he said.

"I'm glad to see myself doing so well, too," Iakovitzes wrote. Krispos snorted. They drank together.

Dara straightened, her face pale. A maidservant wiped the Empress' mouth and chin with a damp cloth, then stooped to pick up the basin at her feet and carry it away. "I wish I just had *morning* sickness," Dara said wearily, "but I seem to be vomiting any time of the day or night."

Krispos handed her a cup of wine. "Here, get the taste out of your mouth."

Dara took a small, cautious sip. She cocked her head and waited, gauging the wine's effect on her stomach. When the first swallow sat well, she drank more. She said, "Maybe I should have nursed Phostis myself after all. The midwives say it's harder for a nursing mother to conceive."

"I've heard that," Krispos said. "I don't know whether it's so. Whether or not, I hope you're better soon."

"So do I." Dara rolled her eyes. "But if I do with this baby as I did with Phostis, I'll keep on puking for the next two months."

"Oh, I hope not." But Krispos knew he would keep a close eye on the date Dara's morning sickness stopped and on the day the baby was born. He did not doubt her, not really. Though he'd been in Videssos the city only a couple of days between the campaigns against Petronas and Harvas, he and she'd been anything but idle during that little while, and her sickness had begun about the right length of time after it—no use reckoning by her courses, which were still disrupted after Phostis' birth.

But he'd watched the days, all the same. Dara had cheated with him, which meant she might cheat against him. He thought that unlikely, but Avtokrators who ignored the unlikely did not reign long.

Dara said, "Phostis sat up by himself yesterday."

"So his nurse told me." Krispos did his best to sound pleased. Try as he would, he had trouble warming to Phostis. He could not help wondering if he was raising a cuckoo's chick. *If this next child is a boy* . . . he said to himself, and in thinking how much he would enjoy raising it, he discovered he was sure it was his.

Dara changed the subject. "How are the tax revenues looking?"

"From the westlands, pretty well. From the island of Kalavria, from the peninsula of Opsikion, from the lands right around the city, pretty well. From the north—" Krispos did not need to go on. Only carrion birds found anything worth picking over anywhere near the Paristrian Mountains.

"Will we have enough to fight Harvas next spring?" Dara asked. She was a general's daughter; she knew armies needed money and everything it bought as much as they needed men.

"The logothetes in the treasury say we should," Krispos answered. "And with Petronas gone at last, we'll be able to bring all our soldiers to bear against him." He shook his head. "How I wish we could have done that this year. We might have saved Imbros. Phos be praised that the Empire is united now."

That might have been a mime show cue. The eunuch Longinos came bustling into the room, moving so fast that sweat beaded his fat, beardless face. "Majesty," he gasped. "There's word of rioting around the High Temple, Majesty."

Krispos got up and glared at him so fiercely that the eunuch flinched back in alarm. With an effort, he took hold of his temper. "Tell me about it," he said.

"Save the news itself, your Majesty, I know no more," Longinos quavered. "A soldier carried the report here; I've brought it to you fast as I could."

"You did right, Longinos; thank you," Krispos said, in control of himself again. "Take me to this soldier. I'll hear what he has to say for myself."

The eunuch turned and left. As Krispos followed him out the door, Dara spoke one word. "Pyrrhos."

"That thought had crossed my mind, yes," Krispos said over his shoulder. He trotted down the hall after Longinos.

When Krispos came out of the imperial residence, the soldier prostrated himself, then quickly got to his feet. He looked like a man who had been caught in a riot; his tunic was torn, the crown of his wide-brimmed hat had been caved in, his nose was bloody, and a bruise purpled his right cheekbone. "By the good god, man, what happened?" Krispos said.

The man shook his head and ran a sleeve under his nose. "The ice take me if I know, your Majesty. I was goin' along mindin' my own business when this crowd boiled out of the forecourt to the High Temple. They was all screamin' and whalin' each other with whatever they had handy. Then they lit into me. I still don't have no notion of what it's all about, but I figured you got to hear of it straightaway, so I came here." He wiped his nose again.

"I'm grateful," Krispos said. "Give me your name, if you would."

"I'm Tzouroulos, your Majesty, file closer in Mammianos' command—Selymbrios is captain of my company."

"You're file leader now, Tzouroulos, and you'll have a reward you can spend, too." Krispos turned to the Halogai, who had listened to the exchange with interest. "Vagn, go to, hmm, Rhisoulphos' regiment in the barracks. Get them over to the High Temple as fast as they can march. Tell them it's riot duty, not combat—if they start slaying people out of hand, the whole city's liable to go up in smoke."

"Aye, Majesty. Rhisoulphos' regiment it is." Vagn saluted and jogged away. His long fair braid flapped against his back at every step he took.

Krispos said to Longinos, "After we get order back—by the good god's mercy, we will—I'll also want to speak with the most holy ecumenical patriarch Pyrrhos, to see if he can shed some light on what might have touched off this fighting. Be so good, esteemed sir, as to draft for my signature a formal summons for him to come to the Grand Courtroom and explain himself."

"Of course, your Majesty. Directly. To the Grand Courtroom, you say? Not here?"

"No. Riots round the temples are a serious business. I want to remind Pyrrhos just how dim a view I take of them. Making my inquiries in the Courtroom should help him understand that."

"Very well, your Majesty." Lips moving as he tasted phrases, Longinos went back into the imperial residence.

Krispos stared east and north, toward the High Temple. The residence and the other buildings of the palace quarter hid its great dome and the gilded spheres that topped its spires, but arson often went with riot. He did not see the black column of smoke he feared. It was the rainy season, after all, he thought hopefully. Even if it was only drizzling today, walls and fences would still be damp.

He went inside. Longinos approached him with the summons. He read it over, nodded, and signed and sealed it. The chamberlain took the parchment away. Krispos waited and worried. He knew he'd given the proper orders. But even the imperial power had limits. He needed others to turn those orders into reality.

The sun was low in the west when a messenger came from Rhisoulphos with word that the disturbances had been quelled. "Aye," the fellow said cheerfully, "we broke some heads. The city folk don't have the gear to stand against us and, besides, they keep on fighting each other. Civilians," he finished with a sneer.

"I'll want to see some prisoners, so I can find out what got these civilians started," Krispos said.

"We have some," the messenger agreed. "They're sending them back to the jail in the government office building on Middle Street."

"I'll go there, then," Krispos said, glad of something he could do. Bu he could not simply walk over to the big red granite building, as any private citizen might. Before he set out from the imperial residence, he required a squad of Halogai and the dozen parasol-bearers. Gathering the retinue took awhile, so that by the time he set out, he needed torchbearers, too.

One of the palace eunuchs must have sent word ahead of his procession, for the warders and soldiers at the government offices were ready when he arrived. They escorted him to a chamber on the ground level, one floor above the cells. As soon as he was settled, two warders hauled in a captive whose hands were chained in front of him. "On your belly before his Majesty," they growled. He went to his knees, then awkwardly finished the prostration. One of the warders said, "Majesty, this here is a certain Koprisianos. He tried to smash in a trooper's skull, he did."

"Would've done it, too, your Majesty, 'cept the bastard was wearing a helmet," Koprisianos said thickly. He had an engagingly ugly face, though now his lip was swollen and split and a couple of teeth looked to be freshly gone.

"Never mind that," Krispos said. "I want to know what started the fighting in the first place."

"So do I," Koprisianos said. "All I know is, somebody hit

me. I turned around and hit him back—at least I think it was him; lots of people were running by just then, all of 'em screaming about heretics and Skotos-lovers and Phos knows what all else. I was giving as good as I got till some stupid soldier broke a spearshaft over my head. After that, next thing I know is, I wake up here.''

"Oh." Krispos turned to the warders. "Take him away. He just looks to have found himself in the middle of a brawl and enjoyed it. Bring me people who saw the riot start, or who made it start, if you can find any who'll admit to that. I want to get to the bottom of how it began.''

"Yes, your Majesty," the warders said together. One of them added, "Come on, you," as they led away Koprisianos. They were gone for some time before they returned with an older man who wore the tattered remnants of what had been a fine robe. "This here is a certain Mindes. He was captured inside the forecourt to the High Temple. On your belly, you!''

Mindes performed the proskynesis with the smoothness of a man who had done it before. "May it please your Majesty, I have the privilege of serving as senior secretary to the ypologothete Gripas,'' he said as he rose.

A mid-level treasury official, Krispos thought. He said, "Having men sworn to uphold the state captured rioting pleases me not at all, Mindes. How did you come to disgrace yourself that way?''

"Only because I wanted to hear the most holy patriarch Pyrrhos preach, your Majesty," Mindes said. "His words always inspire me, and he was particularly vigorous today. He spoke of the need for holy zeal in routing out the influence of Skotos from every part of our lives and from our city as a whole. Even some priests, he said, had tolerated evil too long.''

"Did he?" Krispos said with a sinking feeling.

"Aye, your Majesty, he did, and a great deal of truth in what he said, too.'' Mindes drew the sun-sign as well as he could with his hands chained. He went on, "People talked about the sermon afterward, as they often do while leaving the High Temple. Several priests notorious for their laxness were named. Then someone claimed Skotos could also profit from too much rigor in the holy hierarchy. Someone else took that as a deliberate insult against Pyrrhos, and—'' Mindes' chains clanked as he shrugged.

"And your own part in this was purely innocent?" Krispos asked.

"Purely, your Majesty," Mindes said, the picture of candor.

One of the wanders coughed dryly. "When captured, your Majesty, he was carrying five belt pouches, not counting the one on his own belt."

"A treasury official indeed," Krispos said. The warders laughed. Mindes looked innocent—with the smoothness of a man who has done it before, Krispos thought. He said, "All right, take him back to his cell and bring me someone else who was there at the start of things."

The next man told essentially the same story. Just to be sure, Krispos had one more summoned and heard the tale over again. Then he went back to the imperial residence and spent the night pondering what to do with Pyrrhos. Ordering the patriarch to wear a muzzle at all times struck him as a good idea, but he suspected Pyrrhos would find some theological justification for disobeying.

"He might not, you know," Dara said when he mentioned his conceit out loud. "He might take it for some wonderful new style of asceticism and try to enforce it on the whole clergy." She chuckled.

So did Krispos, but only for a moment. Knowing Pyrrhos, there was always the chance Dara was right.

The Grand Courtroom was heated by the same kind of system of ducts under the floor that the imperial residence used. It was far larger than any room in the residence, though; the ducts kept one's feet warm, but not much more.

Krispos' throne stood on a platform a man's height above the floor; not even his feet were warm. Some of the courtiers who flanked the double row of columns that led up to the throne shivered in their robes. The Haloga guards were warm—they wore trousers. Back in his old village, Krispos would have been wearing trousers, too. He cursed fashion, then smiled as he imagined Barsymes' face if he'd proposed coming to the Grand Courtroom in anything but the scarlet robe custom decreed.

The smile went away when Pyrrhos appeared at the far end of the hall. The patriarch advanced toward the throne with the steady stride of a much younger man. He was entitled to vestments of blue silk and cloth-of-gold, vestments almost as rich as the imperial raiment. All he wore, though, was a monk's simple blue robe, now soaked and dark. As he drew near, Krispos heard his feet squelching in his blue boots; he refused to acknowledge the rain by covering himself against it.

He prostrated himself before Krispos, waiting with his forehead on the ground till given leave to rise. "How may I serve your Majesty?" he asked. He did not hesitate to meet Krispos' eye. If this conscience troubled him, he concealed it perfectly. Krispos did not think it did; unlike most Videssians, Pyrrhos had no use for dissembling.

"Most holy sir, we are not pleased with you," Krispos said in the formal tone he'd practiced for occasions such as this. He stifled a grin of pleasure at remembering to use the first-person plural.

"How so, your Majesty?" Pyrrhos said. "In my simple way, I have striven only to speak the truth, and how can the truth displease any man who has no reason to fear it?"

Krispos clamped his teeth together. He might have known this would not be easy. Pyrrhos wore righteousness like chain mail. Krispos answered, "Stirring up quarrels within the temples serves neither them nor the Empire as a whole, the more so as Harvas Black-Robe alone will profit if we fight among ourselves."

"Your Majesty, I have no intention of stirring up dissent," Pyrrhos said. "I merely aim to purify the temples of the unacceptable practices that have entered over years of lax discipline."

What Krispos wanted to do was scream, "*Not* now, *you cursed idiot*!" Instead he said, "Since these practices you don't approve of have been a long time growing, maybe you'd be wiser to ease them out of the ground instead of jerking them up by the roots."

"No, your Majesty," Pyrrhos said firmly. "These are the webs Skotos spins, the tiny errors that grow larger, more flagrant month by month, year by year, until at last utter wickedness and depravity become acceptable. I tell you, your Majesty, thanks to Gnatios and his ilk, Videssos the city is a place where the dark god roams free!" He spat on the polished marble floor and traced the sun-circle over the sodden wool above his heart.

Several courtiers imitated the pious gesture. Some looked fearfully toward Krispos, wondering how he dared ask the patriarch to restrain his attack on evil.

But Krispos said, "You are wrong, most holy sir." His voice was hard and certain. That certainty made Pyrrhos' eyes widen slightly; he was more used to hearing it in his own voice than from another. Krispos said, "No doubt Skotos sneaks about in Videssos the city, as he does all through the world. But I have seen a city where he roamed free; I see Imbros still in my dreams."

"Exactly so, your Majesty. It is to prevent Videssos the city from suffering the fate of Imbros that I strive. The evil within us, given time, will devour us unless, to use your phrase, we root it out now."

"The evil Harvas Black-Robe loves will devour us right now unless we root it out," Krispos said. "How do you propose to minister to the soul of an impaled corpse? Most holy sir, think which victory is more urgent at the moment."

Pyrrhos thought; Krispos gave him credit for it. At length the patriarch said, "You have your concerns, Majesty, but I have mine, as well." He sounded troubled, as if he had not expected Krispos to make him admit even so much. "If I see evil and do nothing to rid the world of it, I myself have done that evil. I cannot pass it by in silence, not without consigning my soul to the eternal ice."

"Not even if other men, men of good standing in the temples, fail to see anything evil in it?" Krispos persisted. "Do you say that anyone who disagrees with you in any way will spend eternity in the ice?"

"I would not go so far as that, your Majesty," Pyrrhos said, though by the look in his eyes, he wanted to. Reluctantly he continued, "The principle of theological economy does apply to certain beliefs that cannot be proven actively pernicious."

"Then while we are at war with Harvas, stretch it as wide as you can. If you did not go out of your way to make enemies in the temples, most holy sir, you would find many who might be your friends. But think again now and answer me truly: can you see stretching economy to fit Harvas or his deeds?"

Again Pyrrhos paused for honest thought. "No," he admitted, the word expressionless. As much as he wanted to keep his face straight, he looked like a man who suspected, too late, he'd been cheated at dice. He bowed stiffly. "Let it be as you say, your Majesty. I shall essay to practice economy where I can, for so long as this Harvas remains in arms against us."

One or two courtiers burst into applause, amazed and impressed that Krispos had wrung any concession from Pyrrhos. Krispos was amazed and impressed, too, but did not let on; he also noted the qualifying phrases the patriarch used to keep those concessions as small as possible. He said, "Excellent, most holy sir. I knew I could rely on you."

The patriarch bowed again, even more like an automaton than before. He started to prostrate himself once more so he could leave the imperial presence.

Krispos held up a hand. "Before you go, most holy sir, a question. Did the monk Gnatios ask leave of you to come out of his monastery not long ago?"

"Why, so he did, your Majesty—and in proper form, too," Pyrrhos added grudgingly. "I rejected the petition even so, of course: no matter what reasons he gives for wishing to come forth, no doubt he mainly seeks to work mischief."

"As you say, most holy sir. I thought the same."

Pyrrhos' face twisted. For a moment he seemed about to smile. In the end, as befit his abstemious temperament, he contented himself with a sharp, short nod. He performed the proskynesis, rose, and backed away from the throne until he was far enough from it to turn his back on Krispos without giving offense. No sooner had he gone than a servitor with a rag scurried out to wipe up the rainwater that had dripped from his robe.

Krispos surveyed the Grand Courtroom with a broad, benign smile. The courtiers were not shouting, "Thou conquerest, Krispos!" at him, but he knew he'd won a victory, just the same.

Phostis rolled from belly to back, from back to belly. The baby started to roll over one more time. Krispos grabbed him before he went off the edge of the bed. "Don't do that," he said. "You're too smart to be a farmer, aren't you?"

" 'Too smart to be a farmer'?" Dara echoed, puzzled.

"The only way a farmer ever learns anything is to hit himself in the head," Krispos explained. He held Phostis close to his face. The baby reached out, grabbed a double handful of beard, and yanked. "Ow!" Krispos said. He carefully worked Phostis' left hand free, then the right—by which time, the left was tangled in his beard again.

After another try, he was able to put down the baby. Phostis promptly tried to roll off the bed. Krispos caught him again. "I told you not to do that," he said. "Why don't babies listen?"

"You're very gentle with him," Dara said. "I think that's good, especially considering—" She let her voice trail away.

"Not much point to whacking him till he's big enough to understand what he's being whacked for," Krispos said, deliberately choosing to misunderstand. *Considering he might be another man's son*, Dara had started to say. She wondered, too, then. Phostis refused to give either of them much in the way of clues.

The baby tried to roll off the bed once more. This time he almost made it. Krispos snagged him by an ankle and dragged him back. "You're not supposed to do that," he said. Phostis laughed at him. He thought being rescued was a fine game.

"I'm glad you'll be here the winter long," Dara said. "He'll get a chance to know you now. When you were out on campaign the whole summer, he'd forgotten you by the time you came back again."

"I know." Part of Krispos wanted to keep Phostis by him every hour of the day and night, to leave the child, if not Krispos himself, no doubt they were father and son. Another part of him wanted nothing to do with the boy. The result was an uneasy blend of feelings that grew only more complicated as day followed day.

The baby started to fuss, jamming fingers into his mouth. "He's cutting a tooth, poor dear little one," Dara said. "He's probably getting hungry, too. I'll ring for the wet nurse." She tugged the green bell cord that rang back in the maidservants' quarters.

A minute later someone tapped politely on the bedchamber door. When Krispos opened it, he found not the wet nurse but Barsymes standing there. The vestiarios bowed. "I have a letter for you."

"Thank you, esteemed sir." Krispos took the sealed parchment from him. Just then the wet nurse came bustling down the hall. She smiled at Krispos as she brushed past him and hurried over to the baby, who was still crying.

"Who sent the letter?" Dara asked as the wet nurse took Phostis from her.

Krispos did not need to open it to answer. He had recognized the seal, recognized the elegantly precise script that named him the addressee. "Tanilis," he said. "You remember—Mavros' mother."

"Yes, of course." Dara turned to the wet nurse. "Iliana, could you carry him someplace else for a bit, please?" Anthimos had been good at acting as if servants did not exist when that suited him. Dara had more trouble doing so, and Krispos more still—he'd had no servants till he was an adult. Iliana left; Barsymes, perfect servitor that he was, had already disappeared. Dara said, "Read it to me, will you?"

"Certainly." Krispos broke the seal, slid off the ribbon around the letter, unrolled the parchment. " 'Tanilis to his imperial Majesty Krispos, Avtokrator of the Videssians: Greetings. I thank you for your sympathy. As you say, my son died as he lived, going straight ahead without hesitating to look to either side of the road.' "

The closeness of the image to the way Mavros' army had actually been caught made Krispos pause and reminded him how Tanilis saw more than met the ordinary man's eye. He collected himself and read on: " 'I have no doubt you did all you could to keep him from his folly, but no one, in the end, can be saved from himself and his will. Therein lies the deadly danger of Harvas Black-Robe, for, having known the good, he has forsaken it for evil. Would I were a man, to face him in the field, though I know he is mightier than I. But perhaps I shall meet him even so; Phos grant it may be. And may the good god bless you, your Empress, and your sons. Farewell.' "

Dara seized on one word of the letter. "Sons?"

Krispos checked. "So she wrote."

Dara sketched the sun-circle over her heart. "She does see true, you say?"

"She always has." Krispos reached out to set a hand on Dara's belly. The child did not show yet, not even when she was naked, certainly not when she wore the warm robes approaching winter required. "What shall we name him?"

"You're too practical for me—I hadn't looked so far ahead." As Dara frowned in thought, the faintest of lines came out on her forehead and at the corners of her mouth. They hadn't been there when Krispos first came to the imperial residence as vestiarios. She was the same age as he, near enough; her aging, minor though it was, reminded him he also grew no younger. She said, "You named Phostis. If this truly is a son, shall we call him Evripos, after my father's father?"

"Evripos." Krispos plucked at his beard as he considered. "Good enough."

"That's settled, then. Another son." Dara drew the sun-sign again. "A pity Mavros had none of his mother's gift." Her eyes went to the letter Krispos was still holding.

"Aye. He never showed a sign of it that I saw. If he'd had it, he wouldn't have gone out from the city. I know he didn't fear for himself; he was wild to be a soldier when I met him." Krispos smiled, remembering Mavros hacking at bushes as they rode from Tanilis' villa into Opsikion. "But he never would have taken a whole army into danger."

"No doubt you're right." Dara hesitated, then asked, "Have you thought about appointing a new Sevastos?"

"I expect I'll get around to it one of these days." The matter seemed less urgent to Krispos than it had when he'd named Mavros to the post. Now that no rebel was moving against him, he had less need to act in two places at the same time, and thus less need for so powerful a minister. Thinking out loud, he went on, "Most likely I'd pick Iakovitzes. He's served me well and he knows both the city and the wider world."

"Oh." Dara nodded. "Yes, he would make a good choice."

The words were commonplace. Something in the way she said them made him glance sharply at her. "Did you have someone else in mind?"

She was swarthy enough to make her flush hard to spot, but he saw it. Her voice became elaborately casual. "Not that so much, but my father was curious to learn if you were thinking of someone in particular."

"Was he? He was curious to learn if I was thinking of him in particular, you mean."

"Yes, I suppose I do." That flush grew deeper. "I'm sure he meant nothing out of ordinary by asking."

"No doubt. Tell him this for me, Dara: tell him I think he might make a good Sevastos, if only I could trust him with my back turned. As things are now, I don't know that I can, and his sneaking questions through you doesn't make me think any better of him. Or am I wrong to be on my guard?" Dara bit her lip. Krispos said, "Never mind. You don't have to answer. That question puts you in an impossible spot."

"You already know my father is an ambitious man," Dara said. "I will pass on to him what you've told me."

"I'd be grateful if you would." Krispos let it go at that. Pushing Dara too hard was more likely to force her away than to bind her to him.

To give himself something impersonal to do, he read through Tanilis' letter again. He wished she could face Harvas in the field. If anyone could best him, she might be that person. Not only would her gifts of foreknowledge warn her of his ploys, but the loss he'd inflicted on her would focus her sorcerous skill against him as a burning glass focused the rays of the sun.

Then Krispos put the letter aside. From what he'd seen thus far, unhappily, no Videssian wizard could face Harvas Black-Robe in the field. That left Krispos a cruel dilemma: how was he to overcome Harvas' Halogai if the evil mage's magic worked and his own did not?

Posing the question was easy. Finding an answer anywhere this side of catastrophe, up till now, had been impossible.

* * *

Trokoundos looked harassed. Every time Krispos had seen him this fall and winter, he'd looked harassed. Krispos understood that. As much as he could afford to, he even sympathized with Trokoundos. He kept summoning the wizard to ask him about Harvas, and Trokoundos had no miracles to report.

"Your Majesty, ever since I returned from the campaign, the Sorcerers' Collegium has hummed like a hive of bees, trying to unravel the secrets behind Harvas' spells," Trokoundos said. "I've had myself examined under sorcery and drugs to make sure my recall of what I witnessed was perfectly exact, in the hope that some other mage, given access to my observations, might find the answer that has eluded me. But—" He spread his hands.

"All your bees have made no honey," Krispos finished for him.

"No, your Majesty, we have not. We are used to reckoning ourselves the finest wizards in the world. Oh, maybe in Mashiz the King of Kings of Makuran has a stable to match us, but that a solitary barbarian mage should have the power to baffle us—" Trokoundos' heavy-lidded eyes flashed angrily. Being beaten so ate at his pride.

"You have no idea, then, how he does what he does?" Krispos asked.

"I did not quite say that. What makes his magic effective is easy enough to divine. He is very strong. Strength may accrue to any man of any nation—even, perhaps, such strength as his. But he also possesses technique refined beyond any we can match here in Videssos the city. How he acquired that, and how we may meet it . . . well, an answer there will go far toward piecing the puzzle together. But we have none."

Krispos said, "Not too long ago I got a note from our dear friend Gnatios. He claims he has your answers all tied up with a scarlet ribbon. Of course, he would claim dung was cherries if he thought he saw a copper's worth of advantage in it."

"He's a trimmer, aye, but he's no fool," Trokoundos said seriously, echoing Iakovitzes. "What answer did he give? By the lord with the great and good mind, I'll seize whatever I can find now."

"He *gave* none," Krispos said. "He just claimed he had one. As best I could tell, his main aim was escaping the monastery. He thinks I forget the trouble he's caused me. If he hadn't got

Petronas loose, I could have turned on Harvas close to half a year sooner.''

"Would you have won on account of that?'' Trokoundos asked.

"Up till this instant I'd thought so,'' Krispos answered. "If I couldn't beat him then with the full power of Videssos behind me, how may I hope to next spring? Or are you telling me I shouldn't go forth at all? Should I wait here in the city and stand siege?''

"No. Better to meet Harvas as far from Videssos the city as you may. How much good did walls do either Develtos or Imbros?''

"None at all.'' Krispos started to say something more, then stopped, appalled, and stared at Trokoundos. Videssos the city's walls were incomparably greater than those of the two provincial towns. Imagining them breached was almost more than Krispos could do. That was not quite the mental image that dismayed him. Winter was the quiet time of year on the farm, the time when people would do minor repairs and get ready for the busyness that would return with spring. In his mind's eye he saw Harvas' Halogai sitting round their hearths, some with skins of ale, others with their feet up, and every last one of them sharpening stakes, sharpening stakes, sharpening stakes . . . Of itself, his anus tightened.

"What is it, your Majesty?'' Trokoundos asked. "For a moment there you looked—frightened and frightening at the same time.''

"I believe it.'' Krispos was glad he'd had no mirror in which to watch his features change. "This I vow, Trokoundos: we'll meet Harvas as far from Videssos the city as we can.''

Progress paced down Middle Street at a slow walk. Beside the big bay gelding, eight servants tramped along with the imperial litter. Their breath, the horse's, and Krispos' rose in white, steaming clouds at every exhalation.

The city was white, too, white with new-fallen snow. Over his imperial robes, Krispos wore a coat of soft, supple otter furs. He still shivered; he'd lost track of his nose a while before. Dara had a brazier inside the litter. Krispos hoped it did her some good.

Only the Haloga guardsmen who marched ahead of and behind Krispos and his lady literally took winter in their stride. Marched, indeed, was not the right word: they strutted, their heads thrown back, chests thrust forward, backs as resolutely straight as the columns that supported the colonnades running along either side of Middle Street. Their breath fairly burst from their nostrils; they took in great gulps of the air Krispos reluctantly sipped. This was the climate they were made for.

Narvikka turned his head back. "W'at a fine morning!" he boomed. The rest of the northerners nodded. Some of them wore braids like Vagn's, tied tight with crimson cords; these bobbed like horses' tails to emphasize their agreement. Krispos shivered again. Inside the litter, Dara sneezed. He didn't like that. With her pregnant, he wanted nothing out of the ordinary.

The small procession turned north off Middle Street toward the High Temple. When they arrived, one of the Halogai held Progress' head while Krispos dismounted. The litter-bearers and all but two of the guardsmen stayed outside with the horse. The pair who accompanied Krispos and Dara into the temple had diced for the privilege—and lost. Halogai cared nothing for hymns and prayers to Phos.

A priest bowed low when he saw Krispos. "Will you sit close by the altar as usual, your Majesty?" he asked.

"No," Krispos answered. "Today I think I'll hear the service from the imperial niche."

"As you will, of course, your Majesty." The priest could not keep a note of surprise from his voice, but recovered quickly. Bowing again, he said, "The stairway is at the far end of the narthex there."

"Yes, I know. Thank you, holy sir." One Haloga fell in in front of Krispos and Dara, the other behind them. Both guards held axes at the ready, though the service was still an hour away and the narthex deserted but for themselves, the Avtokrator and Empress, and a few priests.

As she went up the stairs, Dara complained, "I'd much rather stay down on the main level. Inside the niche, you have trouble seeing out through the grillwork, you're too far away anyhow, and half the time you can't hear what the patriarch is saying."

"I know." Krispos climbed the last stair and walked forward into the imperial niche. The blond oak benches there were bedecked with even more precious stones than those on which less exalted worshipers sat. Mother-of-pearl and gleaming silver ornamented the floral-patterned grillwork. Krispos stood by it for a moment. He said, "I can see well enough, and Pyrrhos is loud enough so I won't have trouble hearing him. I want to find out what goes on when I'm not at the temple, the kind of things Pyrrhos says when I'm not here to listen.''

"Spies would do that just as well," Dara said reasonably.

"It's not the same if I don't hear it myself." Krispos didn't know why it wasn't the same—probably because he'd been Emperor for less than a year and a half and still wanted to do as much as he could for himself. Come to that, Pyrrhos was not the sort to change his words because Krispos was in the audience.

"You just want to play spy," Dara said.

His grin was sheepish. "Maybe you're right. But I'd feel even more foolish going down now than I would staying." Dara's eyes rolled heavenward, but she stopped arguing.

Down below, worshipers filed into their places. When they all rose, Krispos and Dara stood, too: the patriarch was approaching the altar. "We bless thee, Phos, lord with the great and good mind, by thy grace our protector, watchful beforehand that the great test of life may be decided in our favor," Pyrrhos declaimed. Everyone recited with him, everyone save the two Halogai in the niche, who stood as silent and unmoving—and probably as bored—as if they were statuary.

More prayers followed Phos' creed. Then came a series of hymns, sung by the congregation and by a chorus of monks who stood against one wall. "May Phos hear our entreaties and the music of our hearts," Pyrrhos said as the last echoes died away in the dome far above his head.

"May it be so," the worshipers responded. Then, at the patriarch's gesture, they sank back onto their benches. Dara let out a small sigh of relief as she sat.

Pyrrhos paused to gather his thoughts before he began to preach. "I shall begin today by considering the thirtieth chapter of Phos' holy scriptures," he said. " 'If you understand the commands the good god has given, all hereafter will be for the best: well-being and suffering, the one for the just, the other for the wicked. Then in the end shall Skotos cease to flourish, while those of good life shall reap the promised reward and bask forevermore in the blessed light of the lord with the great and good mind.'

"Again, in the forty-sixth chapter we read, 'But he who rejects Phos, he is a creature of Skotos, who in the sight of the evil one is best.' And yet again, in the fifty-first: 'He who seeks to destroy for whatever cause, he is a son of the creator of evil, and an evildoer to mankind. Righteousness do I call to me to bring good reward.'

"How do we apply these teachings? That the vicious foe who prowls our borders is wicked is plain to all. Yet note how perfectly the holy scriptures set forth his sin: he is a destroyer, an evildoer to mankind, a son of the creator of evil, and one who gives no thought to the commands of the good god. And indeed, one day the eternal ice shall be his home. May it be soon."

"May it be soon," Krispos said. Beside him, Dara nodded. A low mutter also rose from the congregation below.

Pyrrhos went on, "Aye, with Harvas Black-Robe and the savage barbarians who follow him, the recognition of what is good and what evil comes easily enough. Would that Skotos knew no guises more seductive. But the dark god is a trickster and a liar, constantly seeking to ensnare and deceive men into thinking they do good when in fact their acts lead only toward the ice.

"What shall we say, for example—" The patriarch loaded his voice with scorn. "—of priests and prelates who make false statements for their own advantage, or who condone the sins of others, or who remain in concord with those who condone the sins of others?"

"He's whipping Gnatios again," Dara said.

"So he is," Krispos said. "Trouble is, he's using Gnatios to whip all the priests in the whole hierarchy who don't spend every free moment mortifying their flesh, and I told him not to do that." Now he wished he was down by the altar. He could rise up in righteous wrath and denounce the patriarch on the spot— and wouldn't that make a scandal to resound all through the Empire! He laughed a little, enjoying the idea.

The laughter left his lips as Pyrrhos repeated, "What shall we say of these men who have blinded themselves to Phos' sacred words? By the Lord with the great and good mind, here is my answer: a man of such nature no longer deserves the appellation of priest. He is rather a wild animal, an evil scoundrel, a sinful heretic, a whore, one who does not deserve and is not worthy to wear a blue robe. He will spend all eternity in the ice with his true master Skotos. His tears of lamentation shall freeze to his cheeks—and who would deny this is his just desert?"

The patriarch sounded grimly pleased at the prospect. He went on, "This is why we root out misbelievers when and where we find them. For a priest who errs in his faith condemns not only himself to Skotos' clutches, but gives over his flock as well.

Thus a misbelieving priest is doubly damned and doubly damnable, and must not be suffered to survive, much less to preach.''

Krispos did not like the buzz of approval that rose to the imperial niche. Religious strife was meat and drink to the folk of Videssos the city. Pyrrhos might have promised to exercise economy, but the promise went too much against his nature for him to keep it: he was a controversialist born.

''I'll have to get rid of him,'' Krispos said, though saying it aloud made him wince. Pyrrhos had given him his start in the city. Driven by some mystic vision, the then-abbot had taken him to Iakovitzes, thus starting the train of events that led to the throne. But now that Krispos was on the throne, how could he afford a patriarch who kept doing his best to turn Videssos upside down?

''With whom would you replace him?'' Dara asked. Krispos shook his head. He had no idea.

Pyrrhos was finishing his sermon. ''As you prepare to leave the temple and return to the world, offer up a prayer to the Avtokrator of the Videssians, that he may lead us to victory against all who threaten the Empire.''

That only made Krispos feel worse. Pyrrhos remained solidly behind him. But the patriarch threatened the Empire, too. Krispos had tried to tell him so, every way he knew how. Pyrrhos had not listened—more accurately, had refused to hear. As soon as Krispos could decide on a suitable replacement, it would be back to the monastery for the zealous cleric.

The congregation recited Phos' creed a last time to mark the end of the service. ''This liturgy is accomplished,'' Pyrrhos declared. ''Go now, and may each of you walk in Phos' light forevermore.''

''May it be so,'' the worshipers said. They rose from their benches and began filing out to the narthex.

Krispos and Dara also rose. The Halogai behind them unfroze from immobility. One of the northerners muttered something in his own tongue to the other. The second guardsman started to grin until he saw Krispos watching him. His face congealed into soldierly immobility. *Laughing at the ceremony*, Krispos guessed. He wished the Halogai would see the truth of Phos. On the other hand, an Avtokrator who proselytized too vigorously was liable to see the size of his bodyguard shrink.

The Halogai preceded the imperial couple down the stairs. The men and women in the narthex bowed low as Krispos emerged. No proskynesis was required, not here: this was Phos' precinct first. Flanked by watchful guardsmen fore and aft, Krispos and Dara went out to the forecourt.

With a flourish, the chief litter-bearer opened the door to the conveyance so Dara could slip in. Narvikka came over to hold Progress' head. Krispos had his left foot in the stirrup when somebody not far away shouted, "You'll go to the ice with the lax priest you follow!"

"Too much pickiness will send *you* to the ice, Blemmyas, for condemning those who don't deserve it," someone else shouted back.

"Liar!" Blemmyas shouted.

"Who's a liar?" Fist smacked flesh with a meaty *thwock*. In an instant, people all over the forecourt were screaming and cursing and pounding and kicking at one another. Wan sunlight sparkled off the sharpened edge of a knife. "Dig up Pyrrhos' bones!" someone yelled. The ice that walked Krispos' spine had nothing to do with chilly weather—digging up somebody's bones was the call to riot in the city.

A stone whizzed past his head. Another clattered off the side of Dara's litter. She let out a muffled shriek. Krispos sprang into the saddle. "Give me your axe!" he shouted to Narvikka. The Haloga stared, then handed him the weapon. "Good!" Krispos said. "You, you, you, and you—" He pointed to guardsmen. "—stay here and help the bearers keep the Empress' litter safe. The rest of you, follow me! Try not to kill, but don't let yourselves get hurt, either."

He spurred Progress toward the center of the forecourt. The Halogai gaped, then cheered and plunged after him.

The axe was an impossible weapon to swing from horseback—too long, too heavy, balanced altogether wrong. Had Progress not been an extraordinarily steady mount, Krispos' first wild swipe would have pitched him out of the saddle. As it was, he missed the man at whom he'd aimed. The flat of the axehead crashed into the side of a nearby man's head. The fellow staggered as if drunk, then went down.

"Go back to your homes. Stop fighting," Krispos yelled, again and again. Behind him, the armored Halogai were happily felling anyone rash enough to come near them or too slow to get out of the way. From the cries of anguish that rose into the sky, Krispos suspected they weren't paying much heed to his urge of caution.

The riot, though, was murdered before it had truly been born. People in the forecourt broke and ran. They were too afraid of the fearsome northerners to remember why they had been battling one another. That suited Krispos well enough. He held the axe across his knees as he brought Progress to a halt.

When he looked back, he saw about what he'd expected: several men and a woman down and unmoving. The Halogai were busy slitting belt pouches. Krispos looked the other way. Things could have got very sticky had they not waded into the crowd in his wake.

From the top of the steps, priests peered down in dismay at the blood that splashed the snow in the forecourt. Under that snow, old blood still stained the flagstones from the last riot Pyrrhos had inspired. Enough was enough, Krispos thought.

He leaned down from the saddle and returned Narvikka's axe to him. "Maybe one day I show you what to do with it," the Haloga said with a sly smile.

Krispos' ears heated; that stroke had looked as awkward as it felt, then. He pointed to a couple of corpses. "Take their heads," he said. "We'll set them at the foot of the Milestone with a big placard that says 'rioters.' The good god willing, people will see them and think twice."

"Aye, Majesty." Narvikka went about his grisly task with no more concern than if he'd been slaughtering swine. He glanced over to Krispos when he was done. "You go at them like a northern man."

"It needed doing. Besides, if I hadn't, the fighting just would have spread and gotten worse." That was a most un-Halogalike notion. To the northerners, fighting that spread was better, not worse.

Krispos rode the few steps to the litter. The bearers saluted. One of them had a cut on his forehead and a blackened eye. He grinned at Krispos. "Thanks to you, Majesty, we were only at the edge of things. They plumb stopped noticing us when you charged into the middle of 'em."

"Good. That's what I had in mind." Krispos leaned down and spoke into the small window set into the litter door. "Are you all right?"

"I'm fine," Dara answered at once. "I was in the safest place in the whole forecourt, after all." *The safest place as long as the bearers didn't run away*, Krispos thought. *Well, they didn't.* Dara went on, "I'm just glad you came through safe."

He could hear that she meant it. He'd worried about her, too. This was not the fiery sort of love about which lute players sang in wineshops, this marriage of convenience between them. All the same, bit by bit he was coming to see it was a kind of love, too.

"Let's get back to the palaces," he said. The litter-bearers stooped, grunted, and lifted. The Halogai fell into place. Narvikka swaggered along, holding by their beards the two heads he'd taken. City folk either stared at the gruesome trophies or turned away in horror.

Narvikka had fought to defend the Emperor whose gold he'd taken, and had enjoyed every moment of it. How, Krispos wondered uncomfortably, did that make him different from the Halogai who followed Harvas? The only answer he found was that Narvikka's violence was under the control of the state and was used to protect it, not to destroy.

That satisfied him, but not altogether. Harvas could trumpet the same claim for his conquests, no matter how vicious they were. The difference was, Harvas lied.

"A petition for you, your Majesty," Barsymes said.

"I'll read it," Krispos said resignedly. Petitions to the Avtokrator poured in from all over the Empire. Most of them he did not need to see; he had a logothete in aid of requests who dealt with those. But even the winter slowdown did not keep them from coming into the city, and the logothete could not handle everything.

He unrolled the parchment. His nostrils twitched, as if at the smell of bad fish. "Why didn't you tell me it was from Gnatios?"

"Shall I discard it, then?"

Krispos was tempted to say yes, but had second thoughts. "As long as it's in my hands, I may as well read it through." Not the smallest part in his decision was Gnatios' beautifully legible script.

" 'The humble monk Gnatios to his imperial Majesty Krispos, Avtokrator of the Videssians: Greetings.' " Krispos nodded to himself—gone were the fawning phrases of Gnatios' first letter. Having seen they did no good, the former patriarch was wise enough to discard them. They were not his proper style anyhow. Krispos read on:

" 'Again, your Majesty, I beg the boon of an audience with you. I am painfully aware that you have no reason to trust me and, indeed, every reason to mistrust me, but I write nonetheless not so much for my own sake as for the sake of the Empire of Videssos, whose interest I have at heart regardless of who holds the throne.' "

*That might even be true*, Krispos thought. He imagined Gnatios scribbling in the scriptorium or in his own monastic cell, pausing to seek out the telling phrase that would make Krispos relent, or at least read further. He'd succeeded in the latter, if not in the former; Krispos' eyes kept moving down the parchment.

" 'Let me speak plainly, your Majesty,' " Gnatios wrote. " 'The cause of Videssos' present crisis is rooted three hundred years in the past, in the theological controversies that followed the invasions off the Pardrayan steppe, the invasions that raped away the lands now known as Thatagush, Khatrish, and Kubrat. As a result, you will need to consider those controversies and their consequences in contemplating combat against Harvas Black-Robe.' "

The jingling alliteration, though very much the vogue in sophisticated Videssian circles, only irritated Krispos. So did Gnatios' confident "as a result . . ." Of course the past shaped the present. Krispos enjoyed histories and chronicles for exactly that reason. But if Gnatios claimed the Empire's current problems were in fact three hundred years old, he also needed to say why he thought so.

And he did not. Krispos tried to find his reasons for holding back. Two quickly came to mind. One was that the deposed patriarch was lying. The other was that he thought he had the truth, but feared to set it down on parchment lest Krispos use it and keep him mewed up in the monastery all the same.

If that was what troubled him, he was naïve—Krispos could send him back to the monastery of the holy Skirios after hearing what he had to say as easily as he could after reading his words. Gnatios was many things, Krispos thought, but hardly naïve. Most likely, that meant he was lying.

"Bring me pen and ink, please, Barsymes," Krispos said. When the eunuch returned, he took them and wrote, "I still forbid your release. Krispos Avtokrator." He gave the parchment to Barsymes. "Arrange to have this returned to the holy sir, if you would."

"Certainly, your Majesty. Shall I reject out of hand any further petitions from him?"

"No," Krispos said after thinking it over. "I'll read them. I don't have to do anything about them, after all." Barsymes dipped his head and carried the petition away.

Krispos whistled between his teeth. Gnatios was everything Pyrrhos was not: he was smooth, suave, rational, and tolerant. He was also pliable and devious. Krispos had taken great and malicious glee in confining him to the monastery of the holy Skirios for a second time after Petronas' rebellion failed. Now he wondered whether Gnatios had learned enough humility in the monastery to serve as patriarch once more.

When that occurred to him, he also wondered whether he'd lost his own mind. The monastery had changed Petronas not at all, save only to fill him with a brooding desire for vengeance. If Pyrrhos was intolerable on the patriarch throne, what would Gnatios be but intolerable in some different way? Surely it would be better to replace Pyrrhos with an amiable nonentity, the priestly equivalent of barley porridge.

Yet somehow the idea of restoring Gnatios, once planted, would not go away. Krispos got up, still whistling, and went to the sewing room to ask Dara what she thought of it. She jabbed her needle into the linen fabric on her lap and stared up at him. "I can see why you want Pyrrhos out," she said, "but Gnatios has kept trying to wreck you ever since you took the crown."

"I know," Krispos said. "But Petronas is dead, so Gnatios has no reason—well, less reason—for treachery now. He made Anthimos a good patriarch."

"You should have struck off his head when he surrendered at Antigonos. Then your own wouldn't be filled with this moonshine now."

Krispos sighed. "No doubt you're right. His petitions are probably moonshine, too."

"What petitions?" Dara asked. After Krispos explained, her lip curled in a noblewoman's sneer. "If he knows so much about these vast secrets he's keeping, let him tell them. They'd have to be vast indeed to earn him his way out of his cell."

"By the good god, so they would." Krispos bent down to kiss Dara. "I'll summon him and hear him out. If he has nothing, I can send him back to the monastery for good."

"Even that's better than he deserves." Dara did not sound quite happy at having her sarcasm taken literally. "Remember where you'd be, remember where we'd all be—" She patted her belly. "—if he'd had his way."

"I'll never forget it," Krispos promised. He made a wry face. "But I also remember what Iakovitzes told me, and Trokoundos, too: that Gnatios is no one's fool. I don't have to like him, I don't have to trust him, but I have the bad feeling that I may need him.''

Dara stabbed her needle into the cloth again. "I don't like it."

"I don't, either." Krispos raised his voice to call for Barsymes. When the eunuch came into the sewing room, he said, "Esteemed sir, I'm sorry, but I've changed my mind. I think I'd best talk, or rather listen, to Gnatios after all.''

"Very well, your Majesty. I shall see to it at once." Barsymes could make his voice toneless as well as sexless, but Krispos had now had years to learn to read it. He found no disapproval there. More than anything else, that convinced him he was doing the right thing.

# VIII

FREEZING RAIN PELTED DOWN. GNATIOS SHIVERED IN HIS BLUE robe as he walked up to the imperial residence. The troop of Halogai who surrounded him—Krispos was taking no chances on any schemes the ex-patriarch might have hatched—bore the nasty weather with the resigned air of men who had been through worse.

Krispos met Gnatios just inside the entranceway to the residence. Wet and dripping, Gnatios prostrated himself on the chilly marble floor. "Your Majesty is most gracious to receive me," he said through chattering teeth.

"Rise, holy sir, rise." Gnatios looked bedraggled enough to make Krispos feel guilty. "Let's get you dry and warm; then I'll hear what you have to say." At his nod, a chamberlain brought towels and furs to swaddle Gnatios.

Krispos led Gnatios down the hall and into a chamber fitted out for audiences. Gnatios' step was sure, but then, Krispos remembered, he'd been here many times before. Iakovitzes waited inside the chamber. He rose and bowed as Krispos led in the former patriarch. Krispos said, "Since I intend to name Iakovitzes as Sevastos to succeed Mavros, I thought he should hear you along with me."

Gnatios bowed to Iakovitzes. "Congratulations, your Highness, if I may anticipate your coming into your new office," he murmured.

Iakovitzes' stylus raced over wax. He held up what he'd written so Krispos and Gnatios both could read it. "Never mind the fancy talk. If you know how to hurt Harvas, tell us. If you don't, go back to your bleeding cell."

188

"That's how it is, holy sir," Krispos agreed.

"I am aware of it, I assure you," Gnatios said. For once his clever, rather foxy features were altogether serious. "In truth, I do not know how to hurt him, but I think I know who—'what' may be the better word—he is. I rely on your Majesty's honor to judge the value of that."

"I'm glad you do, since you have no other choice save silence," Krispos said. "Now sit, holy sir, and tell me your tale."

"Thank you, your Majesty." Gnatios perched on a chair. Krispos sat down beside Iakovitzes on the couch that faced it. Gnatios said, "As I have written, this tale begins three hundred years ago."

"Go on," Krispos said. He was glad he had Iakovitzes with him. He'd enjoyed the histories and chronicles he'd read, but the noble was a truly educated man. He'd know if Gnatios tried to sneak something past.

Gnatios said, "Surely you know, your Majesty, of the Empire's time of troubles, when the barbarians poured in all along our northern and eastern frontiers and stole so many lands from us."

"I should," Krispos said. "The Kubratoi kidnapped me when I was a boy, and I aided Iakovitzes in his diplomatic dealings with Khatrish some years ago. I know less of Thatagush, and worry about it less, too, since its borders don't touch ours."

"Aye, we deal with them as nations now, like Videssos if neither so old nor so mighty," Gnatios said. "But it was not always so. We had ruled for hundreds of years the provinces they invaded. We—the Empire of Videssos—had a comfortable world then. Save for Makuran, we knew no other nations, only tribes on the Pardrayan steppe and in frigid Halogaland. We were sure Phos favored us, for how could mere tribes do us harm?"

Iakovitzes scribbled, then held up his tablet. "We found out."

"We did indeed," Gnatios said soberly. "Within ten years of the borders being breached, a third of Videssos' territory was gone. The barbarians rode where they would, for once past the frontier they found no forces to resist them. Videssos the city was besieged. Skopentzana fell."

"Skopentzana?" Krispos frowned. "That's no city I ever heard of." Wondering if Gnatios had invented the place, he glanced toward Iakovitzes.

But Iakovitzes wrote, "It's ruins now. It lies in what's Thatagush these days, and the folk there still have but scant use for towns. In its day, though, it was a great city, maybe next greatest in the Empire after Videssos; in no way were more than two towns ahead of it."

"Shall I go on?" Gnatios asked when he saw Krispos had finished reading. At Krispos' nod, he did: "As I said, Skopentzana fell. From what the few survivors wrote afterward, the sack was fearsome, with all the usual pillage and slaughter and rape magnified by the size of the city and because no one had imagined such a fate could befall him till the day. Among the men who got free was the prelate of the city, one Rhavas."

Krispos sketched the sun-circle over his heart. "The good god must have kept him safe."

"Under other circumstances, your Majesty, I might agree with you. As is—well, may I digress briefly?"

"The whole business so far has seemed pretty pointless," Krispos said, "so how am I to know when you wander off the track?" The story Gnatios spun was interesting enough—the man had a gift for words—but seemed altogether unconnected to Harvas Black-Robe. If he could do no better, Krispos thought, he'd stay in his monastery till he was ninety.

"I hope to weave my threads together into a whole garment, Majesty," Gnatios said.

"Whole cloth, you mean," Iakovitzes wrote, but Krispos waved for Gnatios to go on.

"Thank you, your Majesty. I know you have no special training in theology, but you must be able to see that a catastrophe like the invasion off the steppes brought crisis to the ecclesiastical hierarchy. We had believed—comfortably, again—that just as we went from triumph to triumph in the world, so Phos could not help but triumph in the universe as a whole. That remains our orthodoxy to this day—" Gnatios sketched the sun-sign. "—but it was sorely tested in those times.

"For, you see, now so many folk made the acquaintance of misfortune and outright evil that they began to doubt Phos' power. Out of this eventually arose the Balancer heresy, which still holds sway in Khatrish and Thatagush—aye, and even in Agder by Halogaland, which though still Videssian by blood has its own king. But worse than that heresy arose, as well. As I said, Rhavas escaped the sack of Skopentzana."

Krispos' eyebrows rose. "Worse came from the man who was prelate of an important city?"

"It did, your Majesty. Rhavas, I gather, was connected not too distantly to the imperial house of the time, but earned his position by ability, not through his blood. He might have been ecumenical patriarch had Skopentzana not fallen, and he might have been a great one. But when he made his way to Videssos the city, he was . . . changed. He had seen too much of evil when the Khamorth took Skopentzana; he concluded Skotos was mightier than Phos."

Even Iakovitzes, whose piety ran thin, drew the sun-sign when he heard that. Krispos said, "How did the priests of the time take to that?"

"With poor grace, as you might expect." Pyrrhos' reply would have been fierce and full of horror. Gnatios let understatement do the same job. Krispos found he preferred Gnatios' way. The scholarly monk went on, "Rhavas, though, was become as great a zealot for the dark god as he had been for Phos. He preached his new doctrine to all who would listen, first in the temples and then in the streets after the patriarch of the day banned him from the pulpit."

Now Krispos was interested in spite of himself. "They didn't let that go on, did they?" The thought of Videssos the city filled with worshipers of evil filled him with dread.

"No, they didn't," Gnatios said. "But because Rhavas was well connected, they had to try him publicly in an ecclesiastical court, which meant he had the privilege of defending himself against the charges they lodged. And because he was able—well, no, he was more than able; he was brilliant. I've read his defense, your Majesty. It frightens me. It must have frightened the prelates of the day, too, for they sentenced him to death."

"I ask you again, holy sir—how does this apply to the trouble we're in now? If this Rhavas is three centuries dead, then evil as he may have become—"

"Your Majesty, I am not at all sure Rhavas is three centuries dead," Gnatios said heavily. "I am not sure he is dead at all. He laughed when the court sentenced him, and told them they had not the power to be his death. He was left in his cell for the night, to brood on his misbelief and on the crimes he had committed in the belief they furthered his god's ends. Guards came the next morning to take him to the headsman and found the cell empty. The lock had not been tampered with, there were no tunnels. But Rhavas was gone.''

"Magic," Krispos said. The small hairs on his forearms and the back of his neck prickled erect.

"No doubt you are right, your Majesty, but because of the nature of Rhavas' offense the cell was warded by the finest sorcerers of the day. Afterward they all took oath their wards were undisturbed. Yet Rhavas was gone.''

Iakovitzes bent over his tablet. He held it up to show what he had written. "You're saying this Rhavas is Harvas, aren't you?" He screwed up his face to show what he thought of that. But then he lowered the tablet so he could see it himself. When he raised it again, he pointed with his stylus to each name in turn.

For a moment, Krispos had no idea what he was driving at. *Harvas* was an ordinary Haloga name, *Rhavas* an ordinary Videssian one. But was it coincidence that both of them were formed from the same letters? The renewed prickle of alarm he felt told him no.

Gnatios stared at the two names as if he'd never seen them before. His eyes flicked from one to the other, then back again. "I didn't notice—" he breathed.

Iakovitzes set the tablet in his lap so he could write. He passed it to Krispos, who read it aloud: " 'No wonder he wouldn't swear by Phos.' " Iakovitzes believed, too, then.

"But if we're battling a . . . a three-hundred-year-old wizard," Krispos faltered, "how do we, how can we hope to beat him?"

"Your Majesty, I do not know. I was hoping you could tell me," Gnatios said. His voice held no irony. Krispos was the Avtokrator. Defeating foreign foes came with the job.

Iakovitzes wrote again. "If we do face an undying wizard who worships Skotos and hates everything Phos stands for, why hasn't he troubled Videssos long before now?"

That made Krispos doubt again. But Gnatios answered, "How do we know he has not? By the lord with the great and good mind, your Highness, the Empire has suffered its full share of disasters over the years. How many of them might Rhavas have caused or made worse? Our ignorance of the force behind the misfortune fails to prove the force did not exist.''

"Holy sir, I think—I fear—you are right," Krispos said. Only a man—or whatever this Rhavas or Harvas was, after so long— who loved Skotos could have inflicted such brutal savagery on

Imbros. And only a man who had studied sorcery for three centuries could have so baffled a clever, well-trained mage like Trokoundos. The pieces fit as neatly as those of a wooden puzzle, but Krispos cringed from the shape they made.

Gnatios said, "Now do with me as you will, your Majesty. I know you have no reason to love me, nor, truth to tell, have I any to love you. But this tale needed telling for the Empire's sake, not for yours or mine."

"How peculiar," Iakovitzes wrote. "I thought him a man completely without integrity. Shows you can't rely on adverbs, I suppose."

"Er, yes." Krispos handed the tablet back to Iakovitzes. When Gnatios saw he would not be invited to read Iakovitzes' comment, one eyebrow arched. Krispos ignored it. He was thinking hard. At last he said, "Holy sir, this deserves a reward, as you well know."

"Being out of the monastery, even if but for a brief while, is reward in itself." Gnatios raised that eyebrow again. "How ever did you arrange for the most holy ecumenical patriarch of the Videssians—" Gnatios put irony in his voice with a scalpel, not a shovel. "—to acquiesce in my release?"

"That's right, we both had to agree to it, didn't we?" Krispos grinned sheepishly. "As a matter of fact, holy sir, I forgot to ask him, and I gather an imperial summons for you was enough to overawe your abbot."

"Evidently so." Gnatios paused before continuing. "The most holy patriarch will not be pleased with you for having enlarged me so."

"That's all right. I haven't been pleased with him for some time." Only after the words were out of his mouth did Krispos wonder how impolitic it was for him to run down the incumbent patriarch to a former holder of the office.

Not even Gnatios' eyebrow stirred; Krispos admired that. Gnatios chose his words with evident care: "Exactly how great a reward did your Majesty contemplate?"

Iakovitzes gobbled. Gnatios turned his way in surprise; Krispos, by now, was used to the noble's strange laugh. He felt like laughing himself. "So you want your old post back, do you, holy sir?"

"I suppose I should feel chagrin at being so obvious, but yes, your Majesty, I do. To be frank—" Krispos wondered if Gnatios was ever frank. "—the idea of that narrow zealot's possessing the patriarchal throne makes my blood boil."

"He loves you just as well," Krispos remarked.

"I'm aware of that. I respect his honesty and sincerity. Have you not found, though, your Majesty, that an honest fanatic poses certain problems of his own?"

Krispos wondered how much Gnatios knew of Pyrrhos' summons to the Grand Courtroom, of the riots outside the High Temple. *Quite a lot,* he suspected. Gnatios might be confined to his monastic cell, but Krispos was willing to bet he heard every whisper in the city.

"Holy sir, there is some truth in what you say," he admitted. He leaned forward, as if he were in the marketplace of Imbros—back in the days when Imbros' marketplace held life—haggling over the price of a shoat. "How can I hope to trust you, though, after you've betrayed me not once but twice?"

"Always an interesting question." Gnatios sighed, spreading his hands in front of him. "Your Majesty, I have no good answer for it. I will say that I would be a better patriarch than the one you have now."

"For as long as you take to decide someone else would make a better Emperor than the one you have now."

Gnatios bowed his head. "An argument I cannot counter."

"Here is what I will do, holy sir: from now on, you may come and go as you will, subject to the wishes of your abbot. I daresay you'll need something in writing." Krispos called for pen and parchment, wrote rapidly, signed and sealed the document, and handed it to Gnatios. "I hope you'll overlook faults of style and grammar."

"Your Majesty, for this document I would overlook a great deal," Gnatios said. In one sentence, that summed up the difference between him and Pyrrhos. Pyrrhos never overlooked anything for any reason.

"If you find anything more in your histories, be sure to let me know at once," Krispos said.

Gnatios understood the audience was over. He prostrated himself, rose, and started for the door. Barsymes met him there. The vestiarios asked, "Shall the Halogai accompany the holy sir back to his monastery?"

"No, let him go back by himself," Krispos said. He succeeded in surprising his chamberlain, no easy feat. With a bow of acquiescence and an expression that spoke volumes, Barsymes led Gnatios toward the door of the imperial residence.

Krispos listened to the two sets of footsteps fading down the hall. He turned to Iakovitzes. "Well, what now?"

"Do you mean, what now as in giving Gnatios the High Temple back, or what now as in Harvas?" Iakovitzes wrote.

"I don't know," Krispos said, "and by the good god, I never expected the two questions to be wrapped up with each other." He sighed. "Let's talk about the patriarch first. Pyrrhos must go." In the two weeks since Krispos went up into the imperial niche at the High Temple, two more fights had broken out there—both of them, fortunately, small.

Iakovitzes scribbled. "Aye, my dear cousin's not the most yielding sort, is he? If you do want Gnatios back, maybe you can keep him in line by threatening to feed him to the Halogai the first time the word *treason* so much as tiptoes across the back of his twisty little mind."

"Something to that." Krispos remembered how Gnatios had cringed from a guardsman's axe the night he seized the Empire. He looked down at the tablet in his lap, then admiringly over to Iakovitzes. "Do you know, I hear your voice whenever I read what you write. Your words on wax or parchment capture the very tone of your speech. Whenever I try to set thoughts down, they always seem so stiff and formal. How do you do it?"

"Genius," Iakovitzes wrote. Krispos made as if to break the tablet over his head. The noble reclaimed it, then wrote a good deal more. He handed it to Krispos. "If you must have a long answer, for one thing, I came to writing earlier in life than you and have used it a good deal longer. For another, this *is* my voice now. Shall I be silent merely because I can no longer utter the more or less articulate croaks that most men use for speech?"

"I see the answer is no," Krispos said, thinking that Iakovitzes was about as unyielding as his cousin Pyrrhos. Refusing to yield to adversity struck him as more admirable than refusing to yield to common sense. The thought of Iakovitzes' adversity led to the one who had caused it. "Now, what of Harvas?"

Bright fear widened Iakovitzes' eyes, then left them as he visibly took a grip on himself. He bent over the tablet, used the blunt end of his stylus to smooth down the wax and give himself room to write. At last he passed Krispos his words. "Fight him as best we can. What else is there? Now that we have some notion of what he is, perhaps the wizards will better be able to arm themselves against him."

Krispos thumped himself on the forehead with the heel of his hand. "By the lord with the great and good mind, I haven't any mind at all. Gnatios has to tell his tale to Trokoundos before the day is through." He shouted for Barsymes again. The vestiarios transcribed his note and took it to a courier for delivery to Trokoundos.

That accomplished, Krispos leaned back on the couch. He had the battered feeling of a man to whom too much had happened too fast. If Harvas or Rhavas or whatever his proper name was had been perfecting his dark sorcery over half a dozen men's lives, no wonder he'd overcome a mere mortal like Trokoundos.

"To the ice with Harvas or Rhavas or whatever his proper name is," he muttered.

"What about Pyrrhos?" Iakovitzes wrote.

"You like to poke people with pointy sticks, just to see them jump," Krispos said. Iakovitzes' look of shocked indignation might have convinced someone who hadn't met him more than half a minute before. Krispos went on, "I don't wish the ice for Pyrrhos. I just wish he'd go back to his monastery and keep quiet. I'm not even likely to get that, worse luck. He won't bend, the stiff-necked old—"

Krispos stopped. His mouth hung open. His eyes went wide. "What are you gawping at?" Iakovitzes wrote. "It had better be Phos' holy light, to account for that idiotic expression you're wearing."

"It's the next best thing," Krispos assured him. He raised his voice: "Barsymes! Are you still there? Ah, good. I want you to draft me a note to the most holy patriarch Pyrrhos. Here's what you need to say—"

Barsymes stuck his head into the audience chamber. "The most holy patriarch Pyrrhos is here to see you, your Majesty."

"Good. He should be done to a turn by now." Krispos had put off four days of increasingly urgent requests from the patriarch for an audience. He turned to Iakovitzes, Mammianos, and Rhisoulphos. "Excellent and eminent sirs, I ask you to bear careful witness to what takes place here today, so that you may take oath on it at need."

The three nobles nodded, formally and solemnly. Mammianos said, "This had better work."

"The beauty of it is, I'm no worse off if it doesn't," Krispos answered. "Now to business. I hear Pyrrhos coming."

The patriarch prostrated himself with his usual punctiliousness. He glanced at the three high-ranking men who sat to Krispos' left, but only for a moment. His eyes sparked as he swung them back to Krispos. "Your Majesty, I must vehemently protest this recent decision of yours." He drew out the note Krispos had sent him.

"Oh? Why is that, most holy sir?"

Pyrrhos' jaw set. He knew when he was being toyed with. With luck, he did not know why. He ground out, "Because, your Majesty, you have restored to the monk Gnatios—the treacherous, wicked monk Gnatios—as much liberty as is enjoyed by the other brethren of the monastery dedicated to the sacred memory of the holy Skirios. Moreover, you have done so without consulting me." Plainer than words, his face said what he would have answered had Krispos consulted him.

"The monk Gnatios did a great service for me and for the Empire," Krispos said. "Because of that, I've decided to overlook his past failings."

"*I* haven't," Pyrrhos said. "This interference in the internal affairs of the temples is unwarranted and intolerable."

"In this special case, I judged not. And let me remind you that the Avtokrator is Avtokrator over all the Empire, cities and farms and temples alike. Most holy sir, I have the right if I choose to use it, and I choose to use it here."

"Intolerable," Pyrrhos repeated. He drew himself up. "Your Majesty, if you persist in you pernicious course, I have no choice but to submit to you my resignation in protest thereof."

Off to Krispos' left, someone sighed softly. He thought it was Rhisoulphos. It was all the applause he would ever get, but it was more than enough. "I'm sorry to hear that from you, most holy sir," he said to Pyrrhos. Just by a hair's breath, the patriarch began to relax. But Krispos was not finished. "I accept your resignation. These gentlemen will attest you offered it of your own free will, with no coercion whatsoever."

Iakovitzes, Mammianos, and Rhisoulphos nodded, formally and solemnly.

"You—planned this," Pyrrhos said in a ghastly voice. He saw everything, too late.

"I did not urge you to resign," Krispos pointed out. "You did it yourself. Now that you have done it, Barsymes will prepare a document for you to sign."

"And if I refuse to set my signature upon it?"

"Then you have resigned even so. As I said, holy sir—"

Pyrrhos scowled at the abrupt devaluation of his title. "—you resigned of your own accord, in front of witnesses. That may be smoothest all around. I would have removed you if you insisted on staying on—you promised to practice theological economy and tolerate what you could, but none of your sermons has shown even one drop of tolerance."

Pyrrhos said, "I see everything now. You will replace me with that panderer to evil, Gnatios. Without your knowing it, the dark god has taken hold of your heart."

Krispos leaned forward and spat on the floor. "That to the dark god! Look at your cousin here, holy sir. Remember what Harvas Black-Robe did to him. Would he fall into any trap Skotos might lay?"

"Were it baited with a pretty boy, he might," Pyrrhos said.

Iakovitzes used a two-fingered gesture common on the streets of Videssos the city. Pyrrhos gasped. Krispos wondered when that gesture had last been aimed at a patriarch—no, an ex-patriarch, he amended. Iakovitzes wrote furiously and passed his tablet to Rhisoulphos. Rhisoulphos read it: " 'Cousin, the only bait you need is the hope of tormenting everyone who disagrees with you. Are you sure you have not swallowed it?' "

"I know I believe the truth; thus anyone who holds otherwise embraces falsehood," Pyrrhos said, "I see now that that includes those here. Majesty, you may ban me from preaching in the High Temple, but I shall take my message to the streets of the city—"

Now Krispos knew Pyrrhos was no intriguer. A man wiser in the ways of stirring up strife would never have warned what he planned to do. Krispos said, "If what you believe is the truth, holy sir, and if I have fallen into evil, how do you explain the vision that bade you help me like a son?"

Pyrrhos opened his mouth, then closed it again. Rhisoulphos leaned over to whisper to Krispos, "If nothing else, your Majesty, you've confused him."

Grateful even for so much, Krispos nodded. He told Pyrrhos, "Holy sir, I'm going to give you an honor guard of Halogai to escort you to the monastery of the holy Skirios. If you do decide to yell something foolish to the people in the street, they'll do what they have to, to keep you quiet." Pyrrhos could not terrify the heathen northerners with threats of Skotos' ice.

He could not be intimidated, either. "Let them do as they will."

"The monastery of the holy Skirios, eh?" Mammianos said. One eyelid rose, then fell. "I'm sure the holy sir and Gnatios will have a good deal to say to each other."

Having planted his barb, the fat general leaned back to enjoy it. Pyrrhos did not disappoint him. The cleric's glare was as cold and withering as the fiercest of ice storms. Mammianos affected not to notice it. He went on, "Of course, Gnatios will have the blue boots back soon enough."

"The good god shall judge between us in the world to come," Pyrrhos said. "I rest content with that." He turned to Krispos. "Phos shall judge you, as well, your Majesty."

"I know," Krispos answered. "Unlike you, holy sir, I'm far from sure of my answers. I do the best I can, even so."

Pyrrhos surprised him by bowing. "So the good god would expect of you. May your judgment be better in other instances than it is with me. Now summon your northerners, if you feel you must. Wherever you send me, I shall continue to praise Phos' holy name." He sketched the sun-circle over his heart.

In an abstract way, Krispos respected Pyrrhos' sincere piety. He did not let that respect blind him. When Pyrrhos departed from the imperial residence, he did so under guard. Iakovitzes nodded approval. "Just because someone sounds humble is no sure reason to trust him," he wrote.

"From what I've seen at the throne, there's no sure reason to trust anyone."

To his secret dismay, both Rhisoulphos and Mammianos nodded at that. Iakovitzes wrote, "You're learning." Krispos supposed he was, but did not care for the lessons his office taught him.

For the first time since Harvas' magic turned back the imperial army on the borders of Kubrat, Trokoundos seemed something more than gloomy. "I hope you intend to reward Gnatios for what he ferreted out," he told Krispos. "Without it, we'd still be stumbling around like so many blind men."

"I have a reward in mind, yes," Krispos said; at that moment, a synod of prelates and abbots was contemplating Gnatios' name for the patriarchate once more, along with those of two other men whom the assembled clerics knew they had better ignore. "Now that you know more of Harvas, will he be easier to defeat?"

"Knowing a bear has teeth, your Majesty, doesn't take those

teeth away," Trokoundos said. At Krispos' disappointed look, he went on, "still, since we know where he grew them, perhaps we can do something more about them. Perhaps."

"Such as?" Krispos asked eagerly.

"It's a fair guess, Majesty, that if he follows Skotos and draws his power from the dark god, his spells will invert the usages with which we're familiar. That may make them easier to meet than if he, say, truly clove to the Haloga gods or the demons and spirits the steppe nomads revere. Magic from the nomads or the northerners can come at you from any direction, if you know what I mean."

"I think so," Krispos said. "But if their mages or shamans or what have you can invoke their gods and demons and have magic work, does that make those gods and demons as true as Phos and Skotos?"

Trokoundos tugged thoughtfully at his ear. "Majesty, I think that's a question better suited to the patriarch's wisdom, or that of an ecumenical synod, than to one who aspires to nothing more than competent wizardry."

"As you wish. In any case, it takes us off the track. You know the direction from which Harvas' spells will come, you say?"

"So I believe, your Majesty. This aids us to a point, but only to a point. Harvas' strength and skill must still be overcome. The one, I have already seen, is formidable. As for the other, three centuries ago it sufficed to free him from a warded cell. He can only have refined it in all the years since. That he remains alive to torment us proves he has refined it."

"What shall we do, then?" Krispos asked. He'd hoped having a handle on Harvas would give the mages of Videssos the means to defeat him with minimal risk to themselves or to the Empire. But he'd long since found that things in the real world had a way of being less simple and less easy than in storytellers' tales. This looked like another lesson from that school.

Trokoundos' words confirmed his own thoughts. "The best we can, your Majesty, and pray to the lord with the great and good mind that it be enough."

Bad weather settled in not long before Midwinter's Day. Blizzard after blizzard roared into Videssos the city from the northwest, off the Videssian Sea. On Midwinter's Day itself, the snow blew so hard and quick that even Krispos, with the best seat in the Amphitheater, made out little of the skits performed on the track before him. The people in the upper reaches of the huge oval stadium could have discerned only drifting white.

The final troupe of mimes changed its act at the last minute. They came out carrying canes and tapped their way through their routine, as if they'd all suddenly been stricken blind. On the spine of the Amphitheater, Krispos laughed loudly. So did many in his entourage, and in the first few rows of seats around the track. Everyone else must have wondered what was funny—which was just the point the mimes were making. Krispos laughed even more when he worked that out.

On the way back to the palaces after the show in the Amphitheater was done, he leaped over a bonfire to burn away misfortune for the coming year. That fire was but one of many that blazed each Midwinter's Day. This year, though, the good-luck bonfires brought misfortune with them. Whipped by winter gales, two got out of control and ignited nearby buildings.

Now Krispos saw through swirling snow the smudges of smoke he'd feared during the religious riots Pyrrhos had caused. The snow did little to slow the flames. Fire-fighting teams dashed through the city with hand pumps to shoot water from fountains and ponds, with axes and sledgehammers to knock down homes and shops to build firebreaks. Krispos had no great hope for them. When fire got loose, it usually pleased itself, not any man.

The teams amazed him. They succeeded in stopping one of the fires before it had eaten more than a block of buildings. The other blaze, by luck, had started near the city wall. It burned what it could, then came to the open space inside the barrier and died for lack of fuel.

Krispos presented a pound of gold to the head of the team that beat the first fire, a middle-age fellow with a fine head of silver hair and a matter-of-fact competence that suggested years as a soldier. Nobles and logothetes in the Grand Courtroom applauded the man, whose name was Thokyodes.

"Along with this reward from the grateful state," Krispos said, "I also give you ten goldpieces from my private purse."

More applause rose. Thokyodes clenched his right fist over his heart in salute—he *was* a veteran, then. "Thank you, your Majesty," he said, pleased but far from obsequious.

"Maybe you'll use one of those ten on a potion to make your eyebrows grow back faster," Krispos said, soft enough that only he and the team leader heard.

Not a bit put out, Thokyodes laughed and ran the palm of his hand across his forehead. "Aye, I do look strange without 'em, don't I? They got singed right off me." He made no effort to keep his voice down. "Fighting fires is just like fighting any other foe. The closer you get, the better you do."

"You did the city a great service," Krispos said.

"Couldn't've done it without my crew. By your leave, your Majesty, I'll share this with all of them." Thokyodes held up the sack of goldpieces.

"It's your money now, to do with as you please," Krispos said. The applause that rang out this time was unrehearsed, sincere, and startled. Few of the courtiers, men who had far more than this fireman, would have been as generous, and they knew it. Krispos wondered if he would have matched the man had fate led him to an ordinary job instead of the throne. He hoped so, but admitted to himself that he was not sure.

"I think you would have," Dara said when he wondered again later in the day, this time aloud. "This I'll tell you—Harvas wouldn't."

"Harvas? Harvas would have stood next to the fire with his cheeks puffed out, to blow it along." Krispos smiled at his conceit. A moment later the smile blew out. He sketched Phos' sun-circle. "By the good god, how do I know his magic didn't help the blazes spread?"

"You don't, but if you start seeing him under our bed whenever anything goes wrong, you'll have your head down there all the time, because we don't need Harvas to know misfortune."

"That's true," Krispos said. "You have good sense." His smile came back, this time full of gratitude. Harvas was quite bad enough without a fearful imagination making him worse.

Dara said, "I do try. It's nice that you notice. I remember when—" She stopped without telling Krispos what she remembered when. It had to do with Anthimos, then. Krispos did not blame her for steering away from that time; it had not been happy for her. But that meant several years of her life, the ones before Krispos became vestiarios, were almost blank to him, which occasionally led to awkward pauses like this one.

He wondered if every second husband and second wife endured them. *Probably,* he thought. It would have been more awkward yet had her marriage to Anthimos been a good one. A lot more awkward, he realized with an inward chuckle, because then she would not have told him Anthimos intended to kill him.

"Can't get much more awkward than that," he muttered under his breath.

"Than what?" Dara asked.

"Never mind."

Whenever fat Longinos burst in on him on the dead run, Krispos braced for trouble. The chamberlain, to his disappointment, did not disappoint him. "Majesty," Longinos gasped, wiping his brow with a silken kerchief—only a fat eunuch could have been sweaty after so trivial an exertion; it was freezing outside and not a great deal warmer inside the imperial residence. "Majesty, the most holy patriarch Pyrrhos—I'm sorry, your Majesty, I mean the monk Pyrrhos—is preaching against you in the street."

"*Is* he, by the good god?" Krispos sprang up from his desk so quickly that a couple of tax registers fluttered to the floor. He let them lie there. So Pyrrhos' indignation at being removed from the patriarchal throne really had overcome his longtime loyalty, had it? "What's he saying?"

"He's spewing forth a great vomit of scandal, your Majesty, over, ah, over your, ah, your relationship with her Majesty the Empress Dara before you, ah, rose to the imperial dignity." Longinos sounded indignant for his master's sake, though he had known Krispos and Dara were lovers long before they were man and wife.

"*Is* he?" Krispos said again. "He'll spew forth his life's blood before I'm through with him."

Longinos' eyes went large with dismay. "Oh, no, your Majesty. To cut down one but lately so high in the temples, one still with many backers who—begging your pardon, your Majesty— deem him more holy than the present wearer of the blue boots . . . your Majesty, it would mean more blood than Pyrrhos' alone. It would mean riots."

He'd found the word he needed to stop Krispos in his tracks. Dividing the city—dividing the Empire—against itself was the one thing Krispos could not afford. "But," he said, as if arguing with himself, "I can't afford to let Pyrrhos defame me, either. If that nonsense goes on for long, it'll bring some would-be usurper out of the woodwork, sure as sure."

"Indeed, your Majesty," Longinos said. "Were you ten years on the throne rather than two—not even two—you might let him rant, confident he would be ignored. As it is—"

"Aye. As it is, people will listen to him. They'll take him

seriously, too, thanks to his piety." Krispos snorted. "As if anyone could take Pyrrhos any way but seriously. I've hardly seen him smile in all the years I've known him, the somber old—" He stopped, laughing out loud. When he could speak again, he asked, "Where is Pyrrhos giving this harangue of his?"

"In the Forum of the Ox, your Majesty," Longinos said.

"All right; he should be easy enough to find there. Now, esteemed sir, this is what I want you to do—" He spoke for several minutes, finishing. "Do you think you should have something in writing from me, to make sure my orders get carried out?"

"Yes, that would be best." Longinos looked half amused, half scandalized. Krispos wrote quickly and handed him the scrap of parchment. The eunuch read it over, shook his head, then visibly pulled himself together. "I shall have this delivered immediately, your Majesty."

"See that you do," Krispos said. Longinos hurried away, calling for a courier. Krispos prided himself on not wasting time, so he reviewed another tax document before he ambled out to the entrance to the imperial residence. The Halogai there stood to stiff attention. "As you were, lads," he told them. "We're going for a walk."

"Where are your parasol-bearers, then, Majesty?" Geirrod asked.

"They'd just get in the way today," Krispos said. The Halogai stirred at that. A couple of them ran fingers down the edges of their axeblades to make sure the weapons were sharp. One must have found a tiny nick, for he took out a whetstone and went to work with it. When he checked again, the axe passed his test. He put away the stone.

"Where to, Majesty?" Geirrod said.

"The Forum of the Ox," Krispos answered lightly. "Seems the holy Pyrrhos isn't taking kindly to not being patriarch any more. He's saying some rather rude things about me there."

The Halogai stirred again, this time in anticipation. "You want us to curb his tongue for him, eh?" said the one who had sharpened his axe. He examined his edge anew, as if to make certain it could bite through a holy man's neck.

But Krispos said, "No, no. I don't aim to harm the holy sir, just to shut him up."

"Better you should kill him," Geirrod said. "Then he'll not trouble you ever again." The rest of the guardsmen nodded.

Krispos wished he could view the world with the ferocious simplicity the Halogai used. In Videssos, though, few things were as simple as they seemed. Without answering Geirrod, Krispos strode down the stairs. The northerners came after him, surrounding him to hold potential assassins at bay.

The Forum of the Ox was a mile and half, perhaps two miles east down Middle Street from the palace quarter. Krispos walked briskly to keep warm. He was glad of his escort as he passed through the plaza of Palamas; as usual, the Halogai marched in a way that said they would trample anyone who did not get clear. Crowds melted before them, as if by magic.

He hurried down Middle Street. He wanted to catch Pyrrhos in the act of preaching against him; whatever punishment he might mete out after the fact, no matter how savage, would not have the effect he wanted. Making a martyr out of the prelate was the last thing he had in mind.

A few hundred yards past the government office building, Middle Street jogged to the south. The Forum of the Ox lay not far ahead. Krispos sped up till he was almost trotting. To have Pyrrhos get away from him now would be unbearably frustrating. He hoped again that his orders had gone through on time.

In ancient days, the Forum of the Ox had been Videssos the city's chief cattle market. It was still an important trading center for goods bulkier, more mundane, and less expensive than those sold in the plaza of Palamas: livestock, grain, cheap pottery, and olive oil. People here stared at Krispos' escort before they got out of the way. In the plaza of Palamas, close by the palaces, they were used to seeing the Avtokrator. He was a much less frequent visitor in this poorer part of the city.

A quick glance around the square showed him what he sought: a knot of men and women gathered around a man in a blue monk's robe. The monk—even across the square, Krispos recognized Pyrrhos' tall, thin frame and lean face—stood on a barrel or box or stone that raised him head and shoulders above his audience. Krispos pointed. "Over there." The Halogai nodded. They moved on Pyrrhos with the directness of a pack of wolves advancing on a wisent.

Pyrrhos was a trained orator. Long before he reached the rear edge of the crowd that listened to the cleric, Krispos could hear what he was saying. So could half the people in the Forum of the Ox. "He must have learned his corruption from the master he formerly served, for surely depravity was the name by which

Anthimos was better known. Yet in his own way, Krispos outdid Anthimos in vice, first seducing the previous Avtokrator's wife, then using her against her husband to climb over his dead body to the throne. How will—how can—Phos bless our efforts with such a man inhabiting the palaces?''

Pyrrhos must have seen Krispos and his bodyguards approach, but he did not pause in his address. Krispos already knew he had courage. Pyrrhos also did not suddenly break off his speech to point out to his audience that the adulterous monster he had been denouncing was here. That, in his sandals, Krispos might have tried, if he truly aimed to overthrow someone. But Pyrrhos did not deviate from what he had decided to say: his mind was made up, which left no room in it for change.

Krispos folded his arms to listen. Pyrrhos continued his harangue as if the Avtokrator were not there. He paid even less attention to the squad of firemen who dashed into the Forum of the Ox. Others round the square glanced up in some alarm at the sight of the men armed with Haloga-style axes and with a hand pump carried by two men who were sweating even in the chill of winter. Especially after the close escape on Midwinter's Day, fire was a constant fear in the city.

But the fire team made straight for the crowd round the gesticulating monk. ''Make way!'' the fire captain shouted.

People tumbled away from the crew. ''Where's the fire?'' somebody yelled.

''Right here!'' Thokyodes yelled back. ''Leastways, I got orders to put out this incendiary here.'' He waved to his crew. One of them swung the pump handle up and down. The other turned his hose toward Pyrrhos.

Cold water from the hand pump's wooden tub gushed forth. The people nearest Pyrrhos stampeded away from him, cursing and spluttering as they went. Pyrrhos himself tried to speak on through his drenching, but started to sneeze whether he wanted to or not. The fire team kept hosing him down until the tub was empty. Then Thokyodes looked over to Krispos. ''Shall we fill 'er up again, your Majesty?''

Pyrrhos looked as if a little more would drown him. ''No, that's fine, Thokyodes, thank you,'' Krispos said. ''I think he's been cooled down very nicely.''

''Cooled down—*ahhchoo!*—am I?'' Pyrrhos shouted. Water dripped from his beard and from the end of his nose. ''Nay, I've just—*ahhchoo!*—begun to speak the truth about our imperial adulterer. Now hear me, people of Videssos—''

"Go home and dry off, holy sir," someone called, not un-kindly. "You'll take a flux on the lungs if you go on like this."

"Aye, your tale's as soggy as your robe anyhow," someone else said.

A woman added, "Save the fire in your belly to warm your-self."

"No, the crew just doused that fire," a man said. He chuckled at his own wit.

Pyrrhos had lived all his adult life in monasteries or attached to one temple or another. He was used to respect from the laity, not gibes—not even gibes kindly meant. But worse than those gibes was the laughter that sprang from so many throats at the spectacle of a furious, drenched, shivering holy man standing on his perch—it was an overturned box, Krispos saw—trying to keep on with his denunciation through teeth that chattered loud as the wooden finger cymbals Vaspurakaner dancers used to clack out their rhythm.

He might have stood up against being ignored: because they preached the virtues of a way of life more austere than most folk would willingly embrace, monks were often ignored. But laugh-ter he could not endure. Glaring at the crowd in general and Krispos in particular, he awkwardly scrambled down from his box and stalked away. A fresh sneezing spasm robbed even his departure of dignity.

"Phos with you, drippy Pyrrhos!" a man with a loud voice yelled after him. New laughter rang out. Pyrrhos' back, already stiff, jerked as if someone had stuck a knife into him. "Drippy Pyrrhos, good old drippy Pyrrhos," the crowd sang. His de-parture turned to headlong retreat; by the time he reached the edge of the Forum of the Ox, he was all but running.

Geirrod turned to Krispos. "He'll love you no better for this, Majesty," the guardsman said. "Make a man out a fool and he'll reckon himself at feud with you no less than if you'd slashed him with sword."

"He's already at feud with me, and with everyone else who won't think and do just as he does," Krispos answered. "Now, though, the good god willing, people won't take him so seriously. The holy Pyrrhos—until lately, the most holy Pyrrhos—was someone whose notions you'd respect. But how much attention would you pay to good old drippy Pyr-rhos?"

"Ahh, now I see it," Geirrod said slowly. "You've poi-soned his word." He spoke in his own language to his fellow northerners. Their deep voices rose and fell; their eyes swung toward Krispos. Geirrod said, "Who but a Videssian would think to slay a man with laughter?" The other Halogai nodded solemnly.

A few feet away, Thokyodes gestured to his crew. The two men who had hauled the pump around now set it down with grunts of relief. The rest leaned on their fire axes, save for one who strolled off toward a fellow selling roasted chickpeas.

Thokyodes caught Krispos' eye. When Krispos did not look away, the fire captain came over to him. "Well, your Majesty, I hope we put out some trouble for you there," he said. Thokyodes was Videssian and, by his accent, a city man. He required no explanations to understand what Krispos had planned.

"I think you did," Krispos said. "You'll be rewarded for it, too."

"I thank you," Thokyodes said briskly. He did not try to protest his own unworthiness. Business was business.

Krispos raised his voice and called out, "All right, folks, the show is over for today." The crowd that had been listening to Pyrrhos rapidly melted away. A few people averted their faces as they went by Krispos, as if they did not want him to know they had been anywhere near someone who preached against him. More, though, went off chattering happily; as far as they were concerned, Pyrrhos' harangue and Krispos' response to it might have been arranged only for their amusement. City folk were like that, Krispos thought with a touch of exasperation.

By the time he and the Halogai got back to the palaces, winter's short day was almost done. Longinos looked ready to burst from curiosity when Krispos came into the imperial residence. "Your Majesty, surely you didn't—"

"—treat Pyrrhos as if he were a fire that needed putting out?" Krispos broke in. "Oh, but I did, esteemed sir." He explained how Thokyodes and his crew had hosed down the cleric, finishing, "Most of the people who saw it got a good laugh out of it."

Like the fire captain, Longinos caught on in a hurry. "Hard to take a laughingstock seriously, eh, your Majesty?"

"Just so, esteemed sir. I remembered how much trouble Petronas had, trying to get rid of Skombros when he was vestiarios. No matter how plainly he showed Anthimos that Skombros was a scoundrel, Anthimos stood by him. But when he arranged to have Skombros laughed at, he was out of the palaces within a week.''

"Ah, yes, Skombros," Longinos murmured. By his voice, he might have forgotten that the eunuch who was once Petronas' rival as the chief power behind Anthimos' throne had ever existed. Krispos was undeceived. Longinos went on, "The good god willing, your Majesty, Pyrrhos will have been dealt with as, ah, thoroughly as Skombros was."

Krispos sketched the sun-sign. "May it be so."

Iron-shod hooves clattered on cobblestones. Chain mail jingled. "Eyes to the right!" an officer bawled. As the regiment rode past the reviewing stand, the lead troopers looked over to Krispos and saluted.

He put his fist over his heart in return. The crowd that lined both sides of Middle Street cheered. The soldiers, most of them in Videssos the city for the first time, grinned at the cheers and went back to gaping at the wonders of the imperial capital. Awed expressions aside, the young men from the westlands' central plateau looked like solid troops, well mounted and in good spirits despite the long, grueling slog that had at last brought them here to the city.

A raindrop splashed off Krispos' cheek, then another and another. The soldiers riding by reached up to tug the hoods of their surcoats lower on their foreheads. Some spectators opened umbrellas; other retreated under the colonnades that flanked the thoroughfare.

When the last horse had trotted past, Krispos stepped down from the reviewing stand with a sigh of relief. By then he was just about as wet as Pyrrhos had been after Thokyodes turned the pump on him. He was glad to mount Progress and head back to the imperial residence. A brisk toweling, a bowl of hot mutton stew, and a fresh robe worked wonders for his attitude. After all, he thought, it had been rain, not snow. Winter's grip would ease soon. When the roads dried, the army he was assembling here would move north against Harvas. He hoped to have seventy thousand men under arms. Surely the Empire's full weight, backed by the cleverest mages of the Sorcerers' Collegium, could overcome one wicked wizard who somehow refused to die.

Barsymes carried away the silver bowl that had held stew. He paused in the doorway. "Majesty, do I need to remind you that the envoy of the King of Kings of Makuran has arranged for an audience with you this afternoon?''

"I remember," Krispos said, not altogether happily. He wished he could forget about Videssos' great western neighbor, the more so as he was concentrating so much of his army against the Empire's northern foe. He had already discovered that wishes availed little in statecraft.

Chihor-Vshnasp, the Makuraner envoy, was an elegant man of middle years, with a long rectangular face, deep hollows under his cheekbones, and large, soulful brown eyes that looked perfectly candid. Looks, Krispos knew, were not to be trusted. When Chihor-Vshnasp performed the proskynesis before him, the ambassador's headgear, a brimless gray felt hat that looked like nothing so much as a bucket, fell from his head and rolled a few feet away. "That happens every time you come to see me," Krispos observed.

"So it does, your Majesty. A small indignity of no import between friends." Chihor-Vshnasp retrieved the errant hat and replaced it on his head. His Videssian was excellent; only a trace of his native hiss said he was not an educated native of Videssos the city. He went on, "I bring you the greetings of his puissant Majesty Nakhorgan, King of Kings, pious, beneficent, to whom the God and his Prophets Four have granted many years and wide domains."

"I am always glad to have the greetings of his puissant Majesty," Krispos said. "In your next dispatch to Mashiz, please send him mine."

Chihor-Vshnasp bowed in his seat. "He will be honored to receive them. He also wishes me to convey to you his hope for your success against the vicious barbarians who assail your northern frontier. Makuran has suffered inroads from such savages; his puissant Majesty knows what Videssos is enduring now and sympathizes with your pain."

"His puissant Majesty is very kind." Krispos thought he had caught the drift of the conversation. He hoped he was wrong.

Unfortunately, he was right. Chihor-Vshnasp continued, "I add my hopes to his: may your war be successful. Since you have invested so much of Videssos' strength in it, no doubt you will vanquish your foes. Without peace with Makuran, there can be no doubt that some of your armies would have remained in the westlands. Indeed, your decision to commit them speaks well of your confidence in the enduring amity between our two great empires."

Now Krispos knew what was coming. The only question was how expensive it would prove. "Should I think otherwise?" he asked.

"Not all leaders of Videssos have felt as you do," Chihor-Vshnasp reminded him. "Only yesterday, it seems, the Sevastokrator Petronas launched an unprovoked assault against Makuran."

"I opposed that war," Krispos said.

"I remember, and I honor you for it. Nonetheless, you must be aware of what would happen if his puissant Majesty Nakhorgan, King of Kings, chose this summer to avenge himself for the insult offered to Makuran. With your forces directed away from your western border, our brave horsemen would charge ahead, sweeping all before them."

Krispos wanted to bite his lip. He held his face still instead. "You're right, of course," he said. Chihor-Vshnasp's iron-gray eyebrows arched. That was not how the game was played. Krispos went on, "If his puissant Majesty really intended to invade Videssos, you wouldn't come here to warn me. How much does he want for being talked out of it?"

Those eyebrows rose again; the envoy was an artist with them. He said, "It is an intolerable affront to the God and his Prophets Four that Makuran should remain bereft of the valley that contains the great cities of Hanzith and Artaz."

Between them, the two little Vaspurakaner town might have held half as many people as, say, Opsikion. "Makuran may have them back." Krispos said, abandoning with a sentence the valley that was the sole fruit of Petronas' war of three years before, the war Petronas had thought would take him all the way to Mashiz.

"Your Majesty is gracious and generous," Chihor-Vshnasp said with a small smile. "With such goodwill, all difficulties between nations may yet fall by the wayside, and peace and harmony prevail. Yet his puissant Majesty the King of Kings Nakhorgan remains aggrieved that you love other sovereigns more than him."

"How can you say such a thing?" Krispos cried, the picture of shock and dismay. "No ruler could be dearer to my heart than your master."

Chihor-Vshnasp sadly shook his head. "Would that his puissant Majesty could believe you! Yet he has seen you fling great sums of gold to this wretch known as Harvas Black-Robe, who rewarded you with nothing but treachery. And his puissant Majesty, the good and true friend of Videssos, has not known so much as a copper of your great bounty.''

"How many coppers would satisfy him?" Krispos asked dryly.

"You paid Harvas a hundred pounds of gold, not so? Surely a good and true friend is worth three times as much as a lying barbarian who takes your money and then does as he would have had you never paid him. Indeed, your Majesty, I reckon that a bargain.''

"A bargain?" Krispos clapped a dramatic hand to his forehead. "I reckon that an outrage. His puissant Majesty is looking to suck Videssos' blood and asks us to give him a solid gold straw with which to drink.''

The dickering went on for several days. Krispos knew he would have to pay Nakhorgan more than he had given Harvas; the King of Kings' honor demanded it. But paying Nakhorgan a lot more than he had given Harvas went against Krispos' grain. For his part, Chihor-Vshnasp haggled more like a rug merchant than a Makuraner grandee.

At last they settled on a hundred fifty pounds of gold: 10,800 goldpieces. "Excellent, your Majesty," Chihor-Vshnasp said when they reached agreement.

Krispos did not think it was excellent; he'd hoped to get away with something closer to a hundred twenty-five pounds. But Chihor-Vshnasp knew too well how badly he needed peace with Makuran. He said, "His puissant Majesty has an able servant in you.''

"You give me credit beyond my worth," Chihor-Vshnasp said, but his voice had a purr in it, like a stroked cat's.

"No indeed," Krispos said. "I will order the gold sent out today.''

"And I shall inform his puissant Majesty that it has begun its journey to him." Looking as pleased with himself as if the hundred fifty pounds of gold were going to him instead of his master, Chihor-Vshnasp made his elaborate farewells and departed.

"Barsymes!" Krispos called.

The vestiarios appeared in the doorway, prompt and punctual as usual. "How may I help you, your Majesty?''

"What in Skotos' cursed name does puissant mean?''

Phostis toddled out of the imperial residence on uncertain legs. He blinked at the bright spring sunshine, then decided he liked it and smiled. One of the Halogai grinned and pointed. "The little Avtokrator, he has teeth!"

"Half a dozen of them," Krispos agreed. "Another one's on the way, too, so he'll chew your greaves off if you let him get near you."

The guardsmen drew back in mock fright, laughing all the while. Phostis charged toward the stairs. He'd only been able to walk without holding on to something for about a week, but he had the hang of it. Going down stairs was something else again. Phostis' plan was to walk blithely off the first one he came to, just to see what would happen. Krispos caught him before he found out.

Far from feeling rescued, Phostis squirmed and kicked and squawked in Krispos' arms. "Aren't you the ungrateful one?" Krispos said as he carried the toddler to the bottom of the stairway. "Would you rather I'd let you smash your silly head?"

By all indications, Phostis would have preferred exactly that. When Krispos put him down at the base of the stairs, he refused to stay there. Instead, he started to climb back toward the top. He had to crawl to do it; the risers were too tall for him to raise his little legs from one to the next. Krispos followed close behind, in case ascent turned to sudden and unplanned descent. Phostis reached the top unscathed—then spun around and tried to jump down. Krispos caught him again.

In the entranceway to the residence, someone clapped. Krispos looked up and saw Dara. "Bravely done, Krispos," she called, mischief in her voice. "You've saved the heir to the state." The Halogai bowed as she came out into the sunshine. Now no robe, no matter how flowing, could conceal her swelling abdomen.

Krispos looked down at Phostis. "The heir to the state won't live to inherit it unless somebody keeps an eye on him every minute of the day and night." As soon as the words were out of his mouth, he wondered if Dara would take them the wrong way; he'd lived in Videssos the city too long to be unaware that plotting, even ahead of the races in the Amphitheater, was its favorite sport.

She only smiled and said, "Babies are like that." She turned toward the sun and closed her eyes. "During the winter, you think it will never get warm and dry again. I'd like to be a lizard and just stand here and bask." But after she'd basked for a minute or two, her smile faded. "I always used to wish winter would end as soon as it could. Now I half want it to last longer—

the good weather means you'll be going out on campaign, doesn't it?''

"You know it does," Krispos said. "Unless we get another rainstorm, the roads should be dry enough to travel by the end of the week."

Dara nodded. "I know. Will you be angry if I tell you I'm worried?''

"No," he answered after some thought. "I'm worried, too." He looked north and east. He couldn't see much, not with the cherry trees that surrounded the imperial residence in such riotous pink bloom, but he knew Harvas was there waiting for him. The knowledge was anything but reassuring.

"I wish you could stay here behind the safety of the city's walls," Dara said.

He remembered his awe on the day he first came to Videssos the city and saw its massive double ring of fortifications. Surely even Harvas could find no way to overthrow them. Then he remembered other things as well: Develtos, Imbros, and Trokoundos' warning that he should meet Harvas as far from the city as he could. Trokoundos had a way of knowing what he was talking about.

"I don't think there's safety anywhere, not while Harvas is on the loose," he said slowly. After a moment, Dara nodded again. He saw how much it cost her.

Phostis wiggled in his arms. He set the boy down. A Haloga took out his dagger, undid the sheath from his belt, and tossed it near Phostis. Gold inlays ornamented the sheath. Their glitter drew Phostis, who picked it up and started chewing on it.

"It's brass and leather," Krispos told him. "You won't like it." A moment later Phostis made a ghastly face and took the sheath out of his mouth. A moment after that, he started gnawing on it again.

From behind Dara, Barsymes said, "Here are some proper toys." He rolled a little wooden wagon to Phostis. Inside it were two cleverly carved horses. Phostis picked them up, then threw them aside. He raised the wagon to his mouth and began to chew on a wheel.

"Stick him by a river, he'll cut down trees like a beaver," a Haloga said. Everyone laughed except Barsymes, who let out an indignant sniff.

Krispos watched Phostis playing in the sunshine. He suddenly bent down to run a hand through the little boy's thick

black hair. He saw Dara's eyes widen with surprise; he seldom showed Phostis physical affection. But he knew beyond
any possible doubt that, even if Phostis happened to be Anthimos' son rather than his own, he would far, far sooner,
see him ruling the Empire of Videssos than Harvas Black-
Robe.

# IX

THE IMPERIAL ARMY WAS LIKE A CITY ON THE MARCH. AS FAR as Krispos could see in any direction were horses and helmets and spearpoints and wagons. They overflowed the road and moved northward on either side. Yet even in the midst of so many armed men, Krispos did not feel altogether secure. He had gone north with an army before and come back defeated.

"What are our chances, Trokoundos?" he asked, anxious to be reassured.

The wizard's lips twitched; Krispos had asked the same question less than an hour before. As he had before, Trokoundos answered: "Were no magic to be used by either side, Majesty. I could hope to ascertain that for you. As it is, spells yet to be cast befog any magic I might use. I assure you, though, Harvas enters this campaign as blind as we do."

Krispos wondered how true that was. Harvas might have no sorcerous foretelling, but he'd lived as long as five or six ordinary men. On how much of that vast experience could he draw, to scent what his foes would do next?

"Will we have enough mages to hold him in check?"

"There, your Majesty, I can be less certain," Trokoundos said. "By the lord with the great and good mind, though, we now have a better notion of how to try to cope with him, thanks to the researches of Gnatios."

"Thanks to Gnatios," Krispos repeated, not altogether happily. Now instead of a patriarch who backed him absolutely but thought nothing of setting the whole Empire ablaze for the sake of perfect orthodoxy, he had once more a patriarch who was theologically moderate but not to be trusted out of sight—or in it, for that matter. He hoped the trade would prove worthwhile.

Trokoundos continued, "When I faced Harvas last year, I took him for a barbarian wizard, puissant but—why are you laughing, your Majesty?"

"Never mind," Krispos said, laughing still. "Go on, please."

"Ahem. Well, as I say, I reckoned Harvas Black-Robe to be powerful but unschooled. Now I know this is not the case—just the reverse obtains, in fact. Having now, thanks to Gnatios, a better notion of the sort of magic he employes, and having also with me more—and more potent—colleagues, I do possess some hope that we shall be able to defend against his onslaughts."

All the finest mages of the Sorcerers' Collegium rode with the army. If Trokoundos could but hope to withstand Harvas by their combined efforts, that in itself spoke volumes about the evil wizard's strength. They were not volumes Krispos cared to read. He said, "Can we sorcerously strike back at the northerners who follow Harvas?"

"Your Majesty, we will try," Trokoundos said. "The good god willing, we will distract Harvas from the magics he might otherwise hurl at us. Past that, I have no great hope. Because battle so inflames men's passions, magic more readily slips aside from them then and is more easily countered. That is why battle magic succeeds so seldom . . . save Harvas'." Krispos wished the wizard had not tacked on that codicil.

Rhisoulphos rode by at a fast trot. "Why aren't you with your regiment?" Krispos called.

His father-in-law reined in and looked around, as if wondering who presumed to address him with such familiarity. His face cleared when he saw Krispos. "Greetings, your Majesty," he said, saluting. "I just gave a courier a note to a friend in the city, and now I am indeed returning to my men. By your leave . . ." He waited for Krispos' nod, then dug his heels into his horse's flanks and urged the animal on again.

Krispos followed him with his eyes. Rhisoulphos did not look back. He rode as if in a competition of horsemanship, without a single wasted motion. "He's so smooth," Krispos said, as much to himself as to Trokoundos. "He rides smoothly, he talks smoothly, he has smooth good looks and smooth good sense."

"But you don't like him," Trokoundos said. It was not a question.

"No, I don't. I want to. I ought to. He's Dara's father, after all. But with so much smoothness on the top of him, who can be sure what's underneath? Petronas guessed wrong and paid for it, too.''

''Set next to Harvas—''

''Every other worry is a small one. I know. But I have to keep an eye on the small things, too, for fear they'll grow while my back was turned. I wonder who he was writing to. You know, Trokoundos, what I really need is a spell that would give me eyes all around my head and let me stay awake day and night both. Then I'd sleep better—except I wouldn't sleep, would I?'' Krispos stopped. ''I've confused myself.''

Trokoundos smiled. ''Never mind, your Majesty. No wizard can give you what you asked for, so there's no point in fretting over it.''

''I suppose not. Fretting over Rhisoulphos, though, is something else again.'' Krispos looked ahead once more, but the general had vanished—smoothly—among the swarms of riders heading north.

The army did not cover much more ground in a day than a walking man might have. When the troopers moved, they set a decent pace. But getting them moving each morning and getting them into camp every night ate away at the time they were able to spend on the road. That had also been true of the forces Krispos led against Petronas and against Harvas the summer before, but to a lesser degree. One of the things a huge army meant was huge inefficiency.

''That's just the way it goes,'' Mammianos said when Krispos complained. ''We can't move out in the morning till the slowest soldiers are ready to go. If we let quicker regiments just rush on ahead, after a few days we'd have men strung out over fifty miles. The whole point of a big army is to be able to use all the troops you've brought along.''

''Supplies—'' Krispos said, as if it were a complete sentence.

Mammianos clapped him on the shoulder. ''Majesty, unless we crawl north on our hands and knees, we'll manage. The quartermasters know how fast—how slow, if you like—we travel. They've had practice keeping armies this size in bread, I promise you.''

Krispos let himself be reassured. The Videssian bureaucracy had kept the Empire running throughout Anthimos' antic reign and through worse reigns than his in the past. Avtokrators came, ruled, and were gone; the gray, efficient stewards, secretaries, and logothetes went on forever. The army quartermasters be-longed to the same breed.

He wondered what would happen if one day an Emperor died and no one succeeded him. He suspected the bureaucrats would go on ruling competently if unspectacularly . . . at least until some important paper needed signing. Then, for want of a sig-nature, the whole state would come crashing down. He chuckled softly, pleased at his foolish conceit.

The next day the army rode past the field when Harvas' raiders had beaten and killed Mavros. The mass graves Krispos' men had dug afterward still scarred the earth. Now new grass, green and hopeful, was spreading over the squares of raw dirt. Krispos pointed to it. "Like the grass, may our victory spring from their defeat."

"From your lips to the ear of Phos," Trokoundos said, sketching the sun-sign with his right hand. He sent Krispos a sly look. "I hadn't thought your Majesty had so much of a poet in him."

"Poet?" Krispos snorted. "I'm no poet, just a farmer—well, a man who used to be a farmer. The grass will grow tall over those graves, with the bodies of so many brave men manuring the fields."

The mage nodded soberly. "That's a less pleasing image, but I daresay a truer one."

They camped three or four miles past the battlefield, far enough, Krispos hoped, to keep the troopers from brooding on it. As was his habit each evening, Krispos wrote a brief note to Iakovitzes detailing the day's progress. When he was done, he called for a courier.

A rider came trotting up to the imperial tent hardly a minute later. He saluted Krispos and said, "All right, your Majesty, let's have yours, too, and I'll be off for the city."

He sat his horse with a let's-get-on-with-it, don't-waste-my-time attitude that made Krispos smile. That attitude and the blithe cheek of his words left Krispos certain he was a city man himself. "Mine, too, is it, eh? Well, sir, with whose letter is mine lucky enough to travel?"

"It's all in the family, you might say, your Majesty: yours and your father-in-law's will go together, both in the same pouch."

"Will they?" Krispos raised an eyebrow. He knew his use of the gesture did not have the flair that Chihor-Vshnasp, say, put into it, but it got the job done. "And to whom is the eminent Rhisoulphos writing?"

"Just let me look and I'll tell you." Like any man from Videssos the city, the courier took it for granted that he knew things lesser mortals didn't. He opened his leather dispatch pouch and drew out a roll of parchment sealed with enough wax to keep a poor family in candles for a month. He had to turn it between his fingers to find out where the address was. "Here we go, your Majesty. It's to the most holy patriarch Gnatios, it is. Leastways, I think he's most holy patriarch this week, unless you made him into a monk again while I wasn't looking, or maybe into a prawn salad."

"A prawn salad? He'll end up wishing he was a prawn salad when I get through with him." Maybe Rhisoulphos was writing to Gnatios for enlightenment on an abstruse theological point or for some other innocuous reason. Krispos didn't believe it, not for a minute. The two of them were both intriguers, and he the logical person against whom they would intrigue. He plucked at his beard as he thought, then turned to one of the Halogai who stood guard in front of his tent. "Vagn, fetch me Trokoundos, right away."

"The mage, Majesty? Aye, I bring him."

Trokoundos was picking at his teeth with a fingernail as he followed Vagn to the imperial tent. "What's toward, your Majesty?"

"This fellow—" Krispos pointed to the courier. "—is carrying a letter from the excellent Rhisoulphos to the most holy patriarch Gnatios."

"Is he indeed?" No one had to draw pictures for Trokoundos. "Are you curious about what's in that letter?"

"You might say so, yes." Krispos held out a hand. The courier was not a man to be caught napping. With a flourish, he gave Krispos Rhisoulphos' letter. Krispos passed it to Trokoundos. "As you see, it's sealed tighter than a winter grain pit. Can you get it open and then shut again without breaking the seals?"

"Hmm. An interesting question. Do you know, sometimes these small conjurations are harder than the more grandiose ones? I'm certain I can get the wax off and on again, but the first method that springs to mind would surely ruin the writing it shelters—not what you have in mind, unless I miss my guess. Let me think . . ."

He proceeded to do just that, quite intensely, for the next

couple of minutes. Once he brightened, then shook his head and sank back into his study. At last he nodded.

"You can do it, then?" Krispos said.

"I believe so, your Majesty. Not a major magic, but one that will draw upon the laws of similarity and contagion both, and nearly at the same time. I presume privacy would be a valuable adjunct to this undertaking?"

"What? Oh, yes; of course." Krispos held the tent flap open with his own hands, then followed Trokoundos inside.

The wizard said, "You must have some parchment in here, yes?" Laughing, Krispos pointed to the portable desk where he'd just finished his note to Iakovitzes. Several other sheets still curled over one another. Trokoundos nodded. "Excellent." He took one, rolling it into a cylinder of about the same diameter as the sealed letter from Rhisoulphos to Gnatios. Then he touched the two of them together and squinted at the place where their ends joined. "I'll use the law of similarity in two aspects," he explained. "First in that parchment is similar to parchment, and second in that these are two similar cylinders. Now just a dab of paste to let this one hold its shape—can't use ribbon, don't you know, for it wouldn't be in precisely the right place."

Krispos didn't know, but he'd already seen that Trokoundos liked to lecture as he worked. The mage set his new parchment cylinder upright on the desk. "By the law of contagion, things once in contact continue to influence each other after that contact ends. Thus—" He held the letter upright in one hand and made slow passes over it with the other, chanting all the while.

Sudden as a blink, the sealing wax disappeared. Trokoundos pointed to the parchment cylinder he'd made. "You did it!" Krispos exclaimed—that new cylinder wore a wax coat now. Every daub and spatter that had been on the letter was there.

"So I did," Trokoundos said with a touch of smugness. "I had to make certain my cylinder was no wider than the one Rhisoulphos made of his letter. That was most important, for otherwise the wax would have cracked as it tried to form itself around my piece of parchment."

He went on explaining, but Krispos had stopped listening. He held out his hand for the letter. Trokoundos gave it to him. He slid off the ribbon, unrolled the document, and read: " 'Rhisoulphos to the most holy ecumenical patriarch Gnatios: Greetings. As I said in my last letter, I think it self-evident that Videssos would best be ruled by a man whose blood is of the best, not by a parvenu, no matter how energetic.' '' He paused. "What's a parvenu?"

"Somebody able who just came off a farm himself, instead of having a great-great-grandfather who did it for him," Trokoundos said.

"Oh." Krispos resumed: " 'As you are scion of a noble house yourself, most holy sir, I am confident you will agree with me and will seize the opportunity to expound this position to the people when the proper circumstances arise. What with the uncertainty and danger of the campaign upon which Krispos has embarked, that moment may come at any time.' '' He stopped again.

Trokoundos said, "Nothing treasonous so far—quite. He could as well be worrying about what happens if you die in battle as over anything else."

"So he could. But he sends himself to the ice with his next five words. Listen: " 'It might even be hastened.' ''

"Aye, that's treason," Trokoundos said flatly. "What will you do about it?"

Krispos had been thinking about that from the instant he'd learned Rhisoulphos was corresponding with Gnatios. Now he answered, "First, I want you to seal the letter up again." He handed it to Trokoundos.

"Of course, your Majesty." Trokoundos rerolled the letter and put the ribbon around it once more. His left hand shaped a quick pass; he spoke a low-voiced word of command. The ribbon changed place on the parchment. "I've returned it to its exact previous position, your Majesty, so the restored wax will fit over it perfectly."

Without waiting for Krispos' nod, the mage held the letter upright. The ribbon did not stir; evidently the minor magic held it where it belonged. Trokoundos began the chant he had used before to remove the sealing wax. This time, though, his fingers fluttered downward in his passes rather than up toward the ceiling of the imperial tent.

Again Krispos missed the transfer of wax from one parchment to the other. One instant it was on the roll that stood on his desk; the next, back on Rhisoulphos' letter. With a bow Trokoundos returned the letter to Krispos.

"Thanks." Krispos went back outside. The courier was waiting with no sign of impatience; the sorcery could not have taken long. Krispos gave him the letter. "Everything's fine," he said, smiling. "Go on and deliver this to the patriarch; he'll be glad to have it."

The courier saluted. "Just as you say, your Majesty." He clucked to his horse and dug in his heels. With a small snort, the animal trotted away.

Krispos turned to Vagn. "Can you find me, hmm, half a dozen of your countrymen? I need quiet men, men who can not only keep their mouths shut but also move quietly."

"I bring them, Majesty," Vagn said at once.

Trokoundos sent Krispos a curious look. He ignored it. A few minutes later Vagn returned with six more burly blond northerners. For all their bulk, they moved like hunting cats. Krispos held the tent flap open. "Brave sirs, come in. I have a task for you—"

Krispos woke at sunrise every day. *Maybe I'd be able to sleep late if my great-great-grandfather were the one who'd come off the farm,* he thought as he put his feet on the ground. He listened to the camp stirring to life.

He was just buckling on his sword belt when shouts of alarm cut through the usual morning drone of chattering men, clanking mail, and bubbling cookpots. He stuck his head outside, savoring a long breath of cool, fresh air; soon enough the day would turn hot and sticky. "What's going on?" he asked Narvikka, who was standing morning guard duty.

"Majesty, the noble Rhisoulphos seems to have disappeared," the Haloga answered.

"Disappeared? What do you mean, disappeared?"

"He is not in his tent, Majesty, not anywhere about the camp," Narvikka said stolidly.

"That's terrible news. What could have happened to him?" Since Narvikka only shrugged a musical chain mail shrug, Krispos hurried over to Rhisoulphos' tent, which lay not far away. The tent was surrounded by men and officers, all of them agitated. Krispos strode up to Rhisoulphos' second-in-command. "What's happened, excellent Bagradas?"

"Your Majesty!" Bagradas saluted. He was a short, pudgy man of about forty who looked and often acted more like a dressmaker than a soldier. Krispos knew he was one of the two or three best swordsmen in the imperial army. That did not keep him from wringing his hands now. "Your wife the lady Empress' father has been stolen away from us, whether by wicked men or dark sorcery I cannot say."

"Can Harvas' magic have reached into our camp? May Phos prevent it!" Krispos drew the sun-circle over his heart.

So did Bagradas. "Truly I hope not, your Majesty. I am inclined to say not, for the sentry who guarded Rhisoulphos' tent was found unconscious this morning by his relief. Magic might have dealt with the general, but would it have needed to lay low his guard as well? That seems more like the work of ordinary men."

"You reason like a priest explaining Phos' holy scriptures," Krispos said. A broad, pleased grin spread across Bagradas' face. Krispos went on, "Take me to this sentry."

Bagradas led him through the crowd. The officer's rank and shouts were not enough to clear a path. But when Krispos raised his voice, men stumbled backward out of the way. Bagradas said, "Your Majesty, this is the file closer Nogeto, who had the late-night duty outside the eminent Rhisoulphos' tent."

Nogeto drew himself to stiff, indeed trembling, attention. "Tell me what happened to you last night, soldier," Krispos said.

"Majesty, begging your pardon, but everybody's been asking me that, and may the ice take me if I *know* what happened to me. One minute I was standing here not thinking real hard, the way you do when it's late and you know nothing's going to go wrong. Only it did. Next thing I knew I was lying on the ground with my relief shaking me awake. And his eminence the general was gone."

"Did somebody sap you?"

"No, Majesty." Nogeto emphatically shook his head. "I've been sapped before, and I know what it's like. I don't feel like I'm fixing to die now, the way I would be. I just feel like I went to sleep and then got woke up. Only I couldn't have. By the good god, I didn't." The guard's eyes widened with fear. Sentries who fell asleep at their posts earned the sword and the chopping block.

"He's always been a good soldier, your Majesty," Bagradas put in. "He'd not have been chosen to guard the general's tent if he weren't."

"Is there any reason to think you didn't just fall asleep when you were, ah, not thinking real hard, soldier?" Krispos asked sternly.

Nogeto said, "Majesty, for whatever you think it's worth, just before I—" He changed tacks. "Just before whatever happened happened, I mean, I thought I felt—oh, I don't know; I thought

I felt a cobweb blow across my face. I thought I'd picked up my hand to brush it away, but—oh, I don't know.''

Krispos glanced at Bagradas. "He's not making it up as he stands here, your Majesty,'' the officer said. "He said as much before you came.''

"Will you let a wizard examine you to learn if you speak truly?'' Krispos asked Nogeto. The sentry nodded without hesitation. Krispos told Bagradas, "Take him to Trokoundos. If he's not lying—'' Krispos pursed his lips, made a wry face. "—well, we'll just have to look in some other direction, that's all.''

"Aye, your Majesty. Who could have done such a vicious, evil deed?''

"Maybe Nogeto will be able to give us a clue once Trokoundos works on him,'' Krispos said. "Meanwhile, we have to go on as best we can. Excellent Bagradas, do you feel you can lead this regiment until Rhisoulphos turns up again, whenever that may be?''

"Me, your Majesty? Oh, you're far too generous.'' Bagradas realized he might have affected too much humility, for he quickly added, "If you feel I can handle the command, I am honored to accept.''

"I'm sure you'll lead bravely, excellent Bagradas. Good; I'm glad that much is settled, then.'' Krispos turned to go, then stopped, as with an afterthought. "Bagradas, you know my father-in-law and I worked closely together. He was helping to manage some rather delicate business for me in the city. Now that he's disappeared, I'll have to deal with it myself. Can you make sure any letters he gets are sent straight on to me before they're unsealed?''

"I'll see to it, your Majesty,'' Bagradas promised. He spun on his heel and set hands on hips as he glared at the gaggle of men still milling around Rhisoulphos' tent. "Come on, come on, you lugs!'' he shouted. "We still have to ride today, whether the eminent sir is here or not. *Get* cracking, *if* you please!''

The men moved smartly to obey. Krispos nodded to himself; Rhisoulphos had been a canny soldier, but the regiment would not suffer under its new leader.

The army moved out a few minutes later than it might have, but not enough to upset even the veteran underofficers who were responsible for keeping their units in good order. Krispos rode Progress up and down the long line of march. Wherever he went, the troopers were buzzing about Rhisoulphos' disappearance. Some thought Bagradas had got rid of his commander;

others blamed sorcery; others, not surprisingly, were lewd. "He'll be back in a couple of days, all sleepy and with his breeches unbuttoned," one fellow guessed.

"Oh, go on, Dertallos, you've just saying what you'd do in his sandals," a mate replied.

"If I were in his sandals right now, I wouldn't be wearing sandals, if you know what I mean," Dertallos said. Half a dozen voices barked deep male laughter.

One slow mile followed another. Halfway through the day, Krispos reported that Nogeto had been telling the truth. "He was drugged somehow, poor sod," the wizard said.

"How very strange," Krispos answered. "All right, then; let him return to duty."

Scouts rode well in advance of the main imperial army. With them rode wizards, not the journeymen who had accompanied Krispos' last northern foray but masters for the Sorcerers' Collegium. If they could not sniff out a trap, no one could. If no one could, Krispos was uneasily aware, that trap would close on his army. And who then would defend Videssos the city, his wife, his heir, and his son to be? No one. He knew that all too well.

The farther north the army traveled, the fewer the farms Krispos saw being worked. That tore at him. Next to harvesttime, spring should have been the busiest season of the year, with men and oxen in the fields plowing, planting, and watering. But what was the point, when raiders might sweep down at any moment? Many little farming villages stood deserted, their former inhabitants fled to ground they hoped safer. If somehow he beat Harvas, Krispos knew he would have to import peasants to replace the ones who had run away or been slain. Otherwise the whole land would start to go back to wilderness.

As the Paristrian Mountains climbed higher into the northern sky, men began to peer suspiciously at every clump of brush, every stand of elms they passed. Krispos had known that same feeling the summer before as he approached Imbros: wondering how and where Harvas would strike. Now that he neared Imbros again, he knew it again, doubly strong.

About two days south of the murdered city, a scout came galloping back to Krispos. The fellow saluted and said, "Majesty, one of the wizards thinks he senses something up ahead. He can't tell what, he's not even sure it's there, but—maybe something." The scout looked irked at having to report what likely was just a mage's vagary.

The most Krispos hoped for, though, was detecting Harvas' snares at all. Expecting them to announce themselves with bells and whistles was too much to ask. He turned to the army musicians. "Play *Form line of battle*, then *Hold in place*. We'll see what's gong on up ahead." As the music rang out and the soldiers began to move, Krispos reflected that he'd be wasting a good part of a day's travel if the wizard had discovered nothing more than his overactive imagination. But better that than ignoring a true warning and throwing away his army.

He touched Progress' flanks with his heels, urging the horse forward. Soon he had pressed ahead of the main body of soldiery. A few other riders advanced with him—wizards all. They knew what a halt had to mean. Trokoundos waved from atop a gray that trotted with a dancer's grace. Krispos waved back.

He reined Progress in close behind a knot of scouts and sorcerers. To his untrained senses, the country ahead looked no different from that through which the army had been traveling: fields—too many of them untended—punctuated by stands of oak, maple, elm, and fir. Shadows raced over them, keeping time with the fluffy clouds that drifted across the sky. It all seemed too lovely, too peaceful, to have anything to do with Harvas.

"What's wrong?" Krispos asked.

One of the sorcerers, a young, gangly man whose thin beard imperfectly covered his acne scars, bowed and said, "Your Majesty, I'm called Zaidas. I feel—not a wrongness ahead, nor even a lack of rightness, but rather—oh, how best to say it?—an absence of both rightness and wrongness, which could be unusual." He cracked his knuckles and peered nervously at the innocent-appearing countryside.

"If you don't sense anything, who knows what's hiding there? Is that what you're saying?" Krispos asked. Zaidas nodded. Krispos turned to the other mages. "Do you also feel this, ah, absence?"

"No, Majesty," one of them said. "That does not mean it is not there, though. Despite his youth, Zaidas has great and unusual sensitivity, which is the reason we bade him accompany us. What he perceives, or fails to perceive, may well be genuine." Zaidas' larynx bobbed up and down as he shot his colleague a grateful glance.

Krispos made a sour face. " 'May well be' cuts no ice, sorcerous sirs. I could starve, hunting a grouse that may well be there. How do we find out?"

Trokoundos strolled up just then to join the discussion. "We find out by testing. Is it not so, brothers?" The other wizards nodded. Trokoundos went on, "The Lord with the great and good mind willing, we may even surprise Harvas, who should be confident we've noticed nothing."

Trokoundos was an able mage, but no general. "If he's there, he'll know we've noticed," Krispos said. "We don't form line of battle every time a rabbit hops across the road. What we have to find out is, what is our line of battle moving toward?"

"You're right, of course, your Majesty." Trokoundos shook his head in chagrin, then began a technical discussion with the rest of the wizards that lost Krispos by the fourth sentence. He was beginning to wonder if they would spend the whole morning chattering at one another when Trokoundos seemed to remember he was there. The mage said, "Your Majesty, a number of spells could create the illusion of normality ahead. We think one is more likely, given that Harvas could both pervert and amplify its power through blood sacrifice. We will try to break through it now, assuming it to be the one we guess."

"Do it," Krispos said at once. Acting against Harvas instead of reacting to him felt like a victory in itself.

The wizards went to work with the practiced efficiency of a squad of soldiers who had fought side by side for years. Krispos watched Trokoundos, who smeared his eyelids with an ointment another mage ceremoniously handed him. "The gall of a cat mixed with the fat of an all-white hen," Trokoundos explained. "It gives the power to see that which others may not."

He held up a pale-green stone and a goldpiece, touched the two of them together. "Chrysolite and gold drive away foolishness and expel fantasies, the good god willing." Behind him, the voice of the rest of the wizards rose and fell as some invoked Phos while others chanted to bring their building spell to sharper focus.

A wizard threw a gray-green leaf on a brazier; the puff of smoke that arose smelled sweet. Trokoundos set a small, sparkling stone in a copper bowl, smashed it to fragments with a silver hammer. "Opal and laurel, when used with the proper spell, may render a man—or, with sufficient strength, maybe, an army—invisible. Thus we destroy both, and thus we destroy with spell." With the last words Trokoundos' voice rose to a shout. His right finger stabbed out toward the peaceful-looking landscape ahead.

For a long moment, for more than a moment, nothing hap-

pened. Krispos glared at Zaidas, who was watching the unchanged terrain with the same dejected expression his colleagues
bore. Aye, he was very sensitive, Krispos thought—he could
even detect traps that weren't there.

Then the air rippled, as if it were the surface of a rough-
running stream. Krispos blinked and rubbed at his eyes. Trokoundos raised a fist and shouted in triumph. Zaidas looked like
a man reprieved when the sword was already on its way up. And
while the landscape to the north did not change, when the ripples
cleared they revealed a great army of footsoldiers drawn up in
battle array across the road, across the fields, one end of their
line anchored by a pond, the other by a grove of apple trees.
They could not have been more than a mile away.

Horns cried out behind Krispos. Drums thumped. Pipes
squealed. His men shouted. They saw the enemy, too, then. He
gave the wizards a formal military salute. "Thank you, magical
sirs. Without you, we would have blundered straight into them."

Just then Harvas' men must have realized they were discovered. They shouted, too, not with the disciplined hurrah of
Videssian troops but loud and long and fierce, like so many
bloodthirsty wild beasts. The sun sparked cheerfully off axe
blades, helms, and mail coats as they surged toward the imperial
army.

Krispos turned to the wizards once more. "Magical sirs, if
it's to be battle, I suggest you get clear before you're caught in
the middle." That possibility did not seem to have occurred to
some of the sorcerers. They scrambled onto horses and mules
and rode off with remarkable celerity. Krispos rode away, too,
back to where the imperial standard snapped in the breeze at
the center of the imperial line.

Mammianos greeted him with a salute and a wry grin. "Worried for a minute there that I'd have to run this battle without
you," the fat general grunted.

"Nice to know you think I'm of some use," Krispos answered.

Mammianos grunted again. His grin got wider. He said,
"Aye, you're of some use, your Majesty. Fair gave me a turn,
it did, when those buggers appeared out of thin air. If we'd just
walked on into them, well, it could have ruined our whole day."

"That's one way to put it, yes." Krispos grinned, too, at
Mammianos' sangfroid. He ran an eye up and down the Videssian line. It was as he and his marshals had planned, with lancers—some mounted on horses wearing mail of their own—in the

front ranks on either wing and archers behind them, ready to shoot over their heads into the ranks of the enemy. In the center stood the Halogai of the imperial guard.

The guardsmen did not know it, but native units on either side had orders to turn on them if they went over to Harvas. That might suffice to keep the imperial army alive. Krispos knew it would not save him. He drew his saber and scowled at the advancing enemy.

Mammianos spoke to the musicians. New calls rang through the air. The horsemen on either wing slid forward, seeking to envelop Harvas' front. Krispos scowled again, this time when he noticed how broad that front was. "He has more men than we'd reckoned," he said to Mammianos.

"Aye, so he does," the general agreed glumly. "The northerners must have been streaming south from Halogaland ever since Harvas seized Kubrat. To them the land and climate look good."

"True, true." Krispos had entertained the same thought himself. He'd spent several years north of the Paristrian Mountains after Kubrati raiders kidnapped everyone in his village. He remembered Kubrat as bleak and cold. If Halogai found it attractive, he shivered to think what that said of their homeland.

Then he stopped worrying about Halogaland and started worrying about the Halogai in front of him. Harvas' men fought with the same disregard for life and limb—their own or their foes'—as did the northerners who served Videssos. They shouted their evil chieftain's name as they swung their axes in sweeping arcs of death.

The imperials shouted, too. The cry Krispos heard most often was a cry for revenge: "Imbros!" The lines crashed together in bloody collision. After moments of that fight, even men previously uninitiated into the red brotherhood of war could honestly call themselves veterans. A little fighting against the northerners went a long way.

Here a lancer spitted a Haloga, as if to roast him over some huge fire. There another Haloga crashed to the ground, his armor clattering about him, as a cleverly aimed arrow found the gap between shield top and helm. But Harvas' men dealt out deadly wounds as well as suffering them. Here an axeman hewed down first horse and then rider, splashing friend and foe alike with gore. There yet another northerner, already bleeding from a dozen wounds, pulled a Videssian from the saddle and stabbed him before falling in death.

In front of Krispos, the combat was footsoldier against footsoldier, Haloga against Haloga, as the warriors who followed Harvas met those who had given their allegiance to the Avtokrator of the Videssians. As in any battle where brother met brother, that was the fiercest fight of all, a war within the greater war. The Halogai swung and struck and swung again, all the while cursing one another for having chosen the wrong side. Once hatred was too hot even for weapons, as two Halogai who had been screaming abuse as they fought threw aside axes and shields to batter each other with fists.

The northerners who had taken Videssos' gold never wavered; Krispos knew shame for having doubted them. All because they'd sworn they would, they battled and bled and died for a land that was not theirs, with a courage few of its native sons could match.

"How do we fare?" Krispos shouted to Mammianos.

"We're holding them," the general shouted back. "From all I can tell, that's better than Agapetos or Mavros—Phos keep them in his light—ever managed to do. If the wizards can keep Harvas from buggering us while we're looking the other way, we may end up celebrating the day instead of cursing it."

Most of the wizards, by now, clustered behind the imperial line, not far from where Krispos sat atop Progress. They gathered in a tight knot around Zaidas; if any of their number could sense Harvas Black-Robe's next move, the young mage was probably the one. Krispos hoped his skinny shoulders could carry that weight of responsibility.

Even as the thought crossed Krispos' mind, Zaidas jerked where he stood. He spoke rapidly to his comrades, who burst into action. Krispos noted what they did less closely than he might have, for at that same moment he was afflicted by a deep and venomous itch. Put any man in armor and he will itch—sweat will dry on his skin, and he cannot scratch. Rather than go mad, he learns to ignore it. Krispos could not ignore this itch; it was as if cockroaches scrambled over the very core of him. Of themselves, his fingertips scraped against his gilded shirt of mail.

And he was not alone. Up and down the Videssian line, men clawed at themselves, forgetting the foes before them. Harvas' warriors were not afflicted. In the twinkling of any eye, a score of imperial soldiers went down, too distracted by their torment even to protect themselves. The Videssian line wavered.

Ice ran through Krispos, chilling even his itch for an instant.

If this went on for long, the army would fall apart. Even as first blood welled from beneath torn nails, his head turned toward the wizards. Led by Trokoundos, they were incanting frantically. Those not actually involved in shaping the spell scratched as hard as anyone else. The ones who were casting it needed their hands for passes; the discipline they required to carry on would have made Pyrrhos jealous.

All at once, as if a portcullis had fallen, the itching stopped. The imperials looked to their weapons again and cut down the Halogai who, confident they would not be able to resist, had thrust forward into their line.

"A cheer for the mages of the Sorcerers' Collegium!" Krispos yelled. His soldiers took up the cry and made it ring out over the field. From behind the enemy line, an answering scream rose, a scream of such hatred, rage, and frustration that for a moment all other war cries, Videssian and Haloga alike, tremblingly fell silent. That, Krispos thought, was the voice of the man—if man he still was—who wanted to rule Videssos. He shuddered.

Harvas' northerners seemed for a moment dismayed at the failure of their dark chieftain's magic. But with or without Harvas, they were warriors fierce and bold, men who had grown used to winning glory by always crushing their foes in combat; they would have been ashamed to be deprived of it now through defeat at the hands of Videssians. So they fought on, giving no quarter and seeking none.

The Videssians had been more hesitant at the start of the fight. Some had experienced Harvas' sorcery in the campaigns of the summer before. All had heard of it, nor had the tales shrunk in the telling. Only now were they beginning to see, beginning to believe their wizards could counter Harvas, leaving the outcome of the battle to them alone. Battle against merely mortal foes held only terrors they already knew. They pressed against the Halogai with renewed spirit.

Krispos realized Gnatios had done the Empire a great service by discovering Harvas' nature. He hoped for the patriarch's sake that his response to Rhisoulphos would prove benign. If it was not, Gnatios would answer for it, no matter what aid he had rendered in the fight against Harvas.

A fresh charge from Harvas' men yanked his mind back to the immediate. The Halogai seemed to have inhuman endurance, to be as strong and uncomplaining as the horses the Videssians rode. They were roaring again, their blue eyes wide and staring, their faces blood-crimson. By their set expressions, many of them were drunk.

The imperial guards met their cousins breast to breast, defied them to advance a foot. As one guard fell, another deliberately stepped forward to take his place. Fewer ranks stood between Krispos and the enemy than had been in place when the fight began.

The shrieks of the wounded began to drown out war cries on both sides. Some hurt men staggered away from the line, clutching at themselves and biting their lips to hold back screams. Comrades dragged aside others, not least so they could reach over them to fight some more. Healer-priests, gray-faced with fatigue, did what they could for the most desperately hurt. No one helped the horses, whose screams were more piteous than those of the soldiers.

Krispos saw, surprised, how long his shadow had grown. He glanced toward the sun. It had sunk far down in the west. The battle went on, still perfectly balanced. Though night was near, neither side showed any sign of giving way. Krispos had an uneasy vision of the fight coming down to a duel between the last living Videssian and his Haloga counterpart.

Suddenly the wizards stirred again. Krispos ground his teeth. Harvas Black-Robe had his own notions of how the battle should end, and the strength and will to bring those notions to reality. For just an instant, Krispos' sight grew dim, as if night had already fallen. He rubbed at his eyes, nor was he the only Videssian to do so. But then his vision cleared. Once more Harvas screamed in rage and hate.

Trokoundos walked over to Krispos. The mage looked as worn as any healer-priest, but sober triumph lit his eyes. ''Your Majesty, he tried to draw the night and the darkness that is Skotos' down upon us. We foiled him more easily this time than before; that spell is potent, but can come from only one direction. Our strength together sufficed to wall it away.''

The assembled might of the finest wizards of the Sorcerers' Collegium, then, was more or less a match for Harvas Black-Robe alone. In a way, that was encouraging; Krispos had feared nothing and no one could match Harvas. But it was also frightening in and of itself, for it gave some notion of the might the sorcerer had acquired in the long years since he turned away from Phos toward Skotos.

Harvas cried out again, this time in a tone of command. What his dark sorcery had failed to do, the axes of his followers might yet accomplish. The Halogai rushed forward in an all-out effort to break the ranks of their foes. "Steady, men, steady!" officers shouted from one end of the line to the other. It would do, Krispos thought, as a watchword for the Empire of Videssos. The northerners could rage like the sea; like Videssos the city's sea walls, the imperial army would hold them at bay.

Hold them the army did, if barely. As the Haloga surge began to ebb, Mammianos nudged Krispos. "Now's our time to hit back."

Krispos glanced west again. The sun was down now; the sky where it had set was red as the blood that splashed the battlefield. In the gathering gloom above, the evening star blazed bright and clear. "Aye," Krispos said. "Everything we have." He turned to the military musicians. "Sound the charge."

High and sweet and urgent, the notes rang through the battle din. Krispos held his saber high over his head. "Come on!" he cried. "Will you let yourselves be beaten by a bunch of barbarians who fight on foot and don't know the first thing about horsemanship?"

"No!" yelled every Videssian trooper who heard him.

"Then show them what we can do!"

The imperials raised a great, wordless shout and spurred against Harvas' men. For several minutes the Halogai resisted as desperately and as successfully as their foes had not long before. Then, on the imperial left, a band of lancers at last broke through their line and got into their rear. More followed, their voices high and excited in triumph. Beset from front and rear at once, the Halogai could not withstand the Videssian onslaught. They broke and fled northward.

Krispos set spurs to Progress. The big bay gelding snorted and bounded forward through the thinned ranks of the imperial bodyguards. Krispos was far from an enthusiastic warrior; he'd seen war young, and from a peasant's perspective. But now he wanted to strike a blow at the marauders who had done Videssos such grievous harm.

His guardsmen shouted and grabbed for Progress' bridle, trying to hold him back. Krispos spurred the horse again, harder this time. All at once, quite abruptly, no one stood between him and the foe. Progress pounded toward Harvas' Halogai. The Videssian horsemen, seeing Krispos heading toward the fight, cheered even harder than they had before.

A northerner turned to face him. The fellow wore a mail shirt that reached down to his knees, carried a hacked and battered round wooden shield. He was bareheaded; if he'd ever had a helmet, he'd lost it in the fighting. He still had his axe. It was streaked with the brown of drying blood and with fresh red. He chopped at Progress' forelegs.

The stroke was too quick, and missed. Krispos slashed at the Haloga. He missed, too. Then Progress was past the man. Krispos never knew whether the northerner escaped or was finished by other Videssians. Battle, he had discovered, was often like that.

Soon Progress caught up with another foe. This one did not turn. He kept trotting heavily toward the north, intent only on escape. Krispos aimed for the hand-wide gap between the base of his helmet and the collar of his coat of mail. He swung with all his strength. His saber clattered off iron. The blow jolted him in the saddle. The Haloga staggered but did not fall. His dogged trot went on.

Krispos reined in. Even a slight taste of battle burned out the desire for more. As well that as a youth he had ignored others' urgings and refused to become a soldier, he thought. If this was the best he could do, he would have been ravens' meat all too quickly.

Up ahead, a band of Halogai turned at bay, buying time for their countrymen to get free. Now more stars than the evening star shone in the sky; black night was near. In the darkness and confusion, victory could unravel . . . and Krispos would sooner have stepped on a scorpion in the dark than encounter Harvas there. He looked round for a courier, but found none. *This is what I get for running ahead of the people I need*, he thought, feeling absurdly guilty.

Just then a call he knew sang out, loud and insistent: *Hold in place*. His shoulders sagged with relief. Mammianos was thinking along with him. Videssians began pulling up, taking off their helmets to wipe their brows. Those who had come through unhurt started chattering about what a splendid fight it had been.

A Haloga came up beside Krispos. He gasped and started to raise his saber before he realized the fellow wore the raiment of the imperial guard. Geirrod looked at him with doubly reproachful eyes. "Majesty, you should not leave us. We serve to keep you safe."

"I know, Geirrod. Will you forgive me if I admit I made a mistake?"

Geirrod blinked, taken off guard by such quick and abject surrender. "Aye, well," he said, "I suppose the man in you threw down the Emperor. That is not bad.'' He saluted and walked off. But Krispos knew he had made a mistake. He had to be Avtokrator first and man second. If he threw his life away on a foolish whim, far more than he alone would suffer. The lesson was hard. He hoped one day to learn it thoroughly.

Jubilation ran high in camp that night, despite the continuing groans and cries of the wounded. From the excitement the men showed, they were as excited and overjoyed at their victory as was Krispos himself, likely for the same reason: Down deep, they must have doubted they could beat Harvas. Now that they had done it once, the next time might come easier.

''Tonight we feast!'' Krispos shouted, which only made the camp more joyful. Cattle were slaughtered as quickly as they could be led up, adding further to the blood that drenched the area. Soon every trooper seemed to have a big gobbet of beef roasting over a fire. Krispos' nostrils twitched at the savory scent, which reminded him he'd eaten nothing since morning. He stood in line to get some meat of his own.

After he'd eaten, he met with his generals. Several of them had men they wanted promoted for bravery on the battlefield. ''We'll do it right now,'' Krispos said. ''That way everyone will be able to applaud them.''

The musicians played *Assembly*. The troops packed themselves around the imperial tent. One by one Krispos called names. As the soldiers came forward to be rewarded, their commanders shouted out what they had done. Their comrades cheered lustily.

''Who's next?'' Krispos whispered.

''A file leader named Inkitatos,'' Mammianos whispered back.

''File leader Inkitatos!'' Krispos yelled as loud as he could, then again. ''File leader Inkitatos!''

Inkitatos elbowed his way through the crush to stand on the podium between Krispos and Mammianos. Mammianos called to the listening soldiers, ''File leader Inkitatos' brave and well-trained war horse dashed out the brains of four northerners with blows from its hooves.''

''Hurrah!'' the men shouted.

''File leader Inkitatos, I am proud to promote you to troop leader,'' Krispos declared. The soldiers cheered again. Grinning, Krispos added, ''And I promote your horse, too.'' The troops whooped and waved and yelled louder than ever.

''If he's promoted, do I get his new pay?'' Inkitatos asked

with the accent and ready opportunism of a man born in Videssos the city.

Krispos laughed out loud. "By the good god, you've earned
it." He turned to the military scribe who was recording the
night's promotions. "Note that Inkitatos here will draw troop
leader's pay once for himself and once for his horse." The
scribe's indulgent chuckle broke off when he saw that Krispos
meant it. He was shaking his head as he made the notation.

It must have been close to midnight by the time the last pro-
motion was awarded. By then the crowd round the imperial tent
had thinned out. Krispos envied the troopers who could go off
to their bedrolls any time they felt like it. He had to stay up on
the podium until the whole ceremony was done. When he did
finally get to bed, he remembered nothing after he lay down.

Sunrise came far too soon. Krispos' eyes felt gritty and his
head ached. He knew he should have been eager to press on
after Harvas, but found exhausting the prospect of anything more
vigorous than an enormous yawn. Yawning over and over, he
went outside for breakfast.

When the army moved out, archers were in the van, ready to
harass Harvas' men as they retreated. With them rode the wizards, Zaidas in front of them all. Harvas could have left any
number of sorcerous ambushes behind to delay or destroy the
Videssians. Krispos worried even more that the raiders would
choose to stand siege in Imbros. With the leisure that would
bring Harvas, who could guess what wickedness he might in-
vent?

Delays the army found. Haloga rearguards twice stood and
fought. They sold their lives as bravely as Videssians might have
if they were protecting their countrymen. The imperial army
rode over them and pressed on.

Imbros was almost in sight when a wall of darkness, twice
the height of a man, suddenly rose up before the soldiers. Zaidas
waved for everyone to halt. The soldiers were more than willing.
They had no idea whether the wall was dangerous and did not
care to learn the hard way.

The wizards went into a huddle. Trokoundos cast a spell toward that blank blackness. The sorcerous wall drank up the spell
and remained unchanged. Trokoundos swore. The wizards tried
a different spell. The black wall drank up that one, too. Trokoundos swore louder. A third try yielded results no better.
What Trokoundos said should have been hot enough to melt the
wall by itself.

"What now?" Krispos asked. "Are we blocked forever?" The wall stretched east and west, far as the eye could see.

"No, by the lord with the great and good mind!" Trokoundos' scowl was as dark as the barrier Harvas had placed in the imperial army's path. "Were such facile creations as potent as this one appears, the sorcerous art would be altogether different from what in fact it is." He paused, as if listening to his own words. Then, right hand outstretched, he walked up to the black wall and tapped it with a fingertip.

The other mages and Krispos, not believing he would dare do that, cried out in dismay. Zaidas reached out to pull Trokoundos back—too late. Lightning crackled, surrounding Trokoundos in a dreadful nimbus. But when it faded, the wall faded, too. The wizard was left unharmed.

"I thought as much," he said, his voice silky with self-satisfaction. "Just a bluff, designed to keep us dithering here as long as we would."

"You were very brave and very foolish," Krispos said. "Please don't do that again—I expected to see you die there."

"I didn't, and now the way lies open," Trokoundos answered. With that Krispos could not argue. He signaled to the musicians. The call *Advance*, all eager horns and pounding drums, rang forth. The army moved ahead.

What with rearguards and sorcerous ploys, Harvas had succeeded in putting space between himself and his pursuers. When Imbros came into sight late that afternoon, Krispos approached the town with more than a little trepidation, fearing Harvas had used the time he'd gained to establish himself inside.

But Imbros stood empty, surrounded by its forest of stakes. Over the winter, most of the impaled corpses had fallen from them; bone gleamed whitely on the ground. Here and there, though, a mummified body still stood, as if in macabre welcome.

Krispos' soldiers' muttered to themselves as they made camp not far away. They had heard of Harvas' atrocity, but only a relative handful had seen it till now. Stories heard, no matter how vile, could be discounted in the mind. What came before the eye was something else again.

An imperial guardsman stuck his head into Krispos' tent. "The general Bagradas would see you, Majesty."

"Send him in." Krispos stuffed a last large bite of bread and cheese into his mouth, then washed it down with a swig of wine. He waved Bagradas to a folding canvas chair. "What can I do for you, excellent sir? You led your—or rather Rhisoulphos'—regiment bravely against the Halogai.''

"Thank you, your Majesty. I did my best. I find myself embarrassed, though. When the fight was over, I found a pair of letters had come for Rhisoulphos, and it slipped my mind till now that you wanted to see all such.''

"So I did," Krispos said. "Well, no harm done, excellent sir. Let me have them, if you please.''

"Here you are, your Majesty.'' Bagradas sadly shook his head. ''I wish he could have seen how his men fought yesterday. They did him proud, and many used his name as a battle cry, reckoning that Harvas had feared him enough to make away with him. Most mysterious and distressing, his disappearance.''

"Yes, so it was.'' Krispos' voice was abstracted. One of the letters to Rhisoulphos was from the patriarch Gnatios. That one he had been waiting for. The other came as a complete and unpleasant surprise. It was from Dara.

He waited until Bagradas had saluted and bowed his way out, then sat and waited a little longer, weighing the two letters in his hand without opening either of them. He had repeatedly warned the ecumenical patriarch not to betray him again, and he knew all his warnings might well have been wasted. But Dara . . . Ever since he'd taken the throne, he'd relied on her, and she'd never given him any reason to doubt his trust. Yet how did a relatively short connection with him weigh against a lifetime's devotion to her father?

He found he did not want to know, not right away. He set down the letter from Dara and broke the seals on the one from Gnatios. It was daubed with as much wax as if it had come from the imperial chancery. When at last he could unroll it, he held it close to a lamp to read:

"Gnatios, ecumenical patriarch of the Videssians, to the eminent and noble sir Rhisoulphos: Greetings. As you know, I have suffered many indignities at the hands of the peasant whose fundament currently defiles the imperial throne. I have long believed that those of noble birth, confident in their own excellence, can best rule the state without feeling the constant and pressing need to interfere in the affairs of the temples. Thus, eminent sir, should any accident, genuine or contrived, befall Krispos, rest assured that I shall be delighted to proclaim your name from the altar at the High Temple.''

Krispos tossed the letter aside. Sure enough, Gnatios could no more turn away from treachery than a fat man could turn away from sweetness. A fat man's taste just made him heavier. Gnatios, though, would soon be lighter—by a head, Krispos promised himself, not without regret. But he had forgiven his patriarch too many times already.

What of his wife? What was he to do if he found her plotting against him? He put his hands over his face—he had no idea. At last he made himself unseal the letter. He recognized Dara's smooth-flowing script at once:

"Dara to her father: Greetings. May Phos keep you safe through all the fighting that is to come and may he give Krispos the victory. I am well, though enormous. The midwife says second births are easier than first. The good god grant that she be right. Phostis has another tooth, and says mama plain as day. I wish you and Krispos could see him. Give Krispos my love and tell him I will write to him tomorrow. Love to you as well, from your affectionate daughter."

Ashamed of his worries, Krispos rolled up the letter. To be Avtokrator was to be schooled in suspicion. Had he not been suspicious, he might not have found Rhisoulphos' plot till it found him. But to suspect his wife flayed his conscience, all the more so since she had but written her father an innocent, friendly letter.

*Fool*, Krispos said to himself, *would you rather have discovered she was guilty?*

He stepped out into the night. His Haloga guard stiffened to attention. "I'm going over to Mammianos' tent," Krispos said. The guardsman nodded and saluted.

Mammianos' guards were Videssians. They, too, saluted as Krispos came up. "I'd like to see your master," he said. One of the guards went into the tent. He emerged a moment later and held the flap wide.

Mammianos had a roasted chicken leg in one hand and a cup of wine in the other. He gestured to a platter on the ground in front of him. "Plenty more where this came from, your Majesty. Help yourself."

"Later, maybe," Krispos said. "First I want to known the latest word on Harvas' movements."

"I talked with some scouts not a quarter of an hour ago." Mammianos paused for another bite. "They've pushed into the woods that start north of Imbros. By all the signs, Harvas' raiders are in full retreat. The men had that Zaidas with them, so I don't think Harvas could have cozened them the way he did poor Mavros."

"If they aren't making a stand in the woods, that means they have to go all the way back to the mountain pass, doesn't it?"

"I think so, yes." Mammianos paused again, this time thoughtfully. "Once past the woods, there's no place between here and the mountains where I'd care to fight with footsoldiers against horse, at any rate."

"Good enough," Krispos said. "I'm going to leave the army in your hands for a while, then—maybe a week, maybe a little longer. I have to get back to Videssos the city as fast as I can; I've had word of a plot against me."

Too late, he wonder if Mammianos was part of the conspiracy. If so, the army might not be his when he came back to it. But the fat general had certainly had countless chances to overthrow him and had used none of them. Now he only nodded gravely and said, "Gnatios has decided he'd sooner be Emperor-maker than patriarch after all, has he? Or is it someone new this time?"

"No, it's Gnatios," Krispos said. He doubted Mammianos once more, but only for a moment. The general needed no guilty knowledge to make that guess, just the keen political sense he'd shown as long as Krispos had known him.

Mammianos sighed. "He's just like Petronas, Gnatios is: thinks he's cleverer than anyone else. Will you finally go and settle him for good?"

"Yes," Krispos said. "He's wriggled out of what he deserves too often, and then gone and deserved it again. I'll ride the courier relays down to the city and drop on him before he realizes I've come. Meanwhile, I want you to press ahead. If Harvas has fallen back to the pass, don't try to force your way through into Kubrat. We came to grief with that last year. But don't let him back into Videssos, either. With the men and mages you have, that should be no problem."

"No indeed, Majesty," Mammianos agreed. "But it's an expensive way to keep him out, if you'll forgive my being so bold as to say so."

"I know," Krispos said. "I'm beginning to have an idea about that, but it's not ripe yet. I'll talk more about it with you after I get back."

"As you say, Majesty." Mammianos tossed aside a bare bone. "Now, would you care for a chunk of this bird? The white wine I have here goes nicely with it, too. You wouldn't want to set out riding on an empty stomach, would you?"

"No, I suppose not." Krispos ate and drank with Mammianos. Through a mouthful of meat, he said, "I'll even sleep here through the night. Can't go far in the darkness, anyhow."

"True, true. If you don't want anything more there, I'll finish that off for you. Ah, thanks very much." With a little help from Krispos, Mammianos had completely devoured the chicken. He sighed. "I'm still hungry."

"I envy you your appetite," Krispos said.

Mammianos chuckled hoarsely. "I'm getting old, your Majesty. Nice one of my appetites works as it did when I was young, or maybe even better. It's not the one I would have chosen, but then, the choice wasn't up to me."

Krispos went back to his own tent a few minutes later. "I want to be roused at first light," he told the guard. "Tell your relief to have Progress saddled and ready for me."

"It shall be done, Majesty," the guardsman promised.

Done it was, but when Krispos went to climb aboard Progress, he found the scout commander Sarkis and a squad of his men waiting, each of them already mounted. "Best we ride back to the city with you, your Majesty, to keep you safe."

Krispos glared. "By the good god, excellent sir, can I do nothing secret?"

"Not if it puts you in danger," Sarkis answered firmly. His men nodded. Krispos glared again. It did no good. He spurred Progress, moving quickly into a trot and then a gallop. The scouts' horses were nothing special to look at, but had no trouble keeping pace.

Every couple of hours, he and his unwanted companions changed mounts at a courier relay station. His backside and inner thighs grew chafed and sore long before the end of the first day in the saddle—riding hard from dawn to dusk was far different from ambling along at the slow pace of the imperial army. But the miles melted away.

That night Krispos slept like a dead man. The attendants at the relay station had to shake him awake when morning came. He rose grumpily from his bedroll, but managed to say, "Thanks for not worrying about my imperial dignity there."

One of the attendants grinned. "Majesty, right now you smell more like a horse than an Avtokrator, if you know what I mean."

"I hadn't even noticed," Krispos said; after so long in close contact with horses, his nose no longer reported their presence. "It's not a bad smell." He'd spent years in the stables, first for Iakovitzes, then for Petronas.

Sarkis and the scouts were ready to go when Krispos mounted

his latest horse. He scowled at them for being so fresh. His own rear end gave a painful protest as he settled himself in the saddle. He did his best to ignore it. His best was not good enough.

His eyes blurred with tears from the wind of his passage. He rode on. One of the horses he took had a gait hard enough to shake his teeth and his kidneys loose. He rode on. A scout's horse went lame. The fellow rode double to the next station. He got a fresh animal and they all rode on.

When Krispos stopped at last on that second day, he dismounted with the slow, brittle caution of a man twice his age. Even the iron-arsed scouts were less limber than when they'd set out. But Sarkis said, "One day more and we're in the city."

"A good thing, too," Krispos said feelingly, "for I'd never make two days more." None of the scouts laughed at him. That was the best sign he'd done enough to win their respect.

Everyone grumbled the next morning, but everyone wearily scrambled onto a horse and rode south. The horses were fresh. They went hard to the next station, but then got to rest. There was no rest for Krispos and the scouts.

Just when he was convinced he'd been on horseback forever and would stay on horseback forevermore, the walls of Videssos appeared on the southwestern horizon ahead. It was late afternoon. "Under three days," Sarkis said. "Your Majesty, were I the head of the imperial courier service, I'd hire you."

"Oh, no you wouldn't, for it's not work I'd ever seek," Krispos retorted. The scouts laughed. Krispos spurred his horse on toward the capital.

# X

Gnatios stood at the altar in the center of the High Temple, chanting the sunset prayers that thanked Phos for the day's light and bid the sun to return safely on the morrow. The benches were mostly empty; only a few pious souls joined him in the day's last liturgy.

Still wearing the trousers and tunic in which he'd ridden, Krispos strode up the temple aisle toward the ecumenical patriarch. He felt bowlegged and wondered if it showed. Behind him, sabers drawn, came Sarkis and the squad of scouts. Behind them tramped a squad of Halogai, part of the company that had been left behind to protect Dara and Phostis.

Krispos waited in grim silence until Gnatios finished the prayer that was last as well as first: "We bless thee, Phos, lord with the great and good mind, watchful beforehand that the great test of our life may be decided in our favor. This liturgy now is ended. May Phos be with us all." One or two worshipers got up to go. The rest stayed in their seats, curious to see what would happen next. Gnatios bowed to Krispos. "I thought you with the army, your Majesty. How may I serve you?"

"You may not," Krispos said curtly. He turned to the Halogai. "Arrest him. The charge is treason." The guardsmen swarmed forward. Gnatios turned as if to run, then considered their upraised axes and thought better of it. They seized him; their big hands wrapped round his forearms in an unbreakable grip. "Take him to the Grand Courtroom."

The priests and worshipers in the High Temple cried out in dismay as the imperial guards dragged Gnatios away, but the weapons the Halogai and Sarkis' scouts carried kept them from doing anything more than cry out. Krispos had counted on that.

The streets of the city were never empty, but they were less crowded after the sun went down. The party of soldiers marched back to the palace quarter unimpeded. Surrounded by tall Halogai, Gnatios was almost invisible in their midst. Krispos had counted on that, too.

A bonfire blazed in front of the Grand Courtroom. By its light, nobles, courtiers, and high-ranking bureaucrats filed into the building. "Well done, Barsymes," Krispos said. "You look to have gotten just about everyone here."

"I did my best on short notice, your Majesty," the vestiarios said.

"You did fine. Take charge of the guards and Gnatios here, would you? You'll know when to send them out where people can see them."

"Oh, indeed, your Majesty." Barsymes gestured to the Halogai. "Wait here in this alcove for the time being, gentlemen. I shall tell you when to proceed."

Krispos walked down the long central aisle toward the throne. The officials who had been chattering among themselves, wondering why they'd been so abruptly summoned, fell silent when they saw him. They resumed once he was past, this time in whispers.

Closest to the throne stood Iakovitzes. He knew what was toward. "Everything all right at your end?" Krispos asked. At the Sevastos' nod, he went on, "We'll settle that later tonight, with more privacy. Meanwhile—" He climbed the steps to the throne, turned, sat, and looked out at the assembled grandees. They looked back at him.

"Noble sirs," he said, "I apologize for ordering you together so quickly this evening, but what has arisen will not wait. I must get back to the army as soon as I can; we've won a victory against Harvas and hope to win more."

"Thou conquerest, Krispos! Thou conquerest!" the courtiers shouted in union. Echoes reverberated from the high ceiling of the Grand Courtroom. The acclamation sounded more fulsome than usual. News of the victory could only have beaten Krispos to the city by a day, and it was the first victory ever over Harvas.

The outcry ceased at Krispos' upraised hand. He said, "In spite of that victory, I had to leave the army to come here to deal with a dangerous case of treason. That is why you are gathered together now." Somehow, without moving a muscle, on hearing the word *treason* the assembled nobles all contrived to look perfectly innocent. Saddened and amused at the same time, Krispos went on, "Here is the prisoner."

At a slow march, the Halogai led Gnatios, still in his patriarchal robes, down the long aisle to the imperial throne. Gusts of whispers trailed him. No one, though, exclaimed in horror or amazement. That, too, saddened Krispos, but did not surprise him. Everybody knew what Gnatios was like. The guardsmen shoved him forward. He prostrated himself before Krispos.

"I will read a letter Gnatios sent to an officer in the imperial army." Krispos drew Gnatios' letter to Rhisoulphos from his belt pouch and read it without naming Rhisoulphos. Then he cast the letter in front of Gnatios. He also threw down the fragments of the patriarch's seal of sky-blue wax. "Can you deny these are your words, written in your hand, sealed with your seal?"

Gnatios stayed on his belly and did not dare even to raise his head. "Majesty, I—" he began. Then he stopped, as if realizing nothing could save him now.

"Gnatios, you are guilty of treason," Krispos declared. "I have forgiven you before, twice over. I cannot, I do not, I will not forgive you again. Tomorrow morning you will meet the headsman, and your head will go up on the Milestone as a warning to others."

A voiceless sigh rose throughout the Grand Courtroom. Again, though, none of the courtiers seemed surprised or dismayed. Softly, Gnatios began to weep.

"Take him away," Krispos said. The guardsmen lifted Gnatios. They had to bear most of his weight as they marched him back along the central aisle, for his legs could hardly carry him. "Thank you for witnessing the sentence," Krispos told the grandees. "You may go, and may Phos bless you all."

The nobles filed out of the Grand Courtroom, talking quietly among themselves. Krispos picked up the damning letter, then caught Iakovitzes' eye. Iakovitzes nodded.

Krispos went back to the imperial residence. Dara stood in the entranceway, waiting for him. She looked uncomfortable, not least because she also looked as if she could have her baby at any moment. "What did you do with Gnatios?" she asked as he came up the steps.

"He loses his head tomorrow," Krispos said. He walked down the hall.

"Good. He should have lost it a long time ago," Dara said

with a vigorous nod of approval. Then she let worry enter her voice. "Now, what didn't you tell me this afternoon, when you rode in with such a rush?"

Krispos sighed. He'd always been glad Dara was clever. Now he wished, just a little, that she wasn't. He took out Gnatios' letter to Rhisoulphos and showed it to her. She carefully read it through. When she was done, she sagged against him. "No," she whispered. "Not Father."

"I'm afraid so." He drew out the other letter his pouch contained, the one from Rhisoulphos to Gnatios. He handed it to her. "Dara, I'm sorry."

She shook her head back and forth, back and forth, like a wild creature thrashing in a trap. "What will you do?" she asked at last. "Not—" Her voice broke. She could not say the word, but Krispos knew what she meant.

"Not if he doesn't force me to it," he promised. "I have something else in mind." He was glad word of Rhisoulphos' disappearance hadn't yet got back to the imperial city.

A few minutes later the eunuch Tyrovitzes came in and said, "Your Majesty, the Sevastos Iakovitzes is outside the entrance, along with several of his, ah, retainers." The chamberlain sniffed; he had a low opinion of the handsome youths with whom Iakovitzes surrounded himself.

"I'll come out." Krispos turned to Dara. "Wait here, if you would. This has to do with you and with your father. I'll be back in just a moment." He left before she could argue.

Iakovitzes' grooms, all of them stalwart and muscular young men, bent themselves double in deep bows to Krispos. Iakovitzes also bowed, less deeply. That left one man standing straight in the middle of the crowd. Bowing would have been hard for him in any case, for his hands were tied behind his back. He did nod, politely. "Your Majesty," he said.

"Hello, Rhisoulphos," Krispos said. "I daresay you're glad to be anyplace outside of Iakovitzes' basement."

"Yes and no. Given a choice between the basement and the chopping block, I prefer the basement. In fact, I also like the basement rather better than the rolled-up carpet in which I was brought to it."

"You don't need to worry about the carpet anymore. The chopping block is something else again," Krispos said. "Come along with me—you and I and your daughter have a few things to discuss. You come, too, Iakovitzes, if you please."

Iakovitzes nodded. He pulled out his tablet and wrote, "That's all, lads," and showed it to the grooms. They nodded and started away from the imperial residence and out of the palace quarter. Iakovitzes wrote something else and passed the tablet to Krispos. "Such a pity—these days I can only pick from among lads who know how to read." Krispos screwed up his face and gave the tablet back.

When Rhisoulphos came into the chamber where Dara was sitting, she looked up at him and said, "Why, Father? Why?" Her voice trembled; tears stood in her eyes, ready to fall.

"I thought I could," he answered with a shrug. "It appears I was wrong. I would have made your son my heir, for whatever that's worth."

"Nothing," Krispos said flatly. "Gnatios goes to the block tomorrow. Give me one good reason you shouldn't follow him."

"Because I am Dara's father," Rhisoulphos said at once. "How would you dare to fall asleep beside her after you put me to death?"

Krispos wanted to kick him—he was still smooth and still right. "As you say. But if you want to live, it will cost you your hair. You'll go into a monastery for the rest of your days."

"I agree," Rhisoulphos said, again without hesitation.

Iakovitzes scowled furiously and held up his tablet so Krispos could read it. "Are you mad, your Majesty? How many people have you clapped into monasteries, only to see them pop right out again?"

"I wasn't finished yet." Krispos turned back to Rhisoulphos. "It won't be the monastery of the holy Skirios for you. No matter what Iakovitzes thinks, I have learned better than that. If you want to live, you'll serve the good god at a monastery in Prista."

For an instant, Rhisoulphos' smooth façade cracked and revealed raw red rage. The town of Prista lay far to the north and west of Videssos the city, across the Videssian Sea. It sat on the southern tip of a peninsula that dangled down from the steppes of Pardraya and served as the Empire's listening post for the plains. It was also the most Phos-forsaken spot in the Empire to which to exile a man.

"Well, Rhisoulphos?" Krispos said.

"Let it be as you say," Rhisoulphos answered at last, his self-control restored. He nodded again to Krispos. "I appear to have underestimated you, your Majesty. My only consolation is that I'm not the first to make that mistake."

Krispos paid hardly any attention to him after he said yes. He was looking at Dara instead, hoping she could accept the choice he'd made. After some endless time that was less than a minute, she, too, nodded. The gesture was eerily like her father's. Krispos did not care. Now once more he blessed her good sense. She saw what had to be done.

Krispos called Tyrovitzes. When the chamberlain came in, he told him, "We need a priest here, esteemed sir. Tell him to bring along scissors, razor, Phos' holy scriptures, and a new blue robe: the eminent Rhisoulphos has decided to enter a monastery."

"Indeed, your Majesty," was all Tyrovitzes said. He bowed and left the room.

The eunuch chamberlain returned within an hour, a priest at his side. After praying, the priest told Rhisoulphos, "Bend your head." Rhisoulphos obeyed. The priest used scissors first, then the razor. Lock by lock, Rhisoulphos' iron-gray hair fell to the floor. When all his scalp was bare, the priest held out the scriptures to him and said, "Behold the law under which you shall live if you choose. If in your heart you feel you can observe it, enter the monastic life; if not, speak now."

"I will observe it," Rhisoulphos declared. Twice more the priest asked him; twice more he affirmed his will. If he did so with irony in his voice, the priest took no notice of it.

After the third affirmation, the priest said, "Doff your garment." Rhisoulphos obeyed. The priest gave him the monastic robe to put on. "As the garment of Phos' blue covers your naked body, so may his righteousness enfold your heart and preserve it from all evil."

"So may it be," Rhisoulphos said; he formally became a monk with those words.

"Thank you, holy sir," Krispos said to the priest. "Your temple will learn that I'm grateful. Tyrovitzes, escort him back, if you would be so kind, and settle those arrangements. You needn't haggle overmuch."

"As you say, your Majesty," Tyrovitzes murmured. Krispos knew he would haggle anyhow, on general principles. Perhaps this way he would not skin the priest too badly.

When the chamberlain had led the priest away, Krispos turned to Rhisoulphos. "Come with me, holy sir."

Rhisoulphos rose, but said, "A moment, if you please." He put a hand on Dara's shoulder. "Daughter, I wish it had turned out better. It could have."

She would not look at him. "I wish you would have left well enough alone," she said in a voice filled with tears.

"So do I, child, so do I." Rhisoulphos straightened, then dipped his head to Krispos. "Now I will accompany you."

More Halogai than the usual squad of guards stood outside the imperial residence. The extra men converged on Rhisoulphos. Krispos said, "Take the holy sir here to the *Sea Lion*, which is tied up at the Neorhesian harbor. Put him aboard; in fact, stay aboard with him until the *Sea Lion* sails for Prista in the morning."

The guardsmen saluted. "We obey, Majesty," one of them said.

"You have everything ready for me," Rhisoulphos observed. "Nicely done."

"I try," Krispos said shortly. He nodded to the Halogai. They took charge of the new-made monk. Krispos watched them march him down the path till it rounded a corner and took them out of his sight. He sighed and drank in a long lungful of sweet night air. Then he went back inside.

When he walked into the audience chamber, Iakovitzes' eyes flickered from him to Dara and back again. The Sevastos quickly got to his feet. "I'd best be going," he wrote in large letters. He held up the tablet to show it to both Krispos and Dara, then bowed and left with what would have been unforgivable abruptness in most circumstances. As it was, Krispos did not blame Iakovitzes for being so precipitate. He just wished the Sevastos would have stayed longer.

No help for it: he was alone with Dara after sending her father into exile. "I'm sorry," he said, and meant it. "I didn't see what else to do."

She nodded. "If you want to keep the throne, if you want to stay alive, you did what you had to do. I know that. But—" She turned her head away from him; her voice broke. "—it's hard."

"Aye, it is." He came over to her and stroked her lustrous black hair. He was afraid she would shy from him, but she sat steady. He went on, "When I was a peasant, I used to think how easy the Avtokrator must have it. All he needs to do is give an order, and people do things for him." He laughed briefly. "I wish it were that simple."

"I wish it were, too. But it's not." Dara looked up at him. "You seldom speak of your days on the farm."

"Most of them aren't worth talking about. Believe me, this is better," Krispos said. Dara did not pursue it, which suited him fine. The chief reason he rarely mentioned his early days to her was that he did not want to remind her how lowly his origins were. Since explaining would also have brought that to the fore, he was pleased to get away without having to.

"Let's go to bed," Dara said. "The lord with the great and good mind knows I won't sleep much with the baby kicking me and getting me up to make water half a dozen times a night, but I ought to try to get what I can."

"All right," Krispos said. Before long, the last lamp was blown out and he lay in the darkness beside Dara. He remembered Rhisoulphos' gibe. Was he safe next to her now, with Rhisoulphos on a ship bound for Prista? He must have decided he was, for he fell asleep while he was still mulling over the question, and did not wake the rest of the night.

At the northern edge of the palace quarter, not far from the Sorcerers' Collegium, was a small park known to city wits as the hunting ground. It was not stocked with boar or antlered stag. In the center of that hedge-surrounded patch of greensward stood a much-hacked oak stump whose height was convenient for a kneeling man's neck.

His back to the early-morning sun, Krispos waited not far from that stump. A couple of Haloga guards stood by, chatting with each other in their own language. They kept sneaking glances at the headsman, who was leaning his chin on the pommel of his sword. He was a tall man, almost as tall as a Haloga. Finally one of the northerners could hold out no more. He walked over to the headsman and said, "Please, sir, may I try the heft of that great blade?"

"Be my guest."

The headsman watched the guard get the feel of the two-handed grip, smiling at his whistle over the sword's weight. The Haloga backed off and swung it a couple of times, first across at waist level, then up and down. He whistled again, gave it back. "A brave brand indeed, but too heavy for me."

"You handle it better than most," the headsman said. "Must be that you're used to the axe, which isn't light, either. I've seen big strong men, but ones who're used to these cavalry sabers that don't weigh nothin', almost fall over when they try my sword."

They went on talking for a few minutes, two professionals in related fields passing the time until one of them had to do his job. Then more Halogai brought Gnatios into the little park. He wore a plain linen robe, not even blue. His hands were tied behind him.

He stopped when he saw Krispos. "Please, your Majesty, I beseech you—" He fell to his knees. "Have mercy, in the name of Phos, in the name of the service I gave you in the matter of Harvas—"

Krispos bit his lip. He'd come to witness the execution because he thought he owed Gnatios that much. But did he owe him mercy—again? He shook his head. "May Phos judge you more kindly than I must, Gnatios, in the name of the service you gave me in the matter of Petronas, and in the matter of Rhisoulphos. Who would be next?" He turned to the guardsmen. "Take him to the stump."

They dragged Gnatios the last few feet, not kindly but not cruelly either, just going about their business. One told him, "Hold still and it will be over soonest."

"Aye, he's right," the headsman said. "You'd not want to twist and maybe make me have to strike twice."

Still not roughly, the guards forced Gnatios' head down to the stump. His eyes were wide and bright and staring, with white all around the iris. He sucked in great noisy gulps of air; his chest rose and fell against the thin fabric of his robe in an extremity of fear. "Please," he mouthed over and over again. "Oh, please."

The headsman stepped up beside the oak stump. He swung the two-handed sword over his head. Gnatios screamed. The sword came down. The scream cut off abruptly as the heavy blade bit through flesh and bone. Gnatios' head rolled away, cleanly severed at the first stroke. Krispos was appalled to see its eyes blink twice as it fell from the stump.

Every muscle in Gnatios' body convulsed at the instant of beheading. It jerked free of the Halogai. Blood fountained from the stump of his neck as his heart gave a couple of last beats before it realized he was dead. His bowels and bladder emptied, befouling his robe and adding their stenches to the hot iron smell of blood.

Krispos turned away, more than a little sickened. He'd read of bloodthirsty tyrants who liked nothing better than seeing the heads of their enemies—real or imagined—roll. All he wondered was whether the chunk of bread he'd had on the way over would stay down. Watching a helpless man die was worse than anything the battlefield had shown him. How Harvas could have struck down a whole city grew only more mysterious, and more dreadful.

Krispos turned to the headsman, who stood proudly, expecting praise, conscious of a job well done. "He didn't suffer," Krispos said—the best he could do. The headsman beamed, so it must have been enough. Krispos went on, "Take the head—" He would not look at it. "—to the Milestone. I'm going back to the imperial residence."

"As you say, your Majesty." The headsman bowed. "Your presence here honored me this morning."

Not long after Krispos returned to the residence, Barsymes asked him what he wanted for lunch. "Nothing, thanks," he said. The vestiarios did not change expression, but still conveyed that his answer was not an acceptable response. Krispos felt he had to explain. "You needn't fear I'll make a bloodthirsty tyrant, esteemed sir. I find I don't have the stomach for it."

"Ah." Now Barsymes' voice showed he understood. "Will you return to the army later today, then?"

"I have a couple of things to do before I go. Do I remember rightly that Pyrrhos, while he was patriarch, condemned the hierarch Savianos for some tiny lapse or other?"

"Yes, your Majesty, that's so." Barsymes' eyes narrowed. "Am I to infer, then, that you will name Savianos ecumenical patriarch rather than restoring Pyrrhos to his old throne?"

"That's just what I intend to do, if he wants the job. I've had a bellyful of quarrelsome clerics. Will you arrange to have Savianos brought here as quickly as you can?"

"I shall have to find out in which monastery he's been confined, but yes, I will deal with that at once."

Toward evening that day Savianos prostrated himself before Krispos. "How may I serve your Majesty?" he asked as he rose. His face was craggy and intelligent; beyond that, Krispos had learned better than to guess character from features.

He came straight to the point: "Gnatios' head went up on the Milestone this morning. I want you to succeed him as ecumenical patriarch."

Savianos' shaggy gray eyebrows leaped like startled gray caterpillars. "Me, your Majesty? Why me? For one thing, I'm more nearly of Gnatios' theological bent than Pyrrhos', and I even spoke against Pyrrhos when you named *him* patriarch. For another, why would I want the patriarchal throne if you just killed the man who was on it? I have no interest in making the headsman's acquaintance just because I somehow offended you."

"Gnatios didn't meet the headsman for offending me. He met him for plotting against me. If you plan on meddling in politics after you put on the blue boots, you'd best stay where you are."

"If I'd wanted to meddle in politics, I'd have become a bureaucrat, not a priest," Savianos said.

"Good enough. As for the other, I remember your speaking up for Gnatios. That took courage. It's one of the reasons I want you to be patriarch. And my own beliefs aren't as, as—" Krispos groped for a word. "—rigid as Pyrrhos'. I didn't object to Gnatios' doctrines, only to his treason. So, holy sir, shall I submit your name to the synod?"

"You really mean it," Savianos said in a wondering tone. He studied Krispos, giving him a more thorough and critical scrutiny than he was used to getting since he'd become Avtokrator. At last, with a nod, the priest said, "No, you're not one to butcher for the sport of it, are you?"

"No," Krispos answered at once, queasily remembering how Gnatios' head had blinked as it bounced from the stump onto the grass.

"No," Savianos agreed. "All right, your Majesty, if you want to give it to me, I'll take it on. Shall we aim to work without biting each other's tails?"

"By the good god, that's just what we need to do." Krispos felt like cheering. He'd said that to Pyrrhos and Gnatios both, time and again; each in his own way had chosen to ignore it. Now an ecclesiastic was saying it for himself! "Holy sir—most holy sir to be—I already feel I've picked the right man."

Saviano's chuckle had a wry edge to it. "Don't praise the horse till you've ridden him. If you tell me as much three years from now, we'll both have reason to be pleased."

"I'm pleased right now. Let me come up with a couple of truly ghastly names to go along with the rules of the synod and I'll be able to get back to the army knowing the temples are in good hands."

After Savianos left the imperial residence, Krispos summoned the grand drungarios of the fleet, a solidly built veteran sailor named Kanaris. That meeting was much shorter than the one with Savianos. But then, unlike Savianos, Kanaris did not need to be persuaded—when he heard what Krispos wanted, he rushed away as fast as he could go, all eager to start at once.

Krispos wished he could look forward to the ride back to the army with equal anticipation.

The ride north was as fast as the ride south had been, but even harder to endure. Krispos had hoped he would be inured to the endless rolling, jouncing hours in the saddle, but it was not so. By the time he returned to camp, his best walk was a spraddle-legged shamble. Sarkis and the squad of scouts were in hardly better shape. The worst of it was, Krispos knew more long days of riding lay ahead.

The soldiers cheered as he rode up to the imperial tent. He waved back to them and put all the exuberance he had left into that wave. They would have been less flattered to know why he was so pleased, but he kept that to himself. He'd most dreaded coming upon their broken remnants as he hurried north.

"Things have been quiet while you were gone," Mammianos reported that evening, when Krispos met with his officers. "A few skirmishes here, a few there, but nothing major. Oh, the wizards have had a bit to do, too, so they have."

Krispos glanced at Trokoundos. "Aye, a bit to do," the mage said. Krispos concealed a start at the sound of his voice—he sounded more than tired, he sounded old. Battling Harvas had taken its toll on him. But he continued with sober pride, "Everything the Skotos-lover has hurled at us, we have withstood. I'll not deny he's cost us a handful of men, but only a handful. Without us, the army would be in ruins."

"I believe you, magical sir," Krispos said. "All Videssos owes you and your fellows a great debt of thanks. With everything safe here, I can give you my own news from the capital." Everyone leaned toward him. "First, Gnatios is patriarch no more. He plotted against me once too often, and I took his head."

Only nods greeted that announcement, not exclamations of surprise. Krispos nodded, too. Trokoundos and Mammianos had both known why he'd returned to the city in such a hurry, and he hadn't ordered either one of them to keep quiet about it. For that matter, he often thought ordering a Videssian to keep quiet about anything was a waste of breath.

He went on, "Next, I bring word of the eminent Rhisoulphos. He turns out to have given up the soldier's life for that of a monk, and is spending his days in Phos' service at a monastery in Prista."

That produced all the reaction he could have wanted.

"Prista?" Bagradas burst out. "By the good god, what's he doing in Prista? How'd he get there?" Several other officers loudly wondered the same thing. Krispos did not answer. One by one the soldiers and mages noticed he was not answering. They started to use their brains instead of their mouths. No Videssian of reasonable rank ignored politics; ignoring politics was unsafe. Before long they reached the proper conclusion. "I'm to keep my regiment, then?" Bagradas asked.

"I'd say it's very likely," Krispos agreed with a straight face.

"A nice bit of work, that, your Majesty," Mammianos said. Almost everyone echoed him. Nobles and courtiers had an artist's appreciation for underhandedness brought off with panache.

"I did one more brief bit of business while I was in the capital," Krispos said. "I ordered Kanaris to send a fleet of dromons up the Astris River. If the Halogai want to cross into Kubrat to fight for Harvas, why should we let them have an easy time of it?"

Fierce growls of approval rose from the officers. "Aye, let's see 'em take on our dromons with the canoes they hollow out of logs," Mammianos said.

"All this may hurt Harvas indirectly, but how do we do more than that?" Sarkis asked. "We can't go through him; we tried that last summer." He pointed to a map that a couple of stones held down and unrolled on Krispos' portable desk. "The next pass north into Kubrat is easily eighty miles east of here. That's too far to coordinate with a flying column, and if we set the whole army moving, what's to keep Harvas from shifting, too, on his side of the mountains?"

"We could double back—" Mammianos began. Then he shook his head. "No, it's too complicated, too likely to go wrong. Besides, if we march away from here, what's to keep Harvas from just jumping right back down into Videssos?"

"There is a pass closer than eighty miles from here," Krispos said.

Wizards and officers crowded close around the portable desk, peered down. Sarkis pointed out the obvious. "It's not on the map, your Majesty."

"I know it's not," Krispos said. "I've been through it all the same, when I was maybe six years old and the Kubratoi herded my whole village up into their country. The outlet at the southern end is hard to find; a forest and a spur of hillside hide it away unless you come at it from the right angle. The pass is narrow and winding; a squad of troops could hold back an army inside it. But if you gentlemen don't know of it, the odds are decent that Harvas doesn't, either."

"The Kubratoi won't have told him, that's certain," Mammianos said. Everybody nodded at that; by all accounts, Harvas and his Halogai had been no gentler in Kubrat than they were in the Empire of Videssos.

Sarkis said, "I mean no offense, your Majesty, but even if all is as you say, you have not been six years old for some time. How can you lead us to this hidden pass now?"

Krispos looked to Trokoundos. "The good god willing, between them the talented mages here should be able to pull the way from my mind. I traveled it, after all."

"The memory is there," Trokoundos affirmed. "As for bringing it into the open once more . . . We can try, your Majesty. I would not presume to say more than that."

"Then tomorrow you will try," Krispos said. "I'd say tonight, but I'm so tired right now that I don't think I have any mind left to look into." The officers chuckled, all but Sarkis, who had ridden with Krispos. Sarkis was too busy yawning.

Trokoundos ceremoniously handed Krispos a cup. "Drink this, if you please, your Majesty."

Before he drank, Krispos held the cup under his nose. Beneath the sweet, fruity odor of red wine, he caught others smells, more pungent and musty. "What's in it?" he asked, half curious, half suspicious.

"It's a decoction to help loosen your wits from the here-and-now," the mage answered. "There are roasted henbane seeds in it, ground hemp leaves and seeds, a distillate from the poppy, and several other things as well. You'll likely feel rather drunk all through the day; past that, the brew is harmless."

"Let's be about it." With an abrupt motion, Krispos knocked back the cup. His lips twisted; it tasted nastier than it smelled.

Trokoundos eased him down into a folding chair. "Are you comfortable, your Majesty?"

"Comfortable? Yes, I—think so." Krispos listened to himself answer, as if from far away. He felt his mind float, detach itself from his body. Despite what Trokoundos had said, it was not like being drunk. It was not like anything he had ever known. It was pleasant, though. He wondered vaguely if Anthimos had ever tried it. Probably. If anything yielded pleasure, Anthimos would have tried it. Then Anthimos, too, slid away from Krispos' mind. He smiled, content to float.

"Majesty? Hear me, your Majesty." Trokoundos' voice echoed and reechoed inside Krispos' head. He found he could not ignore it, found he did not want to ignore it. The mage went on, "Your Majesty, cast your mind back to journeying through the passes between Videssos and Kurat. I conjure you, remember, remember, remember."

Obediently—he did not seem to have much will of his own—Krispos let his mind spin back through time. All at once he gasped; his distant body stiffened and began to sweat. Halogai chopped down his horsemen at the barricade. A black-robed figure gestured, and boulders sprang from the hillsides to smash his army. "Harvas!" he said harshly.

"Farther, reach farther," Trokoundos said. "Remember, remember, remember."

The lost battle of the summer before misted over and vanished from Krispos' thoughts. He rolled back and back and back, one gray year after another passing away. Then all at once he was in the pass again, the pass he had tried and failed to force—somehow he both knew and did not know that at the same time. A short, plump man in the robes of a Videssian noble rode by. He looked cocky and full of spit. Krispos knew his name, and knew—and did not know—much more than that. "Iakovitzes!" he exclaimed. He exclaimed again, wordlessly, for the voice that came from his lips was not his own but a boy's high treble.

"How old are you?" Trokoundos demanded.

He thought about it. "Nine," the boy's voice answered for him.

"Farther, reach farther. Remember, remember, remember."

Again he whirled through time. Now he emerged from a forest track toward what seemed at first only a spur of hillock in front of the mountains. But shouting men on ponies urged him and his companions on with curses and threats. Beyond that spur was a narrow opening. A man in a tunic of homespun wool steadied him with a hand on his shoulder. He looked up in thanks. Amazement ran through him—he thought he was looking at himself. Then the amazement doubled. "Father," he whispered in a child's voice, a younger child's voice now.

Trokoundos broke into his—vision? "How old are you?"

"I—think I'm six."

"Do you see before you the pass of which your adult self spoke? See it now with adult eyes as well as those of a child.

Mark well everything about it, so that you may find it once more. Can you do this and remember afterward?''

"Yes," Krispos said. His voice was an odd blend of two, of boy's and man's, both of them his own. He did not simply look at the opening to the pass anymore, he studied it, considered the forest from which he'd emerged, contemplated the streak of pinkish stone that ran through the spur, examined the mountains and fixed their precise configuration in his mind. At last he said, "I will remember."

Trokoundos put another cup in his hand. "Drink this, then."

It was a hot, meaty broth, rich with the taste of fat. With every swallow, Krispos felt his mind and body rejoin each other. But even when he was himself again, he remembered everything about the pass—and the feel of his father's strong hand on his shoulder, guiding him along. "Thank you," he said to Trokoundos. "You gave me a great gift. Not many men can say their father touched them long years after he was dead."

Trokoundos bowed. "Your Majesty, I'm pleased to help in any way I can, even that one which I did not expect."

"Any way you can," Krispos mused. He nodded, more than half to himself. "Ride with me, then, Trokoundos. If need be, you can use your magic again to help me find the pass. We'll need a sorcerer along anyhow, to keep Harvas from noticing us as we slip around his flank. If he catches us in that narrow place, we're done for."

"I will ride with you," Trokoundos said. "Let me go back to my tent now, to gather the tools and supplies I'll need." He bowed again and walked away, rubbing his chin as he thought about just what he ought to take.

Krispos thought about that, too, but in terms of manpower rather than sorcerous paraphernalia. Sarkis and his scouts, of course . . . Krispos smiled. No matter how sore Sarkis' backside was, he couldn't complain his Emperor had ordered him to do anything Krispos wasn't also doing. But he'd need more than scouts on this mission . . .

The column rode south out of camp the next day before noon. The imperial standard still fluttered over Krispos' tent; imperial guards still tramped back and forth before it. But some dozens of horsemen concealed blond hair beneath helms and surcoat hoods. They stayed clustered around one man in nondescript gear who rode a nondescript horse—Progress was also still back at camp.

Once well out of view of their own camp and that of the foe, the soldiers paused. Trokoundos went to work. At last he nodded to Krispos. "If Harvas tries to track us by magic, your Majesty, he will, Phos willing, perceive us as continuing southward, perhaps on our way to the imperial capital. Whereas in reality—"

"Aye." Krispos pointed to the east. The riders swung off the north–south thoroughfare and onto one of the narrow dirt tracks that led away from it. The forest pressed close along either side of the track; the column lengthened, simply because the troopers lacked the room to ride more than four or five abreast.

Every so often, even smaller paths branched off from the track and wound their way back toward the mountains. Scouts galloped down each one of them to see if it seemed to dead-end against a spur of hillock with a streak of pink stone running through it. Krispos thought his flanking column was still too far west, but took no chances.

The soldiers camped that night in the first clearing large enough to hold them all that they found. Krispos asked Trokoundos, "Any sign Harvas knows what we're up to?"

He wanted the mage to grin and shake his head. Instead, Trokoundos frowned. "Your Majesty, I've had the feeling—and it is but a feeling—that we are being sorcerously sought. Whether it's by Harvas or not I cannot say, for the seeking is at the very edge of my ability to perceive it."

"Who else would it be?" Krispos said with a scoffing laugh. Trokoundos laughed, too. He was not scoffing. Magicians did not scoff about Harvas. Monster he surely was, but they took him most seriously.

Krispos sent double sentry parties out on picket duty and ordered them to set up farther than usual from the camp. He had doubts about how much good that would do. If Harvas found him out, the first he was likely to know of it would be a magical onslaught that wrecked the flying column. The sentries went out even so, on the off chance he was wrong.

As usual, he got up at sunrise. He gnawed hard bread, drank rough wine, mounted, and rode. As he headed east, he kept peering at the mountains through breaks in the trees. By noon he knew he and his men were getting close. The granite shapes that turned the horizon jagged looked ever more familiar. He began to worry about overrunning the pass.

Hardly had the thought crossed his mind when a sloppily dressed scout came pounding up to him. "Majesty, I found it, Majesty!" the fellow said. "A pink vein of rock on the spur, and when I rode in back of it, sure enough, it opens out. I'll take us there!''

"Lead us,'' Krispos said, slapping the scout on the back. The order to halt ran quickly through the column—horns and drums were silent, for fear Harvas might somehow detect their rhythmic calls at a range beyond that of merely human ears.

The scout led the troopers back to a forest path no different from half a dozen others they'd passed earlier in the day. As soon as Krispos plunged into the woods, he knew he'd traveled this way before. Almost as if it came from the leaves and branches around him, he picked up a sense of the fear and urgency he'd had the last time he used this track. He thought for a moment he could hear guttural Kubrati voices shouting for him to hurry, hurry, but it was only the wind and a cawing crow. All the same, sweat prickled under his armpits and ran down his flanks like drops of molten lead.

Then the path seemed to come to a dead end against a spur of rock with a pink streak through it. The scout pointed and asked excitedly, "Is this it, your Majesty? It looks just like what you were talking about. Is it?''

"By the lord with the great and good mind, it is,'' Krispos whispered. Awe on his face, he turned and bowed in the saddle to Trokoundos. The place looked as familiar as if he'd last seen it day before yesterday—and so, thanks to the mage's skill, he had. Before he ordered the army into the pass, he asked Trokoundos, "Are we detected?''

"Let me check.'' After a few minutes of work the wizard answered, "Not so far as I can tell. I still think we may be sought, but Harvas has not found us. I do not say this lightly, your Majesty: I stake my life on the truth of it no less than yours.''

"So you do.'' Krispos took a deep breath and brought up his arm to point. "Forward!''

The pass was as narrow and winding as he remembered. If the sides did not seem quite so overwhelmingly high, he was now a full-grown man on horseback rather than a boy stumbling along afoot. He was as afraid now as then, though. A squad of Harvas' Halogai could plug the pass; if men waited up above with boulders, the evil wizard would need no wizardry to rid himself of this entire column.

The troopers felt the danger as starkly as he did. They leaned forward over their horses' necks, gently urging the animals to more and more speed. And the horses responded; they liked being in that narrow, echoing, gloomy place—it was so steep, the sun could not reach down to the bottom—no better than did their riders.

"How long till we're through?" Sarkis asked Krispos as the gloom began to deepen toward evening. "By the good god, Majesty, I don't want to have to spend the night in this miserable cleft."

"Neither do I," Krispos said. "I think we're close to the end of it."

Sure enough, less than an hour later the advance guard of the column burst out of the pass and into the foothill country on the northern side of the mountains. Looking north, Krispos saw nothing but those hills leading down to a flatter country of plains and patches of forest. He turned round to the granite mass of the mountains. To have them behind him instead of before seemed strange and unnatural, as if sky and land had changed places on the horizon.

Full darkness was close at hand. The evening star dominated the western sky, though a thin fingernail-paring of moon also hung there. More and more stars came out as crimson and then gray faded into black.

The soldiers buzzed with excitement as they set up camp. They'd flanked Harvas and he didn't know it. Day after tomorrow they would crash into his unguarded rear; he and his men would be caught between their hammer and the anvil of the main imperial army. One trooper told his tentmate, "They say the bastard's a good wizard. He'll need to be better than good to get away from us now."

"He is better than good," the second soldier answered.

Krispos sketched Phos' sun-circle over his heart to avert any possible omen. Then he went to check with Trokoundos. The mage said, "No, we are not found. I still feel we are sought, but I would also have that feeling because of Harvas' sorcerous scrutiny of the supposed southward journey of this army."

"How much longer can that trick hold up?" Krispos asked.

"Long enough, I hope. The farther Harvas' magic has to reach, the less omniscient it becomes. There are no guidelines, I admit, the more so for a unique sorcerer like Harvas. But as I say, what we have done should suffice."

That was as much reassurance as Krispos could reasonably expect. He arranged himself in his bedroll confident that Harvas would not turn him into a spider while he slept. And sleep he did; despite aches in every riding muscle, he went out like a blown lamp while he was still trying to get a blanket up to his chin.

Camp broke quickly the next morning. Everyone knew the column had stolen a march on Harvas, and everyone wanted to take advantage of it. Underofficers had to warn men not to wear out their horses by riding too hard too soon.

Off in the distance Krispos saw other small mounted parties. They saw his men, too, and promptly fled. He did not know what to feel as he watched them gallop away. So these were the fierce Kubratoi who had scourged Videssos' northern provinces all through his childhood! Now they only wanted to escape.

His pride at that was punctured when Trokoundos remarked, "I wonder whether they think we're really who we are or some of Harvas' men."

Near noon a band of about a dozen nomads approached the column instead of running away. "You horsemen, you imperials?" one of them called in broken Videssian.

"Aye," the soldiers answered, ready to kill them if they turned to take that news to Harvas Black-Robe.

But the Kubrati went on, "You come to fight Harvas?"

"Aye," the soldiers repeated, with a yell this time.

"We fight with you, we fight for you." The nomad held his bow over his head "Harvas and his axemen, they worst in world. You Videssians, you gots to be better. Better you rule over us than Harvas any day, any day better." He spoke to his companions in their own language. They shouted what had to be agreement.

Krispos lifted his helmet so he could scratch his head. *Kubratoi* had meant *enemies* to him since he was six years old. Even imagining them as comrades came hard. But the nomad had spoken the truth in a way he probably did not suspect. The land of Kubrat had been Videssian once. If the imperial army beat Harvas, it would become Videssian again—Krispos did not intend to turn it over to some Kubrati chieftain who would stay grateful until the day he thought he could safely raid south of the mountains, and not a moment longer. Gnatios had taught him some hard lessons about how long loyalty was apt to last.

Still, if he did succeed in annexing—reannexing, he reminded himself—Kubrat, the goodwill of the locals would be worth something. "Aye, join us," he told the nomads. "Help drive the invaders out of Kubrat." He did not say *out of your land*. None of the Kubratoi noticed the fine distinction.

Most of the nomads who saw the flying column continued to

avoid it. But several more groups came in, so that by the end of the day close to a hundred Kubratoi camped with the Videssians. Their furs and boiled-leather cuirasses contrasted oddly with the linen surcoats and iron shirts the imperials wore. Their ponies also looked like nothing much next to the bigger, handsomer horses that came from south of the mountains. But those ponies hadn't breathed hard while they kept up with the column, and Krispos knew the Kubratoi could fight. He was glad to have them.

"We can't be more than three or four hours away from Harvas," Krispos said to Sarkis, "but we haven't seen a single Haloga. He doesn't know we're here."

"So it seems, your Majesty." Sarkis' white teeth flashed in the firelight, very bright against his thick black beard and mustaches. "I said a couple of years ago, when I first served under you, that things wouldn't be dull. Who else would have found a way to sneak up on the nastiest wizard the world's ever seen?"

"I hope we *are* sneaking up on him," Trokoundos said. "My feeling of being sought grows ever stronger. It worries me, and yet surely Harvas would assail us if he knew we were here. I wish Zaidas were along, to tell me all my fears are so much moonshine. The good god grant that I hold Harvas befooled yet a little longer."

"So may it be," Krispos and Sarkis said in the same breath. They both sketched the sun-sign.

Sarkis added, "This also shows the risk of depending too much on magic. If Harvas had his scouts properly posted, he'd already know we were loose in his country."

"It's not his country," Krispos said. "It's ours." He explained the thoughts he'd had when the first Kubrati party attached itself to the column, finishing, "We'll never have another chance like this to bring Kubrat back under our rule."

Sarkis let out a soft, approving grunt. Trokoundos cocked his head to one side and studied Krispos. "You've grown, your Majesty," he said. "You've come into the long view of things you need to make a proper Avtokrator. Who but a man with that long view would say that taking Kubrat, which has been a thorn in our flesh for three centuries now, is bringing it *back* under our rule?"

Both pleased and amused, Krispos said, "The good god willing, I've learned a bit from that long past of ours." He yawned. "Right now, this whole day seems a very long past all by itself. It's hard to remember when I've been out of the saddle except to squat by the side of the road or to sleep, which is what I'm going to do now."

"This is a sound strategy," Sarkis said, his voice filled with such military seriousness that Krispos came to attention and saluted. Then, laughing, he went off to spread out his blankets.

The next morning the troopers checked their swords' edges and made sure their arrows were straight and well fletched, as they did when they were certain they would be going into battle before long. They leaped onto their horses and stormed westward. Krispos knew the only thing that made veterans hurry toward a fight was confidence they would win.

All that kept his own confidence from soaring equally was Trokoundos' attitude. The mage kept looking back over his shoulder, as if he expected to see Harvas on the horse right behind him. "We are sought," he said over and over again, his voice haunted.

But despite his forebodings, neither Krispos nor any of the soldiers in the flying column had any sense that Harvas knew they were there. He'd posted no guards, not in land he thought his own. And there, ahead in the distance, lay the northern mouth of the pass through the mountains in which the wizard and his Halogai were about to be bottled.

"Unfurl our banner," Krispos said. The imperial standard, gold sunburst on blue, fluttered free at the head of the column.

But before the men could even begin to raise a cheer, Trokoundos went white as milk. "We are found," he whispered. His eyes were huge and frightened.

"Too late," Krispos said fiercely, trying to restore his spirit. "We have Harvas now, not the other way round." The words were hardly out of his mouth before a wall of blackness sprang up in front of the column. It stretched north and south, far as the eye could see. The troopers in the lead quickly reined in to keep from running into it headlong.

It did not dishearten Krispos. "There, you see?" he said to Trokoundos, "it's the same paltry trick he used to slow down the army south of the mountains. One touch from you then and the whole silly wall just disappeared. Does he think to fool us the same way twice?"

Trokoundos visibly revived. "Aye, you're right, your Majesty. He must indeed be panicked, to forget he already used this illusion against us. And a panicked sorcerer is a weakened sorcerer. Let me get rid of this phantasm, and then on to the attack."

The soldiers in earshot yelled and clapped. They swatted Trokoundos on the shoulder as his smooth-gaited gray approached the barrier with mincing steps. The mage dismounted a few feet away, walked straight up to it. He stretched out a hand, leaned forward, shouted, "Begone!"

Far, far off in the distance, Krispos thought he heard a woman's voice crying, "No! Wait!" He shook his head, annoyed at his ears' playing tricks on him. In any case, the cry came too late. Trokoundos' forefinger had met the wall of blackness.

As they had before, lightnings crackled round the mage. Men who had not been close by when he pierced the barrier south of the mountains cried out in alarm and dismay. Krispos sat smiling on his horse, waiting for the barrier to dissolve.

Trokoundos screamed, a raw, wordless sound of terror and agony. His spine spasmed and arched backward, as if it were a bow being bent. He screamed again, this time intelligibly. "Trap!" He flung his arms out wide. His back bent still farther, impossibly far. He cried out one last time, again without words.

His hands writhed. The motions reminded Krispos of sorcerous passes. If they were, they did no good. With a sound like that of a cracking knuckle but magnified a thousand times, Trokoundos' backbone broke. He fell to the ground, limp and dead.

The black wall—Harvas Black-Robe's black wall—remained.

Along with his soldiers, Krispos stared in consternation at Torkoundos' crumpled corpse. What would happen to him now, with his own chief wizard slain and Harvas all too aware of exactly where he was? *You'll die in whatever dreadful way Harvas wants you to die* was the first answer that sprang to mind. He cast about for a better one, but did not find any.

Shouts came from the right flank of the column. The Kubratoi who had briefly attached themselves to Krispos' force were galloping off as fast as their little ponies would take them. "Shall we pursue?" Sarkis asked.

"No, let them go," Krispos answered wearily. "You can't blame them for changing their minds about our chances, can you?"

"No, Majesty, not when I've just changed my own." Sarkis managed a grin, but not of the cheery sort—it looked more like the snarl of a hunting beast brought to bay. "What do we do now?"

To his relief, Krispos did not have to answer that at once. A trooper from the rearguard rode up, saluted, and said, "Your

Majesty, there's a party of maybe fifteen or twenty horsemen coming up on us from behind.''

"More Kubratoi?" Krispos asked. "They'll turn tail when they see the mess we're in." His eyes flicked to Trokoundos' body again. Soon, he knew, he would feel the loss of a friend as well as that of a mage. He had no time for that, not now, not yet.

The trooper said, "Your Majesty, they don't look like Kubratoi, or ride like 'em, either. They look like Videssians, is what they look like.''

"Videssians?" Krispos' rather heavy eyebrows drew together over his nose. Had Mammianos sent men after him for some reason? If he had, would Harvas have spotted the party because it was not warded? And could the evil wizard have been led from that party to the flying column Krispos led? The chain of logic made all too much sense. Cold anger in his voice, Krispos went on, "Bring them here to me, this instant.'

"Aye, your Majesty." The trooper wheeled his horse and set spurs to it. The animal squealed a loud protest but quickly went into a gallop. Clods of dirt flew up from its hooves as it bounded away.

Krispos fought down the urge to ride after the fellow, making himself wait. Before long the trooper returned with the band of which he'd spoken. By their horses, by their gear, they were Videssians, as he'd said. As they drew closer, Krispos' frown deepened. He recognized none of them that he could see, though some were hidden behind others. Surely Mammianos would have sent out someone he knew.

"Who are you people?" he said. "What are you doing here?"

The answer came from the back of the group. "Majesty, we are come to give you aid, as we may."

Krispos stared. So did every man who heard that light, clear voice or saw the beardless, sculptured profile beneath that conical cavalry helm. Tanilis might don chain mail, but no one anywhere would ever mistake her for a man.

With an effort, Krispos found his own voice. "My lady, the good god knows you're welcome and more than welcome. But how did you track us here? Trokoundos was sure he'd screened off the column from sorcerers' senses. Of course, Trokoundos proved not to know everything there was to know." His mouth twisted; he jerked his chin toward the mage's corpse.

Tanilis' eyes moved with his gesture. A slim finger sketched the sun-circle above her left breast. She said, "Honor to his skill, for had I depended on finding your soldiers, I should not have been aware of their true path till far too late. But I sought *you* with my magic, your Majesty; our old ties of friendship made that possible where the other would have failed.''

"Aye, friendship,'' Krispos said slowly. Their ties had been more intimate than that, back a decade before when he'd wintered in Opsikion, helping Iakovitzes recover from a badly broken leg. He studied her. She was ten years older than he, or a bit more; her son Mavros had been only five years younger. Some of her years showed, but not many. Most of them had only added character to a beauty that had once been almost beyond needing it.

She sat her horse quietly, waiting under his scrutiny. She did not wait long; that had never been her way. "However skilled your mage was, in Harvas Black-Robe he found one stronger than himself. Do you think Harvas sits idly on the other side of that wall he made, that wall black as his robes, black as his heart?''

"I very much fear he doesn't,'' Krispos said, "but with Trokoundos slain, how can I answer him? Unless . . .'' His voice trailed away.

"Just so,'' Tanilis said. "I tried to warn your wizard, there at the end, but he was too full of himself to hear or heed me.''

"*I* heard you,'' Krispos exclaimed.

"I thought you might have. Harvas is also stronger than I am. This I know. I will stand against him all the same, for my Emperor and for my son.'' She slid down from her horse and approached the barrier Harvas had set in front of the flying column. After some minutes' study, she turned back to Krispos. "Considering what you may find on the other side, your warriors would be well advised to form line of battle.''

"Aye.'' Krispos waved. The command ran down the column. The troopers moved smoothly into place. They still sent wary glances toward the black wall, but the routine of having orders to follow soaked up some of their fear.

Instead of stabbing at the barrier with a peremptory index finger, Tanilis gently touched it with the palm of her hand. Krispos held his breath; his heard pounded as he wondered if the livid lightnings would consume her as they had Trokoundos. The lightnings flashed. Some of the soldiers groaned—they had no great hope for her.

"Is she mad?'' one man said.

"No, she knows what she's about,'' another answered, his

eastern accent hinting that he came from somewhere not far from Opsikion. "That's the lady Tanilis, that is, mother to Mavros the dead Sevastos and a sorceress in her own right, if the tales be true." His words went up and down the line, faster than Krispos' command had: rumors were more interesting than orders.

Tanilis' back stiffened, arched . . . but only a little. "No, Harvas, not now," she said, so softly Krispos barely heard. "You have already hurt me worse than this." It was as if she did not fight against whatever torment the black barrier dealt out, but rather accepted it, and in accepting defeated it.

The wall seemed to sense that. The lightnings blazed ever brighter around Tanilis as it sought to lay her low. But she refused to topple. "No," she said again, very clearly. Again the lightnings increased, this time to a peak of such brilliance that Krispos had to turn his head away, his eyes watering. "No," Tanilis said for a third time from the heart of that firestorm.

Through slitted eyelids, Krispos looked back toward her. She still stood defiant—and all at once the black wall's force yielded to her stronger will. The lightning ceased; the barrier melted into the thin air from which it had sprung.

The imperial soldiers cried out in triumph at that. Then, a moment later, they cried out again. The black wall's vanishing revealed the Halogai who had been advancing on the flying column under its cover. Harvas, too, would have let the barrier disappear, no doubt, but at a time of his own choosing.

"Forward!" Krispos shouted. "The cry is 'Mavros'!"

"Mavros!" the Videssians thundered. They rolled toward Harvas' Haloga, then rolled over them. The northerners were caught in loose order, confident they would find foes ripe for the slaughter. Some of them turned tail when the downfall of the barrier showed that Krispos' men were more ready for battle than they. More stood and fought. They followed a wicked leader, but kept their own fierce pride. It availed them nothing. The imperials rode them down, then rode on toward the northern mouth of the pass. "Mavros!" they shouted again and again, and another cry: "Tanilis!"

"We may yet bottle Harvas up in there," Sarkis yelled to Krispos, his black eyes snapping with excitement.

"Aye." When Krispos' horse even thought of slowing, he roweled it with his spurs. Normally he was gentle to his mounts, but now he would not willingly lose so much as an instant. A solid line across the outlet to the pass and Harvas' army was done for.

The exultation in the thought almost made Krispos drunk. Almost. That army would be done for unless Harvas magicked it free. Despite Tanilis, despite all the mages from the Sorcerers' Collegium, the possibility remained real. Any time Krispos was tempted to forget it, he had only to think of Trokoundos' twisted body, now more than a mile behind him.

He saw the mouth of the pass ahead. Get his men across it and— "Rein in!" he shouted, and followed that with a volley of curses. Harvas' Halogai were already streaming north out of the trap. Some carried axes at the ready, others bore them over their shoulders. The long files of fighting men were ready for action, unlike the now-shattered band that had been on the way to deal with Krispos' column.

"Too many for us to head," Sarkis said, gauging the enemy's numbers with a practiced eye.

"I fear you're right, worse luck for us," Krispos answered. "He's pulled them out just in time. Maybe he could tell when his wall went down, or some such. Even if we can't keep him there, though, let's see how much we can hurt his soldiers. They're giving us their flank for a target."

Sarkis nodded and brought up his hand in salute. "Mammianos said you were learning the trade of war. I see he's right." The scout commander raised his voice. "Archers!"

Shouting enthusiastically, the bowmen began to ply their trade. Shooting from horseback did not make for accurate archery, but with a massed target like the one they had, they did not need to be accurate. Halogai screamed; Halogai stumbled; Halogai fell.

Some of the northerners awkwardly shifted their shields to their right sides to help ward themselves from the arrows that rained down on them. Others, singly and then by troops and companies, rushed toward their tormentors. The archers could not come close to shooting all of them before they closed the gap and began to swing axe and sword. Imperial lancers spurred forward to protect the bowmen. Half a dozen melees developed all along the imperial line. As more and more Halogai poured out of the pass, Krispos' men found themselves outnumbered.

"Pull back!" he shouted. "We didn't come here to take on Harvas' whole bloody army by ourselves. He's out of the pass, and that's what counts. Do you think he can hold all the rest of our own troops out of Kubrat with just a rearguard? Not likely!"

An army of Halogai would either have ignored Krispos' order or taken it as a signal to panic. They fought as much for the joy of fighting as to gain advantage. The Videssians were less ferocious and more flexible. They drew back, stinging Harvas' footsoldiers with more arrows as they did so. The lancers nipped in to cut off and destroy bands of Halogai who pursued with too much spirit. Again and again the Halogai paid in blood to learn that lesson.

"I don't think Harvas is leaving much of a rearguard in there," Sarkis said late that afternoon. By then the running fight had moved close to ten miles into Kubrat; Krispos was hard-pressed to stretch the limited manpower of his column to cover all of Harvas' army.

Like wildfire, a cheer ran up the Videssian line from the south. At last it—and the news that caused it—reached Krispos, who was near the northern end of his force as it skirmished with Harvas' scouts and vanguard. "Our own men are coming up out of the pass!" someone bawled in his ear.

"That's good," Krispos said automatically. Then the full meaning of what he'd heard sank in. He let loose with a yell that made his horse sidestep and switch its ears in reproach. "We have him!"

But as Harvas had shown south of Imbros, he was general as well as wizard. Reaguards had to be beaten down; sorcerous screens had to be cautiously probed and even more cautiously eliminated. By the time night fell, he had succeeded in breaking off contact between his army and most of his Videssian pursuers, though the flying column still hung just off his right flank.

Krispos made his way back to where the main imperial army was setting up camp. He smiled to find his own tent erect and waiting for him. He invited Mammianos over. When the fat general arrived, he clapped him on the back. "You couldn't have done a better job of timing your attack on Harvas' barricade," he said.

"I thank you kindly, your Majesty." But Mammianos did not sound as proud as he might have. In fact, he shuffled from foot to foot like an embarrassed schoolboy. "It, uh, wasn't exactly my idea, though."

"Oh?" Krispos raised an eyebrow. "What then?"

"Might as well hear it from me instead of somebody else, I suppose," Mammianos said. He shifted his weight again before he went on. "That Zaidas—you know, the young wizard—he came up and told me he didn't think things were going any too well for you this morning.''

"He was right," Krispos said, remembering the sound Trokoundos' spine had made as it snapped and his own fear when the wizard died. Trokoundos had a wife—a widow, now—in Videssos the city. Krispos reminded himself to provide for her, not that gold could make up for the loss of her man.

"I figured he might be, seeing as he was the one who sniffed out Harvas' army down south of Imbros," Mammianos said. "So I asked him if we could help you by having a go at the barricade, and he said yes. So we had a go, and maybe Harvas was distracted on account of trying to deal with your lot, because we broke through. The rest I guess you know.''

"I'm just glad you listened to Zaidas," Krispos said.

Mammianos rumbled laughter. "Now that you mention it, your Majesty, so am I.''

# XI

KRISPOS AND TANILIS RODE SIDE BY SIDE. THEY'D RIDDEN SIDE by side ever since the imperial army entered Kubrat. By now, more than a week later and half the way to the Astris River, no one even gave them a sidelong glance. No one had ever had the temerity to say anything to Krispos about it.

Perhaps someone might have, had Tanilis not proven her worth so solidly. The mages from the Sorcerers' Collegium—all, Krispos noted, save Zaidas—had muttered when she included herself in their labors against Harvas, but the mutters died away soon enough. Inside of a day she became as much their spearhead as Trokoundos had ever been. Again and again Harvas' sorcerous assaults failed. Again and again his army, outflanked by the more mobile Videssians, had to retreat.

"I think he's falling back on Pliskavos," Krispos said. "In all of Kubrat, it's the only place where he could hope to stand siege." The prospect of Harvas under siege still worried him. A siege would give the evil wizard the leisure he needed to exercise his ingenuity to the fullest. Krispos grimaced at the prospect of facing whatever that exercised ingenuity came up with.

Tanilis' gaze became slightly unfocused. "Yes," she said, a few seconds too late for a proper reply. "He is falling back on Pliskavos." She sounded as certain as if she'd said the sun would rise the next morning. A moment later she came back to herself, a small frown on her face. "I have a headache," she remarked.

Krispos passed her his canteen. "Here's some wine," he said. As she drank, he ran his hands over her arms, trying to smooth down the gooseflesh that had prickled up at her foretelling. He'd seen the mantic fit take her far more strongly than that, not least on the day when he'd first met her, the day she'd terrified him by calling him *Majesty*.

Then he'd wondered if she saw true. Now he knew she did. Knowing that, he thought to take advantage of her gift. He called for a courier. "Get Sarkis over here," he said. The courier saluted and rode away.

He soon returned with the scout commander. "What can I do for you, your Majesty?" Sarkis asked.

"Time to send out another column," Krispos said, and watched Sarkis grin. "Harvas *is* on his way back to Pliskavos." Sarkis caught his certainty and glanced over to Tanilis. Krispos nodded. He went on, "If we can put a few thousand men into the place before he gets there, say, or burn down a good part of it—"

Sarkis' grin got wider. "Aye, your Majesty, we can try that. We can swing wide and get around behind his men, the good god willing. Horses go faster than shank's mare. It should work. I'll get right on it."

"Good." Krispos grinned, too, savagely. Let Harvas find out for a change what being hunted was like, feel what it meant to move to someone else's will, to move in fear lest the tiniest error bring the fabric of all his designs down in ruin. He'd inflicted misery on Videssos for too long—perhaps for the whole span of his unnatural life. Only fitting and proper to mete misery out to him at last.

The column clattered away from the main Videssian army late that afternoon, heading off to the west to circle round Harvas' Halogai. The troopers who stayed on the primary line of march whooped as their comrades departed. One outflanking move had forced Harvas out of his strong position in the pass. Another might ruin him altogether. The soldiers were cheerful as they encamped for the night.

As was his habit, Krispos picked a line at random and patiently advanced toward the cookpot at the end of it. Anthimos, with his love of rare delicacies, would have turned up his toes at army fare. Used to worse for much of his life, Krispos minded it not at all. Peas, beans, onions, and cheese made a savory stew, enlivened, as it had seldom been in his peasant days, with small chunks of salty sausage and beef. He slapped his stomach and raised a belch. The men around him laughed. They knew they ate better because he shared their food.

After he had eaten, Krispos walked along the lines of tethered horses, stopping to chat now and then with a trooper grooming his mount or prying a pebble out from under a horseshoe. His years as a groom after he came to Videssos the city made him easy with horsy talk, though he was not one of the fairly common breed who cared for nothing else by day or night. For the most part, the men treated their animals well; their lives might depend on keeping the beasts in good condition.

The short, full darkness of summer night had fallen by the time Krispos made his way back to his own tent, which stood, as always, in the center of the camp. The Haloga guardsmen in front of it came to attention as he approached. "As you were," he said, and ducked through the flap. Unlike the heavy canvas under which most of the troopers sweltered, his summer tent was of silk. He got whatever breeze there was. Tonight there was no breeze.

He was not ready to sleep yet, not quite. He sat down in a folding chair of wood and wicker, set his chin in his hand, and thought about what the coming days would bring. He no longer believed Harvas would be able to enspell his army this side of Pliskavos. He'd had to summon most of the sorcerous talent in the Empire to match the undying renegade, but he'd done it. He thought Harvas was beginning to understand that, too. If his magic would not serve him, that left his soldiers. Some time soon he might try battle. If he found a piece of ground that suited him—

Outside the tent, the sentries shifted their weight. Their boots scuffed the dirt; their mail shirts rang softly. The small sounds so close by made Krispos glance up toward the entrance. His right hand stole toward the hilt of his saber. Then one of the sentries said, "How do we serve you, my lady?"

In all the sprawling imperial camp, there was only one "my lady." Tanilis said, "I would speak with his Majesty, if he will see me."

One of the guardsmen stuck his head into the tent. Before he could speak Krispos said, "Of course I will see the lady." He felt his heartbeat shift from walk to trot. However they rode during the day, Tanilis had not come to his tent at night before.

The guard held the flap wide for her. Silk rustled as it fell after she came in. Krispos got to his feet, taking a step toward a second chair so he could unfold it for her. Before he reached it, Tanilis went smoothly to her knees and then to her belly. Her forehead touched the ground in the most graceful act of proskynesis he had ever seen.

He felt his face grow hot. "Get up," he said, his voice so soft the guards could not listen but rough with emotions he was still sorting through. "It's not right—not fitting—for you to prostrate yourself before me."

"And wherefore not, your Majesty?" she asked as she rose with the same liquid elegance she had used in the proskynesis. "You are my Avtokrator; should I not grant you the full honor your station deserves?"

He opened the other chair. She sat in it. He went back to the one in which he had been sitting. His thoughts refused to muster themselves into any kind of order. At last he said, "It's not the same. You knew me before I was Emperor. By the lord with the great and good mind, my lady, you knew me before I was much of anything."

"I gave you leave long ago, as a friend, to call me by my name. I could scarcely deny my Emperor the same privilege." A tiny smile tugged up the corners of Tanilis' mouth. "And you seem to have become quite a lot of something, if I may take a friend's privilege and point it out."

"Thank you." Krispos spoke carefully, to ensure that he did not stammer. Being with Tanilis took him back to the days when he had been more nearly boy than man. He did not want to show that, not to her of all people. Now he made himself think clearly and said, "And thank you also for making sure I left Opsikion—and you—that spring, whether I wanted to or not."

She inclined her head to him. "Now you have come into a man's wisdom, to see why I did as I did. I could tell that Opsikion was too small for you—and I, at the time I was rather too large. You were not yet what you would become."

Her words so paralleled his own thoughts that he nodded in turn. As he did, he gazed at her. She had held her beauty well enough to remain more than striking even in harshest daylight. Lamps were kinder; now she seemed hardly to have aged a day.

Seeing her, hearing her, also reminded him of how they had spent a good part of their time together. He'd gone on campaign before without seriously wanting to bring a woman into his tent to keep his cot warm. Part of that, he admitted to himself with a wry grin, was nervousness about Dara. But another part, a bigger part, came from fondness for his wife.

Now he found he wanted Tanilis. None of what he felt for

Dara had gone away. It just did not seem relevant anymore. He'd known Tanilis, known her body, long before he'd ever imagined he would meet Dara. Wanting to take her to bed again did not feel like being unfaithful; it felt much more like picking up an old friendship.

He did not stop to wonder what his taking Tanilis to bed would feel like to Dara. He got up, stretched, and walked over to the map table in one corner of the tent. Videssos had not ruled in Kubrat for three hundred years; the imperial archives nevertheless held detailed if archaic maps of the land, stored against the day when it might become a province of the Empire once more.

But he only glanced at the ragged parchment with its ink going brown and pale from age. He stretched again, then walked about as if at random. It was no accident, though, that he ended up behind Tanilis' chair. He rested a hand on her shoulder.

She twisted her head up and back to look at him. Her small smile grew. She made a pleased noise, almost a purr, deep in her throat. Her hand covered his. Her skin was smooth, her flesh soft. A ruby ring on her index finger caught the dim lamplight and glowed like warm blood.

Krispos bent down and lightly kissed her. "Like old times," he said.

"Aye, like old times." Her pleased purr got louder. Her eyes were almost all pupil. Then, suddenly, those huge eyes seemed to be looking past Krispos, or through him. "For a little while," she said in a voice altogether different from the one she'd used a moment before. That distant expression faded before Krispos was quite sure he'd seen it. Her voice returned to normal, too, or better than normal. "Kiss me again," she told him.

He did, gladly. When the kiss ended, she got to her feet. Afterward he was never sure which of them took the first step toward the cot. She pulled her robe over her head, slid out of her drawers, and lay down to wait while he undressed. She did not wait long. "Do you want to blow out the lamps?" she whispered.

"No," he answered as softly. "For one thing, it would tell the guardsmen just what we're doing. For another, you're beautiful and I want to see you." Even more than her face, her body had retained its youthful tautness.

Her eyes lit. "No wonder I recall you so happily." She held up her arms to him. He got down beside her.

The cot was narrow for two; the cot, in truth, was narrow for one. They managed all the same. Tanilis was as Krispos remembered her, or even more so, an all but overwhelming blend of passion and technique. Soon his own excitement drove memory away, leaving only the moment.

Even after they were spent, they lay entangled—otherwise one of them would have fallen off the cot. Tanilis' hand stole down his side and stroked him with practiced art. "Another round?" she murmured, her breath warm in his ear.

"In a bit, maybe," he answered after taking stock of himself. "I'm older than I was when I visited Opsikion, you know. I wasn't spending long days in the saddle then, either." One of his eyebrows quirked upward against the velvety skin of her throat. "At least, not on horseback."

She bit him in the shoulder, hard enough to hurt. He started to yelp, but checked himself in time. The small pain seemed to spur him, though; sooner than he had expected, he found himself rising to the occasion once more. Tanilis let out a voiceless sigh as they began again.

From outside the tent one of the guardsmen called, "Majesty, a courier is here with a dispatch from the city."

Krispos did his best not to hear the Haloga. "Don't be foolish," Tanilis said; she retained as much self-control as Krispos remembered. She made a small pushing motion against his chest. "Go on; see what news the rider brings. I'll be here when you get back."

Knowing she was right helped only so much. More than a little grumpily, he separated from her, climbed off the cot, dressed, and went out into the night. "Here you are, your Majesty," the courier said, handing him a sealed roll of parchment. After a salute, the fellow twitched his mount's reins and headed out toward the long lines of tethered horses.

Krispos ducked back into the tent. As he did so, his cheeks started to flame. The Halogai had never been shy about sticking their heads inside when they needed him to come out. If they called now, it had to be because they knew what he was doing in there. "Oh, to the ice with it," he muttered. The longer he ruled, the more resigned he became to having no privacy.

The sight of Tanilis waiting for him drove such minor annoyances clean out of his mind. He yanked off his robe and let it fall to the ground. Tanilis frowned. "The dispatch—"

"Whatever it is, it will keep long enough."

She lowered her eyes in acquiescence. "Then hurry here, your Majesty." Krispos hurried.

Afterward, languid, he wanted to forget about the roll of parchment, but he knew Tanilis would think less of him for that—and he would think less of himself when morning came. He got into his robe again and broke the seal on the message. Tanilis projected an air of silent approval as she, also, put her clothes back on.

His impatient thoughts full of her, he hadn't bothered to hold the dispatch up to a lamp to find out who'd sent it. Now, as he read the note inside, he learned: "The Empress Dara to her husband Krispos, Avtokrator of the Videssians: Greetings. Yesterday I gave birth to our second son, as Mavros' mother Tanilis foretold. As we agreed, I've named him Evripos. He is large and seems healthy, and squalls at all hours of the day and night. The birth was hard, but all births are hard. The midwife acts pleased with him and me both. The good god grant that you are soon here in the city once more to see him and me."

Krispos had felt no guilt before. Now it all crashed down on him at once. When he said nothing for some time, Tanilis asked, "Is the news so very bad, then?" Wordlessly he passed the letter to her. She read quickly and without moving her lips, something Krispos still found far from easy. "Oh," was all she said when she was done.

"Yes," Krispos said: only two words between them, but words charged with a great weight of meaning.

"Shall I come here to your tent no more then, your Majesty?" Tanilis asked, her voice all at once cool and formal.

"That might be best," Krispos answered miserably.

"As you wish, your Majesty. Do recall, though, that you knew of the Empress'—your wife's—condition before this dispatch arrived. I grant that knowing and being reminded are not the same, but you had the knowledge. And now, by your leave—" She tossed Dara's letter onto the cot, strode briskly to the tent flap, ducked through it, and walked away.

Krispos stared after her. Minutes before they had been gasping in each other's arms. He picked up the letter to read it again. He had another son, and Dara was well. Good news, every bit of it. Even so, he crumpled the parchment into a ball and flung it to the ground.

\* \* \*

Scouts pushed ahead before dawn the next morning, probing to make sure no ambushes lay ahead of the imperial army. The main force soon followed, a long column with its supply wagons, protected by a sizable knot of mounted men, rattling along in the middle.

The unwieldy arrangement never failed to make Krispos nervous. "If Harvas had even a few Kubrati horse-archers on his side, he could give us no end of grief," he remarked to Bagradas, who led the force guarding the baggage train. Concentrating on the army's affairs helped Krispos keep his mind off his own, and off the fact that today Tanilis had chosen not to ride beside him, but rather with the rest of the magicians.

Bagradas did not notice that—or if he did, had sense enough not to let on. He said, "Whatever Kubratoi still have fight in them want to come in on our side, your Majesty, not against us. We picked up another few dozen yesterday. Of course, when it comes to real fighting, they may do us as little good as that group that stayed with you out of the pass all the way up until things looked dangerous and then took off." The regimental commander lifted a cynical eyebrow.

"As long as they aren't raiding us, they can do as they please," Krispos said. "We brought along enough of our own folk to do our fighting for us." He lifted a hand from Progress' neck to pluck at his beard. "I wonder how that column I sent out is faring."

"My guess would be that they are still out swinging wide, your Majesty," Bagradas said. "If they turn north too close to us, Harvas might be able to position men in front of them."

"They were warned about that," Krispos said. One more thing to worry about—

He urged Progress ahead toward the group of sorcerers. They were, he saw without surprise, gathered around Tanilis. Zaidas, who had been animatedly chattering with her, looked over with almost comic startlement as Krispos rode up beside him.

"A good thing I'm not Harvas," Krispos remarked dryly. He bowed in the saddle to Tanilis. "My lady, may I speak with you?"

"Of course, your Majesty. You know you have only to command." She spoke without apparent irony and flicked the reins to get her horse into a trot and away from the wizards. Krispos did the same. Zaidas and the other wizards stared after them in disappointment. When enough clear space had opened up to give them some privacy, Tanilis inclined her head to Krispos. "Your Majesty?"

"I just wanted to say I feel bad about the way things ended between us last night."

"You needn't trouble yourself about it," she replied. "After all, you are the Avtokrator of the Videssians. You may do just as you wish."

"Anthimos did just as he wished," Krispos said angrily. "Look what it got him. I want to try to do what's right, so far as I can see what that is."

"You've chosen a harder road than he did." After a small pause, Tanilis went on in a dispassionate tone of voice, "Few would say that bedding a woman not your wife falls into that category."

"I know, I know, I know." He made a fist and slammed it down on his thigh just below the bottom edge of his coat of mail. "I don't make a habit of it, you know."

"I would have guessed that, yes." Now she sounded amused, perhaps not in an altogether pleasant way.

"It isn't funny, curse it." Doggedly, clumsily, he went ahead: "I'd known you—loved you for a while, though I know you didn't love me—for such a long time, and now I'd seen you again, when I never expected to, well, I never worried about what I was doing till I'd done it. Then that note came, and I got brought up short—"

"Aye, you did." Tanilis studied him. "I might have guessed your marriage was one of convenience only, but two sons born close together argues against that, the more so as you've spent a good part of your reign in the field."

"Oh, there's something of convenience in it, for me and for her both," Krispos admitted, "but there turns out to be more to it than that, too." He laughed without mirth. "You noticed that, didn't you? But all the same, when we'd made love and the courier brought the letter, I had no business treating you the way I did. That's not right, either, and I'm sorry for it."

Tanilis rode on for a little while in silence. Then she remarked, "I think riding into battle might be easier for you than saying what you just said."

Krispos shrugged. "One thing I'm sure of is that putting a crown on my head doesn't make me right all the time. The lord with the great and good mind knows I didn't learn much from

Anthimos about how to rule, but I learned that. And if I was wrong, what's the point in being ashamed to say so?"

"Wherever you learned to rule, Krispos—" He warmed to hear her use his name again, rather than his title. "—you appear to have learned a good deal. Shall we return to being friends, then?"

"Yes," he answered with relief. "How could I be your enemy?"

Mischief sparkled in Tanilis' eyes. "Suppose I came to your tent again tonight. Would you take up saber and shield to drive me away?"

In spite of all his good intentions, his manhood stirred at the thought of her coming to his tent again. He ignored it. *I'm too old to let my prick do my thinking for me,* he told himself firmly. A moment later he added, *I hope.* Aloud, he said, "If you're trying to tempt me, you're doing a good job." He managed a smile.

"I would not seek to tempt you into something you find improper," Tanilis answered seriously. "If that is how it is, let it be so. I said back in Opsikion, all those years ago, that we would not suit each other over the long haul. It still seems true."

"Yes," Krispos said again, with no small regret. He still wondered if he and Dara suited each other over the long haul. Ever since he became Emperor, he'd been away on campaign so much that they'd had scant chance to find out. He went on, "I'm glad we can be friends."

"So am I." Tanilis looked around at the Kubrati countryside through which they were riding. Her voice sank to a whisper. "Being friendless in such a land would be a dreadful fate."

"It's not that bad," Krispos said, remembering his childhood years north of the mountains. "It's just different from Videssos." The sky was a paler, damper blue than inside the Empire. The land was a different shade of green, too, deeper and more like moss; the gray-green olive trees that gave Videssos so much of its distinctive tint would not grow here. The winters, Krispos knew, had a ferocity worse than any Videssos suffered.

But perhaps Tanilis was not seeing the material landscape that was all Krispos could perceive. "This land hates me," she said, shivering though the day was warm. Her sepulchral tone made Krispos want to shiver, too. Then Tanilis brightened, or rather grew intent on her prey. "If we can pull Harvas down, let it hate me as much as it will."

With that Krispos could not argue. He gazed out at Kubrat again. Far off in the northwest, he spied a rising smudge of dirty gray smoke against the horizon. He pointed to it. "Maybe that's the work of the column I sent out," he said hopefully.

Tanilis' gaze swung that way. "Aye, it is your column," she said, but she did not sound hopeful. Krispos tried to make himself believe she was still fretting over the way the land affected her.

But the next morning, as the main body of the army was getting ready to break camp, riders began straggling in from the west. Krispos did not want to talk with the first few of them; as he'd learned, men who got away first often had no idea what had really gone wrong—if anything had.

Sarkis came in about midmorning. A fresh cut seamed one cheek; his right forearm was bandaged. "I'm sorry, Majesty," he said. "I was the one who made the mistake."

"You own up to it, anyhow," Krispos said. "Tell me what happened."

"We came across a village—a town, almost—that isn't on our old maps," the scout commander answered. "I'm not surprised—it looked as if the Halogai were still building it: longhouses are their style, anyhow. Not a lot of men were in it, but those who were came boiling out, and their women with them, armed and fighting as fierce as they were."

Sarkis picked at a flake of dried blood on his face. "Majesty, beating them wasn't the problem. We had plenty of men for that. But I knew our true goal was Pliskavos and I wanted to get there as quick as I could. So instead of doing much more than skirmishing and setting the village ablaze—"

"We saw the smoke," Krispos broke in.

"I shouldn't wonder. Anyhow, I didn't want to lose time by riding around the place, either. So I swung us in on this side instead, and we rode straight north—right into a detachment from Harvas' army. They had more troopers than we did and they beat us, curse 'em."

"Oh, a plague," Krispos said, as much to himself as to Sarkis. He thought for a few seconds. "Any sign of magic in the fight?"

"Not a bit of it," Sarkis answered at once. "The northerners looked to be heading west themselves, to try to cut us off from riding around their army. Thanks to that miserable, stinking flea-farm of a village, they got the chance and they took it. Let me have another go at them, your Majesty, or some new man if you've lost faith in me. The plan was good, and we still have enough room to maneuver to make it work.''

Krispos thought some more and shook his head. "No. A trick may work once against Harvas if it catches him by surprise. I can't imagine him letting us try one twice. Something ghastly would be waiting for us; I feel it in my bones.''

"You're likely right.'' Sarkis hung his head. "Do what you will with me for having failed you.''

"Nothing to be done about it now,'' Krispos answered. "You tried to pick the fastest way to carry out my orders, and it happened not to work. May you be luckier next time.''

"May the good god grant it be so!'' Sarkis said fervently. "I'll make you glad you've trusted me—I promise I will.''

"Good,'' Krispos said. Sarkis saluted and rode away to see the men who were still coming in from the column. Krispos sighed as he watched him go. It would have to be the hard way, then, with the butcher's bill that accompanied the hard way.

He'd already thought about putting peasants back into the border regions south of the mountains. He would also have to find soldiers to replace those who fell in this campaign. Where, he wondered, would all the men come from? He laughed at himself, though it wasn't really funny. Back in his days on the farm, he'd never imagined the Emperor could have any reason to worry, let alone a reason so mundane as finding the people to do what needed doing. He laughed again. Back in his days on the farm, he'd never imagined a lot of things.

Harvas skirmished, screened, avoided pitched battle. He seemed content to let the war turn on what happened after he got to Pliskavos. That worried Krispos. Even the Kubratoi and the Videssian-speaking peasants who flocked to his army and acclaimed him as a liberator failed to cheer him. Kubrat would return to imperial rule if he beat Harvas, aye. If he lost, the nomads and peasants both would only suffer more for acclaiming him.

As his force neared Pliskavos, he began sending out striking columns again, not to cut Harvas off from the capital of Kubrat but rather to ensure that he and his army went nowhere else. One of the columns sent men galloping back in high excitement. "The Astris! The Astris!'' they shouted as they returned to the main force from the northwest. They were the first imperial soldiers to reach the river in three hundred years.

Another column came to the Astris east of Pliskavos a day later. Instead of sending back proud troopers to boast of what they'd done, they shouted for reinforcements. "A whole raft of Halogai are crossing the river on boats," a rider gasped as he rode in, mixing his metaphors but getting the message across.

Krispos dispatched reinforcements on the double. He also sent a company of soldiers from the first column that had reached the Astris to ride west along its bank toward the Videssian Sea. "Find Kanaris and bring him here," he ordered. "This is why we have ships on the Astris. Let's see the northerners put more men across it once he sails up."

He saw the Astris himself the next day. The wide gray river flowed past Pliskavos, which lay by its southern bank. The stream was wide enough to make the steppes and forests on the far bank seem distant and unreal. Unfortunately quite real, however, were the little boats that scurried across it. Each one brought a new band of Halogai to help Harvas hold the land he'd seized. Krispos raged, but could do little more until the grand drungarios of the fleet arrived. While he waited, the army began to built a palisade around Pliskavos.

"Something occurs to me," Mammianos said that evening. "I don't know as much as I'd like about fighting on water or much of anything about magic, but what's to keep Harvas from hurting our dromons when they do come up the Astris?"

Kristos gnawed on his lower lip. "We'd better talk with the magicians."

By the time the talk was done, Krispos found himself missing Trokoundos not just because the mage had been a friend. Trokoundos had been able to make sorcerous matters clear to people who were not wizards. His colleagues left Krispos feeling as confused as he was enlightened. He gathered, though, that sorcery aimed at targets on running water tended to be weakened or to go astray altogether.

He didn't care for the sound of that *tended to*. "I hope Harvas has read the same magical books you have," he told the wizards.

"Your Majesty, I see no sorcerous threat looming over Kanaris' fleet," Zaidas said.

"Nor do I," Tanilis agreed. Zaidas blinked, then beamed. He sent Tanilis a worshipful look. She nodded to him, a regal gesture Krispos knew well. The force of it seemed to daze Zaidas, who was younger and more susceptible than Krispos ever had been when he knew her. Krispos shook his head; noticing how young other people were was a sign he wasn't so young himself. But he had as much assurance from his wizards as he could hope for. That was worth a slight feeling of antiquity.

The palisade around Pliskavos grew stronger over the next couple of days. The troopers dug a ditch and used the dirt from it to build a rampart behind it. They mounted shields on top of the rampart to make it even higher. All the same, the gray stone wall of Pliskavos stood taller still.

The Halogai sallied several times, seeking to disrupt the men who were busy strengthening the palisade. They fought with their folk's usual reckless courage and paid heavily for it. Each day, though, dugouts brought fresh bands of northerners across the Astris and into Pliskavos.

"Halogaland must be grim indeed, if so many of the northerners brave the trip across Pardraya in hopes of settling here," Krispos observed at an evening meeting with his officers.

"Aye, true enough, for the lands hereabouts are nothing to brag of," Mammianos said. Krispos did not entirely trust the fat general's sense of proportion; the coastal lowlands where Mammianos had been stationed were the richest farming country in the whole Empire.

Sarkis put in, "I wonder how many villages like the one that gave me trouble have been planted on Kubrati soil. We'll have to finish the job of uprooting them once we're done here." A gleam came into his dark eyes. "I wouldn't mind uprooting one or two of those gold-haired northern women myself."

Several of the men in Krispos' tent nodded. Fair hair was rare—and exotically interesting—in Videssos. "Have a care now, Sarkis," Mammianos rumbled. "From what you've told us, the Haloga wenches fight back."

Everyone laughed. "You should have tried sweet talk, Sarkis," Bagradas said. The laughter got louder.

"I hadn't gone there to woo them then," Sarkis answered tartly.

"Back to business," Krispos said, trying without much success to sound stern. "How soon can we be ready to storm Pliskavos?"

His officers exchanged worried looks. "Starving the place into submission would be a lot cheaper, your Majesty," Mammianos said. "Harvas can't have supplies for all the men he's jammed in there, no matter how full his warehouses are. His troops'll start taking sick before long, too, crowded together the way they must be.''

"So will ours, in spite of everything the healer-priests can do," Krispos answered. Mammianos nodded; camp fevers could cost an army more men than combat. Krispos went on, "Even so, I'd say you were right most of the time. But not against Harvas Black-Robe. The more time he has to ready himself in there, the more I fear him.''

Mammianos sighed. "Aye, some truth in what you say. He is a proper bugger, isn't he?" He glanced around to the other officers, as if hoping one of them would speak out for delay. No one did. Mammianos sighed again. "Well, Majesty, we have ladders and such in the baggage train, and all the metal parts and cordage for siege engines. We'll need some time to knock down trees for their frames and cut the wood to fit, but as soon as that's done we can take a crack at it.''

"How long?" Krispos insisted.

"A week, maybe a day or two less," Mammianos said, obviously reluctant to be pinned down. "Other thing is, though, that Harvas'd have to be blind not to see what we're up to as we prepare. He's a lot of nasty things, but blind isn't any of them.''

"I know," Krispos said. "Still, he knows what we're here for anyhow. We didn't fight our way across Kubrat to offer to harvest his turnips. Let's get those engines started." Mammianos and the rest of the officers saluted. With orders given, they would obey.

The next morning, armed parties rode out to chop timber. By midday horses and mules began hauling back roughly trimmed logs. Under the watchful eyes of the engineers who would assemble and direct the use of the catapults and rams, soldiers cut the wood to proper lengths. The noise of carpentry filled the camp.

Mammianos had been right: the Halogai on Pliskavos' walls had no doubt what the imperials were doing. They jeered and waved their axes and swords in defiance. The ones with a few words of Videssian yelled out what sort of welcome the attackers were likely to receive. Some of Krispos' soldiers yelled back. Most just kept working.

A tall, thin pillar of smoke rose into the sky from somewhere near the center of Pliskavos. When Zaidas saw it, he turned pale and drew the sun-circle over his heart. All the wizards with the imperial army redoubled their apotropaic spells.

"What exactly is Harvas up to?" Krispos asked Zaidas, reasoning he would be most likely to know because of his sensitive sorcerous vision.

But the young mage only shook his head. "Nothing good," was the sole answer he would give. "That smoke—" He shuddered and sketched the sun-sign again. This time Krispos did the same.

The wizards' concern made Krispos more and more edgy. Nor was his temper improved when a dozen more dugouts full of Halogai landed at Pliskavos' quays before the sun reached its zenith. In the late afternoon, Videssian watchers on the shore of the Astris spied another small flotilla getting ready to set out from the northern bank.

The news went straight to Krispos. He slammed his fist down onto his portable desk and scowled at the messenger. "By the good god, I wish we could do something about these bastards," he growled. "Every one of them who gets into town means another one who'll be able to kill our men."

Seldom in a man's life are prayers answered promptly; all too seldom in a man's life are prayers answered at all. But Krispos was still fuming when another messenger burst into his tent, this one fairly hopping with excitement. "Majesty," he cried, "we've spotted Kanaris' ships rowing their way upstream against the current!"

"Have you?" Krispos said softly. He rolled up the message he'd been reading. It could wait. "This I want to see for myself." He hurried out of the tent, shouting for Progress. He booted the gelding into a gallop. In a few minutes, the horse stood blowing by the riverbank.

Krispos peered west, using a hand to shield his eyes from the sun. Sure enough, up the river stormed the lean shark-shapes of the imperial dromons. Their twin banks of oars rose and fell in swift unison. Spray flew from the polished bronze rams the ships bore at their bows. Sailors and marines hurried about on the decks, readying the dromons for combat.

The Halogai had paddled their dugout canoes scarcely a quarter of the way across the Astris. They might have turned around and got back safe to the northern shore, but they did not even try: retreat was a word few northerners knew. They only bent their backs and paddled harder. A few of the dugouts sported small masts. Sails sprouted from those now.

For a moment Krispos thought the Halogai might win their race into Pliskavos, but the Videssian warships caught them a couple of hundred yards from the quays. Darts flew from the catapults at the dromons' bows. So did covered clay pots, which trailed smoke as they arced through the air. One burst in the middle of a dugout. In an instant the canoe was ablaze from one end to the other. So were the men inside. Thinned by long travel over water, their screams came to Krispos' ears. The Halogai who could plunged into the Astris. Their mail shirts dragged them to the bottom, an easier end than one filled with flame.

A dromon's ram broke a dugout in half. More Halogai, these unburned, thrashed in the water, but not for long. Videssian marines shot those who did not sink at once from the weight of their armor.

Another canoe broke free from the midriver melee and sprinted for the protection of Pliskavos' docks. Halogai on the walls of the town cheered their countrymen on. But a dromon quickly closed on the canoe. Instead of ramming, the captain chose a different form of fire. A sailor aimed a wooden tube faced inside with bronze at the fleeing dugout. Two more men worked a hand pump similar to the ones the fire brigades used in Videssos the city. But they did not pump water—out spurted the same incendiary brew that had incinerated the first Haloga canoe. This one suffered a like fate, for the sheet of fire that covered it was nearly as long as it was. The northerners writhed and wilted in the fire like moths in a torchflame.

Krispos' head swiveled back and forth as he looked around for more dugout canoes. He saw none. In the space of a couple of minutes, the imperial dromons had swept the river clear. Only a couple of chunks of flaming debris that drifted downstream and were gone said any folk but the Videssians had ever been on the Astris.

The soldiers by the water who had watched the fight yelled themselves hoarse as the dromons came in to beach themselves on the riverbank. Inside Pliskavos, the Halogai were as silent as if the town were uninhabited.

The grand drungarios' barred pennant snapped at the stern of a galley not far from Krispos. He rode Progress over to the dromon and got there just as Kanaris was coming down the gangplank to the ground. "Well done!" Krispos called.

Kanaris waved to him, then saluted more formally. "Well done yourself, Majesty," he answered, his deep, gruff voice pitched to carry over wind and wave. "Sorry we were west of here, but who thought you'd push all the way to Pliskavos? Well done indeed."

Praise from a longtime warrior always made Krispos proud, for he knew what an amateur he was in matters military. He called for a messenger. When one came up, he told the fellow, "Fetch some of the wizards here. The fleet will need them."

As the messenger rode away, Kanaris said, "We have our own wizards aboard, Majesty."

"No doubt," Krispos aid. "But I've brought the finest mages from the Sorcerers' Collegium up with the army. Harvas Black-Robe is no ordinary enemy, and you've given him special reason to hate you and your ships right now."

"Have it your way, then, Majesty," the grand drungarios said. "By the look of things, you've been right so far."

"Aye, so far." Krispos sketched the sun-sign to turn aside any evil omen. He also reminded himself never to take anything for granted against a foe like Harvas.

Krispos raised his cup. "To tomorrow," he said.

"To tomorrow," the officers in the imperial tent echoed. They, too, held their wine cups high, then emptied them and filed out. Twilight still tinged the western sky, but they all had many things to see to before they sought their bedrolls. Tomorrow the imperial army would attack Pliskavos.

Krispos paced back and forth, trying again to find holes in the plan he and his generals had hammered out. For all their planning, there would be holes and the attack would reveal them. War, he had learned, was like that. If he could find one or two of them before the trumpets blew, he would save lives.

But he could not. He kept pacing for a while anyhow, to work off nervous energy. Then he blew out all the lamps save one, undressed, and lay down on his cot. Sleep would be slow coming. Best to start seeking it early.

He was warm and relaxed and just drifting off when Geirrod poked his head into the tent. "Majesty, the lady Tanilis would see you," the imperial guardsman said.

"*Must* see you," Tanilis corrected from outside.

"Wait a minute," he said muzzily. Cursing under his breath at having rest jerked out from under him, he pulled a robe on over his head and relit a couple of the lamps he'd put out not long before. As he went about that homely labor, his bad temper eased and his wits began to clear. He nodded to Geirrod. "Let her come in."

"Aye, Majesty." The Haloga managed to bow and hold the tent flap open at the same time. "Go in, my lady," he said, his voice as respectful as if Tanilis were of imperial rank.

Any thought that she was seeking to seduce him for her own advantage disappeared when Krispos got a good look at her face. For the first time he saw her haggard, her hair awry, her eyes hollow and dark-circled, lines harshly carved on her forehead and at the corners of her mouth. "By the good god!" he exclaimed. "What's wrong?"

Without asking leave—again most unlike her—Tanilis sank into a folding chair. The motion held none of her usual grace, only exhaustion. "You will assail Harvas in his lair tomorrow," she said.

It was flat statement, not question. She had not been at the officers' conclave, but the signs of a building attack were hard to hide. Krispos nodded. "Aye, we will. What of it?"

"You must not." Again Tanilis' voice held no room for doubt; only Pyrrhos, perhaps, pronouncing on some point of dogma, could have sounded as certain. "If you do, much the greater part of the army will surely be destroyed."

"You've—seen—this?" Even as the words passed his lips, Krispos knew how foolish they were. Tanilis would not trouble him with ordinary worries.

She did not twit him for stupidity, either, as she might have were the matter less urgent and she less worn. She simply answered, "I have seen this." She rested for a moment, slumped down with her chin in her hands. Then, drawing on some reserve of resolution, she straightened. "Yes, I have seen. When I wrote you after Mavros was slain, I said I know Harvas' power was greater than mine, but I hoped to face him nonetheless. Now I have faced him. His power—" She shivered, though the night was warm and muggy. When she slumped again, the heels of her hands covered her eyes.

Krispos went to her and put his hand on her shoulder. He'd done the same just before they made love, but this touch had nothing of the erotic to it. It was support and care, as he might have given any friend brought low by killing labor. He said, "What did you do, Tanilis?"

The words dragged from her, one by one. "Since Harvas was willing to stand siege, I sought to spy, to seek—aye, to sneak—

from his mind how he aimed to answer us when the time came. I did not plan to confront him directly; had I done so, I would now be lying dead in my tent. I came near enough to that as it was.''

She paused to rest again. Krispos poured her a cup of wine. She seemed a little restored after she drank it. Her voice was stronger as she went on, ''Even entering the corners of that mind is like tiptoeing through a maze of death. He has shields and spike-filled snares in his head, snares beyond counting. Be thankful you are mindblind, dear Krispos, that you never need to touch such evil. I made myself very small, hoping he would not notice me . . .'' Tears ran down her cheeks. She did not seem to know they were there.

''What did you do?'' Krispos asked again.

''I found what I sought. Were Harvas less arrogant, less sure of himself, he would have caught me no matter what I did. But down deep, he will not believe any mere mortal truly able to challenge him. And so, beneath his notice, I found what he intended—and I fled.''

Of themselves, Krispos' hands curled into fists. ''And what is waiting for us?'' he demanded.

''Fire.'' Tanilis answered. ''I know not how—nor did I stay to try to learn—but Harvas has made the city wall of Pliskavos a great reservoir of flame. At his will or signal, the wall can be ignited. Most likely he would wait until our men are on it everywhere, perhaps beginning to drop down into Pliskavos. Then he could burn those on the wall and climbing up it, and also trap the intrepid souls who aimed to take the fight farther.''

''But he'd burn the defenders on the wall, too,'' Krispos said.

''Would he care?'' Tanilis asked brutally.

''No,'' Krispos admitted, ''not if they served his purpose. It would, too—he wouldn't have to have many Halogai up there, just enough to slow us, to make us think we were overpowering them because of our might. And then—'' He did not want to think about ''and then,'' not so soon after watching what the dromons' invincible fire did to dugout canoes and men.

''Exactly so,'' Tanilis said. ''You see you must delay the attack, then, until our mages devise some suitable countermeasure to abate the menace of this—''

''Hold on,'' Krispos said. Tanilis tried to continue. He shook his head at her. ''Hold on,'' he repeated, more sharply this time. A couple of ideas rattled around in his head. If he could bring them together . . . He did, with almost an audible click. His eyes widened. "Suppose we lit the wall first," he whispered. "What then?"

Fatigue fell from Tanilis like a discarded cloak as she surged to her feet. "Yes, by the lord with the great and good mind!" She and Krispos hugged, not so much like lovers as like conspirators who realized they'd hatched the perfect plot.

Krispos stuck his head out of the tent. Geirrod came to smart attention. "Never mind that," Krispos said. "Get me Mammianos and then get me Kanaris."

Drawn up in full battle array, the imperial army ringed the entire landward perimeter of Pliskavos. Horns and drums and pipes whipped the soldiers toward full martial fury. The men shouted Krispos' name and bellowed abuse and threats at the Halogai on the walls.

The Halogai roared back, crying defiance to the sky. "Come on, little men, try us!" one shouted. "We make you littler still!" He threw his axe high in the air and caught it with a flourish.

Siege engines bucked and snapped. Stones and great darts flew toward Pliskavos. Engineers returned the machines' throwing arms to their proper positions, checked ropes, reloaded, then hauled on windlasses to tighten the cordage to the point where the engines could cast again. Meanwhile archers skipped forward to add their missiles to those of the catapults.

Not many Halogai were bowmen; the fighting they reveled in was hand to hand. Those who had bows shot back. A couple of Videssians fell; more northerners tumbled from the wall. The main body of imperial troops shouted and made as if to surge toward the wall. The Halogai roared back.

Krispos watched all that from the riverbank west of Pliskavos. It was a fine warlike display, with banners flying and polished armor gleaming under the morning sun. He hoped Harvas found it as riveting as he did himself. If all the wizard's attention focused there, he would pay no heed to the pair of dromons now gliding up the Astris toward his town.

With their twin banks of oars, thirty oars to a bank, the war galleys reminded Krispos of centipedes striding over the water. Such smooth motion seemed impossible. As with anything else, it came by dint of endless practice.

Closer and closer to the quays at the bottom of the wall came the two dromons. Krispos watched the marines who were busy at their bows. A few Halogai watched, too, watched and jeered. A whole fleet of dromons might have carried enough warriors to attack Pliskavos from the river. Two were no threat.

Aboard each vessel, an officer raised his hand, then let it fall. The marines at the hand pumps swing their handles up and down, up and down. Twin sheets of flame belched from the wood-and-bronze siphon tubes. The quays caught at once. Black smoke shot skyward. Then the flames splashed against the wall.

For most of a minute, as the marines aboard the dromons kept pumping out their incendiary mixture, Krispos could not tell whether Tanilis had stolen the truth from Harvas' mind, whether his own scheme could disrupt the wizard's plan. Then the tubs of firemix went dry. The fiery streams stopped pouring from the siphons. The wall still burned.

Slowly at first, then quicker and quicker, the flames spread. The dromons backed oars to get away from a conflagration greater than any they were intended to confront. The Halogai atop the river wall poured buckets of water down onto the fire. It kept burning, kept spreading. The Halogai poured again, with no better luck. Krispos saw them stare down, the images of their bodies wavering through heat-haze. Then they gave up and ran away.

The flames were already running as fast as a man could. They burned a brilliant yellow, brighter and hotter than the orange-red fire that had spawned them. They reached the top of the wall and threw themselves high into the air, as if in play.

"By the good god," Krispos whispered. He sketched Phos' sun-sign. At the same time, he narrowed his eyes against the growing glare from Pliskavos. His face heated, as if he were standing in front of a fireplace. So he was, but several hundred yards away.

Halogai ran all along the wall now, even where the flames had not yet reached. Their terrified shouts rose above the crackle and hiss of the fire. Then the flames that had gone one way around Pliskavos met those that had gone the other, and there was nowhere to run anymore. Harvas' city was a perfect ring of fire.

The wall itself burned with a clean, almost smokeless flame. Before long, though, smoke did start rising up from inside Pliskavos—and no wonder, Krispos thought. By then he had already moved back from the fire twice. Houses and other buildings could not move back. So close to so much heat, they had to ignite, too.

Kanaris came up to Krispos. The grand drungarios of the fleet pursed his lips in a soundless whistle as he watched Pliskavos burn. "There's a grim sight," he said. As a lifelong sailing man, he feared fire worse than any foe.

Krispos remembered the fright fire had given him the winter before, when wind whipped Midwinter's Day blazes out of control. All the same he said, "It's winning our war for us. Would you sooner have watched our soldiers burn as they tried to storm those walls? Harvas intended the flames for us, you know."

"Oh, aye, he and his deserve them," Kanaris answered at once, "and the ice they'll meet in the world to come, as well. But there are easier ways of dying." He pointed toward the base of the wall.

Some Halogai had chosen to leap to their deaths rather than burn. As is the way of such things, not all had killed themselves cleanly. They burned anyway, most of them, and had the added torment of splintered bones and crushed organs to accompany the anguish of the fire that ate their flesh. The strongest and luckiest tried to crawl away from the flames toward the Videssian line. Forgetting for a moment that they were deadly enemies, imperial troopers darted out to drag two or three of them to safety. Healer-priests hurried up to do what they could for the Halogai.

The fire burned on and on. Krispos ordered his men out of their battle line. Until the flames subsided, they screened Pliskavos better than the wall from which they sprang. The soldiers watched the fire with something approaching awe. They cheered Krispos almost frantically, whether for having raised the fire or for having saved them from it he could not tell.

He wondered what Harvas was doing, was thinking, there inside his burning wall. After three hundred years of unnatural life, did the evil wizard have teeth left to gnash? Whether or no, his hopes were burning with the wall. A sudden savage grin twisted Krispos' mouth. Maybe Harvas had even been on the wall when it went up. That would be be justice indeed!

Afternoon came, and evening. Pliskavos kept burning. The sky grew dark; the evening star appeared. It might still have been noon in the Videssian camp, so brilliant was the firelight. Only its occasional flicker said that light was born of flames rather than the sun.

Krispos made himself go into his tent. Sooner or later the flames would die. When they did, the army would need orders.

He wanted to be fresh, to be sure he gave the right ones. But how was he to sleep when the glow that came through the silk fabric of his tent testified to the fearful marvel outside?

And outside one of the guards said, "Aye, my lady, he's within." The Haloga looked into the tent. "The lady Tanilis would see you, Majesty. Ah, good, you're up and about." Krispos hadn't been, but hearing *my lady* had bounced him from his cot faster than anything short of a sally out of Pliskavos.

When Tanilis came in, Krispos pointed to the bright light that played on the silk. "That victory is yours, Tanilis," he said. Then he gave her the salute properly reserved for the Emperor alone: "Thou conquerest!" He took her in his arms and kissed her.

He'd intended nothing more than that, but she returned the kiss with a desperate intensity unlike anything he'd known from her before. She clung to him so tightly that he could feel her heartbeat through her robe and his. She would not let him go. Before long, all his continent intentions, all his promises to control himself and his body, were swept away in a tide of furious excitement that seemed as hot and fiery as Pliskavos' flaming wall. Still clutching each other, he and Tanilis tumbled to the cot, careless of whether it broke beneath them, as it nearly did.

"Quickly, oh, quickly," she urged him, not that he needed much urging. The cool, practiced competence she usually brought to bed was gone now, leaving only desire. When she arched her back beneath him and quivered at the final instant, she cried out his name again and again. He scarcely heard her. A moment later, he, too, cried out, wordlessly, as he spent himself.

The world apart from their still-joined bodies returned to him little by little. He leaned up on his elbows, or began to, but Tanilis' arms tightened round his back. "Don't leave me," she said. "Don't go. Don't ever go."

Her eyes, scant inches from his own, were huge and staring. He wondered if she was truly looking at him. The last time— the only time—he'd seen eyes so wide was when Gnatios met the executioner. He shook his head; the comparison disturbed him. "What's wrong?" He stroked her cheek.

She did not respond directly. "I wish we could do it again, right now, one last time," she said.

"Again?" Krispos had to laugh. "After that, Tanilis, I'm not sure I could do it again in a week, let alone right now." Then he frowned as he listened again in his own mind to all of what she'd said. "What do you mean, one last time?"

Now she shoved him away from her. "Too late," she whispered. "Oh, too late for everything."

Once more Krispos hardly heard her. This time, though, it was not because of passion but rather pain. Agony such as he had never known filled every crevice of his body. Again he thought of the burning walls of Pliskavos. Now that fire seemed to blaze within his bones, to be consuming him from the inside out. He tried to scream, but his throat was on fire, too, and no sound came forth.

A new voice echoed in the tiny corner of his mind not given over to torment: "Little man, thinkest thou to thwart me? Thinkest thou thy fribbling futile mages suffice to save what I would slay? Aye, they cost me effort, but with effort cometh reward. Learn of my might as thou diest, and despair."

Tanilis must have heard that cold, hateful voice, too, for she said, "No, Harvas, you may not have him." Her tone now was as calm and matter-of-fact as if the wizard were in the tent with them.

Krispos felt a tiny fragment of his anguish ease as Harvas shifted his regard to Tanilis. "Be silent, naked slut, lest I deal with thee next."

"Deal with me if you can, Harvas." Tanilis' chin went up in defiance. "I say you may not have this man. This I have foreseen."

"Damnation to thy foreseeing, and to thee." Harvas returned. "Since thou'dst know the wretch's body, know what it suffereth now, as well."

Tanilis gasped. With a great effort of will, Krispos turned his eyes toward her. She was biting her lip to keep from crying out. Blood trickled from the corner of her mouth. But she would not yield. "Do your worst to me," she told Harvas. "It cannot be a tithe of the harm Krispos and I worked against your wicked scheme this day."

Harvas screamed then, so loudly that for a moment Krispos wondered why no guardsmen burst in to see who was slaying whom. But the scream sounded only in his mind, and in Tanilis'. More torment lifted from him. Tanilis said, "Here, Harvas. As you give, so shall you get. Let me be a mirror, to reflect your gifts. This is what I feel from you now."

Harvas screamed again, but in an altogether different way. He was used to inflicting pain, not to receiving it. Krispos' anguish went away. He thought Tanilis had forced the wizard to yield, simply by making him experience what he was used to handing out. But when Krispos glanced over at her, he saw her fine features were still death-pale and twisted in torment. Her struggle with Harvas was not yet done.

Krispos drew in a long, miraculously pain-free breath. He opened his mouth to shout for more wizards to come to Tanilis' rescue. No sound emerged. Despite everything Tanilis was doing to him—everything he was doing to himself—Harvas still had the strength to enjoin silence on Krispos. And Tanilis agreed. "This is between the two of us now, Krispos." She returned her attention to her foe. "Here, Harvas: This is what I felt when I learned you had slain my son. You should know all your gifts in full."

Harvas howled like a wolf with its leg crushed in the jaws of a trap. But he was trapper as well as victim. He had endured a great deal in his sorcerously prolonged span of days. Though Tanilis wounded him as he had never been wounded before, he did not release her from agony he, too, felt. If he could bear it longer than she, victory would in the end be his. Krispos caught an echo of what he whispered, longingly, again and again to Tanilis: "Die. Oh, die."

"When I do, may you go with me," she answered. "I will rise to Phos' light while you spend eternity in the ice of your master Skotos."

"I usher in my master's dominion to the world. Thy Phos hath failed; only fools feel it not. And thou hast not the power to drag me into death with thee. See now!"

Tanilis whimpered on the cot beside Krispos. Her hand reached out and clutched his forearm. Her nails bit into his flesh, deep enough to draw blood. Then all at once that desperate grip went slack. Her eyes rolled up; her chest no longer rose and fell with breath. Krispos knew she was dead.

While the link with Harvas held, he heard in his mind the beginning of a frightened wail. But the link was abruptly cut, clean as a cord sword-severed. Had Tanilis succeeded in taking the evil wizard down to death with her? If not, she had to have left him hurt and weakened. But the price she'd paid—

Krispos bent down to brush his lips against those that had so recently bruised his. Now they did not respond. "May you be avenged," he said softly.

A new and bitter thought crossed his mind: he wondered if she'd foreseen her own doom when she set out from Opsikion to join the imperial army. Being who and what she was, she must have. Her behavior argued for it—she'd acted like someone who knew she had very little time. But she'd come all the same, heedless of her safety. Krispos shook his head in wonder and renewed grief.

He heard rapid footsteps outside, footsteps that came to a sudden stop in front of the imperial tent. "What do you want, wizard?" a Haloga guardsman demanded.

"I must see his Majesty," Zaidas answered. His young, light voice cracked in the middle of the sentence.

"You must, eh?" The guardsman did not sound impressed. "What you must do, young sir, is wait."

"But—"

"Wait," the guard said implacably. He raised his voice, pitching it so Krispos would notice it inside the tent. "Majesty, a wizard out here would have speech with you." The guard did not poke his head right into the tent now, not after Tanilis had gone in. Yes, he had his own ideas about what was going on in there. Krispos wished he was right.

Wishing did as much good as usual, no more and no less. Krispos slowly got to his feet. "I'll be with you soon," he called to the guard and Zaidas. He put on his robe, then covered Tanilis' body with hers. He straightened. No help for it now. "Let the wizard come in."

Zaidas started to fall to his knees to prostrate himself before Krispos but broke off the ritual gesture when he saw Tanilis lying dead on the cot. Her eyes were still open, staring up at nothing.

"Oh, no," Zaidas whispered. He sketched the sun-sign over his heart. Then he looked at Tanilis again, this time not in shocked surprise but with the trained eye of a mage. He turned to Krispos. "Harvas' work," he said without hesitation or doubt.

"Yes." Krispos' voice was flat and empty.

Lines of grief etched Zaidas' face; in that moment, Krispos saw what the young man would look like when he was fifty. "I sensed the danger," Zaidas said, "but only the edges of it, and not soon enough, I see. Would I had been the one to lay down life for you, Majesty, not the lady."

"Would that no one ever needed to lay down life for me," Krispos said as flatly as before.

"Oh, aye, your Majesty, aye," Zaidas stammered. "But the lady Tanilis, she was—she was—something, someone special." He scowled in frustration at the inadequacy of his words. Krispos remembered how Zaidas had hung on everything Tanilis said when the wizards gathered together, remembered the worshipful look in the younger man's eye. He'd loved her, or been infatuated with her—at his age, the difference was hard to know. Krispos remembered that, too, from Opsikion.

Love or infatuation, Zaidas had spoken only the truth. "Someone special? She was indeed," Krispos said. Harvas had cost him so many who were dear to him: his sister Evdokia, his brother-in-law, his nieces, Mavros, Trokoundos, now Tanilis. But Tanilis had hit back, hit back harder than Harvas could have expected. How hard? Now Krispos' voice held urgency. "Zaidas, see what you can sense of Harvas for me."

"Of his plans, do you mean, your Majesty?" the young mage asked in some alarm. "I could not probe deeply without his detecting me; probing at all is no small risk—"

"Not his plans," Krispos said quickly. "Just see if he's there and active inside Pliskavos."

"Very well, your Majesty; I can do that safely enough, I think," Zaidas said. "As you've seen, even the subtlest screening techniques leave signs of their presence, the more so if they screen a presence as powerful as Harvas'. Let me think. We bless thee, Phos, lord with the—"

Zaidas' voice grew dreamy and far away as he repeated Phos' creed to focus his concentration and slide into a trance, much as a healer-priest might have done. But instead of laying hands on a wounded man, Zaidas turned toward Pliskavos. His eyes were wide and unblinking and seemed sightless, but Krispos knew they sensed more than any normal man's.

After a couple of minutes of turning ever so slightly this way and that, as if he were a hunting dog unsure of a scent, Zaidas slowly came back to himself. He still looked like a puzzled hound, though, as he said, "Your Majesty, I can't find him. I feel he ought to be there, but it's as if he's not. It's no screen I've ever met before. I don't know what it is." He did not enjoy confessing ignorance.

"By the good god, magical sir, I think *I* know what it is. It's Tanilis." Krispos told Zaidas the whole story of her struggle against Harvas Black-Robe.

"I think you're right, your Majesty," Zaidas said when he was through. The young mage bowed to the cot on which Tanilis lay as if she were a living queen. "Either she slew Harvas as she herself was slain, or at the very least hurt him so badly that his torch of power is reduced to a guttering ember too small for me even to discern."

"Which means all we face in Pliskavos is an army of ferocious Halogai," Krispos said. He and Zaidas beamed at each other. Next to the prospect of battling Harvas Black-Robe again, any number of berserk, fearless axe-swinging northerners seemed a stroll in the meadow by comparison.

# XII

The walls of Pliskavos burned all through the night. Only when morning came again did the flames begin to subside. Smoke still rose here and there inside the town from the fires the blazing wall had started.

Two heralds, one a Videssian, the other from Krispos' force of Haloga guards, approached the wall as closely at its heat would allow. In the imperial speech and the tongue of Halogaland, they called on the northerners inside Pliskavos to yield, "... the more so," as the Videssian-speaker put it, "since the evil wizard who brought you to this pass can no longer aid you."

Krispos held his breath at that, afraid in spite of everything that Harvas had been laying low for reasons of his own and would now reappear with redoubled malice and might. But of Harvas there was no sign. The Halogai did not yield, either. The heralds called out their message again and again, then withdrew to the imperial lines. Pliskavos remained silent, smoky, and enigmatic the whole day long.

At the officers' meeting just after sunset, Krispos said, "If the walls have cooled enough by morning, we'll send men up onto them to see what's going on in there."

"Aye," Mammianos said. "It's not like the cursed northerners to keep so quiet so long. They're up to something we'll likely regret—unless they've all been roasted, but that's too much to ask for, worse luck."

The rest of the generals loudly and profanely agreed with him. Then Bagradas raised his wine cup and said, "Let's drink to the brave lady Tanilis, who made sure they were the ones who roasted rather than us, and who made Harvas choke on his own bile.''

''Tanilis!'' The officers shouted out her name. Krispos spoke it with the rest of them and drank with them as well. The meeting broke up soon afterward. The soldiers filed out of the imperial tent, leaving him alone.

He sat down on the edge of the cot. He shook his head. The night before, Tanilis and he had shared the cot first in triumph, then in terror. Now she was dead, and Bagradas' well-meaning toast did not, could not, begin to do justice to what she'd accomplished. Zaidas understood far more. Krispos wondered how much he understood himself.

Too much had happened too fast—his emotions were still several jumps behind events. Instead of victorious or full of grief, he mostly felt battered, as if he'd gone through rapids without a boat.

He drained his cup, then poured another and drained that. Then he set down the jar of wine. Tanilis would have wanted him to stop, he thought: he'd need a clear head come morning. He undressed and lay down where he had lain with Tanilis; the scent of her still clung to the blanket. Tears filled his eyes. He angrily brushed them aside. Tears were no fit monument for Tanilis. Finishing what she'd made possible was. He did his best to sleep.


''Majesty!'' a Haloga guard boomed. ''There's stirring inside Pliskavos, Majesty.''

Krispos woke with a grunt. A guttering lamp gave the tent all the light it had; the sun was not yet up. ''I'll be out soon,'' he called. He got out of bed, used the chamber pot, and put on his gilded coat of mail.

He saw the eastern sky had turned gray. ''What's toward?'' he asked the guardsman.

''That we don't yet know, Majesty. But through the grates of the portcullises some scouts have spied the warriors within Pliskavos milling about. Come the dawn, we'll have a better notion of why.''

''True enough,'' Krispos said. ''We'd best be ready for the worst, though.'' Night or day, a detachment of military musicians remained on duty. Krispos went over to them. ''Call the men from their tents and to assembly.'' As the martial music rang out, he hurried up to the palisade to see what was going on for himself.

As the guard had said, no one could tell just what was going on in Pliskavos, but something definitely was. The wooden gates had been burned to ashes when the wall caught fire, but the portcullises' iron grills survived. Through the grillwork Krispos saw shadowy motion. He could not make out more than that, even as twilight brightened toward dawn.

Behind him, noise quickly built as the imperial army readied itself for whatever might come. Men called back and forth; underofficers shouted; swords and quivers and armor rattled; horses snorted and complained as troopers tightened girths. Through it all, the musicians kept playing. Their music got louder, too, as more of them came on duty.

The sun rose. Krispos sketched Phos' circle over his heart as he murmured the creed. It was also on other men's lips as they caught the day's first sight of the chiefest symbol of the good god.

Mammianos came up to Krispos. He said, "If they are going to try to break out, your Majesty, do you want to meet them behind the palisade or before it?"

"If everything goes well, meeting them behind the palisade would be cheapest," Krispos mused. "But we'd be stretched all along the line around Pliskavos, and they might well rush their men at one point and smash their way through us." He rubbed his chin. "I hate to say it, but I think we have to meet them face to face. What do you say, Mammianos? I halfway hope you can talk me out of it."

The fat general grunted, far from happily. "No, I fear you have the right of it, your Majesty. I was hoping you could talk me round to the other way, but you see the same dangers I do." He grunted again. "I'll pass on the word, then."

"Thank you, eminent sir."

The musicians' calls changed from *Assembly* to *Battle Stations*. Officers' orders amplified the music. "No, not behind the rampart, lads. Today we're going to let them see what they'll be tangling with if they have the stones for it."

Krispos made his own way back through the crowd to the imperial tent. As he'd expected, Progress was saddled and waiting for him. He checked the straps under the saddle for tightness, then swung his left foot into the stirrup. Climbing onto Progress reminded him how Mavros had helped him choose the big bay gelding, and helped haggle the price down, too.

"One more win, foster brother of mine—one more win and you and your mother are both avenged," he said softly.

He rode out through a gap in the palisade and took his place at the center of the imperial army that was rapidly forming up in front of Pliskavos. He thought about sending his heralds up to the town to call once more for the Halogai to surrender, but decided not to. Soon enough the northerners would show what they intended to do.

The thought had hardly crossed his mind when the portcullises began to rise. They did not move smoothly; one, indeed, warped by the heat of the burning wall, stuck in its track with its spiked lower edge about four feet off the ground. That did not keep hundreds of armed Halogai from ducking under it as they filed out of Pliskavos. More of the big blond warriors came through other gates.

"They don't look like men about to yield," Mammianos said.

"No, they don't," Krispos agreed glumly. The leading ranks of Halogai carried big shields that protected them almost from head to foot. Behind that shield wall—almost a palisade in itself—the rest of the northerners began to deploy. Krispos swore. "If we had all our men in place, we could break them before they got set up themselves." He scowled at the Halogai. "By the good god, let's hit them anyway. With us mounted, we can choose when and where the attack goes in."

"Aye, Majesty." Mammianos opened his mouth to shout orders, then stopped, staring in amazement at one of the gates where the portcullis had gone all the way up.

Krispos followed his gaze. He started, too. A company of Halogai on horseback was coming out. "I didn't think any of them were riders," he said.

"I didn't, either." Mammianos made a noise half cough, half chuckle. "By the look of them, they aren't too sure themselves."

The Halogai were on Kubrati ponies, the only sort of horses they could have found inside Pliskavos. Some of the blond warriors so outmatched their mounts in size that their feet almost brushed the ground. They brandished swords and axes as they formed a ragged line. From his own experience in the courtyard of the High Temple, Krispos knew a footsoldier's axe was no proper weapon for a cavalryman.

"They do try to learn new things, don't they?" Mammianos said in a thoughtful tone. "That makes them more dangerous, or rather dangerous in a different sort of way, than, say, the Makuraners, who do what they do very well, but always in the same old way."

"If they want to learn, let's see that they pay for their first lesson." Krispos turned to a courier. "Order Bagradas to send one of his companies out into the ground between our army and the barbarians. We'll find out what sort of riders they are." The courier grinned nastily as he hurried away.

Bagradas' troopers, a band of archers and lancers about equal in numbers to the mounted Halogai, rode into the no-man's-land. There they stopped and waited. After a moment the Halogai understood the challenge. They yelled and spurred their horses toward the imperials.

The Videssians also raised a shout. They urged their horses forward, too. The archers used their knees to control their mounts as they let fly again and again. A couple of Halogai fell from the saddle. More ponies were wounded and went bounding out of the fight, beyond the ability of their inexperienced riders to control.

But the archers could account for only so many of their foes before the two companies came together. Then it was the lancers' turn. Their long spears gave them far greater reach than the northerners. They spitted Halogai out of the saddle without getting close enough for their foes to strike back. The imperials had also mastered the art of fighting as a unit rather than man by man. The Halogai fought that way afoot, but had never practiced it on horseback. As Krispos had been sure they would, they paid dearly for instruction.

Finally, however brave they were, the Halogai could bear no more. They wheeled their horses and fled for the protection of their comrades on foot. The imperials pursued. The archers accounted for several more men before they and their comrades turned about and rode back to their own lines. The Videssians cheered thunderously. The Halogai, with nothing to cheer about, advanced on the imperial army in grim silence.

"They must be getting desperate, to challenge us mounted when they can barely stay on their horses," Mammianos observed.

"Our cavalry's beaten them again and again, first south of the mountains and now up here," Krispos answered. "If they are desperate, we've made them that way. And now, remember, they don't have Harvas to help them any more." *I hope they don't,* he added to himself.

"Aye, that's so." Mammianos cocked his head to one side. "From what I hear, we have the lady Tanilis and you to thank for it, your Majesty."

"Give the lady the credit," Krispos said firmly. "If it had just been me, you'd be looking for a new Emperor right now, or more likely in too much trouble to worry about finding one."

Companies of horse archers cantered forward to pour arrows into the oncoming Halogai. They could not miss such a bunched target, but did less damage than Krispos had hoped. The first ranks of northerners had those head-to-foot shields; the men behind them raised their round wooden bucklers high to turn aside the shafts. Some got through, but not enough. Inexorable as the tide, the Halogai tramped forward.

The Videssian archers withdrew into the protection of their line. The musicians sounded the charge. Lancers couched spears, dug spurs into horses' flanks. Slowly at first, then faster and faster, they rumbled toward the Halogai.

"This isn't going to be pretty," Mammianos shouted over the thunder of hoofbeats.

"So long as it works," Krispos shouted back. The two lines collided then. Videssian horsemen spitted northerners, using their mounts to bowl over and ride down others. Unlike the cavalry fight, they did not have it all their own way, not for a moment. At close quarters, the axes of the Halogai hewed down men and horses alike; those big, swift strokes bit through mail shirts to hack flesh and split bones.

The battle line did not move twenty yards forward or back for some time. Halogai pressed forward as their comrades were killed. They blunted charge after charge by fresh troops of lancers. Each side dragged its wounded to safety as best it could. Dead horses and soldiers hindered the living from reaching one another to slay some more.

Shouts of alarm rose from the far right as the northerners, borrowing from the Videssian book, tried to slide round the imperial army's flank. After a few tense minutes, a messenger reported to Krispos. "We've held 'em, Majesty, looks like. A good many bowmen had to pull out their sabers before we managed it, though."

"That's why they carry them," Krispos answered.

The imperials shouted his name over and over. They also had another cry, one calculated to unnerve the Halogai. "Where's Harvas Black-Robe?" The northerners were not using the wizard's name as their war cry. When they shouted, they most often called the name Svenkel.

Krispos learned soon enough who Svenkel was. An enormous Haloga, tall even for that big breed, swung an axe that would have impressed the imperial headsman. No one came within its length of him and lived. After he felled a Videssian with a stroke that caved in the luckless fellow's chest, all the northerners who saw cried out his name. He had presence as well as strength and warrior's skill: before he went back to battle, he waved to show he heard the cheers.

"Shall we send one of our champions against him?" Mammianos asked.

"Why risk a champion?" Krispos said. "Enough arrows will take care of him. Give the archers word to shoot at him till he goes down."

"That's not sporting," Mammianos said with a laugh, "but it's the right way to go about war. Let's just see how long Svenkel the hero lasts."

But along with being a warrior bold even by Haloga standards, Svenkel the hero was far from a fool. When three or four arrows in quick succession pincushioned his shield and another glanced off his helm, he knew he was a marked man. Instead of drawing back among his comrades, as most might have done, he led a wedge of northerners into the center of the imperial line against his countrymen who warded Krispos. They were axemen like himself; when they tried to slay him, he could strike back.

The imperial guards had seen hard fighting in all the clashes since the campaign began south of Imbros. The Halogai who were hale still fought as fiercely as ever, but their ranks had been thinned. Svenkel's wedge punched deep. If it broke through, it would cut the imperial army in half.

Krispos drew his saber. He looked at Mammianos. The fat general also had his sword out. He shrugged. "Ah, well, your Majesty, sometimes we have to be sporting, whether we want to or not."

"So we do." Krispos raised his voice and cried, "Videssos!" He spurred Progress toward the sagging line of guardsmen. Mammianos rode with him. So did the couriers who had congregated around them.

By then, only a handful of Halogai in imperial service stood in Svenkel's way. He must have seen victory just ahead. His mouth flew open in a great snarl when horsemen rode up to aid the guards. Then he realized who led the makeshift band. In Videssian, he shouted to Krispos: "Leader to leader, then!"

It didn't quite work that way; war was too chaotic a business to conform to anyone's expectations, even a hero's. Krispos got into the battle a few feet to Svenkel's right, against a Haloga almost as big as the northern chieftain. The fellow swung up his axe to chop at Progress. Before he could, Krispos slashed at his face. He missed, but made the Haloga shift his weight backward so his own stroke fell short. Krispos slashed again. This time he felt his blade bite. The Haloga howled and reeled away, clutching a forearm gashed to the bone.

Seeing Krispos in the fight made his surviving guardsmen redouble their efforts. Svenkel's men still battled for all they were worth, but could push forward no farther. The guards threw themselves at Svenkel, one after another. One after another he beat them back. His strokes never faltered; he might have been a siege engine himself, powered by twisted cords rather than flesh and sinew.

As the guardsmen sought to cut down Svenkel, so his warriors went for Krispos. Krispos fought desperately, trying for nothing more than staying alive. He knew he was no great master of the soldier's art and was very glad when Geirrod came up to stand by Progress' right flank and help him beat back the foe.

Step by step, some of Svenkel's men began to give ground. Others, stubborn with the peculiar Haloga stubbornness, preferred dying where they stood to falling back. Die they did, one after another, along with the imperial guardsmen and Videssian troopers they slew before they went down.

There at the forefront of the fighting, what scholarly chroniclers would later call a line hardly deserved such a dignified name. It was more like knots of grunting, cursing, sweating, bleeding men all entangled with one another. Krispos struck and struck and struck—and knew most of his strokes were useless, either because they clove only air or because they rebounded from mail. He did not much mind; no one in that crush could have hoped to do better.

Then he saw a Haloga close by swing up an axe to chop at one of the guardsmen. He lashed out with his saber. It cut deep into the northerner's wrist. The axe flew from his hand. The Haloga bellowed in pain and whirled around.

Krispos was startled to see it was Svenkel. Svenkel looked startled, too, but was neither too startled nor too badly hurt to raise his shield before Krispos could cut at him again. But that did not save him for long. Geirrod's axe bit into the shield, once, twice . . . on the third blow, the round slab of wood split in two. Geirrod struck once more. Blood sprayed. Svenkel's armor clattered as he fell.

The imperials raised a great cheer. The Halogai still fought ferociously, but something at last went out of them with their chieftain's death. Now the fighters in the wedge that had been his drew back more quickly. As they did so, Geirrod turned to Krispos and said, "Out of the line for you now, Majesty. You did what was needful; we'll go on from here."

Krispos was not sorry to obey. He'd never been an eager warrior. He'd also learned that the Emperor, like any other high-ranking officer, usually was more useful directing the fighting than caught in the thick of it.

He looked round for Mammianos and was relieved to see the general had also got out of the press. But Mammianos had not come through unscathed; he bared his teeth in a grimace of pain as he awkwardly tried to tie a strip of cloth around his right forearm. The cloth was soaked with red.

"Here, let me help you," Krispos said, sheathing his saber. "I have two free hands."

"Thank you, your Majesty. Aye, get it good and tight. There, that should do it." The fat general shook his head. "I'm lucky it's not a bloody stump, I suppose. Been too long since I last tried trading handstrokes."

"What was it you said? Sometimes we have to be sporting? But trooper's not your proper trade anymore."

"Too right it isn't. And a good thing, else I'd long since be dead." Mammianos grimaced. "As is, this arm's the only thing that's killing me."

Shouts rang out, far off at the end of the imperial army's left wing. Krispos and Mammianos both stared in that direction. For the moment, that was all they could do—their couriers were still battling to drive back Svenkel's men. Some of the shouts were full of excitement, others of dismay. From several hundred yards off, Krispos could not tell which came from the Halogai, which from the imperials.

He kept his neck craned leftward, fearing above all else to see the Videssians driven back in rout. He saw no soldiers fleeing on horseback, which he took as a good sign. All the same, he fidgeted atop Progress for the next several minutes, until at last a rider came galloping his way from the left.

The horseman's grin told him most of what he needed to know before the fellow began to speak. "Majesty, we've flanked them! Sarkis got his scouts round their right and now we're rolling 'em up."

"The good god be praised," Krispos said. "That's what I

most wanted to hear. Go back there and tell all the officers on that wing to pour as many men after Sarkis as they can spare without thinning their line too much."

"Majesty, they're already doing it," the messenger said.

"They're good soldiers, most of them," Mammianos put in. The rider's news banished pain from his face. "A good soldier doesn't wait for orders when he sees a chance like that. He just ups and grabs it."

"It's all right with me," Krispos said. His grin stretched wider than the one the messenger was wearing. "In fact, it's better than all right."

Faster even than he'd dared hope, the Haloga right came to pieces. The northerners faced a cruel dilemma. If they turned at bay and formed an embattled circle, nothing would keep the Videssians from simply riding into Pliskavos. But if they fell back toward the gates, they risked fresh breakthroughs as the imperials probed flimsy, makeshift lines.

Some turned at bay, some fell back. The Videssians did break through, repeatedly, forcing more and more Halogai to make the unpalatable choice. Sarkis could easily have seized Pliskavos. Instead, with even deadlier instinct, he urged his men—and the other imperials in their wake—all around the rear of the Haloga army. Krispos traced their progress by the panic-filled yells that rose first from the northerners' shattered right, then the center, and then their left—the imperial right. A few minutes later, the imperials on the right yelled, too, in triumph.

"By the lord with the great and good mind, they're in the sack," Mammianos said. "Now we slaughter them." He did not sound as if he took any great joy in the prospect, merely as if it was a job that needed doing. The imperial headsman plied his trade in that matter-of-fact, deadly fashion.

The Videssian army went about its business the same way, methodically using bows, lances, and sabers against the northerners. As Mammianos had said, it was a slaughter. Then all the Halogai suddenly turned round and rushed against the Videssians who stood between them and Pliskavos. That part of the imperial line remained thinner than the rest. Shouting wildly, the northerners hacked their way through.

"After them!" Krispos yelled. Quite without orders, the musicians played *Charge*. They were soldiers, too, and out to grab the chance.

The Videssians surged forward in pursuit of their fleeing foes. Here and there a Haloga stood and fought. Those who did were beset by several men at once and quickly fell. Many more were cut down or speared from behind. And more than one, rather than dying at the imperials' hands or doffing his helm in token of surrender, plunged a sword into his own belly or a knife between his ribs. The way the northerners so deliberately killed themselves chilled Krispos.

"Why do they do that?" he asked Geirrod.

"We Halogai, we think that if a man be slain by an enemy, he serves him in the world to come," the guardsman answered. "Some of us, we would liefer live free after we die, if you take my meaning, Majesty."

"I suppose I do." Krispos sketched the sun-sign over his heart. He wished the Halogai could be persuaded to follow Phos. Every so often zealous priests went to preach the good god's doctrines in Halogaland. If they were fearless men, the northerners generally let them live. But they won few converts; the Halogai stubbornly clung to their false gods.

Such reflections ran through his mind and then were gone, lost in the chase. Now he wished Sarkis had sent men to secure Pliskavos' gates. A few Videssians made for them, but the rush of Halogai overwhelmed the riders. The big blond men streamed into the town. More turned at bay, to give their comrades the chance to save themselves.

Krispos swore. "If we had ladders ready, we could storm the place. It would fall at the first rush."

"Aye, likely so, your Majesty," Mammianos said, "but ladders aren't of much use in a pitched battle, which is what we were set to fight. This isn't one of those minstrels' romances, where the bold hero always thinks of everything ahead of time. If it were, I wouldn't have this." He held up his bandaged arm.

The imperials charged again and again at the Haloga rearguards. Then some of the northerners gained the walls of Pliskavos and began shooting at their foes and pelting them with stones. Under the cover of that barrage, most of the Halogai managed to withdraw into the city. Portcullises slammed down in the Videssians' faces.

Only when the fighting finally died away did Krispos notice how far toward the east his shadow stretched. The sun was nearly set. He looked over the battlefield and shook his head in wonder. Softly he said, "How many Halogai are down!"

"That's the way of it when one side breaks," Mammianos said. "Remember, Agapetos and Mavros paid in this coin for us."

"I remember," Krispos said. "Oh, yes, I remember."

The Videssians ranged over the field. They dragged and carried their wounded countrymen back to their healer-priests. Most of the Halogai not yet dead got shorter shrift. Some—those who had been seen to fight with special bravery and those who looked rich enough to be worth ransoming—were spared.

Horse leeches went here and there, doing what they could for injured animals. Other soldiers went here and there, too, plundering the dead. Piles of Haloga shields, too big and bulky to be of use to horsemen, grew and grew. Krispos saw so many that he ordered a count made, to give him some idea of how many northerners had fallen. He also wondered what his horsemen would do with the war axes and heavy swords they were happily taking away.

"Some will be inlaid with gold, and so worth something," Geirrod said when he spoke that thought aloud. "As for the others, well, Majesty, even you southrons deem it worth recalling that you overcame brave men." Krispos had to nod.

Burial parties began their work—a pit that would make a mass grave for the fallen Halogai, individual resting places for the far smaller number of Videssians who had died. Krispos told the soldiers to dig a special grave for Tanilis, apart from all the others. "Set a wooden marker over it for now," he said. "When this land is ours and peaceful once more, the finest marble will be none too good for her."

The men counting northern shields came to him with their total: over twelve thousand. He knew fewer Halogai than that had died; some would have discarded their shields to flee the faster. It was still a great total, especially when set against imperial losses, which were under two thousand.

That evening, as the army rested in camp, Krispos went to see some of the Haloga prisoners. Archers stood guard over them as they dejectedly sat around in their linen drawers and undertunics—their armor was already booty. They stirred with interest as he approached. Some of them glowered at their countrymen who guarded him.

He ignored that, announcing "I need a man who understands Videssian to listen to my words and take them to your comrades in Pliskavos. Who will do this for me?" Several northerners raised their hands. He chose a solid-looking fellow with gray mixed in his golden hair and beard. He asked the man, "What is your name?"

"I am Soribulf, Videssian emperor," the Haloga said, politely but without the elaborate respect imperials used.

"Well, Soribulf, tell this to your chiefs in Pliskavos: if they yield the city and set free any Videssian prisoners they are holding, I will let them cross to the north shore of the Astris without ordering my fleet to burn their boats."

"We are the Halogai," Soribulf said, drawing himself up proudly. "We do not yield."

"If we weren't already burying them, you could see all the Haloga corpses on today's field," Krispos said. "If you don't yield, every one of you inside Pliskavos will die, too. Do you think we can't take the town with our siege engines and our ships that shoot fire?"

Soribulf's mouth puckered, as if he were chewing on something sour. "How do we trust you not to burn us even so, when we are on the water and cannot ward ourselves?"

"My word is good," Krispos said. "Better than that of the evil mage you followed."

"Aye, you speak truth there, Videssian emperor. He told us you would burn with the wall, but our warriors were the ones the bright blaze bit. And then after, he helped us no more; some say he fled. I know not the truth of that, but we saw none of him today when swords struck."

"Pass on what I say, then, and my warning," Krispos urged.

Soribulf swayed back and forth. "He mourns," a guardsman whispered to Krispos. Soribulf spoke in his own language. The guard translated: "The glory of Haloga arms is dead. Will we now yield ingloriously to Videssos and travel back to our homeland in defeat? Never have we done so—braver to conquer or die."

"Die you will, if you fight on," Krispos said. "Shall I choose someone else as my messenger?"

"No." Soribulf returned to the imperial speech. "I will bear your words to my people. Whether they choose to hear, I could not guess."

Krispos nodded to a couple of the archers who guarded the Haloga prisoners. "You men take him to the rampart and let him go to Pliskavos." He turned back to Soribulf. "If your chiefs are willing to speak of yielding, tell them to show a white-painted shield above the central gate first thing tomorrow morning."

"I shall tell them," Soribulf said. The guards led him away. Krispos sent an order to Kanaris the grand drungarios of the fleet: to have his dromons sailing back and forth on the Astris by dawn, as a warning that the trapped northerners had no way out unless the imperials granted it to them. Then, while the rest of the army celebrated the great victory they had won, Krispos went to bed.

When he woke the next morning, he looked to the walls of Pliskavos. Halogai marched along them, but he saw no truce shield. Glowering, he ordered the engineers to ready their dart-shooters and stone-throwers. "Don't make any secret of what you're doing, either," he told them.

The Halogai watched from the walls as the artisans ostentatiously checked the ropes and timbers of their engines, made sure they had plenty of stones and sheaves of outsized arrows close at hand, and squinted toward Pliskavos as if checking range and aim for the catapults. Dew was still damp on the grass when a shield went up over the gate.

"Well, well." Krispos let out a long sigh of relief. Even without magic used against his men, storming the town would have been desperately expensive. "Have Progress saddled up for me," he said to his guardsmen. "I'll parley with their chief."

"Not alone!" the guards said in one voice. "If the foe sallies—"

"I hadn't intended to go out there alone," Krispos answered mildly, "not for fear of treachery and not for my dignity's sake, either."

He approached Pliskavos in the midst of a full company of Haloga guards. Another company, this one of Videssian horse-archers, flanked the guards on either side. The horsemen had arrows nocked and ready in their bows.

He reined in about a hundred feet from the wall. "Who will speak with me?" he called.

A Haloga stood atop one of the low stretches of battlement. "I am Ikmor," he called back. "Those inside will obey me." His Videssian was good; a moment later he explained why: "Years ago, in my youth, I served in the city as guard to the Avtokrator Rhaptes. I learned your speech then."

"You served Anthimos' father, eh? Good enough," Krispos said. "Soribulf brought you my terms. Will you take them, or will you go on with a fight you cannot win?"

"You are a hard man, Videssian Emperor, harder than Rhaptes who was," Ikmor answered. "I grieved the whole night long at the ruin of our grand army, struggling with my spirit over whether to yield or battle on. But I saw in the end that I must give over, though it is bitter as wormwood to me. Yet a war leader must not surrender to sorrow, but try in every way to save the lives of the warriors under him."

"Spoken like a wise man," Krispos said. *Spoken like a man who indeed spent time in Videssos,* he thought. A Haloga fresh from his native land would have been unlikely to take such a long view.

"Spoken like a man who finds himself without choice," Ikmor answered bleakly. "To show I am in earnest, I will send out the captives from your people whom we hold."

The Haloga chieftain turned, shouting in his own language. The portcullis beneath him creaked up. One by one dark-haired men came through the gateway, most of them in rags, many pale and thin as only longtime prisoners become. Some rubbed at their eyes, as if unused to sunlight. When they saw the imperial banner that floated above Krispos' head, they cheered and pelted toward him.

His own eyes filled with tears. He called to the officer who led the cavalry company. "Take them back to our camp. Feed them, get clothes for them. Have the healer-priests check them, too, those who aren't too worn from work with our wounded." The captain saluted and told off a squad to take charge of the newly released Videssians.

No sooner was the last imperial out of Pliskavos than the portcullis slammed down again. Ikmor said, "Videssian emperor, if we come out ourselves, how do we know you will not treat us as . . . as—" He hesitated, but had to say it: "—as we treated Imbros?"

"Do you not trust my pledge?" Krispos said.

"Not in this," Ikmor answered at once. After a moment's anger, Krispos reluctantly saw his point: having done deeds that deserved retribution, no wonder the Halogai feared it. Ikmor went on, "Let us come forth in arms and armor, to ward ourselves at need."

"No," Krispos said. "You could start the battle over then, looking to take us by surprise." He stroked his beard as he thought. "How's this, Haloga chief? Wear your swords and axes, if you will. But leave shields behind and carry your mail shirts as part of your baggage, rolled up on your backs."

It was Ikmor's turn to ponder. At last he said. "Let it be as you will. We shall need our weapons against the Khamorth nomads as we trek north over the plains to Halogaland."

With luck, Krispos thought, the nomads would take a good bite out of the Halogai before they made it back to their own cold country. That might them think twice about moving south against Videssos again. Come to that, he might help luck along. Aloud, he said, "One other thing, brave Ikmor."

"What would you, Videssian Emperor?"

"When you northerners come out of Pliskavos, you will all come through this same gate through which you let out your Videssian prisoners. I want to post wizards there, to make sure Harvas Black-Robe doesn't sneak out among you."

Ikmor's laugh was unkind. "Then you should have checked the captives, too, eh?" Krispos ground his teeth—the Haloga chieftain was right. Ikmor continued, "But we will do as you say once more, though for our own sake rather than yours. If you do find Harvas, let our axes drink his blood, for he betrayed us." He spoke in his own tongue to the men on the wall with him. They growled and hefted their weapons in a way that left no doubt of what they thought of Harvas.

Krispos said, "If you love him so well, why didn't you turn on him before?"

"Before, Videssian Emperor, he led us to victory and helped us settle this fine new land. Even a war leader with the soul of a carrion crow will hold his followers thus," Ikmor said. "But when his fires turned against his own folk, when after that he vanished from our ken instead of staying to battle on as a true man would, he showed us he had not even a carrion crow inside himself, only the splattered white turd one leaves behind after it has fed and flown on."

Some of the Halogai on the wall—the ones who followed Videssian, Krispos supposed—nodded vigorously. So did some of the soldiers with Krispos, impressed by Ikmor's ability to revile without actually cursing.

"If you agree, Ikmor, we will bring the wizards into place tomorrow," Krispos said.

"No, give us four days' time," Ikmor answered. "We will use timber from the town to knock together rafts and go out through the river gates to put them at the quays."

"If you try to escape on them before the day we agreed to, the dromons will burn you," Krispos warned.

"We have seen the fire they fling, the fire they spit. We will hold to these terms, Videssian Emperor."

"Good enough." Krispos gave Ikmor a Videssian salute, clenched fist over his heart. He was not surprised to see the

Haloga return it. As quickly as ceremony permitted, or maybe a little quicker, he withdrew to the camp. The first thing he did there was to summon Zaidas.

By the time he was done talking, the young mage's face mirrored the concern he knew his own showed. "Aye, your Majesty, I'll attend to it directly," Zaidas said. "It would be a dreadful blow if Harvas the accursed profited thus from the misery of our own people. But if he is among them, I shall sniff him out." The picture of determination, he started away from the imperial tent.

"Take a squad of soldiers, in case you need to do more than sniff," Krispos called after him. Zaidas did not turn around but waved to show he had heard.

Krispos spent the rest of the day worrying, half afraid he would hear of trouble from where the liberated Videssians sat and ate and talked and marveled at being free, half afraid he wouldn't because Harvas had managed to outfox Zaidas. But toward sunset Zaidas reported, "He is not among those who are there, your Majesty. On that I would take oath by the lord with the great and good mind. If no other captives came from Pliskavos, we may rest easy. The officers and men who have dealt with them believe them to be all the ones the Halogai released."

"The good god be praised," Krispos said. He could not be perfectly sure Harvas hadn't been among the freed captives, but the older he got, the less he was perfectly sure of anything. With a nod toward Zaidas, he said, "Ready yourself and your comrades to study the Haloga when they leave Pliskavos."

"We shall be fully prepared," Zaidas promised. "Harvas hale could hope to stand against us. Harvas as he is after the lady Tanilis smote him—" His voice softened as he spoke her name, but his eyes flashed. "—is small beer, as the saying goes. If he is there, we will smoke him out."

"Good." Krispos was not usually vindictive, but he wanted to lay hands on Harvas, to make him suffer for all the suffering he had inflicted on Videssos. Then he remembered a saying himself: "To make rabbit stew, first catch a rabbit."

The Halogai inside Pliskavos gave no sign of breaking the terms to which Ikmor had agreed. Kanaris brought word that the northerners really were building rafts. All the same Krispos held off sending word of his victory south to the city. Once he'd caught his rabbit—or, in this case, seen it across the Astris— would be time enough.

On the fourth morning, he ordered his army to advance on Pliskavos. The soldiers came fully armed and ready for battle. He had strong forces covering each gate, not merely the one through which Ikmor had promised the Halogai would march. Mammianos nodded at that. "If we show 'em we're set for everything, they're less likely to try anything."

Zaidas and the rest of the wizards took their place outside the central gate. They waved to Krispos to show they were ready. He peered into the town through the grid of the portcullis. A lot of men looked to be lined up there. Then the portcullis rose, screeching in its track every inch of the way.

One man came through alone. He tramped past the Videssian mages without sparing them a glance and made straight for the imperial banner. He saluted Krispos. "I am Ikmor. For my folk I stand before you. Do as you will with me if we play you false."

"Go with your people," Krispos said. "I did not ask this of you."

"I know that. I give it to you, for my honor's sake. I shall stay."

Krispos had learned better than to argue about a Haloga's prickly sense of honor. "As you will, northern sir." He undid his canteen, swigged, and passed it to Ikmor. "Share wine with me."

"Aye." Ikmor drank. A couple of drops splashed on his white tunic, which was already none too clean. The Haloga was a well-made man of middle height, snub-nosed and gray-eyed. He was bald on top of his head, but let the hair above his ears grow long. His mustaches were also long, though the rest of his beard was rather thin. In each ear he wore a thick gold ring set with pearls—Iakovitzes would have wanted a pair of them, Krispos thought irrelevantly. When he handed the canteen back to Krispos, it was empty.

The Halogai filed out of Pliskavos a few at a time, walking between Zaidas and the other wizards. Most of the northerners made Ikmor seem immaculate by comparison. More than a few showed the marks of burns from when the wall caught fire, wounds from the latest battle, or both. They glared at the imperials who had overcome them, as if they still could not believe the campaign had gone against them.

Looking at them, Krispos also wondered how he'd won. The Halogai were big, fierce men who might have been specially made for war. Fighting came less naturally to Videssians. In the end, though, trained skill had overcome ferocity.

Mammianos was thinking along similar lines. He remarked, "They want another chance at us. You can see it in their eyes."

"They won't have such an easy time trying again," Krispos answered. "Now that we rule all the way up to the Astris again, I expect we'll keep a flotilla of dromons patrolling the river. I wouldn't want to try crossing it in the face of them."

He spoke as much to Ikmor as to Mammianos. Out of the corner of his eye, he saw the Haloga chief's mouth turn down. The message had got through, then.

A few minutes later a warrior broke ranks and strode toward Krispos. He touched his sword. His guardsmen tensed, readying themselves to cut the fellow down. But he paused at a safe distance and spoke loudly in his own language. Krispos glanced at Ikmor. "What does he say?"

Ikmor looked even less happy. "He wants to take service with you, Videssian Emperor."

"What? Why?"

Ikmor spoke to the Haloga, then listened to his reply. "He says his name is Odd the son of Aki, and that he will only fight among the best soldiers in the world. Till now he thought those were his own people, but you have beaten us, so he must have been wrong."

"For that I'll find him a place," Krispos said, grinning. Ikmor translated. Odd the son of Aki dipped his head to Krispos, then stepped aside. A Videssian officer took charge of him.

As the day went on, more Halogai broke ranks and asked leave to join the imperial army. Most of them gave the same reason Odd had. By the time the last northerner filed out of Pliskavos, Krispos found he had recruited a good-sized company. Ikmor turned his back on the men who had gone over.

The Halogai marched around Pliskavos toward the quays. More evidence of imperial might awaited them there: Kanaris' warships, holding their place against the current of the Astris like so many sparrowhawks hovering above a mousehole.

Krispos rode Progress up toward the riverbank so he could watch the northerners embark on their rafts. Ikmor paced alongside him, though two guardsmen made sure they were between the chieftain and the Avtokrator at all times.

The Halogai paddled the first raft out onto the Astris a little past noon. A dromon shadowed it all the way across the river, the fearsome siphon tube pointing straight at it. The wallowing raft was completely at the dromon's mercy. No one, Haloga or imperial, could doubt it. More than anything else, that first river crossing brought home who had won and who had lost.

More and more rafts set out. Not all of them enjoyed the attentions of a dromon all the way across the Astris, but the warships stayed close enough to leave no question of what they could do at need. Destroying the northerners' dugout canoes had been an unequal struggle. Attacking the rafts would have been a massacre.

Zaidas made his way through the crowd to Krispos. "All the Halogai passed before me, your Majesty. I found no sign of Harvas' presence."

"Go rest, then," Krispos told him. The young mage had always been reedy. Now he was a thin reed indeed.

Even so, he tried to protest. "I ought to go into the town, to see whether the evil wizard still lurks within." He weakened his own words with an enormous yawn.

"The shape you're in, you're likelier to fall asleep than find him," Krispos said. "I'll keep wizards posted at each gate. If he's in there, he won't get out." He did his best to look stern and imperial. It probably wasn't a very good best; Zaidas winked at him. But the mage went back toward the camp, which was what Krispos had in mind.

The rafts the Halogai had built carried only a fraction of them over the Astris that first day. The northerners who were left behind spread their bedrolls outside of Pliskavos. The countrymen's campfires blazed from the far shore. Between the two groups, up and down, up and down along the river, the dromons of the imperial fleet prowled all night long.

Videssian archers stood guard through the night on the southern bank of the Astris, alert in case the Halogai proved treacherous. But most of the imperial army returned to the camp on the other side of the palisade. At the officers' meeting that evening, Sarkis gave Krispos a sly look. "May I read your mind, Majesty?"

"Go ahead," Krispos told him.

"You're wishing a nice big band of Khamorth would pitch into the Halogai on their way north and finish the job we started."

"Who, me?" As he tried to look imperial to Zaidas, now Krispos tried to look innocent. "That would be a terrible fate to wish on a foe we've just made peace with."

"Aye, so it would, Majesty." Sarkis' eyes twinkled. "But didn't I see you send a couple of men with horses to the north

shore of the Astris? Unless they're going to keep the northerners company on their way back to Halogaland, they're
probably up there to talk with one of the local Khamorth
khagans.''

"With more than one," Krispos admitted. "One of the local
clan leaders by himself wouldn't have enough men to risk tangling with such a big Haloga army. Three or four together might,
in hopes of getting gold from us for the favor. I'd sooner spend
gold than soldiers; we've spent enough soldiers against the Halogai.''

A low mutter of approval ran through the officers. Bagradas
turned to Krispos and said, "Your Majesty, you are truly what
an Avtokrator of the Videssians should be." The rest of the
commanders solemnly nodded. Krispos felt himself swell with
pride.

Sarkis asked, "What would you have done had Ikmor made
you pledge not to send envoys to the Khamorth?''

"I would have kept my word," Krispos answered. "But since
he didn't think of it, I saw no reason to bring it up myself.''

"Aye, a Videssian indeed," Sarkis murmured, reminding
Krispos that the scout commander sprang from Vaspurakan. A
moment later Sarkis softened his words. "No blame to you,
though, Majesty, not after what the northerners have done to
Videssos. They've earned whatever they catch.''

Again the officers nodded and called out, many with fierce
eagerness. But Krispos asked, "Whatever they catch? What of
Imbros?''

Abrupt silence fell inside the imperial tent. Krispos was relieved to hear it. No one who preferred Phos to Skotos could
feel easy about imagining Imbros' fate for any group, no matter
what its crimes, and he was glad none of his officers thirsted so
much for revenge as to forget it.

Zaidas seemed much more his old self when morning came.
Along with several other wizards, he entered Pliskavos to continue the search for Harvas Black-Robe. A substantial armed
band went along to guard them: the Halogai were out of Pliskavos and in the process of crossing the Astris, but some of the
folk who had lived there before Harvas, before the Halogai, still
remained.

The guard party would have been smaller had Krispos not
decided to go into Pliskavos with the mages. Not only did he
want to be in at the kill if Harvas was captured, he also wanted

to see what would be needed to restore the town to a provincial capital after its occupation first by the Kubratoi for centuries and then by the evil wizard and the northerners.

His first horrified thought was that everything inside the fortifications should be torched, to cleanse the place and start again. The fires that had spread from the burning wall had done some of that, but not enough. Half-burned wooden buildings were everywhere, along with the stenches of stale smoke and of burned and rotting flesh. Once or twice heads peeked out of ruins to eye the newcomers. Krispos saw more than one glint of weapons in the shadows and was glad for his armed escort.

"This was once a Videssian town of note?" he said, shaking his head. "I can't believe it."

"It's true, your Majesty." Zaidas pointed. "See that stone building, and that one, and what's left of that one over there? You'll find the same sort of work in Videssos the city. And the streets, or some of them, still keep to the square grid pattern we usually use."

"You know town planning as well as wizardry?" Krispos asked.

Zaidas flushed. "My older brother is a builder."

"If he serves his craft as well as you do yours, he'll be one of the best," Krispos said, which made the young mage turn pink all over again.

As they rode on toward the center of town, they came across more and more stretches of unburned buildings. Now people did emerge to stare. Some were of Kubrati blood, stocky, the men heavily bearded. Others, slimmer, their features more sharply sculpted, could have been poor Videssians by the look of them. They all watched soldiers, wizards, and Emperor as if wondering what fresh misfortunes these newcomers would bring down on them.

"How will you sniff out Harvas from among them and from among others who may be hiding?" Krispos asked Zaidas.

"I will have to ride through the whole of Pliskavos, I think," the wizard answered. "I know the reek of his magic, and I know the blankness with which he seeks to disguise it. To detect either, I will have to be close to it, for thanks to the lady Tanilis his power is less than a shadow of what it once was."

"If he is here at all," Krispos added.

"Aye, your Majesty, if he is here at all."

In a park in the heart of Pliskavos stood an ornately carved wooden palace, the former residence of the khagans of Kubrat.

A new carving was set above the doorway: twin three-pronged lightning flashes. Zaidas' finger stabbed toward them. "That is Skotos' mark!" He sketched Phos' sun-circle.

So did Krispos. "Harvas laired here, then?" he asked.

"Harvas once laired here," Zaidas agreed. "Be thankful you cannot feel the effluvium of his past power." He grew thoughtful. "I wonder if now he seeks to hide there, hoping no one will notice his present small bad odor in the great stench of the past. We must closely examine that building."

One of the other Videssian mages, a stout, middle-age man named Gepas, stirred in the saddle and said, "Do pray remember we're not your servants, Zaidas."

"Are you the Empire's servants, Gepas?" Krispos asked sharply. The wizard stared, startled. His eyes fell. He nodded. "Good," Krispos said. "For a moment there, I wondered. Do you deny that Zaidas speaks good sense, or do you just wish you'd spoken before he did? Does Harvas' palace need looking at, or not?"

"It does, your Majesty," Gepas admitted.

"Then let's look at it." Krispos urged Progress forward and tied the horse at the rail in front of the palace.

Neither his guards nor the mages would hear of his going in first. He'd wondered if the doors would be locked, but they opened at the guards' touch. Zaidas turned to Gepas. With unaffected politeness, the young wizard asked, "Sir, would it please you to stand guard here at the doorway, to ensure that Harvas cannot sneak past you?"

"Better, youngling." Gepas puffed out his chest and pulled in his belly. His voice got deeper. "Aye, I'll do that. He shan't escape by this road."

"Good." Zaidas' face was perfectly straight. Krispos had to work to keep his the same way. He wondered whether Zaidas was a natural innocent or a schemer subtle beyond his years. Either way, he got results.

Wizards fanned out through the wooden palace. Krispos stayed with Zaidas. The guards, naturally, stayed with him. Together they made their way into the hall that was, Krispos supposed, the equivalent of the Grand Courtroom back at the capital. He pointed to the white throne that stood out against the gloom at the far end. "Is that ivory, like the patriarch's throne?"

Zaidas studied it, murmuring briefly to himself. His large larynx worked. "It's—bone," he said at last. Just then Krispos saw Skotos' symbol on the wall above the high seat. He decided not to ask what sort of bone.

The hall held a sour, metallic smell. Without much enthusiasm, Krispos walked down the hard dirt aisleway toward the throne. A few feet in front of it, his boot heels sank into a soggy spot. The smell got worse. "That's blood," he said, hoping Zaidas would contradict him.

Zaidas didn't. He said, "We already knew Harvas practiced abominations. We also know now that he is not in this hall, which was our purpose in coming here. Let's go on to see where he may be."

"Yes, let's," Krispos said in a small voice, admiring the young mage's ability to stay calm in the face of horror.

To the left of the bone throne was a door. In the twilight that filled the hall with all torches dark, its outline was invisible until one came right up to it. Again, Krispos' guards would not let him go in first. One of them tugged at the latch. The door did not open. The guardsman used his axe with a will.

Moments later he tried the door again. This time he easily pulled it open. When he did, he and everyone else in the hall drew back a pace, or more than a pace, for darkness seemed to well out toward them. Krispos' hand shaped the sun-circle. Loudly and clearly Zaidas declared, "We bless thee, Phos, lord with the great and good mind, watchful beforehand that the great test of life may be decided in our favor."

The spreading darkness faded. Krispos wondered if it had really been there. Even after it was gone, the open doorway remained black and forbidding. He glanced toward Zaidas. The young wizard licked his lips and seemed to gather his courage. Then he strode into the room. Remembering Trokoundos, Krispos started to shout for him to come back.

But Zaidas said, "Ah, as I thought," with such scholarly satisfaction that Krispos knew he'd come to no harm. The mage went on, "It is a shrine dedicated to Skotos. They speak of them at the Sorcerers' Collegium, but I'd never seen one before."

Krispos had never seen one, either, or wanted to see one. But his pride would not let him stay back while Zaidas was inside. He was glad to have his guardsmen form up around him. They went into the small room together.

The hall of the throne had been dark. Even so, his eyes needed a minute or so to adapt to the deeper shadow inside. As the eye went to the altar in one of Phos' temples, so it did here. Indeed, this altar at first glance resembled one from a temple—not surprising, Krispos supposed, since Harvas the evil mage, the apostate, had in his earlier days been Rhavas the prelate of Skopentzana. But no altar dedicated to Phos would have had knives lying on it.

One of Phos' temples would have been full of icons, holy images of the good god and his work in the world. As Krispos' vision adapted to the gloom, he saw icons on the wall above the altar here, too. He saw the dark god, wreathed in blackness, fighting Phos, driving him, and slaying him. He saw other things, as well, things he thought no man could have dreamed of taking brush to panel to portray. He saw things that made the forest of stakes outside Imbros seem a mercy. One of his guardsmen, a warrior who delighted in battle like most Halogai, lurched out into the great hall and was noisily sick there.

"This is what he would have brought to Videssos the city," Zaidas said quietly.

"I know," Krispos said. But knowing and seeing were not the same. He'd found that out in a different context when he'd got word of Evripos' birth while Tanilis was in his bed. He looked at the icons again, and at the altar. He saw small bones among the knives. His little sister Kosta would have had bones about that size, a couple of years before cholera killed her. For a moment he thought he would be sick himself.

"A pity the flames from the wall didn't reach here," he said. "We'll just have to fire this building ourselves." More than anything else, he wanted Phos' icons to burn.

One of the guardsmen clapped him on the back, hard enough to stagger him. Zaidas said, "Excellent, your Majesty. Fire and its light are gifts from Phos, and will cleanse the evil that has put its roots down here. May something better arise from the ashes. And," he added, his voice suddenly hopeful, "if Harvas has managed to elude us here, fire will cleanse the world of him as well."

"So may it be," Krispos said. After that, he was not ashamed to leave the dark chapel. Zaidas followed close on his heels. The young mage carefully closed the splintered door behind him, as if to make sure what dwelt inside stayed there.

All the wizards gathered by the entrance that Gepas still guarded. They'd not found Harvas, nor had any of the rest of them stumbled onto anything as black as Skotos' altar. Not one, however, offered a word of protest at what Krispos proposed to do to the palace.

He unhitched Progress and led the gelding well away from the wooden building. The mages still kept a close watch on it, as if they could sense even at a distance the evil Harvas had brought into it. Very likely they could, Krispos thought. Most of his guardsmen stayed by him, but one hurried back to the imperial camp.

The guard returned fairly soon. He was carrying a jar of lamp oil and a smoking torch. He handed Krispos the torch, unstoppered the jar, and splashed oil on the palace wall. "Light it, Majesty," he urged.

As Krispos touched the torch to the oil, he reflected that the dromons' incendiary mix would have served even better. But the lamp oil did the job. Flames walked across the weathered surface of the wooden wall, crept into cracks, climbed over carvings. Before long the wood caught, too. No hearth logs could have been better seasoned than the old timbers of the palace. They burned quick and hard and hot. A pillar of smoke rose to the sky.

Imperials ran and rode up in alarm, fearing the blaze had broken out on its own. Krispos kept some of them close by, to help fight the fire in case it spread. But the palace was set apart from Pliskavos' other buildings, as if to give the khagans of Kubrat the sense of space they might have enjoyed on the steppe. It had plenty of room in which to burn safely.

Krispos watched the fire for a while. He wished he could know whether Harvas was burning with those flames. Whether or not, though, the power he had forged to strike at Videssos was broken; those of his raiders who lived were boarding rafts under the eyes and arrows of imperial troops. And Harvas' own power was broken, as well, thanks to Tanilis. Krispos shook his head, wishing for the thousandth time the price of the latter breaking had not been so high.

But he knew that Tanilis had willingly paid the price, and that she would not have wanted him to grieve in victory. The knowledge helped—some. He swung himself up onto Progress and twitched the reins. The horse turned till Krispos felt the warmth of the burning palace on his back. He touched Progress' flanks with his heels and rode away.

With a hand shading his eyes to ease the glare, Krispos peered across the Astris. Tiny in the distance, the last of Harvas' Halogai trudged away from the northern back of the river. "This land is ours now," Krispos said, slightly embarrassed to hear slight surprise in his voice. "Ours again," he amended.

Mammianos was also watching the Halogai go. "A very neat campaign, your Majesty," he said. "The provincial levies will be back on their farms in time to help with the harvest. Very neat indeed."

"So they will." Krispos turned to the fat general. "And what of you, Mammianos? Shall I send you back to your province, too, to govern the coastal lowlands for me?"

"This for the coastal lowlands." Mammianos yawned a slow, deliberate, scornful yawn. "The only reason I was there is that Petronas sent me to the most insignificant place he could think of." The yawn gave way to a smug expression. "Turned out not to be so insignificant after all, the way things worked out, eh, your Majesty?"

"You're right about that," Krispos said. Mammianos had given him the opening he'd hoped for. "If you're bored with the lowlands, eminent sir, will you serve as my governor here, as the first governor of the new province of Kubrat?"

"Ah. That job wouldn't soon grow dull, now would it?" Mammianos didn't sound surprised, but then Mammianos was no one's fool. His voice turned musing. "Let's see, what all would I be doing? Keeping the nomads on their side of the Astris, and the Halogai, too, if they think about getting frisky again—"

"Cleaning up the Haloga settlements that got started here, like the one that gave Sarkis so much trouble," Krispos put in.

"Aye, and the Kubratoi might decide to rise up again, once they get over being grateful to us for ridding them of dear Harvas, which is to say any time starting about day after tomorrow."

"Oh, we ought to be good until next week," Krispos said. Both men chuckled, although Krispos knew he wasn't really joking. He went on, "We'll start resettling farmers, too, to start giving you enough men to use as a balance against the Kubratoi. People will want to come if we forgive, say, their first five years' taxes after they get here. It's not the worst farming country, not if the Kubratoi don't come by every fall to steal half your crop."

"You'd know about that, wouldn't you, your Majesty?"

"Oh, yes." Even across more than two decades and the vast gulf that separated the man he was from the boy he had been,

Krispos could still call up the helpless fury he'd felt as the nomads plundered the peasants they'd kidnapped.

Mammianos glanced over to the walls of Pliskavos not far
away. "I'll need artisans to help set the town right, and merchants to come live in it, aye, and priests, as well, for the good
god—" He sketched Phos' sun-circle. "—seems mostly forgotten here." He hardly seemed to notice he'd agreed to take the
job.

"The artisans will come," Krispos promised, "though Imbros needs them, too." Mammianos nodded. Krispos continued, "I'll see that priests come, too. They'll be happier if we
have a temple ready for them." He snapped his fingers in happy
inspiration. "And I know just where—on the spot where the old
wooden palace stood."

"That's very fine, your Majesty. The traders'll come, too, I
expect. They'll be eager for the chance to do direct business
with the nomads north of the Astris instead of going through
Kubrati middlemen. Come to that, there'll be trade down the
Astris, too, in the days ahead, from Pliskavos to Videssos the
city direct by water. Aye, the merchants will come."

"I think you're right," Krispos said. "You'll be busy, making
all of that happen."

"I'd sooner be busy than bored, unlike half the useless drones
back in the city," Mammianos said. His eyes narrowed as he
studied Krispos. "You think you'll stay busy yourself, your
Majesty, without a civil war and a foreign one to juggle?"

"By the good god, eminent sir, I hope not!" Krispos exclaimed. Mammianos stared at him, then started to laugh. Krispos said, "Trouble is, though, something always comes along.
By the time I'm back to the capital, I'll have something new to
worry about. One thing I can think of right away: before too
long, I have to decide whether to keep paying tribute to Makuran
or take the chance on another war by cutting it off."

"We're not ready for another war," Mammianos said seriously.

"Don't I know it! But we can't let the King of Kings go on
sucking our blood forever, either." Krispos sighed. "This Avtokrator business is hard work, if you try to do it the way you
should. I understand Anthimos better than I used to, and why
he forgot about everything save women and wine. Sometimes I
think he had the right idea after all."

"No, you don't," Mammianos said.

Krispos sighed again. "No, I suppose I don't. But there are times when packing it in can look awfully good."

"A farmer can't afford to pack it in, and he only has to deal with one plot of land," Mammianos said. "You have the whole Empire to look out for. On the other hand, you get rewards that poor farmer will never see, starting with the parade down Middle Street when you do get back to the city."

"Anthimos arranged for people to cheer him, too."

"Ah, but there's a difference. You'll have earned these cheers—and you know it." Mammianos thumped Krispos lightly on the back. Krispos thought it over. At last, he nodded.

# XIII

THE GREAT VALVES OF THE SILVER GATE SWUNG OPEN. TRUM-peters on the wall above blared out a fanfare. Krispos flicked Progress' reins. Along with his victorious army, he rode into Videssos the city.

As he passed through the covered way between the outer and inner walls, his mind went back to the day, now more than a decade behind him, when he'd first walked into the great imperial capital. Then no one had known—or cared—he was arriving. Now the whole city waited for him.

He came out of the shadow of the covered way and into the city. Another fanfare blew. Ahead of him in the procession, a marching chorus began to chant. "Behold, Krispos comes in triumph, who subjected Kubrat! Once he served the folk north of the mountains, but now they serve him!"

People packed both sides of Middle Street. They jeered the chained Haloga prisoners who dejectedly clanked along in front of Krispos. When they saw him, the jeers turned to cheers. "Thou conquerest, Krispos!" they shouted. "Thou conquerest!"

In his two years as Avtokrator, he'd heard that acclamation many times. As often as not, it was as much for form's sake as a cobbler's giving his neighbor good morning. Every once in a while, though, people sounded as if they truly meant it. This was one of those times.

He smiled and waved as he rode up the city's main thoroughfare. Protocol demanded that an Emperor stare straight ahead, looking neither to the left nor to the right, to emphasize how far above the people he was. Barsymes would probably scold him when he got back back to the palaces, but he didn't care. He wanted to feel the moment, not to pretend it wasn't happening.

On either side of Progress marched more Halogai, members of the imperial guards. Some wore crimson surcoats that matched Krispos' boots, others blue ones that went along with the banner of Videssos. The guardsmen seemed to ignore the people they strode past, but the axes they carried were not just for show.

Behind Krispos clattered the iron-shod hooves of Sarkis' unit of scouts. The scouts were looking into the crowd, all right, and didn't pretend otherwise. They knew what they were looking for, too. "Hey, pretty lass, I hope I find you tonight!" one of them called.

Hearing that, Krispos made a note to himself to make sure extra watchmen were on the street after the procession was done. Wine shops and joyhouses would both be jumping, and he wanted no trouble to mar the day. His smile turned ironic for a moment. Automatically thinking of such things was part of what it meant to be Avtokrator.

Then he thought of Dara and how good it was not to be just one more man prowling the city for whatever he could find for a night. When he came to the palaces, he was coming home. He wondered what Evripos looked like. Soon enough he'd find out. He even wondered how Phostis was doing. About time his heir got to know him.

"Kubrat is ours again!" the people shouted. Some of them, he was certain, had no idea in which direction Kubrat lay or how long it had been out of Videssian hands. They shouted anyway. If he'd got himself killed in the campaign, they would have shouted just as hard for whichever general seized the throne. Some of them would have shouted just as loud for Harvas Black-Robe, were he riding down Middle Street in triumph.

Krispos' smile disappeared altogether. Ruling over the Empire was making him expect the worst in men, because the consequences of misfortune were so often what he saw and had to try to repair. Folk who led good and quiet lives seldom came to his notice. But he needed to remember the good still existed; if he forgot that, he began to walk the path Harvas had followed. And if he needed to remember the good, he had only to think of Tanilis.

The procession moved on along Middle Street, past the dog-leg where it bent more nearly due west, through the Forum of the Ox, and on toward the plaza of Palamas. After a while Krispos grew bored. Even adulation staled, when it was the same adulation again and again. He did his best to keep smiling and waving anyhow. While he heard the same praise, the same chorus over and over, the parade was fresh and new to each person he passed. He tried to make it as fine as he could for all of them.

The sun was a good deal higher in the sky by the time he finally reached the plaza of Palamas. Much of the big square was packed as tight with people as the sidewalks of Middle Street had been. A thin line of watchmen and soldiers held the crowd back from its center, to give all the units in the parade room to assemble.

A temporary wooden platform stood close to the Milestone. Atop it paced a shaven-headed, gray-bearded man in a robe of blue and cloth-of-gold. Krispos guided Progress toward the platform. He caught the eye of the man on it and nodded slightly. Savianos nodded back. He looked most patriarchal. Of course, so had Pyrrhos and Gnatios. As Savianos himself had said, how well he would wear remained to be learned. All the same, seeing his new patriarch in full regalia for the first time sent hope through Krispos.

He rode up to the stairs on the side of the platform nearest the red granite obelisk that was the center of distance measure throughout the Empire. Geirrod stepped forward with him and held Progress' head while he dismounted.

"Thanks," he said to the Haloga guard. He started for the stairway, then stopped. Gnatios' severed head was still displayed on the base of the Milestone, along with a placard that detailed his treacheries. After some weeks exposed to the elements, the head was unrecognizable without the placard. *Your own fault,* Krispos said to himself. He went up the steps with firm, untroubled stride.

"Thou conquerest, Majesty!" Savianos said loudly as Krispos reached the top of the platform.

"Thou conquerest!" the crowd echoed.

Savianos prostrated himself before Krispos, his forehead pressed against rough boards.

"Rise, most holy sir," Krispos said.

Savianos got to his feet. He turned half away from Krispos to face the crowd. His hands rose in benediction. He recited Phos' creed: "We bless thee, Phos, lord with the great and good mind, watchful beforehand that the great test of life may be decided in our favor."

Krispos spoke the creed with him. So did the great throng

who watched them both. Their voices fell like rolling surf with the rhythms of the prayer. Krispos thought that if he listened to that oceanic creed a few times, he might discover for himself how healer-priests and mages used the holy words to sink into a trance.

But instead of repeating the creed, Savianos addressed the people who packed the plaza of Palamas. "We call our Avtokrator the vice-regent of Phos on earth. Most often this strikes us as but a pleasant conceit, a compliment, even a flattery, to the man who sits on the high throne in the Grand Courtroom. For we know that, while he does rule us, he is but a man, with a man's failings.

"But sometimes, people of the city, sometimes we find the fulsome title enfolds far more than fulsomeness. I submit to you, people of the city, that we have just passed through such a time. For great evil threatened from the north, and only through the good god's grace could his champion have overcome it."

"Thou conquerest, Krispos!" The shout filled the square. Savianos kept facing the crowd, but his eyes slid to Krispos. Krispos waved to the people. The shouts redoubled. Krispos waved again, this time for quiet. Slowly, slowly, the noise faded.

The patriarch resumed his speech. Krispos listened with half an ear; the opening had been enough to tell him Savianos was indeed the man he wanted wearing the blue boots: intelligent, pious, yet mindful that only the Emperor was the chief power of Videssos.

Instead of listening, Krispos watched the people who were watching him. He also finally got to watch his parade, as unit after unit entered the plaza. After the imperial guards and the scouts came the northerners who had chosen to serve Videssos rather than returning to Halogaland. After them rode Bagradas' company, which had routed the Halogai who tried to fight on horseback. A contingent of Kanaris' marines marched behind them; without the grand drungarios' dromons, the northerners could have crossed the Astris in safety and lingered near Kubrat, ready to swoop down again at any moment. A unit of military musicians had played all the way up Middle Street. The men fell silent as they came into the plaza of Palamas, so as not to drown out Savianos.

The patriarch finished just as the last troop of horsemen entered the square. He waved his hand toward Krispos and said, "Now let the Avtokrator himself tell you of his dangers, and of his triumphs.'' With a deep bow, he urged Krispos to the forward edge of the platform.

Krispos' attitude toward speeches was the same as his attitude toward combat: they were a part of being Avtokrator he wished he could do without. Along with the people, polished courtiers would be weighing his words, smiling at his unsophisticated phrases. *Too bad for them,* he thought. He attacked speeches as if they were armored foes and went straight at them. The approach was less than elegant, but it worked.

"People of the city, brave soldiers of Videssos, we have won a great victory,'' he began. "The Halogai are bold warriors. No one would say otherwise, or we would not want them as the Emperor's guards. We should applaud the Halogai who fought for me and for the Empire. They served as loyally as any of our men, though they fought their own countrymen. Without their courage, I would not be talking to you today.''

He pointed down at his guardsmen and clapped his hands together. The assembled units of the army were the first to join him in paying tribute to the Halogai; they'd seen the northerners in action. More slowly, cheers filled the rest of the plaza of Palamas. Some of the imperial guards grinned. Others, not used to such plaudits, looked at their boots and shuffled half a step this way and that.

Krispos went on, "We should also cheer our own brave soldiers, who made the fierce men from the north yield for the first time in history. Some of the Halogai you see now are their captives. Some joined Videssos' army of their own free will after their chief Ikmor surrendered Pliskavos to us—we'd shown them we were the better soldiers.''

The soldiers cheered first again. Many of them cried, "Hurrah for us!'' The rest of the crowd joined in more quickly this time; cheering their fellow Videssians made the people of the city happier than applauding foreigners, even foreigners in imperial service.

."We did not face danger from the Halogai alone,'' Krispos said when something not far from quiet returned once more. "We also faced a wizard who worshiped Skotos.'' As always in Videssos, the dark god's name brought forth first shocked gasps, then complete, attentive, almost fearful silence. Into that silence, Krispos continued, "Truth to tell, the accursed one did us more harm than the Halogai. But in the end, the mages of the Sorcerers' Collegium were able to stymie his wicked attacks, and one, the brave sorceress Tanilis of Opsikion, broke his power, though she herself died in that combat.''

People sighed when they heard that. Krispos heard a few women weep. Some of the soldiers called out Tanilis' name. All of that was as it should be. None of it was close to what she deserved.

"What we've won is important," he said. "Kubrat is ours again; wild horsemen will raid south of the mountains no more. And the Astris is a broad, swift river. The nomads will not easily slip over it to steal away the land we've regained. With this victory, Videssos is truly stronger. It's no sham triumph, unlike some you may have seen in the past." He could not resist the dig at Petronas, who had celebrated his undistinguished campaign against Makuran as if he'd overthrown Mashiz.

"People of the city, you deserve more than a parade to mark what we have done," Krispos proclaimed. "That's why I declare the next three days holidays throughout the city. Enjoy them!"

This time the ordinary people in the plaza of Palamas cheered faster and louder than the soldiers. "May Phos be with us all!" Krispos shouted through the din.

"May Phos be with you, your Majesty!" the people shouted back.

Savianos stepped close to Krispos. "You've made them like you, your Majesty," he said, too quietly for anyone but Krispos to hear in the turmoil.

Krispos eyed him curiously. "Not 'love,' most holy sir? Most men would say that, if they aimed to pay a compliment."

"Let most men say what they will and curry favors as they will," Savianos answered. "Wouldn't you like to have at least one man around who tells you what he thinks to be the truth?"

"Now I have two," Krispos said. It was Savianos' turn to look curious. Krispos went on, "Or has Iakovitzes died in the last quarter of an hour?" He knew perfectly well that Iakovitzes hadn't died. Were the Sevastos still able to speak, he'd have been on the platform with Krispos and the patriarch.

Savianos dipped his head. "There you have me, your Majesty." One of his bushy eyebrows lifted. "At least I won't envenom it before I give it to you."

"Ha! I ought to tell him you said that, just to see some venom come your way. But since the good god knows you're not altogether wrong, I'll let you get away with it."

"Your Majesty is merciful," Savianos said. His eyebrow went up again.

"Oh, hogwash," Krispos said with a snort. He and his patriarch smiled at each other. Then he turned to face the crowd once more. He raised his hands. A few at a time, people noticed him, pointed. The plaza of Palamas grew if not quiet, quieter. "People of the city, soldiers of the Empire, as far as I'm concerned, this gathering is done," he said. "Go on and celebrate!"

One last cheer, louder than the rest, filled the square and reverberated from the Milestone and the outer wall of the Amphitheater. Krispos waved to the crowd, then started for the stairs that led down from the platform. "And how will you celebrate, your Majesty?" Savianos called after him.

"Not with revels like the ones Anthimos enjoyed," Krispos answered. "Me, I'm just another man with a family, coming back from the war. All I want to do right now is see my new baby and my wife."

The palm of Dara's hand cracked against Krispos' cheek. He caught her wrist before she could hit him again. "Let me go, you bastard!" she screamed. "You think you can pull off your robe as soon as you go on campaign, do you? And with Mavros' mother, of all people? By the good god, she must be old enough to be your mother, too."

*Hardly,* Krispos thought, but he knew better than to say that out loud. What he did say was, "Will you listen to me, please?" He was more than a little appalled. He'd thought of so much on the campaign just past; he hadn't thought that rumors about Tanilis and him would get back to Videssos the city so fast.

"What's there to listen to, curse you?" Dara tried to kick him in the shins. "Did you take her to bed with you or not?"

"Yes, but—" She punctuated the sentence by trying to kick him again. This time she succeeded.

"Aii!" he said. The pain roused his own anger. When she started screaming at him again, he outyelled her. "If it weren't for Tanilis, I'd be dead now, and the whole army with me."

"Bugger the army, and bugger you, too."

"Why are you so furious at me?" he demanded. "Anthimos was unfaithful to you twice a day—three or four times, when he could manage that many—and you put up with him for years."

Dara opened her mouth to screech more abuse at him but hesitated. He enjoyed a moment of relief—the first moment he'd enjoyed since he walked into the imperial residence. In slightly softer tones than she'd used thus far, she said, "I expected it from Anthimos. I didn't expect it from you."

Krispos heard the hurt in her voice along with the outrage. "I didn't expect it from me, either, not exactly," he said. "It's just that, well, Tanilis and I knew each other a long time ago, before I ever came to the palaces."

"*Knew* each other?" Now it was all outrage again. "That makes it worse, not better. If you missed her so much, why didn't you just send for her when you got the urge?"

"It wasn't like that," Krispos protested. "And it wasn't as if I set out to seduce her for the first time. It was just—" The more he talked, the deeper in trouble he found himself. He gave up and spread his hands in defeat. "I made a mistake. What can I say? The only thing I can think of is that it's not the sort of mistake I'm likely to make again."

Dara twisted the knife. "There aren't another threescore women you *knew* in those long-lost and forgotten days out there pining for you now?" But then she hesitated again. "I don't think I ever heard Anthimos say he made a mistake."

One of the things Krispos had learned from repeated meetings with his officers was to change the subject when he didn't have all the answers. He said, "Dara, could I please see my new son?"

He'd hoped that would further soften her. It didn't work. Instead, she flared up again. "*Your* new son? And what were *you* doing while *I* was panting like a dog and screaming like a man on the rack to make *your* son come into the world? You don't need to tell me with whom you were doing it. I already know that."

"By the letter you sent, on the day Evripos was born, the army was fighting its way north from the mountains into Kubrat. And I wasn't doing anything more with Tanilis then than traveling in the same army." What he'd been doing when her letter arrived . . . but she hadn't asked him that.

"*Then,*" she said, a word that spoke volumes all by itself. She went on bitterly, "You even had the brass to acclaim her to the people today."

He wondered how she'd learned that. Nothing in Videssos the city flew faster than gossip. He said, "Whatever you think of me, whatever you think of her, she deserved to be acclaimed to them. I told you once, you'd be a widow now if not for her."

Dara gave him a long, cold, measuring stare. "That might be better. I warned you not to trifle with me."

Krispos remembered what Rhisoulphos had asked him—how would he dare fall asleep beside her? He said, "Careful, there. You'd have had no joy bargaining with Harvas Black-Robe over the fate of the Empire."

"I would have bargained with someone besides Harvas." She was angry enough to add one thing more: "I still may. I brought you the throne, after all."

"And you think you can take it away again, is that what you're saying? That the only reason I belong on it is because I married you?" He shook his head. "Maybe that was so two years ago. I don't think it is anymore. I beat Petronas, I beat Harvas. People are used to me with a crown on my head, and they see I can manage well enough." Now he glared coldly at her. "And so, if I wanted to, I expect I could send you to a convent, go on about my affairs here, and get away with it quite handily. Do you doubt me?"

"You wouldn't."

"To save myself, I would. But I don't want to. If we only had a marriage of convenience—" As he groped for the phrase, he remembered Tanilis using it. He shook his head, wishing he hadn't come up with the memory at exactly this moment. "—I think I could put you aside now and not have much trouble over it. I just told you that. I could have arranged it as I was on the way home from Kubrat. I came back here, though, because I love you, curse it."

Dara was not ready to give in, or to let him down easy. "I suppose you'd say the same thing if Tanilis had come back with you."

He winced, as if from a low blow. For all his wishing that Tanilis had lived, he hadn't thought about how he would handle her and Dara both. *Badly* was the answer that sprang to mind; between the two of them, they'd have made mincemeat of him in short order. Dara was doing a good job by herself.

He answered as best he could: "Might-have-beens don't matter. They aren't real, so how can you tell what's true about them? That just makes for more arguments. We don't need more arguments right now."

"Don't we? I trusted you, Krispos. How am I ever supposed to trust you again, now that I know you've been unfaithful?"

"It comes in time, if you give it a chance," he said. "I grew to trust you, for instance."

"Me? What about me?" Dara's eyes flashed dangerously. "Don't go twisting things. I've never been unfaithful to you, by the good god, and you'd better know it, too."

"I'm not twisting things, and I do know that," Krispos said. "But you were unfaithful to Anthimos with me, so I've known all along that you could be unfaithful to me, too. It used to worry me. It used to worry me a lot. It took a long time for me to decide I didn't need to worry about it anymore."

"You never let on," Dara said slowly. She looked at him as if she were seeing him for the first time. "You never let on at all."

"What would have been the point? I always figured that showing I was worried would have made things worse, not better, so I just kept quiet."

"Yes, that's like you, isn't it? You would have just kept quiet about Tanilis, too, and gone about your business." But some of the heat finally left Dara's voice. She kept studying Krispos. In spite of her temper—and in spite of the good reason he'd given her for losing it—she was thoroughly practical down deep. Krispos waited. At last she said, "Well, you may as well have a look at Evripos."

"Thank you." The two words took in much more than her last sentence alone. He'd known her a long time. He counted on her to hear that.

Not a servant was in sight when Krispos and Dara emerged from the imperial bedchamber. His mouth twisted wryly. He said, "All the eunuchs and women must be afraid to get anywhere near us. What with the row we were having, I can't blame them."

"Neither can I," Dara said, with the first half smile she'd given him. "They're probably waiting to find out which one of us comes out of there alive—if either of us does."

The nursery was around a couple of corners from the bedchamber. Only when Krispos and Dara rounded the last corner did they encounter Barsymes in the hallway. The vestiarios bowed. "Your Majesties," he said. With the subtle shifts of tone of which he was a master, he managed to make the innocuous greeting mean something like, *Are your majesties done sticking knives in each other yet?*

"It's—" Krispos started to say it was all right, but it wasn't. Maybe in time it would be. "It's better, esteemed sir." He glanced toward Dara, wondering if she would make a liar of him.

"It's some better, esteemed sir," she said carefully. Krispos clicked his tongue between his teeth. That would have to do.

"I'm pleased to hear it, your Majesties." Barsymes actually did sound pleased. He had to see the palm-size patch of red on Krispos' cheek, but he made sure he did not notice it. He bowed again. "If you will excuse me—" He walked past Krispos and Dara. Palace servants had a magic all their own. Within minutes everyone in the imperial residence would know what the vestiarios knew.

Krispos opened the nursery door and let Dara precede him through it. The woman sitting inside quickly got up and started to prostrate herself. "Never mind, Iliana," Krispos said. The wet nurse smiled, pleased he remembered her name. He went on, "Everything's quiet, so Evripos must be asleep."

"So he is, your Majesty," Iliana said. She smiled again, in a different way this time: the haggard smile of anyone who takes care of a baby. She pointed to the cradle against one wall.

Krispos walked over to it and peered in. Evripos lay on his stomach. His right thumb was in his mouth. His odor, the peculiar mix of inborn baby sweetness and stale milk, wafted up to Krispos. Krispos said the first thing that came into his mind. "He doesn't have as much hair as Phostis did."

"No, he doesn't," Dara agreed.

"I think he's going to look like you, your Majesty," Iliana said to Krispos. She seemed oblivious to the fight he and Dara had just had. If she'd been here by herself with Evripos all the while, maybe she was. If so, she had to be the only person in the imperial residence who was. She continued, "His face is longer than Phostis' was at the same age, and I think he'll have your nose."

Krispos examined Evripos again. He found himself shrugging. For one thing, he'd been in the field when Phostis was this age, so comparing the two little boys was hard for him. For another, he didn't think Evripos' button of a nose looked anything like his own formidable beak. He asked, "How old is he now?"

"Six weeks, a couple of days more," Dara answered. "He's a bigger baby than Phostis was."

"Second babes often are," Iliana put in.

"Maybe he does look like me," Krispos said. "We'll have to train him to be always at his brother's right hand when the time comes for Phostis to rule." That won him a genuinely grateful look from Dara: here with a son surely his, he said nothing of removing Phostis from the succession.

The nursery door opened. Phostis came in, accompanied by Longinos the eunuch. The little boy was much more confident on his feet than he had been when Krispos set out on campaign. He looked at Krispos, as much at his robes as at his face. "Dada?" he said, tentatively.

*Maybe he's not sure, either,* Krispos thought. He scowled at himself, then smiled his biggest smile at Phostis. "Dada," he said. Phostis ran to him and hugged him around the legs. He reached down to ruffle Phostis' hair. "How does he know who I am?" he asked Dara. "Do you suppose he remembers? I've been gone a long time, and he's not very big."

"Maybe he does. He's clever," Dara said. "But I've also shown him the pictures of old-time Avtokrators in their regalia and said 'Emperor' and 'dada.' If he didn't recognize you, I wanted to be sure he recognized the robes."

"Oh . . . That was thoughtful of you," Krispos said. Dara didn't answer. Just as well, Krispos thought. If she had answered, she'd have been only too likely to come back with something like, *Yes, and look what you were doing while I was busy reminding him who you were.*

"Up," Phostis said. Krispos picked him up and held him out at arm's length so he could look him over. Phostis kicked and giggled. Krispos had no idea whom Evripos looked like. Phostis looked like Dara: his coloring, the shape of his face, that unusual small fold of skin at the inner corner of each eyelid all recalled her.

Krispos tossed him a couple of feet into the air, caught him, then gently shook him. Phostis squealed with glee. Krispos wanted to shake him harder, to shake out of him once and for all who his father was.

"Dada," Phostis said again. He stretched out his own little arms to Krispos. When Krispos drew him close, he wrapped them around Krispos' neck. Krispos hugged him, too. From whosever seed he sprang, he was a fine little boy.

"Thank you for helping him to keep me in mind," Krispos said to Dara. "He seems happy to see me."

"Yes, so he does." Dara's voice softened, most likely because she was talking about Phostis.

Longinos handed Krispos an apricot candied in honey. "The young Majesty is especially fond of these."

"Is he?" Krispos held the fruit where Phostis could see it.

The toddler wiggled in delight and opened his mouth wide. Krispos popped in the apricot. Phostis made small *nyum-nyum-nyum* noises as he chewed. Krispos said, "I think he has more teeth than he did when I left the city."

"They do keep growing them," Dara said.

Phostis finished the candied apricot. "More?" he said hopefully. Laughing, Krispos held out his hand to Longinos. The chamberlain produced another apricot. Krispos gave it to Phostis. *"Nyum-nyum-nyum."*

"You'll spoil his supper," Iliana said. Then she remembered to whom she was speaking, and hastily added, "Your Majesty."

"One spoiled supper won't matter," Krispos said. He knew that was true, but also wondered how often it was wise to say such things. He suspected no one had ever said no to Anthimos about anything. He didn't want Phostis to grow up that way.

Barsymes stuck his head into the nursery. "As the afternoon is drawing on, your Majesty, Phestos the cook wishes to know how you care to dine this evening."

"By the good god, one big, fine supper won't spoil me either, not after eating camp food ever since I left the city," Krispos said. "Tell Phestos to let himself go."

"He'll be pleased to hear that, your Majesty," Barsymes said. "He told me that if you asked him to do up a pot of army stew, he'd leave the palaces."

"He'd better not," Krispos exclaimed, laughing. "I like good food all the time, and I've come to enjoy fancy meals now and again, too. This one will be the more welcome after eating plain for so long."

The vestiarios hurried away to carry his word back to the kitchens. Krispos tossed Phostis in the air again. "And what do you want to eat tonight, your Majesty?"

Phostis pointed to the pocket where Longinos kept the candied apricots. With a frown of regret, Longinos turned the pocket inside out. "I'm dreadfully sorry, young Majesty," he said. "I have no more." Phostis started to cry. Krispos tried cuddling him. Against the tragedy of no more candied fruit, cuddling did no good. Krispos turned him upside down. He decided that was funny. Krispos did it again. Phostis chortled.

"I wish we could so easily forget the things that hurt us," Dara said.

Krispos thought that *we* was really an *I*. He said, "We can't forget. The best we can do is not let them rankle."

"I suppose so," Dara said, "though vindictiveness has a bit-

tersweet savor in which so many Videssians delight. Many nobles would sooner forget their names than a slight.'' Krispos
knew some small measure of relief that she did not include
herself in that number.

Just then Evripos woke up with a whimper. Phostis pointed
to the cradle. ''Baby.''

''That's your baby brother,'' Krispos said.

''Baby,'' Phostis repeated.

Evripos cried louder. Iliana picked him up. Krispos turned
Phostis upside down again, lowered him to the floor, and set
him down. ''Let me hold Evripos,'' he said.

Iliana passed him the baby. He took a gingerly grip on his
son. ''Put one hand behind his head, your Majesty,'' Iliana said.
''His neck still wobbles.''

Krispos obeyed. He examined Evripos anew. The cheek on
which the baby had been sleeping was bright red. Evripos' eyes
would be brown; already they were several shades darker than
the blue-gray of a newborn's. He looked at Krispos. Krispos
wondered if he'd ever seen anyone with a beard before. Then he
wondered if the baby was old enough even to notice it.

Evripos' eyes opened wide, as if he was really waking up
now. His face worked— ''He smiled at me!'' Krispos said.

''He's done it a few times,'' Dara said.

''Give him to me, if you please, your Majesty,'' Iliana said.
''He'll be hungry.'' Krispos returned the baby to her. He averted
his eyes as she undid her smock. He did not want Dara to see
him look at another woman's breasts, not now of all times.
Evripos seized the wet nurse's nipple and started making sucking and gulping noises.

''Milk,'' Phostis said. ''Baby.'' He stuck out his tongue.

''You were fond of it till not so long ago,'' Iliana told him, a
smile in her voice. Phostis paid no attention to her. With such
delicious things as candied apricots in the world, he cared for
the breast no more.

''Well, what do you think of your son?'' Dara asked.

''I think well of both my sons,'' Krispos said.

''Good.'' Dara sounded truly pleased. Maybe she knew the
words were an offer of truce, but they were the right one to
make. She went on, ''Evripos should stay awake for a while.
Do you want to play with him a bit longer when he's done nursing?''

''Yes, I'll do that,'' Krispos said.

Soon Iliana presented him with the baby. ''See if you can get him to burp," she said. He patted Evripos on the back. At the same time as Iliana said, "Not so hard, your Majesty," Evripos let out a surprisingly deep belch. Krispos grinned a vindicated grin.

He held the baby for a while. Evripos was still too small to give back very much. Every so often his eyes would focus intently on Krispos' face. Once, when Krispos smiled at him, he smiled back, but his attention drifted away again before long.

Phostis tugged at Krispos' robe. "Up," he demanded. Krispos passed Evripos back to Iliana and lifted Phostis. After the baby, the older boy seemed to weigh quite a lot. He threw himself backward to show he wanted to play the upside-down game again.

Krispos lowered him to the floor, then picked him up so they were nose to upside-down nose. "You trusted me there, didn't you?" he said.

"Why shouldn't he?" Dara said. "You never dropped him on his head." Krispos clicked tongue between teeth, hearing her unspoken *as you did me*.

Before long Phostis got bored with going upside down. Krispos returned him to solid ground. He ran over to a toy chest, where he drew out a carved and painted wooden horse, dog, and wagon. He neighed, barked, and did an alarmingly realistic impression of the squeak of a big wagon's ungreased wheels.

Krispos bent down. He barked and neighed, too. He made the dog chase the horse, then made the horse jump into the wagon. Phostis laughed. He laughed louder when Krispos made loud wheel-squeaks and had the toy dog run off in pretended terror.

He played with Phostis a bit longer, then held Evripos again until the baby started to fuss. Iliana took him back and gave him her breast. He fell asleep while he was nursing. She set him in the cradle. By then Krispos was playing with Phostis again.

Dara said, "This must be your most domestic afternoon in a long time."

"This is my most domestic afternoon ever," Krispos said. "It has to be. I never had two sons to play with before." He thought for a few seconds. "I like it."

"I see that," Dara said quietly.

Barsymes came into the nursery. "Your Majesty, Phestos is ready for you and your lady."

"Is it that time already?" Krispos said, startled. He looked at where the sunlight stood on the nursery wall, considered his stomach. "By the good god, so it is. All right, esteemed sir, we'll come with you." Dara nodded.

Phostis started to wail when Krispos and Dara walked to the door. "He's tired, your Majesties," Longinos said apologetically. "He should have had a nap some time ago, but he was too excited playing with his father."

Dara's eyes flickered to Krispos. All he said was, "I enjoyed it, too." No matter who Phostis' father was, he was a delightful little boy. Krispos realized he should have noticed that long ago. In the end, it was what counted.

Barsymes took Krispos and Dara to the smallest of the several dining chambers in the imperial residence. Lamps already burned there against the coming of evening. A jar of wine stood in the center of the table, a silver goblet before each place. As he sat, Krispos glanced down into his. "White wine," he observed.

"Yes, your Majesty," Barsymes said. "As you've been so long inland, Phestos thought all the courses tonight should come from the sea, to welcome you back to the fare of Videssos the city."

When the vestiarios had gone, Krispos raised his goblet to Dara. "To our sons," he said, and drank.

"To our sons." She also held the cup to her lips. She looked at Krispos over it. "Thank you for picking a toast I can drink to."

He nodded back. "I did try." He was glad to have any truce between them, no matter how fragile.

Barsymes brought in a crystal bowl. "A salad with small squid sliced into it," he announced. "Phestos bids me tell you it is dressed with olive oil, vinegar, garlic, oregano, and some of the squids' own ink: thus the dark color." He served a portion to Krispos, another to Dara, and bowed his way out.

Krispos picked up his fork and smiled, trying to remember the last time he'd used any utensil but spoon or belt knife. The last time he'd been in the city, he decided. He ate a forkful of salad. "That's very good."

Dara tasted hers, too. "So it is." As long as they talked about something safe like the food, they were all right together.

At precisely the proper moment, Barsymes reappeared to clear away the salad. He came back with soup bowls and a gold tureen and ladle. A wonderful odor rose from the tureen. "Prawns, leeks, and mushrooms," he said, ladling out the soup.

"If this tastes as good as it smells, tell Phestos I've just raised his pay," Krispos said. He dipped his spoon and brought it to his lips. "It does. I have. Tell him, Barsymes."

"I shall, your Majesty," the vestiarios promised.

The sharp taste of leeks, though lessened by their being boiled, made a perfect contrast to the prawns' delicate flavor. The mushrooms added the earthy savor of the woods where they'd been picked. Krispos used the ladle himself, until the tureen was empty. When Barsymes returned to take it away, Krispos held out his bowl to him. "Take this back to the kitchens and fill it up again first, if you please, esteemed sir."

"Of course, your Majesty. If I may make so bold, though, do not linger with it overlong. The other courses advance apace."

Sure enough, as soon as that last bowl was done, Barsymes brought in a covered tray. "What now, esteemed sir?" Krispos asked him.

"Roast lampreys stuffed with sea urchin paste, served on a bed of cracked wheat and pickled grape leaves."

"I expect I'll grow fins by the time I'm done," Krispos said with a laugh. "What's that old saying? 'When in Videssos the city, eat fish,' that's it. Well, no one could hope to eat better fish than I am tonight." He raised his cup to salute Phestos. When he set it down, it was empty. He reached for the jar. That was empty, too.

"I'll fetch more directly, your Majesty," Barsymes said.

"Can't go through a feast like this without wine," Krispos said to Dara.

"Indeed not." She drained her own cup, put it down, then stared across the table at Krispos. "As well I hadn't had any to drink earlier this afternoon, though. I'd have tried to put a knife in you, I think." He eyes fell to the one with which she'd been cutting her lamprey.

"You—didn't do badly as it was," he said cautiously. He looked at her knife, too. "You're not trying to carve me now. Does that mean—I hope that means—you forgive me?"

"No," she said at once, so sharply that he grimaced. She went on, "It does mean I don't want to kill you just this minute. Will that do?"

"It will have to. If we had some wine, I'd drink to it. Ah, Barsymes!" The vestiarios brought in a new jar and used a knife to slice through the pitch that held the stopper in place. He poured the wine. Krispos said, "Here's to letting knives cut up fish and not people."

He and Dara both drank. Barsymes said, "That, your Majesty, is an excellent toast."

"Isn't it?" Krispos said expansively. He touched the end of his nose. It was getting numb. He smiled. "I can feel that wine." He took another sip.

Barsymes cleared the table. "I shall return shortly with the main course," he said. As usual, he was as good as his word. He set down the latest tray with a flourish. "Tuna, your majesties, poached in resinated wine with spices."

"I *will* grow fins," Krispos declared. "I'll enjoy every bit of it, too." He let Barsymes serve him a large piece of flaky, pinkish-white fish. He tasted it. "Phestos has outdone himself this time." Dara was busy chewing, but made a wordless noise of agreement.

"He will be pleased to know he has pleased you, your Majesties," Barsymes said. "Now, would you care for some boiled chickpeas, or beets, or perhaps the parsnips in creamy onion sauce?"

After the tuna, Barsymes brought in a bowl of red and white mulberries. Krispos was normally fond of them. Now he rolled his eyes and looked over at Dara. She was looking at him with a similarly overwhelmed expression. They both started to laugh. In an act of conscious—and conscientious—bravery, Krispos reached for the bowl. "Have to eat a few, to keep from hurting Phestos' feelings."

"I suppose so. Here, let me have some, too." Dara washed them down with another swallow of wine. She set down her cup harder than she might. "Strange you worry about the cook's feelings more than mine."

Krispos grunted, looking down at the mulberries. "It wasn't something I made a habit of."

"Bad enough once," she said.

Being without a good answer to that, Krispos kept quiet. Barsymes came in and took away the bowl of fruit. He seemed willing not to see that it had hardly been touched. "Would you care for anything else, your Majesties?" he asked.

Dara shook her head. "No, thank you, esteemed sir," Krispos said. The vestiarios bowed to him and Dara, then strode silently out of the dining chamber. Krispos hefted the wine jar. "Would you like some more?" he asked Dara.

She pushed her cup toward him. He filled it, then poured what was left in the jar into his own. They drank together. Only the lamps lit the dining chamber; the sun was long down.

"What now?" Krispos asked when the wine was gone.

Now Dara would not look at him. "I don't know."

"Let's go to bed," he said. Seeing her scowl, he amended, "To sleep, I mean. I'm too full and too worn to think about anything else tonight anyway."

"All right." She pushed her chair back from the table and got up. Krispos wondered if he ought to check the cutlery to make sure she hadn't secreted a knife up her sleeve. *You're being foolish,* he told himself as he, too, rose from the table. He hoped he was right.

In the bedchamber, he pulled off the imperial boots, then let out a long sigh of relief as he clenched and unclenched his toes. He took off his robe and noticed he hadn't spilled anything on it at dinner—Barsymes would be pleased. He lay down on the bed, sighing again as the mattress enfolded him in softness.

Dara was also undressing, a little more slowly; she'd always had the habit of sleeping without clothes. Krispos remembered the first time he'd been her, the first time he'd come into this chamber as Anthimos' vestiarios. Her body had been perfect then. It wasn't quite perfect anymore. After two births, her waist was thicker than it had been. And with the second one so recently past, the skin on her belly hung a little loose, while her breasts drooped softly.

Krispos shrugged. She was still Dara. He still found himself wanting her. As he'd told Tanilis, it was rather more than a marriage of convenience. If he wanted it to remain so, he suspected he ought to stop thinking about what he'd told Tanilis. That seemed dreadfully unfair, but he'd learned a good deal of life was unfair. He shrugged again. Unfair or not, you went on anyway.

"Get up, please," Dara said. When Krispos did, she pulled back the spread, leaving just the sheet and a light coverlet. "It's a warm night."

"All right." He slid under the sheet and blew out the lamp that stood on the night table. A moment later Dara got into bed with him. She blew out her lamp. The bedchamber plunged into darkness. "Good night," Krispos said.

"Good night," she answered coolly.

The bed was big enough to leave a good deal of space between them. *Here I am, returned in triumph, and I might as well be sleeping alone,* Krispos thought. He yawned enormously. His eyes slid shut. He slept.

* * *

He woke at sunrise the next morning with a bladder full to bursting. He glanced over at Dara. She'd kicked off the covers some time during the night, but was still peacefully asleep. Carefully, so as not to wake her, he got out of bed and used the chamber pot. He lay down again. Dara did not wake.

He slid toward her. Very, very gently, his tongue began to tease her right nipple. It crinkled erect. She smiled in her sleep. All at once her eyes opened. She stiffened, then twisted away from him. "What are you trying to do?" she snapped.

"I thought that would be plain enough," he said. "Your body answered mine, or started to, even if you're angry with me."

"Bodies are fools," Dara said scornfully.

"Aye, they are," Krispos said. "Mine was, too."

She'd opened her mouth to say something, and likely something harsh. That made her shut it. Even so, she shook her head. "You think that if I lie with you, we'll be fools together and I'll forget about what you did."

"I don't think you'll forget." Krispos sighed. "I wish you could, but I know better. Not even the mages have a magic to make things as if they'd never happened. But if we do lie together, I hope you will remember I love you." He nearly finished that sentence *I love you, too*. One hastily swallowed syllable stood between him and disaster, a nearer brush than in any fight against the Halogai.

"If we are to live as man and wife, I suppose we'll have to be man and wife," Dara said, as much to herself as to Krispos. Her lip curled. "Otherwise, you'd surely take your nets and go trolling for other women. Very well, Krispos; as you will." She lay back and stared up at the ceiling.

He did not go to her. Sucking in a deep, irritated breath, he said, "I don't want you just to be having you, curse it. That was Anthimos' sport. I don't care for it. If we can't meet halfway, better not to bother when we're angry at each other."

She lifted her head from the mattress to study him. "You mean that," she said slowly.

"Yes, by the good god, I do. Let's just ring for the servants and start the new day." He reached for the crimson bell pull by his side of the bed.

"Wait," Dara said. His hand stopped. He raised a questioning eyebrow. After a moment she went on, "Let it be a—a peace-offering between us, then. I can't promise to enjoy it, Krispos. I will do more than endure it."

"Are you sure?" he asked.

"I'm sure . . . Be gentle, if you can. I'm not that long out of childbed."

"I will," he promised. Now he reached out to clasp her breast. Her hand closed on his.

Their lovemaking was, perhaps, the strangest he'd known—certainly the most self-conscious. Both her physical frailty and knowing she remained just this side of furious at him constrained him until he was almost afraid to touch her. Despite her pledge, she lay still and unstirred under his caresses.

Her jaw was clamped with apprehension when he entered her. "Is it all right?" he asked. She hesitated, considering. Finally she nodded. He went on, as carefully as he could. At last he gasped and jerked, even then cautiously. He realized he was lying with all his weight on her. He slid out of her, then away from her. "I'm sorry," he said. "I'd hoped to please you better."

"Never mind—don't worry about it," she answered. He looked at her in some surprise, for she sounded serious. Then she nodded to show she was. She went on, "I told you I doubted I was happy enough with you to take full part in it now. But I noticed how you did what you did, how you were careful with me. Maybe I even noticed that more because I wasn't swept away. You wouldn't have been so . . . regardful if I were just so much convenient flesh to you."

"I've never thought of you like that," Krispos protested.

"A woman often wonders," Dara said bleakly, "especially a woman who has known Anthimos, and most especially a woman who, when her husband goes away while she must stay behind, learns he's found some other convenient flesh with which to dally for a while. Me, I mean."

Krispos started to say, "It wasn't like that." But knowing when to hold his tongue had served him well through the years. This was as good a time as any, and better than most. He knew he was right—what he and Tanilis had done together was far more than dallying with convenient flesh. At the moment, though, being right mattered little; if he pressed it, being right was indeed liable to be worse than being wrong. Peace with Dara was worth giving her the last word.

What he did say, not even a beat late, was, "I'm no Anthimos. I hope you've noticed."

"I have," she said. "I was quite sure of it till you went on campaign. Then—" She shook her head. "Then I doubted everything. But maybe, just maybe, we can go on after all."

"I want us to," Krispos said. "I've packed a lifetime's worth of upheavals into the last two years. I don't need any more."

Suddenly Dara made a wry face. She quickly sat, then looked down between her legs. Krispos took a few seconds to be sure the snort she let out was laughter. She said, "The maidservant who changes the bed linen will be sure we've reconciled. I suppose we may as well."

"Good," Krispos said. "I'm glad."

"I . . . think I am, too."

With that Krispos had to be content. Considering how Dara had greeted him the day before, it was as much as he could have hoped for. Now he did yank at the bell pull. Barsymes appeared as promptly and silently as if he'd been conjured up. "Good morning, your Majesty. I trust you slept well?"

"Yes, thank you, esteemed sir."

The vestiarios brought him a pair of drawers and pointed to a robe in the closet. Krispos nodded at his choice. Barsymes drew out the robe. Krispos let the eunuch dress him. Dara must have used her bell pull, too, for a serving maid came in while Barsymes was fussing over Krispos. She helped Dara into her clothes and combed out her shining black hair.

"And how would you care to break your fast this morning, your Majesty?" Barsymes asked.

Krispos slapped his belly with the flat of his hand. "Seeing that I ate enough for three starving men last night, I hope Phestos won't be put out if I just ask for a small bowl of porridge and half a stewed melon."

"I trust he will be able to restrain his chagrin, yes," the vestiarios agreed blandly. Krispos gave him a sharp look—Barsymes' wit was drought-dry. The chamberlain turned to Dara. "And you, your Majesty?"

"The same as for Krispos, I think," she said.

"I shall so inform Phestos. No doubt he will be pleased to find the two of you in accord." With that oblique comment on yesterday's fight, Barsymes strode out of the imperial bedchamber.

When the vestiarios cleared away the few breakfast dishes, Krispos knew he ought to start in on all the scrolls and parchments that had piled up at the palaces while he was on campaign. The most pressing business had followed him even to Pliskavos, but much that was not pressing remained important—and would swiftly become urgent if he neglected it. But he could not make himself get up and attend to business, not on his first full day back in Videssos the city. Hadn't he earned at least one day of rest?

He was still arguing with himself when Longinos brought Phostis into the dining room. "Dada!" Phostis exclaimed, and ran to him. Krispos decided the parchments could wait. He scooped up Phostis and gave him a noisy kiss.

Phostis scrubbed at his cheek with the palm of his hand. After a moment, Krispos realized the boy was not used to being kissed by anyone who wore a beard. He kissed him again. Phostis rubbed again.

"You're doing that on purpose, just to confuse him with your whiskers," Dara said.

"If he gets to know me, he has to get to know my beard, too," Krispos answered. "The lord with the great and good mind willing, I'll be able to stay in the city long enough now to keep him from forgetting me."

Dara yielded. "May Phos hear that prayer." Phostis stood up on Krispos' lap. He wrapped his arms around Krispos' neck and made a loud kissing noise. Krispos found himself grinning. Dara smiled a mother's smile. She said, "He seems fond of you."

"He does, doesn't he? That's good." Krispos glanced to Longinos, then to the doorway. The eunuch, trained to the nuances of palace service, gave a half bow that turned his plump cheeks pink, then stepped into the hall. Krispos lowered his voice and said to Dara, "You know, at last I find I don't care who his father really was. He's a fine little boy, that's all."

"I've thought so all along," she answered. "I never wanted to say it very often, though, for fear of making you worry more about that than you would have otherwise." She studied him, nodding thoughtfully as if he'd passed a test.

He wondered if he had. Was he showing maturity about Phostis' lineage, or merely resignation? He didn't know himself. Whatever it was, it seemed to please Dara. That practical consideration carried more weight with him than any fine-spun point of philosophy.

He chuckled. "What?" Dara asked.

"Only that I'd never make a good sorcerer or theologian," he said.

"You're probably right," she replied. "On the other hand, precious few sorcerers or theologians would make a good Avtokrator, and you're shaping pretty well for that."

He dipped his head to her in silent thanks. Then, all unbidden,

Harvas rose to the surface of his mind. Harvas had been theologian and sorcerer both, and wanted to rule the Empire of Videssos. What sort of Avtokrator would he have made? Krispos knew the answer to that and shuddered at the knowledge.

But Harvas was menace no more, thanks to Tanilis; even if he could not speak of her to Dara, Krispos reflected, how could he erase her from his memory? Maybe one day the sorcerer would arise and threaten Videssos again, but Krispos did not think it would be any year soon. If it did happen, he would deal with it as best he could, or Phostis would, or Phostis' son, or whoever wore the Avtokrator's crown in some distant time.

With the infallible instinct palace servants develop, Longinos knew he could come back into the dining room. "Shall I take charge of the young Majesty again?" he asked Krispos.

Krispos expected Phostis to go to the eunuch, with whom he was far more familiar. But Phostis stayed close by. "I'll keep him awhile, if it's all right with you, Longinos," Krispos said. "He's mine, after all."

"Indeed, your Majesty. Phos has blessed you—blessed you twice now." The chamberlain's voice, not quite tenor, not quite alto, was wistful. Phos would not bless him, not that way.

When Krispos got up from the table and went out into the hall, Phostis toddled after him. He slowed his steps to let the little boy keep up. Phostis walked over to a carved marble display stand and tried to climb up it. Krispos didn't think he was strong enough to knock it over, but took no chances. He lifted Phostis into his arms.

Displayed on the marble stand was a conical helm once worn by a Makuraner King of Kings, part of the spoil from a Videssian triumph of long ago. On the wall above the helmet hung a portrait of the fierce-looking Avtokrator Stavrakios, who had beaten the Halogai in their own country. Every time Krispos saw it, he wondered how he would measure up in Stavrakios' uncompromising eyes.

Phostis pointed to the portrait and frowned in intense concentration. "Emp'ror," he said at last.

"Yes, that's true," Krispos said. "He was Emperor, a long time ago."

Phostis wasn't finished. He pointed to Krispos, almost sticking a finger in his eye. "Emp'ror," he said again, adding a moment later, "Dada."

Krispos hugged the little boy. "That's true, too," he agreed gravely. "I am the Emperor, and your dada. Come to think of it, young Majesty, you're an emperor yourself." Now he pointed at Phostis. "Emperor."

"Emp'ror?" Phostis laughed, as if that were the funniest thing he'd ever heard. Krispos laughed, too. It was a preposterously unlikely notion, when you got right down to it. But it was also true.

Krispos hugged Phostis tighter, till the boy squirmed. Every year, so many, many peasants left their farms and came to Videssos the city to seek their fortunes. Unlike almost all of them, he'd found his.

"Emperor," he said wonderingly. He lowered Phostis to the floor. They walked down the hall together.

## ABOUT THE AUTHOR

Harry Turtledove is that rarity, a lifelong southern Californian. He is married and has three young daughters. After flunking out of Caltech, he earned a degree in Byzantine history and has taught at UCLA and Cal State Fullerton. Academic jobs being few and precarious, however, his primary work since leaving school has been as a technical writer. He has had fantasy and science fiction published in *Isaac Asimov's Amazing, Analog, Fantasy Book*, and *Playboy*. His hobbies include baseball, chess, and beer.